ALSO BY JACK LIVINGS

The Dog: Stories

The Blizzard Party

The Blizzard Party

Jack Livings

FARRAR, STRAUS AND GIROUX

NEW YORK

Farrar, Straus and Giroux
120 Broadway, New York 10271

Library of Congress Cataloging-in-Publication Data
Names: Livings, Jack, 1974– author.
Title: The blizzard party / Jack Livings.
Description: First edition. | New York : Farrar, Straus and Giroux, 2021.
Identifiers: LCCN 2020044655 | ISBN 9780374280536 (hardcover)
Classification: LCC PS3612.I949 B55 2021 | DDC 813/.6—dc23
LC record available at https://lccn.loc.gov/2020044655

Designed by Gretchen Achilles

Our books may be purchased in bulk for promotional, educational,
or business use. Please contact your local bookseller or the Macmillan Corporate
and Premium Sales Department at 1-800-221-7945, extension 5442, or by email
at MacmillanSpecialMarkets@macmillan.com.

www.fsgbooks.com
www.twitter.com/fsgbooks • www.facebook.com/fsgbooks

1   3   5   7   9   10   8   6   4   2

Anna and Eleanor,
who traveled great distances

Prologue, you barrel-crouching rodeo clown, you sleight of hand, you basket viper, you abortion of a knock-knock joke. Foul whisperer, gossipmonger, ear poison enthusiast. Begone! Let me speak clearly in my own voice: something terrible is about to happen.

—*from the prologue to* The Blizzard Party *by E. Saltwater*

Blah, blah, blah.

—*H. Saltwater*

Part I

I.

I am Hazel Saltwater, daughter of Erwin and Sarah Saltwater, a citizen of the borough of Manhattan, proprietor, researcher, part-time recluse, widow, fury, known to the waiters at Wavy Grain Bistro (formerly the Cosmic Diner) as Ms. Patel, known to the co-op board at the Apelles as a compliant and reliable neighbor, among resident children of same known to be a Halloween enthusiast, known to my dry cleaner Tio as a generous December tipper, to my acquaintances a person of pleasant demeanor, to my lenders an exemplary credit risk, to my friends a mystic, a crazy woman, an apopheniac, a rationalist, an open wound.

It is a gray morning. The men working on the building across the street have arrived with their coffee in paper cups and egg sandwiches wrapped in foil. They've staked out the stoop, draping themselves variously over the railing, across the steps, boots on balustrades, shooting the shit, their voices pinwheeling like kids in a schoolyard. The contractor's big Ford pickup, outfitted with racks and rails, drooping lengths of PVC pipe, assorted proofs of masculinity and patriotism affixed to the window, idles at the curb. They're in and out. The doors squeak open, slam shut. It is 31.7 degrees Fahrenheit according to the website upon which I rely for semi-accurate readings, a hub formerly owned and operated by the University of Michigan and in accordance with the rules of academio-subversive nomenclature dubbed the Weather Underground back in the dork days of Telnet. The site was later purchased by the Weather Channel, an acquisition that precipitated the degradation of the Underground's predictive qualities. These days storms blow in without warning, prophesied rain never falls, it's hot when it's supposed to be cold, snowing when it's supposed to be hailing, tsunamis never show, hurricanes lose focus and drift out to sea. My handheld device, which came preset to display the Edenic atmospheric conditions over the city-state of Cupertino, the Holy See of our sparkling new aluminum universe, is equally worthless at making predictions. However, though it's as useless as a crystal ball, the Underground is invaluable for historical readings.

I am alone, and the first to admit that I have not handled well the loss of my husband. I haunt the internet, as do we all, though perhaps I leave behind, pixelated, more of myself than most. Occasionally I chat with strangers on sites where I expose my body to the blue light of the screen, the empty cyclopean eye that so coolly observes whatever I can throw at it. The chats take a familiar, comforting route, along the lines of, Hey bb. Hey bb. Show tits? And I do. I am aware of government and extra-governmental surveillance, the great electronic blanket that shields and suffocates, and I do like to imagine an NSA agent on his or her break scrolling over to my feed and, while popping peanuts somewhere deep within the recesses of that shiny black rectangle in Maryland, possibly flipping through NBA trade rumors on a handheld, one eye on the monitor, one on Kevin Durant's latest tweet, lingering just for a moment, just to see how far I'll go. The thought strikes me like a depth charge. Here's how far I'll go. How about this? And this? Do you see this?

In the years after my husband's disappearance, I froze up a little. I wouldn't say I've ossified. I don't leave the building much, though I'm not, strictly speaking, afraid of anything outside, not the way my father was. This is the same apartment where I grew up, which might be a signal that even before Vikram disappeared I was a creature of habit. New York, so fanatically public, is the world's best place to hide. If I so choose, I may live unseen. But that's not what twists my lemon. I want to be seen, to be observed, but without the knowledge that I am being observed. Like the lady said, I want to be alone. By which I'm pretty sure she meant, Think of Me Always.

Anonymous friend, please watch and see how far I'll go.

Vik's specialty was the assessment of undervalued companies. They called him Old Mother Hubbard, the lax bros and big swinging dicks who staffed his firm. He was the worrier, the detail-sweater, a man of the people who could be trusted to come back from the factory break room with the real story. He traveled a lot. He traveled so that he could sit in a sawdust-floor bar with the drill press operator, or the warehouse associate, or the Logistics Tech II who, after a few drinks, after Vik had listened more patiently to their catalogue of complaints than anyone had listened in their life, might begin to feel that maybe Vik wasn't just some asshole vampire from New York who'd come to suck the life out of the factory that put food on his family's table, but that this guy might actually be sympathetic to the plight of the workingman. Maybe he'd flown all that way because he wanted to do right by them.

They weren't wrong for thinking such a thing. Vik had a soul. He was an avid conversationalist. And if he determined, after a period of information collection, that a distressed company might be made more profitable, his firm would purchase it and set to restructuring. Big deal, so management took a haircut. No one needed to worry about those guys. They parachuted into new Aeron chairs in new offices at new companies without putting so much as a single wrinkle in their khakis. My husband's firm was not a buy-and-burn operation. And they did fine, just fine. They did fine, I should say, until the day they were obliterated, every last one of them.

Thus, by the grace of my husband's good worry, I was allowed to remain on the island of my birth, in the only home I've ever known. I was two months out of Amherst, living in my childhood bedroom, when Vikram hired me as an analyst. He was seven years older than I. We were connected by a long history, though we didn't know each other very well. At first our ages served as a natural barrier. We were formal, respectfully awkward. I told myself he was no different than his colleagues. Nice suits, tall collars, Breitlings, wallets fat as hamburgers parked on their desks lest their spines go crooked from twelve-hour days on misaligned hips. Strange men. Men of practiced masculinity, no subtlety, all of them silently yearning for a lost boyhood. I told myself I had no interest in a man who'd chosen such a life for himself. I told myself I was disappointed in how he'd turned out. We were married three years later.

Vik looked good in a convertible. He looked good in shorts and sunglasses, no shirt, hair blown back. He looked good at the console of Bo Vornado's old Boston Whaler, which he'd scored at a sweet discount. Bo had tried to recruit him when he was twenty-five. The boat had been part of the mating dance. Bo had an eye for talent, but it never would have worked, which Vik recognized long before Bo did. Bo liked to hit the jugular with his fangs out. My husband was a gentleman. He met your eye and listened. He might touch your shoulder on parting. A spy, not a hairy forearm-to-the-face type. On a flight to Tulsa he could talk crop rotation with the Aggie on his right, then turn and talk shoelace production with the Sooner on his left. Mostly he listened, and for his patience he'd been rewarded with a mind that was a warehouse of the arcane. What good does a working knowledge of the lacing patterns attractive to the suburban Caucasian male American 13–17 demo do you? None until you need to assess the financial viability of Oklahoma's last shoelace factory. That kind face, which was absent the menace that men manufacture to scare away the other dogs—it put people at ease. He had brown eyes, elegant bovine eyelashes.

When he traveled for work, I often wished his plane would go down. This was after we were married. I was still in my twenties and hadn't yet developed the competencies that I assume would have allowed me to navigate a long marriage. I didn't know why I wanted him to die. I only knew that I wanted a blank slate. I was getting a bead on it all when he disappeared. He could do a great French accent. He could roll *bastard* around in his mouth and I'd be in agony. I loved him and I wished he would vanish and he did.

After he disappeared, I told the counselor that I'd often wished he would die in a plane crash. She said I'd felt abandoned. She said I was angry at him for traveling. I said that a plane crash was cheaper than a divorce. Ha. You're essentially a solitary person, she said, and I said, Yes, that's true. She said, Do you feel guilty now for wishing that he would die in that manner? No, I said. It was just a fantasy, I said, an escape fantasy, and I knew that much even then. Okay, the counselor said. That's probably what I would have told you. It's a normal fantasy. You know, parents sometimes wish their children would be abducted. Well-adjusted, normal, decent people. Fleeting thoughts, the counselor said, but worth examining. I can imagine, I said. Sometimes, she said, as a reaction to overwhelming life events—the unpredictable nature of love, for instance—our psyches create scenarios that allow us to relieve the pressure. Sometimes that's all we need, a stress valve. If you sometimes feel relief that he's gone, that's normal. It's fine to feel that way. As valid as any other emotion. Do you ever feel that way?

Relieved? I said.

Yes, relieved, she said.

My counselor was named Lana and she was terrible.

S urely he's easier to love retrospectively. Would we have stayed married if he hadn't disappeared? Doesn't matter. Do I still love him only because he's gone? Doesn't matter. Is his existence within me a form of love? Doesn't matter. I'm well trained in the analysis of markets, art, literature, and I'm capable of accurately extracting motivations, intentions, and presuppositions from a wide range of people, and none of that matters, either. It's all mechanics, gears and grease; the only thing that matters is the feeling itself. The how of feelings—even the why of them—is a distraction, a game for college kids reading Descartes, something for a neuroscientist to build a career on.

The ability to experience an emotion without labeling it—that's what I'm talking about. I know it's not cool to say this, but Vik is a living, breathing thing within my every feeling and my every action, and while I recognize that (as I have been told by a number of counselors) I do not have to allow loss to define me, I believe the righteous path is one of memorialization. Of course, I have some experience serving as a vessel for memories of the dead, and perhaps that has influenced my feelings on the matter. Perhaps I've chosen the comfort of the familiar.

How did it all start? Me, six years old, at a party, asleep on the Vornados' guest bed, the coverlet imprinting my cheek and arm with arpeggios of pointillist nonsense, the TV accompanying my heavy, magnetic sleep, my brain dreamlessly emitting spindle waves, delta waves, my consciousness a receptive void. Vik deposited the old lawyer Albert Caldwell into that same room. After Vik left, Albert lay down next to me. He took my hand and he bestowed on me the archive of his life. I had within me a new landscape, both unusual and instantly familiar, as though I'd been on a dark trail all along, following his bootheels. I had become a file cabinet for Albert's history.

So it would seem that Albert carved himself a snug little slot in my head. I have his memories, but the fog blurring his final year obscures his intentions. I can only speculate. Maybe he meant only to hold my hand, to establish a human connection as his final act on earth. Albert was a difficult man, short-tempered, intolerant, made wicked by the erosion of his reason. Yet it's possible he meant me no harm. Albert, being Albert, would point out that intentionality is the only means of judging his actions.

For as long as I can remember, Albert has been with me. I know things about his family that even his children do not know. His life with Sydney. His life before Sydney. The smell of Langdell Hall, the sound of law students' fingers on the pages of those old books. The terrible power his father held over him. The pervasive calm of standing among horses on the farm where he grew up. The infant faces of his children. I have questioned his surviving children, and I have known the answers before they've spoken.

We absorb our parents' grief whether that grief is spoken or not.

The workmen across the street have finished their breakfasts and gone inside the building. They begin work at 8:00 a.m. Soon they will be on the roof, where they've been banging on the HVAC units all week. They will have the best view in the city, but there will be no gifs of the incident passed around social. No conspiracy theories will coalesce around mismatched metadata from one of their phones, somehow calibrated incorrectly, out of sync with central internet time, an outlier, a time traveler, a visitor from another dimension. They will deliver no eyewitness accounts to brisk reporters with sharply parted hair. No helicopters will arrive to provide the bird's-eye view. No wailing fire engines at the curb. No one will claim to have seen black-suited men fleeing the building. But there will be reverberations. One of the workmen might inexplicably return to the religion of his childhood. One might begin a study of geology. Another might quit the trades and move to Jamaica. They will not know it, but they will bear witness to my act of genesis.

2.

oor, sweet Vikram Patel. A boy of thirteen, all wrists and ears, a good son, studious, generous with friends, helpful around his father's office, solicitous of strangers in need, respectful of his elders, just the wrong package entirely. A calamity, when you come right down to it. It was on Vik's arm that Albert Caldwell entered the stately lobby of the Apelles, whereupon the two found themselves on the rump of a mob, a steaming mass of humanity, everyone dripping with melting snow, their cross-country skis, poles, snowshoes, toboggans, sleds clattering and barking against the marble floor with each forward surge.

Everyone but Vik and Albert had assembled for a party. Everyone but Vik and Albert was wearing party-conducive vestment, genre choices informed by a murky matrix of personal politics, pharmaceutical proclivity, alma mater, what was on the closet floor from the not-so-distant New Year's: gorilla suits, tuxedos, deerskins, accessories, and headgear straining the walls of plastic Fairway bags and waxed canvas backpacks—Viking horns, Coneheads, habits, the inevitable Afros, stovepipe hats, Iron Eyes Cody headdresses. Many had traversed great distances, their sufferings a sign of their devotion. Those from the east had braved the tundra of Central Park, those from the south, deep drifts, a persistent headwind. And those hearty souls who had descended from points north had embarked on a passage that would have ensured their murders on any other night of the year. They had come on foot across the frozen wastes of the city, and every last one of them was now jockeying for position at the elevator doors, each car of which could accommodate, in a configuration that would have pleased an orgy efficiency officer, twenty adults, give or take.

Albert was shivering with such violence that he appeared to be vibrating. Vik had only just met the old man. Had the two been better acquainted, he would have been suspicious of Albert's acquiescent behavior. Oh, waters, said Albert. Oh, stars! These were the last words he ever spoke aloud. He had gone down through a trapdoor, vacated the premises, mentally speaking, while Vik pogoed in hopes of putting eyeballs on a doorman or porter, someone who could help. No surprise to him, a watchful kid, that the inside of so grand an apartment building was a complete nuthouse, but didn't he expect a zookeeper or two, a uniform who might acknowledge him, even if only to ask what the hell he thought he was doing there? There had to be someone in charge.

A howl of snow poured through the lobby door behind them, more bodies squeezing Vik and Albert against the wall of people in front of them, the sudden weather on the assembled mass inciting screams, hoots, cheers. And, Ding! the elevator thunk-rumbled open, inhaled a nostril full of partygoers. Whining expletives, more hoots, dramatic screams of Rape! and soprano trills as fingers goosed and rumble-thunk Get those fucking skis in! as the doors did their rattling chomping thing and heavenward groaned another muzzleful to the Vornados' penthouse.

Vik, who'd sacrificed his queen and along with everyone else was playing with nothing but pawns, stopped looking around and shoved his hands in his pockets to protect his cargo, his precious Tami microscope in one, and in the other the leather pouch containing checks and deposit slips from his father's import concern, scientific inquiry and capital of equal value in his Stuyvesant-bound mind, while Albert, whose last bright bulb had sizzled, flickered, and died, slipped into a comatose state, quietly shuffled forward, his arm draped over Vik's, as each new fraction of the crowd disappeared into the wall, speechless, his face a heavy, wet cloth that threatened to slip right off his skull and land with a slap on the slick floor. The firm surface of the present had finally split and he'd fallen into the dark ravine of the past, never to be heard from again.

Their turn came. They were absorbed by the vacuum. Hustle, crush, the doors closed, a hush fell as everyone divided into tribes, those marble pillars who trained their eyes downward, those saintly souls who peered slightly upward at their ethereal destination, those dead-ahead bastions of cool whose refusal to acknowledge the alien nature of vertical transport signaled that they had achieved a divine state of pure, exquisite boredom. Everyone observed the protocol of silence. The wet chinchilla coat in front of Vik tickled his nose. Albert stood as if on review, eyes closed, swimming in his history, at least what he could recall of it, a fourth tribe unto himself. His teeth were chattering like a speed freak's.

Thunk-rumble, the passengers poured into the vestibule outside PH1 and began adding to the graveyard of boots and coats, the precarious teepee of cross-country skis by the door. The coats had formed a mountain slope descending from the ceiling at the right-hand wall, somewhere at its core a wheeled rack on which early arrivals had hung theirs with care, draping scarves just so over lapels, taking pains to insert gloves in pockets, hats folded and tucked securely into a sleeve . . . there was movement on one side of the wedge, an excavation, a poor bastard who'd left a dime bag in the pocket of his coat. Knee-deep in wet wool, he dug deeper into the flank, the thick aroma rising in stinking waves around him as the new arrivals pitched their coats onto the pile. Though harried, he continued to dig. On the other side, boot arrangement likewise had initially followed some ordered system that had collapsed as footwear piled up like a slag heap, rising, shearing, rising again, shearing, absorbing new artifacts as each fresh batch of travelers arrived: a bag of wine, a plastic toboggan, backpacks filled with snacks and brandy for the voyage across Central Park, pulped copies of the *Post* that had been stuffed beneath sweaters as extra insulation, things that slipped free from breast pockets while de-booting: bifocals, Watermans, receipts, prayer beads, boxes of Camels, Marlboros, condoms, lighters, pouches, papers, baggies of weed, baggies of reds, blues, greenies, so that the boot pile was densely populated with excavationists—in fact, a sizable contingent of partygoers were tromping around on the site, mashing and squishing everything in their increasingly frantic attempts to recover the buried mind-altering substances, and, unfortunately, contributing to serious stratum disarray so that, had there been at one time a controlled, archaeological approach to recovering lost items, there was no chance now, as the whole pile was a contaminated context, goulash.

No way was Vik taking his hands out of his pockets, not now, and the pair moved hopelessly along with the crowd, squirting through the bottleneck at the doorway, Albert shuffling along like a trained seal.

Inside, the entrance gallery was dim and thick with smoke—not the painterly striations that hang suspended in opium dens like the gossamer robes of angels, but a searing, heavy storm of smoke that had established itself as the essential medium through which all commerce would be conducted. The Joan Mitchell hanging directly across from the door was nothing but a hint of blue through a fogbank. Entire bricks of marijuana had been combusted and were presently lounging around in cottony clouds, mingling with enough R. J. Reynolds' bright leaf and burley to balance the North Carolina state budget. Here and there, microclimates, the sharp masculinity of Cohibas, Toros, Presidentes, Ascots, Perfectos, Chisels canoodling with feminine curls of Drum, Sir Walter Raleigh, Borkum Riff, Sutliffe Vanilla Custard, Prince Albert. Like a descant, the mysterious perfume of cloves everywhere, nowhere. In darker corners, the harsh burn of bidis.

Enterprising young Tanawat Kongkatitum, known to his friends at Columbia as Hiwatt, after P. Townshend's customary stack, had set up a pair of multi-hose hookahs in the library and was charging the exorbitant sum of eight dollars U.S. for a bowl of shisha and hash. He was doing a bang-up business but it was getting crowded as the remains of his previous customers were taking up all the floor space. They were great for marketing but— Christ on a bicycle, Hiwatt said to a woman in four-inch spikes who was walking across an unresponsive carpet of bodies. Step right up!

Vik, looking for somewhere to stow Albert while he inquired about where exactly in the building the old man lived, was blown away from the pulsing heart of the party like a sloop caught in a squall, toward the residential wing, by the excruciating volume of the song, Iggy Pop grinding out "Lust for Life," on about its eighth curtain call. To the east were six bedrooms and three bathrooms that branched off a dark central hall lined with Cubist paintings, couples making out, triangular shadows, more smoke, one of Hiwatt's customers sleeping Pompei-style atop a Nelson bench, and underfoot a foreboding tangle of clothing.

The doors were all closed, and Albert stood docile at Vik's side as he rapped on the first one. Impossible to hear anything over the noise, he cracked and peeked and saw, oh yeah, an orgy, or group action, at least, definitely XXX if not a full-scale Dionysian revel, pumping asses and hairy bellies, the juxtaposition and rejuxtaposition of arms over legs over arms, the dull flash of jewelry glinting in the oily light from the bedside lamp, which had been boudoired with an orange paisley silk. He lingered, but withdrew before the shoe hit the door.

Too amped up now to rethink his process, he tried the next one. It was a bathroom. A couple was in the tub. Another was attempting to destroy the toilet with their ride-'em-cowboy antics. Water everywhere. Yipping. It smelled like sandalwood and patchouli. The next, a bedroom, another group fling, a more Germanic arrangement, two women on the bed, five men around the edges, pants pooled at their ankles, and what appeared to be a game of cribbage under way at the table beneath the window. Albert lingered dreamily at Vik's side.

Hot damn, Vik thought as he reached for door number four, his fingers trembling with voyeuristic ecstasy. Alas, the room he was about to enter was virtually empty; I was the stain on that virtue, sleeping peacefully on the bed beneath a blanket of cyan TV snow, alone, unperturbed because no matter how perverse the diabolical plans in the drug-soaked brains of the partiers, by some miracle none of them, none of them, included getting it on in front of, with, or around a little girl.

So it was that with a mixture of relief and disappointment Vik parked Albert on a creaky teak chair next to a wooden statue of a Maasai herder, taking care not to wake the kid sacked out atop the coverlet. He had no idea how old I was—a little kid, that was how I registered—and he whispered to Albert that he'd be back soon. What a thoughtful boy. Having secured the addled old man, he closed the door behind him and went to find an adult who might be able to tell him where Albert, who had nothing to say on the matter, lived.

3.

pproximately three hours earlier, Mr. Albert Haynes Caldwell, partner emeritus, former head of litigation, Swank, Brady & Plescher, an editor of the *Harvard Law Review*, class of '26, father of three, widower, atheist, fiscal conservative, moralist, known to the tailors at Paul Stewart as Cheese on account of his habit of expelling toxic nebulas while being taped for trousers, known to the waiters at the Cosmic on 81st and Broadway as Bark (as in, tight as), on account of his miserly tipping and insistence on instant coffee (kept in a glass jar labeled AHC behind the counter, to be wordlessly delivered with one cup hot water, one spoon), magnet for single-fingered farewells, known to his grandchildren as Grumps, known to longtime residents of the Apelles as Albie, for whom co-op meetings were but a canvas on which he might paint his opinions in re the emancipated woman, the ghetto issue, the Soviet threat, the Israel issue, the New York City Department of Sanitation issue, tree huggers, the A-building lobby rug issue, the Head Peanut Hizzoner Jimmy Carter, the Transit Authority conspiracy—in short, anything that happened to tumble across the cerebral threshold of this man known to haggle over the price of Girl Scout cookies and whose five bathrooms, it was rumored, were furnished exclusively from a stockpile of four-star hotel courtesy soaps—had cried into the mouthpiece of his black Bell telephone, I can't feel my hands!

Numbness! Tremors! Again, quaveringly: *Tremors.*

I have a shooting pain in my abdomen!

Tightness—(light gasping)—rib cage.

He was reading from a short monologue he'd composed on the legal pad resting on his rumpled corduroy lap, plotted to convey nothing so specific as heart attack or stroke, but leaving the door open to the possibility of a panoply of life-threatening failures of the body's major systems. When he hung up, he tore off the topmost sheet, folded it in two, and dropped it into the drawer of the side table. He drummed his fingers on his knees, then endeavored to assume a supine position on the rug, a position he achieved with some difficulty, owing both to his age and his sedentary lifestyle, but also to the hour (it was nearly his bedtime), and, despite a healthy dose of scotch, the stiffness that set like epoxy in his joints late in the day. Some blessed mornings he found his body almost completely devoid of pain, limbs loose, his blood warmed from sleep and rippling through his veins with Balanchine-like effervescence, but now, so late in the day, he was a museum of tortures. He hadn't been stretched out on the Oriental long when, gazing absently at the trompe l'oeil ceiling (manganese blue sky, cirrus, a few orioles in flight, elm leaves in the corners), he realized he'd neglected to pocket the slip of paper on which he'd written his final destination. And so he reversed the procedure, rolling from back to front, raising his posterior by shuffling forward on his knees, favoring the tender left one, walking his hands back into a cat's arch, at which point he reached out to the sofa and steadied himself before maneuvering his rear onto the cushions and embarking on phase two: standing. A feat of epic proportions, he thought, that he'd remembered the paper. His memory was a junkyard, heaps of scrap as far as the eye could see.

By the time he was up, he'd forgotten why he was up.

Thus, when the ambulance crew arrived, he was still standing fully erect, still trying to recall what he was looking for, and he greeted the paramedics with a yelp of surprise that they interpreted correctly as surprise, an anomalous reaction from a man who had himself phoned for an ambulance fifteen minutes earlier, therefore diagnostically significant, confusion being a symptom of stroke, and he was quickly apprehended, strapped to an exceedingly uncomfortable stretcher, and wheeled out of his apartment sporting a grimace that the plastic oxygen mask transmuted into a knifeish smile, past the doorman Manny, who'd escorted the crew to 12C, and to whom it appeared that Mr. Caldwell had winked, onto the elevator, down, out, and through the lobby, not yet stuffed to the gills with party people, and across the wet cobblestones, where he was shunted into the back of the rig like a slice of pizza into an oven. The snow swirled in, the doors slammed shut. In the sudden stillness of the medical bay, the snowflakes sashayed down and melted into the fat wales of Albert's pants. Strapped tight, he nonetheless bounced on the stretcher as the snow chains scrabbled against cobblestones, found purchase, and the ambulance scooted through the archway and onto Broadway for its skidding voyage to Roosevelt, where doctors administered a bevy of tests, a second wave of which presumed to measure Albert's mental acuity (D-minus, dunce cap), and where, owing to his advanced age, inebriation, what appeared to be memory impairment, his inability to provide the phone numbers of any relatives, no answer at his home address, and the deteriorating weather conditions, the chief resident declared he should be held overnight for observation.

When the physician had asked if there was anyone they could contact, Albert had patted helplessly at his trouser pockets until a nurse inserted her fingers and plucked out a storm of paper—slips of memory, most numerical: account numbers, dates, times, ages of his grandchildren (without corresponding names), phone numbers (also without corresponding names), all scrupulously inscribed before being pitched into the abyss. Had he remembered to pick up the scrap of paper bearing the name of his final destination, it's unlikely Albert would have been able to make heads or tails of it. He had no memory of copying it onto the paper. At the moment he had no memory of why he'd done anything. His plan was nothing more than a little turbulence on the surface of rough seas.

He had only a feeling that, like a migrating goose, he was to travel south. An image of water.

Is there a number here we can call? A relative? the doctor said, probing the pile, which had been deposited on an instrument tray, with the tip of a pen.

Albert opened his mouth. He closed his mouth.

What was he trying to remember, again? He'd given the doorman the slip, but then what? Perhaps that alone had been the goal. He stared up at the big lights. His shirt was splayed open, the skin of his torso so loose that it appeared to be draining over his sides like melted icing. Oh, the hands that palpated that papery skin and his narrow bones, his stringy muscles, so many hands. His flickering nerves, relit and glowing brightly, bright as a twenty-year-old's, buried within this worn-out machinery. Birds alighting on a lake at dawn.

No immediate relations, Mister Caldwell? No one to call?

He moaned when they touched him, not with pain or sexual delight, but as only a lonesome being can moan, with sorrow and joy at once, in communion with his fellow man, in thanks for their affection. The body is made to be handled. It aches to be embraced. Oh, the hands.

Immediate relations?

Albert shook his head at the doctor. No relations.

Then allow me to invite you to join us here at Camelot, said the chief resident. Albert stared back at him. None of the nurses laughed. The chief resident's hapless witticisms were an endless source of embarrassment for him, yet he couldn't stop himself, and he thought of the ways he'd injure himself later, when he was home alone with his alligator clips and lighter. Admit 'im, he said, before thudding off to another failed interaction with the rest of the species.

Once the hands went away, Albert tried to bring his thoughts into focus. If his brain was a collection of millions of tiny light bulbs, and if certain bulbs lit up in sequence to indicate certain actions that were to take place, the series of bulbs in his brain assigned to light up when it was time to enact his plan were, at best, faulty. All his bulbs were faulty. Their sockets were rusty, their filaments carbonized. They lit erratically, if at all. By the time his comedic failure of a doctor admitted him, half of his bulbs were burned out. The other half could barely get it together long enough to form an unbroken beam pointing to the Hudson River, his final destination.

The problem with so many bulbs having burned out was that the bulbs that *did* work had to pull double-time, which meant that when he tried to remember his plan, bulbs that had nothing to do with the plan lit up, just trying to help out. Lying there on the examination table, he wondered: What happens next? And, seeing that the plan bulbs were as dark and unexcited as jars of molasses, the bulbs in charge of remembering a case he tried in Germany in the 1940s, just pitching in, just trying to be good neighbors, would light up, and he'd be back in Nuremberg, time-warped, which was not where he wanted to be at all.

Constant use had preserved a few of the most important bulb sequences, but he was down to only a handful of those, which meant that the same old memories kept coming back to him no matter what he was trying to think of. The most common was the memory of his grandson, and when that sequence lit up, it pointed at the first step of the plan. That first step never failed to light bright and true. It was a bulb that said it was time for Albert to die.

From there he could piece the plan together, but it was a laborious process, and because of his rusted-out jalopy of a brain, he'd have to re-create the plan from scratch every single time the memory of his grandson relit, which was about fifty times a day. Thus, for the last week he'd spent entire days conceiving and reconceiving the plan. Sometimes he'd think to write the plan down, but even an hour later, the sequence of events would make no sense to him. Oddly enough, from one reconception to the next, the plans were strikingly similar.

The plan was this: Escape the Apelles, where the doormen were paid extra to hold him captive, by introducing an irresistible force in the form of a medical emergency. He would then escape the hospital. Finally, he'd make his way to the Hudson, where he would drown himself.

Albert had several bathtubs in his apartment. With minimal effort he could have drowned himself in any one of them. He also had at his disposal an assortment of curtain rods, doorframes, and an exposed hot water pipe that ran parallel to the ceiling in the kitchen from which he could have successfully hanged himself. He had drawers full of knives. Merely by asserting that he was having trouble sleeping, he could have accumulated enough sleeping pills to finish himself off. And while the doormen would not allow him to take the elevator down and exit through the lobby of his building without a minder, no one would stop him from taking the elevator up, accessing the roof through one of several fire doors, and effecting his best swan dive onto West End Avenue. But no. He intended for his death, an escape from the comfort of forgetfulness, to meet certain requirements, topmost of which was that he die as his grandson had died.

Besides, remember that his plan, so heavy on escape and deception, was formulated in a brain with half its bulbs burned out.

Operationally speaking, so far, so good. He was wheeled out of the ER, down a bright hall, and onto an elevator. His shirt hung open still, and as the car shuddered up the shaft, he endeavored to close it, blindly feeling his way up and down the placket and inserting buttons into whatever hole he happened across, in the process creating an innovatively disordered pattern in the fabric, something out of a differential geometry textbook or a dressing guide for drunks. To Albert's right was a nurse, to his left an orderly, a skinny white man with a lump of quartz for an Adam's apple. The nurse looked down at Albert briefly, looked at the orderly, and moved her mouth at the corner to register amusement. The veins in the orderly's ropy forearms bulged against his muscles and ligaments, vulgar, penile. Albert turned his face away. Obviously the man was an addict. The elevator hitched at the seventh floor and the doors rattled open. The orderly rolled the gurney out, and here Albert took care to mark the location of the elevator, the nurses' station. One wheel was doing that damn spinning thing, floating millimeters from the linoleum, catching, pirouetting, catching, pirouetting. Concentrate, Albert thought. They entered Room 733 and the orderly docked the gurney alongside the bed. Albert pushed away the man's awful veined hands when he tried to facilitate the transfer to the bed.

Do you need help? the nurse said, holding out an oversized wafer of green paper. The druggie left with the gurney.

I do not, Albert said, snapping the gown from her hands. Whether due to his brief and harsh childhood or unbalanced neurological chemistry or a simple unwillingness to part with the warm comfort of selfishness, his reaction to offers of help had always been the same: a petulant outburst, a denial of his own human needs, a refusal to admit that he found comfort comforting, or that he experienced helplessness, or that vulnerability of any stripe could survive in the arctic environment of his heart. Such had been the state of his existence. Offers of union to which he responded with rocket fire. Kind words torched as they floated, delicate as butterflies, from the lips of admiring young associates. Gestures of friendship splashed with acid.

He couldn't keep up with his thoughts anymore. He was flailing, drowning in a sea of his own worst impulses. He'd nearly lost his ability to strategize.

Nearly. It hadn't disappeared entirely. He stopped his hands, yet again working at the buttons on his shirt, as it had occurred to him to make an ordeal of the task. He plucked weakly at one mother-of-pearl disk until the nurse moved to help. Again the hands, oh, the hands. A flash from a memory that had not yet rotted away: He was eight and his cousin Sadie was absently scratching the back of his head while they sat out by the edge of the field watching dust devils, his scalp buzzing beneath her fingernails. That she meant nothing by it transformed the act into an exquisite experience, and he understood even then that her disinterest lent her touch all its power.

The shirt's cuffs had three buttons each, thin nacreous disks that required the nurse to cup his hand against her wrists while she manipulated the closures. Getting all six securely closed was among Albert's daily triumphs. The cuffs required a wife, or else ambidexterity on the order of a card sharp. Her hands lingered as she struggled with them. Her bottom lip disappeared between her teeth. Well, I don't know about this, she said, shaking her head. Albert was in ecstasy. Then she caught on to the method, a crumpling of the fabric that opened the eyelet enough to push the button through, and the cuffs were open.

There we go. Up now.

He rose slowly from the bed, venturing to rest his hand on her shoulder as she helped him off with his pants. He was wearing white cotton boxers with blue pinstripes, and when he inserted his thumb between the elastic and his bony hip and began to pull them down, she said, It's not that kind of party, Mr. Caldwell.

The elastic snapped as he jerked his hand away. No doubt she'll return to the nurses' station and they'll all have a good laugh at the sack of bones who tried to get a tug, he thought. Just as well. Dismiss me. Think nothing of me. He got into the gown and turned so she could tie the neck and back, and when she finished, he turned again and settled his buttocks onto the mattress and reclined into the bed. She took his wrist and pressed, eye on her watch. Satisfied, she leaned over him—a wave of flowery deodorant and beneath it a close, familiar female acridity—and pressed a button on the wall above his head. The overheads went out and he saw through the window the Hudson and, across the ice-clotted river, the lights of Union City. Heaving gusts of snow ticked against the window, and lying quietly in his Arco adjustable, Albert breathed normally as the nurse pulled up his covers, hovered with her hands on her hips, attempting to assess what category this one fell into, exactly: trigger-happy with the call button, a flop-and-roller, a halluciné.

You're not going to give us any trouble, Mr. Caldwell?

I wouldn't dream of it, my dear.

She had a keen sense about her patients, something akin to a Secret Service agent's eye for the pearl of sweat that gives up the assassin in a jubilant throng. For someone who showed up wearing Turnbull & Asser and cashmere socks, this old man wasn't copping nearly enough attitude with the help.

Albert closed his eyes and concentrated on the hallway layout, and when he concentrated, his face screwed up like someone twisting water out of a towel. He unscrewed it. Concentrate. Wait. He opened his eyes a sliver, detected the outline of the nurse, still there; still there when he checked again, and after a time he adjusted his breathing to signal that he had been overtaken by slumber, and he waited for her to go. He was in a hospital. There was water to the south.

4.

The Blizzard Party. Published 1981 to critical acclaim, a laurel collector, bestseller, kingmaker, an unforgettable, an unputdownable. A cathedral of the mind, a masterstroke, a high-wire act, a virtuoso performance, a breakthrough, a brave and compelling intermingling of autobiography and fiction, a capstone, a new standard, a blah, a staggering blow to those sounding the novel's death knell, a blah, a bright star in the blah firmament, a singular blah, an act of blah, a blah pointing the way to a new blah, a blah blah, a blah, a blah blah blah blah blah blah blah blah blah blah blah blah blah blah blah blah.

My father shipped my story to the far corners of the world. He turned that night in 1978 into art, a thing to be passed around by strangers, dismantled and reconstructed, used as an intellectual bludgeon, argued over. A thing that determined the weight of my worth. He'd done some remodeling in the name of fiction, and insisted on calling it a novel, but, as usual, he couldn't leave well enough alone. He had to complicate things. His heart had been pierced by the gleaming needle of veracity, and thusly afflicted, he chose not to change anyone's name, so that suddenly I—the flesh-and-blood I who ate oatmeal from a pink plastic bowl at the scarred kitchen table, who struggled to align the seam of her tights with the tips of her toes and demanded obedience of her stuffed animals—collided with the inky I my father had conjured on the page. I became a photo negative, a child-shaped hole into which anyone who'd read the book tried to fit the Hazel they'd met in those pages. The real Hazel. Here's how it would go: On introduction, adults would repeat my name slowly, eyes narrowed, and I'd get the feeling that I was naked before them, even if I didn't know why. They had knowledge about me I didn't have about myself.

This went on for years, until I was old enough to read the book myself and learn what they knew. Surprise: My father's version of the night didn't match mine. Some memories generate their own language, their own peculiar logic and associations, coded so that only the bearer of the memory can understand them. I'd developed a juvenile idio-glossia to describe that night, a mix of sound and dream and flashes of vision, a language with no English analogue, and here I discovered that my father had published a terrible translation. Not just terrible—he'd translated my story without even consulting the original. It was an invention. Who cared what he remembered? Who cared about his record of events? Who asked him? He'd gotten everything wrong.

Yet, wrong as it was, I was seduced by his perfect description of the Vornados' apartment and the people in it, the blizzard, the heaviness of Albert Caldwell's heart. He'd treated me with love, if not with accuracy. To read his novel was to be dropped into an exact reproduction of that night, yet one in which the actors had gone off script and were playing out a completely different story than the one I knew to be true. Reading it was an oddly dreamlike experience, not unlike being caught in an unending state of déjà vu.

He claimed that the things he'd changed, he'd changed so that I could preserve my own past. He'd done it, he said, to protect me, but the disjunction had turned out to be anything but protective. I was fifteen when I first read *The Blizzard Party*, as unsure of myself as any fifteen-year-old, and I quickly seized on the book as the root of all my problems. Thanks to my father's novel, no one I'd met since its publication could have experienced the true me. All they'd met was a puzzle, a twin, a chance to speculate. It explained everything, from alienation to acne.

Oh, the pleasures of unfettered indignation. I unleashed my rage on him. I denounced his parentage, made threats to "go public" with my own version, and, finally, treated him to long bouts of silence (silence

I'm sure he was only too happy to suffer). It was during one of these interstices, which could last a week or more, that I realized my memory of the night in question had begun to erode. The act of reading his story was destroying my own. Not only destroying it, but rebuilding a new city atop it. My father always said that the more you repeat a lie, the more it sounds like the truth. I would amend thus: writing down a lie *makes* it the truth. What chance did a teenager have against the foremost narrative wizard of his generation?

I'd read and reread, underlined and crossed out, censored entire pages with thick black Sharpie, crammed notes into the margins and gutters, tagged lies and half-truths, fury driving me back again and again to certain passages until I knew them by heart. I'd flooded notebooks with outraged responses without noticing that his rhythms and inflections were trampling my own. I was horrified to discover later that his linguistic tics had seeped into my English essays; in class discussions, I'd insisted on Salinger's intentions using terms I'd picked up from critical essays about my father's work, arguments sagging with prolepsis and discursion, my father's favorite diversionary tactics. I'd promised myself that I wouldn't forget, that I would keep the two versions separate, and all the while I was reading and rereading until my own story was buried deep beneath his. I'd shoveled so much dirt onto my memories that I'd never be able to perform a successful exhumation. It's hard to believe I hadn't done it all on purpose.

So my memory is water-warped and faded. I've executed my best vanishing act on my father's defective translation. I have rewritten and rewritten so that I—not the hole in the world—might appear in the cracks between his paragraphs, in the gap between a comma and an *I*. So that *I* might appear in fiery letters blazing against the sky. I appear here. If I embellish, if I fail to account for certain facts, if I speak through the mouths of the dead, you'll remember that my father spoke for me without so much as a knock on my bedroom door. Many of you read what he wrote, and you believed. Do me the service of reconsidering.

5.

The night of the party, I'd fallen and hit my head, and because of the blizzard my mother couldn't track down my pediatrician, so she'd taken me upstairs to see her friend Dr. Jane Vornado. She hadn't intended to stay any longer than it took to have Jane look me over, but there she was, putting away her third rum and Coke. My mother and Jane had been friends for decades, yet my mother arrived wearing the apologetic smile she put on anytime she had to involve a third party in my care and comfort, the smile meant to give the impression she was a reasonable and pliant woman, not one given to hysterics or undue demands. She hoped that the smile would, in turn, transform her so this attitude of agreeability would become her genuine state of being. Jane was the one who put the first drink in her hand.

Her reflexes are fine, Jane had said. Coordination's fine. It's a little cut. I'm going to put some Loctite on it.

Do I need to ask? my mother said.

Something I picked up from an OB at City. He picked it up from a midwife.

Isn't that remarkable, my mother said, sucking down half the drink.

For tearing. Better than stitches. Right, Hazel?

Tearing what? I said.

In a percentage of births, the perineum sustains tearing during delivery, Jane said. Do you know what your perineum is?

I shook my head.

It's the area between the bottom of your vaginal opening and your anus, Jane said. Sarah, you've got to get in there on this stuff. These days there's no telling where they'll pick up things if you don't get in there first.

Can you stop saying I have to get in there? my mother said.

That would hurt, I said.

What would? my mother said.

Tearing your vagina, I said.

Yep, Jane said, dabbing my wound with gauze. And then you have to get stitches. But for first-degree lacerations like this one, sometimes you can use glue. That's better, right?

Right, I said.

Okay, hold still. She pinched the wound and dropped a dot of the clear cement onto the skin. Toothpick, she said to my mother, who handed it over, and Jane smoothed the adhesive around. Done, she said.

My mother knocked back the rest of her rum and Coke.

Hey, Jane said to me. You get dizzy or you feel like you're going to throw up, you tell your mom right away, understand?

I crossed my eyes and stuck out my tongue. I got brained! I said.

That had been hours ago. Days, years ago. I had happily ensconced myself in a guest bedroom to watch TV. My mother felt the party stretching out, becoming leaner as it settled into accumbency for the long night ahead. Though still early in the life cycle—people were standing around in clusters, and only a couple of guests—a man and woman, both white-haired, who looked like they'd just gotten off the Concorde from de Gaulle—were dancing to the Stooges album pounding through the speakers. They were both wearing silk scarves and platform shoes. Once the party got a little older, the sofas would fill up, someone would dim the lights, the crowd's id would emerge. These parties, if they were any good, went backward in time, the guests urging the river back upstream, toward their coolest years, always bygone, and they'd land on "I Can't Explain" or Cavern-era Beatles and they'd abandon conversation for dancing when that frenzy of physical memory shot through their spines, everyone young again for three minutes and twenty-seven seconds. That would come later. They were still on punk, music for corporate cools, according to my mother's students, all of whom listened to reggae. Donna Summer would put in an appearance before a sustained bout of Bowie, depending on when Bo relinquished control of the stereo. No time soon, judging by the gunslinger's slouch he'd assumed against the wall next to the cabinet. As long as he was manning the controls, it would be mood music for the cubes.

A young party, then, and it would pass through the stages with inevitable predictability, the same as every other party. What a sad thing, always striving to be unique, a party unlike all those that had gone before, a vanguard moment in communal relations, a night that charted, a memory. My mother had always thought of parties as events designed to foster collective amnesia, so that what you wanted in the end was a memorable place for forgetting. Cute.

She was in a clutch of five, the right number, the configuration at which two-by-two intimacy (always man-woman, man-woman, wasn't it?) broke apart into the impersonal, performative stage-and-audience situation, a five-way conversation being a mythical Loch Ness sort of thing, because in reality, wasn't it always just one guy speechifying while the other four stood there and swizzled, which was exactly what she was doing, swizzling, absently observing the varieties of digital combinations employed to cradle a wineglass, almost as individual as the faces above them, each one a signal, her mind wandering, fingernail polish color, prominence of hair between knuckles or lack thereof, presence and make of watch, style of bracelet, wedding ring.

Thank god we look at the nose when we're talking, she thought. Thank god we don't actually have to look into people's eyes.

In her little flight of five (three women, two men), one woman and one man were married, one of each sex was not, and my mother was, but absent her spouse. They were all about the same age, steered toward one another by Jane, who'd then veered off in search of other lost souls, and they'd talked for a while about how consummate Jane was, and one of the men was funny, the married one, and the other one less so, thus playing catch-up, hard to watch, and both of the other women were perfectly nice, though one, wearing a huge white hat made out of an arctic fox, was overselling her boredom, making no effort to conceal her scans for a better option, a naked disregard for the feelings of the other guests that my mother admired, possibly because she herself was lashed to politic behavior like a sailor to the mast. I suppose it was that same appreciation for brutalist behavior that attracted her to my father. And, naturally, everyone was doing it, checking over the shoulder of whoever was standing opposite, just in case. Three knew each other (the couple and the fox hat), all had Jane and Bo in common, and they had talked out the blizzard and the married man was explaining the Coriolis effect—inaccurately, my mother thought, but what did it matter? She crunched an ice cube and heard the echo of her own mother's voice, You'll crack a tooth, and at the same time a more ventrally located dialogue, the morbid drone of Henry Kissinger lecturing her on Viennese-era sexual frustrations.

Low-pressure systems. Low pressure, the man was saying.

I've never understood any of it, his wife said. Nothing but a bunch of wavy lines to me, she said, smiling with her whole face, beaming, shooting rays of sunlight out of her mouth.

Lows bring precipitation. And now here's the interesting part. The Coriolis effect makes wind blow counterclockwise around a low.

Good god, Terry, his wife said, are you trying to get us thrown out of here with all this subversive talk?

Everyone laughed.

Come on, this is interesting, isn't it? It's—it's—it's human history, it's ancient seafaring knowledge. Someday it might come in handy. Like when we get tossed out into the blizzard because of *your* big mouth. He swatted his wife on the ass. She made a Kewpie doll face and said, Did you say counter *cock* wise?

Good grief, Marg, said that fox hat.

If you stand with your back to the wind, the low-pressure system will be on your left—left for low—and the high-pressure system will be on your right, so when you're rounding, say, the Cape of Good Hope, making for Madagascar, you'll know how to avoid those nasty low-pressure hurricanes I'm sure you've all heard so much about.

Fascinating, the other man said.

See? the first man said to his wife. See? Fascinating! Buys-Ballot's law.

God, take me now, she said.

Say their names again? the second man said.

Buys-Ballot. One guy. Buys like Bosch Tools. Danish.

Dutch, my mother said, took a drink, smiled in apology.

Oh? the wife said.

That's right! Of course, the husband said. Dutch.

And, my mother said, grimacing.

What? Oh shit. What? said the husband, laughing at his impending execution.

It's reversed in the southern hemisphere. Sorry.

Flush a toilet in Australia? the other man said, but no one bit.

So you drowned us all within sight of Madagascar, you asshole, the fox hat said, slapping at the husband, who cowered, laughing.

Leave it to me to find the climatologist in the crowd, he said.

Just a crusty old sea dog, my mother said.

The fox hat said, That man over there, bald, tweed, don't everyone look at once, come on, guys. You'll never believe it, but that's Lee Warshaw.

Where? said the husband.

There, bald, tweed jacket.

The guy who?

Speaking of drowning within sight of Madagascar.

The second man looked at my mother, shot his eyebrows, shrugged.

Um—he was—do you want to? my mother said to the hat.

Lee Warshaw. Lee Warshaw? No?

The man laughed and shook his head. I don't follow sports.

Oh dear god, what sport would Lee Warshaw play? HA! the fox hat said. She did not laugh so much as bark the word itself.

Distance swimming? the husband said.

For Christ's sake, Terry, the wife said, slugging him in the arm. He's standing right there.

Paging Warshaw! Warshaw to the lifeboats! the husband announced in the direction of Lee Warshaw, who did not indicate that he'd heard.

Oh my god, shut up, you fuckwit! his wife said, pounding him on the chest while he laughed and dodged, wiggling his drink overhead like a maraca. The other three members of the group all leaned back. Lee Warshaw did then turn slightly, having caught sight of the lofted drink, and he smiled and waved his glass, and my mother saw that he had the eyes of a beagle, trustworthy but mournful. He raised his free hand to the woman in the fox hat, who waved back and gave him the teeth.

Lee Warshaw, she said. Lee Warshaw? The banker? Come on, she said, all before she'd even dropped her hand. He was on that charter flight that went down in the Caribbean. She turned her attention back to the second man. How did you not read about this, you dummy?

I'm functionally illiterate, he said.

Fox hat laughed again: HA!

He was the only survivor, the fox hat said. His firm's entire executive suite was on the plane.

Domestic executive suite, the husband corrected.

Yes, because *that's* important to the story, the wife said.

The fox hat, undeterred, said, So the plane goes down and somehow, by some miracle, he's not killed. He survived. Him! Can you imagine?

He extricates himself from the fuselage, the husband said, which is filling with water, and presumably he tries to save the other passengers, but the thing goes down to Davy Jones's before he can get anyone out. He climbs onto some wreckage, a wing or something, and floats around until eventually he washes up on an island.

Five months he was on the island, the wife said.

Three, I think, the husband said.

Five, the fox hat said.

Not a soul but him on that island. Five months! And sea snakes! the wife said.

You're making that up. There were no sea snakes, her husband said.

Should I fucking go ask him? Hm? she said. Should I go over and fact-check it?

He foraged for grubs and roots. Learned to spearfish, the husband said.

Unbelievable, said the second man. I should buy him a drink.

He ate bats. And eels, the wife said.

A fishing boat picked him up, the husband said. Dominicans.

Cubans! the wife said. My god, how do you mess *that* up?

He winds up in Havana, the wife said. Havana, *Cuba?* Heard of it? He meets Castro. And do you know what Castro says to him?

The second man shook his head.

He says, You should have flown Cubana de Aviación!

They all laughed.

Sí, el Comandante, the husband said.

Five months on a desert island, said the fox hat, and he's just as boring as he was before the crash. Everything I know about it, I know from the papers. And I've had dinner with the man. That story in *New York?* That's the one that had the eels in it, right?

He had to dive for them at night, said the wife.

The second man said, Fire? He figured out how to make fire?

Yep, said the fox hat. Five months by himself. I go a Sunday morning without seeing someone for brunch and I'm suicidal.

There was a hurricane. A hurricane completely blew away this little hut he'd built, said the wife.

Jesus, said the second man. Are you making this up?

How in the *world* do you not know about this? the fox hat said.

I've been in Hong Kong? the second man said.

I've had dinner with the man, the fox hat said, and do you know he's never spoken a word about it? Not a single word. Like it never happened. I don't understand people like that, she said. But then there are *so* many things I don't understand. She fluttered her eyelashes and swooned.

Oh my, said the second man.

People who don't make reservations, said the husband. That's what I don't understand.

I realize this will sound idiotic, said his wife, but I've always wondered what he did about his nails? I guess he just bit them off? But if you're alone all day with nothing to do, that's the sort of thing that could really push you over the edge. Do you know what I mean? Maybe it's just me. I can't stand my nails being too long.

The Volkswagen Beetle, said the second man.

Say what? said the husband.

That's what I don't understand. The Beetle.

What the hell's wrong with the Beetle?

Here in the colonies we're having a gas crisis, you know, said the fox hat. Or do the papers in Hong Kong only cover the chow mein markets?

I hope no one has a Beetle, the second man said. Sorry. I should have kept my mouth shut.

No! said the wife. No. No. No. You say your piece.

So you're the one! said the husband. The voice of the anti-Beetle lobby! I've heard so much about you!

We have a Lincoln, said the wife.

It's nothing profound. I just find them aesthetically displeasing, the man said. I like to think I'm a practical person, and I could generally care less about what things look like, but something about a Bug just drives me nuts. It's nebbishy.

Well, it's more Nazi, isn't it? the husband said, which invited a new fusillade from his wife.

It's no Carrera, that's for sure, said the fox hat.

Well, bravo, said the wife. Bravo, I say. Everyone's afraid to have an opinion about anything anymore. We're all so afraid of offending everyone else. I say down with Beetles!

And Nazis, said the fox hat.

Aren't you full of political fire tonight, said the husband.

It's Lee Warshaw, said the fox hat. I get this way whenever he's near.

May I just ask, when did this Warshaw thing happen? the second man said.

Oh, a year, two years ago, said the husband.

How did I not know this? You all knew about this? said the second man.

They all nodded.

It was two years ago, the fox hat said. Moira had a funeral, for god's sake. It was awful. She thought, you know, shark food. The wreckage washed up two hundred miles outside the flight path. She buried a casket with his photo in it. I was there.

Astonishing, said the second man.

Two weeks to recuperate, said the fox hat. He goes from the desert island to Castro to New York. A week at Mount Sinai, a week at home. And then he's back at work.

Firm was decimated. They lost the entire domestic executive suite! It's a miracle the place didn't collapse, the husband said. He didn't have any choice but to run back into the fray.

Isn't that remarkable, said the second man.

And still just as boring as ever, said the fox hat. The man will talk golf until your tits fall off.

Everyone laughed.

But it's true. And you wish they would, just so you have an excuse to get up from the table, she said. It's just golf golf golf, for hours. I bet the first thing he did on that goddamned island was build a putting green.

Or a sand trap, said the second man. The fox hat smiled. HA.

My mother's drink was gone and she raised her glass to signal that she was taking her leave. Have to go check on my daughter, she said.

She's tending bar? the husband said.

I hope not. She makes a crappy martini. She's probably out on the terrace getting stoned, my mother said.

A little bit she wished my father were there, if only to insert his cranky old man routine between herself and these people, to put on the Erwin Saltwater show. He'd have an admirer or two in the crowd. But getting him out of his study for anything less than a nuclear event required negotiations—endless negotiations—and since he'd only days earlier done his worst at the Vornados' Montauk house, it was, for everyone's sake, better for him to take the night off.

At parties, my father tended to moor himself by the bar. My mother was better at working the crowd, and could convince him to pull up anchor, but platonic flirtations bored him, the requirements of engagement and polite interest made him crazy, and his manner—he tended to leer, hanging just outside the edge of a conversation, so that no one knew whether to address or ignore him—could unbalance even the most carefully calibrated group of small-talkers.

During his serious drinking days, he'd gotten a reputation as a sawtooth blade, an inveterate dismantler of psyches, but that wasn't anything more than a reputation, one he'd cultivated by venting to journalists, whose attention wandered if he spoke reasonably on any subject for too long; as far as keeping strangers at bay, it happened to work to his favor. He was like a contaminated landmass observed from a passing ferry, off-limits by government decree. In a public setting, only the most ardent young fans were willing to risk it. Old hands who knew a duck blind when they saw one might consider approaching, but to what end? It was easier to find someone they actually wanted to talk to. Obviously he wanted to be left alone, but being alone in public was as bad as the spotlight. It *was* the spotlight.

Never had he himself been able to approach a stranger and strike up a conversation. Once, when my father was young, after observing him ineptly navigate a book party for the better part of a Saturday night, Kurt Vonnegut grabbed his arm. Son, don't take this wrong, he said, but it's like watching a bird fly into the same damn window over and over, and you're breaking my heart. Here's some advice: Find the piano. Sit down. Shoot your cuffs. Play. It'll at least give you something to do with your hands.

I don't play the piano, my father said.

Call it jazz, Vonnegut said. These people will believe anything.

What he learned to do with his hands was hold drinks, which found their way down his throat so quickly that by the time my mother had dropped off her coat, stopped to peck the cheeks of a couple of friends, and swung back around to find him, he would often be gearing up for his third scotch. Regardless of where it shows up, bartop bender or wake, a third scotch is the opening scene of a long drama that no one wants to hang around to see the end of.

My father drunk was a good impression of a snowbank: silent, immemorial. Adequately dulled, he could bear almost any line of conversation, though he'd perk up a little if the subject turned to the designated hitter or Berryman. It almost turned him into a piece of furniture my mother could maneuver around the room.

Almost. Except when he got so drunk he dismantled her friends to their faces.

Definitely better, she thought, that he's not here.

To get to the bedroom where I was watching TV, my mother had to cross the packed dining and living rooms, spaces as large as the foredeck of a cruise ship. She dipped in and out of various ecosystems, the haze of Cohibas lingering over a pack of men in ski sweaters, the dark and light of French perfumes, Charlie, Estée, aftershaves that dropped the needle on jingles in her head, backslapping, roaring laughter, groin to satin ass as she squeezed through the narrow channel beside the baby grand, nods, waves, I'll be back, pointing at glass, the only respectable reason to be on the move, an act of weirdness, tacking into the wind, atop it all the noise of Iggy Pop dedicating "Rich Bitch" to the Hebrew ladies, and atop that, trilling soprano laughter, glass clashing, and near one of the bar tables, positioned by the doors that led to the foyer, she had to decide, Get a refill or check on the kid first? Priorities, old girl.

Franklin was behind the bar wearing his lightly toasted shirt and clip-on bow tie, and she wondered what they'd had to pay him to come out in weather like this. Not enough; he was doleful as ever. Ma'am, he said, and she ordered another rum and Coke. She turned back to the crowd, which was whitecapping now that the Stooges were back in the throes.

Her drink came to her two-handed, fluttering napkin skirt, a mournful smile, another signal, she understood, that it was early, he was still fishing for tips. What was it to be without your spouse at a party? A relived experience? A journey into the past, to the days before Erwin? She knew women who wouldn't even leave the house by themselves for a cup of coffee, but, then, they'd been brought up somewhere else, in those places where a lone woman was a meal, an invitation to get up to mischief. It didn't matter that she understood. She still couldn't stand them.

She turned toward the foyer, sliding sideways through the crowd, changing course to avoid Sonia Kasgard, who would get your forearm like a bear trap and whose eyes would bore into yours until you submitted to her crumbling eyeliner and bloodshot, crazed whisperings—in a room where you couldn't hear your own voice—drawing you closer, closer, until those waxen red lips were intimately involved with your ear. She was New York batshit crazy. Checked all the boxes. Health-food nut. Cats. Dressed like a bag lady. Millions in the bank. Never shut up about real estate. It was never anything but what was up for sale at the Dakota and how she really felt that just a little more space, just one more bedroom, a tad more square footage . . . She had a three-bedroom in the Apelles and six on twenty acres in Westport, next to the Lindberghs, no less. Space was an infection, and you didn't want to catch it from her.

Arriving unassailed in the foyer, a marble-floored gallery space big enough to execute a three-point turn in, yes, a Volkswagen Beetle, an advertisement to anyone entering the apartment that the residents were urbane, rich, thoughtful collectors of modern art, my mother encountered a man still wearing his parka, water pooling around his boots. He was facing the large canvas opposite the door and mutter-ing to himself, a bridge troll between her and her daughter. As she approached, he addressed her with his attention still focused on the painting.

They put it right here to slap you when you walk in.

She narrowed her eyes. It's exactly what she'd thought when she'd first come in. Yet another painting they'd bought instead of hers.

I suppose so, she said. How often did the city subject her to the free associations of men who had her captive attention for ten seconds in an elevator, ten minutes in a cab? Five times a day? Fifteen? You plied them with affirmations until you were set free. The cabbie, the suit and tie, the doorman at the building next door, a man she passed multiple times a day, Hey, momma.

Ha! the man exclaimed. There it is, he said, stabbing his finger at the canvas. There it is, goddamnit. Look. Right there. A goddamn question mark. He nodded ruefully, having made short work of the incompre-hensible painting so cruelly thrust upon him without an instruction manual, without an apology for being something that existed beyond the scope of his imagination.

My mother had the feeling he was the sort who did battle with ab-straction in all its forms. What redeeming quality could possibly exist in someone who sought out punctuation from a Joan Mitchell, who took a piece of art as a call to arms, its mere existence a direct challenge to his supremacy? He was one of Bo's friends, obviously.

Perhaps it was the rum, perhaps it was the only sane response, but she said, That's the stupidest thing I've ever heard.

The man, his eyes still trained on the painting, said, Well, stick around, because I'm just getting started. He unzipped his coat and dug around inside until he'd located a pack of Camels. He shook them and presented to her the extended finger of a filter, which she waved off. Without remark, he brought the packet to his mouth and caught the cigarette with his lips, replaced the packet, lit the cigarette, and dropped the match to the floor, where it sizzled in his boot puddle. All the while, studying the painting as though it were a plaque affixed to a building in a foreign city, written in a language he didn't speak. He leaned closer, exhaled smoke, squinted, flexed his teeth.

See this patch here? He waved the cigarette. Indecision. Couldn't figure out whether to let the blue dominate or soften it with white, and what she ends up with is this purple morass, but instead of painting over it there's this little wedge of red over here, and it looks like an accident but it's a lifeboat. It keeps that purple from bringing down the whole painting. She left that mark of confusion in on purpose. It's pretty bold to leave the question mark right there for everyone to see.

What? my mother thought. Um, she said.

No, you're absolutely right. A stupid criticism. The indecision is what makes the painting. The rest of the painting's smoke, and there's the fire, right there.

Could be, my mother said.

Ah well. Nice knowing you, Joan Mitchell, the man said to the painting. For the first time since they'd been talking he looked away from the canvas. I tell you another thing, he said. I had a painting like this, I'd put it in a room with a chair in front of it, and I'd close the door and watch it move in the light.

Would you? my mother said, taking a sip and crossing her arms.

You better believe it. Having it out here where you pass it on the way to the can? Philistines.

You and my husband would get along just fine.

No philistine, he?

Oh no, he's definitely a philistine. Just one with a chip on his shoulder.

She painted this last year, the man said. She asks me if I want it. I can't decide—it's that purple, you know. I didn't understand it then, but it's the purple that put me off. I bought another one instead.

You have that one locked up in a room with a chair?

I use it as a dartboard. I tape Bo's photo to it and . . . It's nothing compared to this one. He looked back at the painting. You probably think I only want it because I can't have it. But this really is the superior painting. It might be *the* superior painting. And I've got four Rothkos.

Oh, be still my beating heart.

This one is better, is all I'm saying.

Hm, my mother said.

You don't go in for rankings. I get it. I don't agree with you, but I get it. You think you can't rank art like you can't rank your children, right? Something like that? Lies we tell ourselves. You can line them up one to ten, and you do. You're just lying to yourself if you say you don't.

Spoken like a man with too many Rothkos.

And too many kids. I'm not saying the Rothkos aren't sublime, I'm just saying that I know which canvas goes with me when I wake up and smell smoke, and it ain't one of the Rothkos.

Is this before or after you get your kids out?

Ah, they can take care of themselves. I don't need them all, anyway. That's why you order in bulk.

They eat everything, you know? They eat everything in the cabinets and then they eat the cabinet doors, and then they start gnawing on the furniture.

I only have one.

Consider yourself blessed. You know, he said, you're going to crack a tooth doing that.

Yeah, yeah, she said around an ice cube. You know what they say.

That it's a sign of intelligence?

Right.

He looked back at the painting. I would never put good art out in the—what is this? The forum—

Foyer.

Yeah. I might be a philistine, but I'm not a philistine like this philistine, he said, jerking his thumb in the general direction of the party. Even worse, he'd never even know who she was if I hadn't introduced them while we were over there.

There being Paris?

Paris. Paris. Yes. Bo never would have left the hotel. I had to drag him to the Louvre. Then I drag him to the Centre Pompidou. Then I drag him to her studio. It's wall-to-wall canvases; they're on the floor, they're everywhere, and he's whispering to me about how it's all finger painting. We leave, and do you know what he says? *Was that smell her or the dogs?* Can you believe this guy? Next thing I know, this.

The man pointed at the canvas. Bastard was playing me, he said. He knew exactly who Mitchell was. He knew exactly what he was looking at. I love him to death but what a complete piece of shit he is.

I thought I detected the odor of sulfur, said a voice behind my mother.

Speak his name and he appears, yea verily, the man said.

Hello, Sarah, Bo said, hand on shoulder, kiss on cheek. I see you've met the esteemed Doctor Jonas Salk.

Yeah, said the man. He extended his hand to my mother. Neil. Neil Ford.

I had no idea you were out, Bo said. I'd heard syphilis was three months, but god bless you, looks like they cured you in two.

Entirely based on advances they made treating you, Neil said. Said they'd never seen anything like it. Pushed the absolute limits of scientific knowledge.

He hasn't tried to rape you, has he? Bo said to my mother.

Only a little, she said.

Well, he was passed around like an old sock at Sing Sing, so it's not entirely his fault.

How Christian of you to vouch for him, my mother said.

Sarah Saltwater, Bo said to Neil.

I know, he said, prompting my mother to raise an eyebrow. Hey, what? he said. I know good work.

I guess you do, she said.

All right, Ford, let her loose, Bo said. She's got better places to be. I heard there's a bris around the corner. And didn't you see the sign outside? No boots and coats in here. Bad dog.

You're crazy if you think I'm leaving my stuff out there, Neil said, pointing at the door.

Gentlemen, a pleasure, my mother said. And in a way, it had been. She headed off in the direction of the bedrooms. She was aware of their silence as she went, the fact that they were watching her, probably staring at her ass, and just before she turned into the hallway she casually flipped them off over her shoulder.

She knows Joan Baez, Bo said.

No shit, Neil said.

She's older than she looks.

Baez?

Sarah.

Okay, Neil said.

Husband's a complete fucking weirdo. I can't figure it out. We had them out to the house over the weekend and among other things he obliterates a tray of my grandfather's crystal tumblers, wandering around in the middle of the night, wakes up the whole house.

I heard he's a drunk.

Drinker, not a drunk. Said he was looking for a pencil because he didn't want to disturb anyone with his typewriter. He makes me nervous. Just a weird weekend. Sarah was trying to talk Jane into buying one of her paintings.

Did she go for it? Neil said.

Nah. Don't mix business and friendship.

Rookie mistake. She's a good painter, Neil said. I might know someone who's in the market.

Don't do it, Bo said. She's not like that.

I'm not doing anything. *I'm* not going to buy it. When I say I know someone I mean I know someone.

Client? Bo said.

Yeah, Neil said.

You like the painting? Bo said, nodding at the wall.

What painting? Where?

I put it up. Just. For. You, Bo said, tagging him on the nose with his index finger.

Fascist bastard.

Bo waggled his fingers in double Vs. I've got some stuff in the study. Want a puff?

Markets went into the shitter, Neil said. Explain to me what four feet of snow has to do with the Dow.

It'll be back tomorrow. Let's go get obliterated. You poor dear. The things you must have done to survive at Rikers.

I'm still full from all the dick I ate, Neil said, patting his belly. He unlaced his boots and pitched them underneath a Louis XV table atop which was a display of Bo and Jane's wedding photos.

Neil stuck out his elbow and the two men walked back into the party arm in arm.

A study in orange and brown, the room where I was lying facedown on the chenille bedspread. The TV was on. My mother sat down next to me and watched. A young Hari Krishna walked beside his father, a nattily dressed man in a raincoat carrying a pile of books on the new religion his son had adopted. Conciliatory tones from a piano, wide-angle, the pair receding into the distance. Fade to black. A still of Lou Grant as the theme saxed over the credits.

Don't talk to the TV, Mommy, I said into the bed.

I wasn't talking to the TV, she said.

Don't turn it off, I said.

I think I should take you downstairs, she said.

Can I stay?

In here? With the statue? She nodded at the Maasai herder and poked his beaded loincloth.

Please? I said. They have cable.

How's your head? Does it hurt? Headache?

No, I believe it's quite fine, I said. I was the age at which children weave adult constructions into their speech, something overheard, something from TV, and I was also old enough to know that my mother found it endearing, and that it could thus be used to my advantage.

You'll stay in here, then, madam? No wandering? my mother said.

I'll stay here, I said without undue solemnity, without any affect at all. She knew I'd comply. She often said to other adults that she admired my forthrightness, that I never resorted to baby talk or whining to get what I wanted. She said I was a straight shooter. I doubt she cared whether or not I had merely figured out how to play the game to my best advantage. What was important to her was that I was no baby.

Okay, my mother said. You'll be watching the news, I presume?

Nooo, I said.

She flipped around until she found *The Odd Couple*. The picture was crisp and clean.

Good? she said.

Good, I said.

You want to get under the covers?

I'm okay, I said, propped up on my elbows, already lost in the show. My mother hugged me, then looked at herself in the mirror on the back of the door. With a pinkie nail she scooped the lipstick at the corners of her mouth, floated her hair, tugged at the black turtleneck, adjusted the gold pendant against her breastbone.

You sure? she said.

What? I muttered.

You sure you don't want me to take you home?

No, Mommy. Close the door. It's noisy.

Please?

Please.

Get under the covers if you get cold. She glanced at the TV, the granular perfection of the images, as if the station were right next door. How many more representational permutations would they have to go through before the images became so clear they lost all recognizable form? Would there someday be an abstract channel, formless swaths of pulsing color, sounds from an auto repair shop piped in? Someday we'll get over our childish insistence on mimesis but we'll never get over the advertisements for disposable razors and luggage and cars with insides like Marie Antoinette's boudoir. We'll move forward to something better, won't we? We'll move forward and we'll be in exactly the same place. That's progress, isn't it, a walk around the block? Progress isn't anything but a retrospective device, anyway, a name on the wax and wane, representational overtaking abstract, abstract overtaking representational, the rules thrown out the window and the old molds broken so we can bake up something brand-new that in the end tastes suspiciously like a childhood memory. You'll crack a tooth, Sarah. Don't think you know how other people think. Back straight, eyes up.

The party ricocheted through the foyer, a hollow, Victrola wash, and she felt that she was acting in a TV drama, her flats clapping against the marble, as though she alone knew the true nature of existence, the depths of everyone else's ludicrous vanity and endless pursuit of distraction. The foyer was filling with people, yet she stopped in front of the Mitchell and backed away from it, nearly to the door, so that the paint no longer moved like electrons but formed larger, sweeping planes of color. She hated the word *beautiful* and she hated the limitations of her intelligence, which always tried to turn everything into words that she could convey to students or to Erwin, when what was on the wall was indescribable. To reduce it to a linguistic description was to destroy it. Wasn't that the hallmark of good work, anyway? A thing that could be only itself, a thing that defied adaptation or explanation?

What is it about us, she wondered, that compels us to speak the most on subjects about which we know the least? Is it because language is how we exercise our misunderstanding? Once we understand something, we don't talk about it anymore—we set it in action. Even Jefferson, declaring those truths he claimed to be self-evident, was speaking to a point of personal contention, giving voice to an argument within himself, an argument with his god. All men created equal? Surely not in the tobacco fields. Surely not at Monticello.

Someone had taken off Iggy Pop and put on the *White Album*, "Dear Prudence" droning along peacefully while my mother alternated between meditation on the painting and arguing with the rowdy, disagreeable visitor parked at the kitchen table in her mind. Shouldn't she be able to look at a painting without ruining it? What the hell kind of painter was she, who couldn't simply experience a work of art? Too many years of practice. Her muscles had warped and knotted to perform the specific task of disassembly and now there was no other way to see. There was no other way to paint, either, and that was why Mitchell, and not Saltwater, was hanging on the wall, no matter what Jane said about not mixing money and friendship. The Mitchell was better.

6.

The more weed he smoked, the more people Bo called. By the time I'd fallen asleep, the party had become a sweeping, pulsing organism that had oozed into every room of the penthouse, consuming whatever lay in its path, vacuuming up all the drugs, all the food, all the liquor, the people. And as it grew, the party moved backward in time, as my mother had known it would, the guests collectively regressing to the age of their greatest beauty, the pinnacle of their intellectual and sexual potency. Corners and quiet rooms were colonized so that flirtations could flourish. Faces appeared in the doorway of the bedroom where I was watching TV and moved on.

Bo believed that there came a time for every party at which its alleged purpose fell away like a trapdoor to reveal its actual purpose, which was to facilitate sex. Whether you just wanted someone to tell you you're pretty, or whether you wanted to fuck the living daylights out of someone half your age against the sink in the laundry room, a party's soul was made of those who stuck around for the pheromones. Sometimes everyone left when the trapdoor fell open. Sometimes everyone dove right in.

This one was a diver, Bo could feel it. These people were in for the long haul. This party had motivation. In the blizzard, it had a reason to exist. The thick haze of infinite possibility had formed. These people imagined they were partying their way through the fall of civilization, like Brits groping each other in an alley as the air raid sirens screamed, possessed of the reckless courage that was born of hopeless terror. In the absence of bombs, a blizzard was a good enough excuse. And that's all you needed, an excuse.

Hiwatt had finally pulled himself together and showed up with the Guerrero Gold, and every time Bo looked up, more people were streaming through the doors—strangers, people in jester hats and bonnets and propeller beanies. He'd made a pass by the bars and both were stocked to hold out for about another hour or two before he'd have to make a run to the basement for reinforcements. For now, his mission was to get the goddamn Beatles off the air before everyone under the age of thirty packed up and left. He do-si-doed, left hand lady, right hand rounded his way through the crowd, and was halfway across the expanse when he saw the Iranians talking to Daisy Walker.

She had them pinned down twenty feet from the bar. The heaving crowd left no chance of retreat. Daisy was the wife of a partner at Sullivan and Cromwell, a pearl-handled penknife whose Charlestonian lilt dropped just enough shadow over her incursions to make her a decent spy. Associates at Sullivan called her Death by a Thousand Cuts. At the moment she was trying to charm the Iranians, no doubt excavating tunnels beneath whatever fortification they might have erected in the name of privacy, and Bo only knew that he needed to get to them and derail the inquisition before Daisy breached their walls. He'd seen them first. They belonged to him. What were they doing here? Had Jane invited them or had they washed in under the door with the rest of the backed-up sewage?

Daisy would have said, And now how do *you* know the Vornados? in that little-girl voice, and Shahin, cross-eyed goon that he was, would have said, Ah, we are in business together! and that would be that. Daisy would hightail it home and tell the old sturgeon that Bo was in cahoots with some Iranians and he'd get on the phone to Paris, and Paris would pass it along to the Texans who'd been camped out on the Shah's doorstep since all the trouble started, and they'd do a big fat belly flop on his plan to tap the vein when everything fell apart in Tehran.

Iranians had been bugging out all year. The Upper East Side had turned into little Elahieh. Entire buildings full of them, and they all burned hundreds to light their fireplaces. Looking around, somehow half of them were in his living room. Did they charter a fucking bus? Jesus, had he invited them? He couldn't even remember.

Get ahold of yourself. Go smoke another spliff and sort this out logically. So Iran is here. They're not stupid. Maybe they're not stupid. How stupid are they? Not the sharpest tool in the shed, not Shahin. He would ruin the whole deal. Nelofar might keep him in check, though, sweet Jesus, please keep his tongue wrapped around your pinkie, you beautiful bitch.

Bo landed all teeth and eyeballs, two hands for Daisy Walker, a kiss, hands to shoulders for Nelofar, she went to school in England, lips to right cheek, lips to left cheek, dear god the woman smells like honey and she's barely even here, she's like water under my hands how do they do that, and her hair like water sweet mother of Christ what does she do with herself when Shahin's out with his girls at 54? How does a wiry little prick like that get away with it? Money. Money uncurdles the milk. A strong handshake for the little shifty-eyed shit, a pat on the shoulder, you little Persian pissant.

Shahin pulled him into an embrace and Bo felt the disagreeable scrape of a stubbly cheek against his. *Get her away from us*, Shahin whispered in Bo's ear as he thumped him on the back.

This good man, Shahin said to Daisy, has been an absolute prince, guiding us around the city, and he asks for nothing—nothing—in return. A gentleman in the finest sense of the word.

Well, don't I know it, Daisy said. Such a dear.

Bo dipped his head and smiled at Daisy. He saw that lipstick had bled into the creased flesh around her lips, absolutely repulsive, yet his eyes locked on her mouth as she raised her wineglass for another dose, and he watched the waddles beneath her chin undulate as she worked the liquid down her esophagus, and the powder in drifts on her cheek. Repulsive. A horror.

First he took us to the Statue of Liberty, then the Empire State Building. Oddly enough, as many times as we've been to New York, we'd never had occasion to visit either one, Shahin said.

Well, that just makes you a true New Yorker, doesn't it? I lived here fifteen years before I ever set foot on Liberty Island, Daisy said. And do you know, I wept when I did. That's the truth. I wept.

It's quite moving, Nelofar said.

Yes, a complete tour, Shahin said. Bo left no stone unturned.

We'd been discussing the situation, Daisy said.

Yes, a seemingly intractable situation, Shahin said, shaking his head somberly.

We met through a mutual friend—a friend from college days, Bo said.

Of course, Daisy said.

Why had he said that?

My old roommate from Boston days, he said. There's a terribly funny story behind it—I'll have to tell you when there's time. Neil Ford. He's at JPM and as it happens does some work for Mr. Jahanbani's family.

Shut up, he thought. Stop talking.

Yes, I'm afraid we're all but permanent residents now, said Shahin.

It's awful, what's happening, Daisy said. Bo forced himself not to sneer. Is the old bag actually bringing her little fucking embroidered hankie up to her nose, the mere thought of revolution too much for her delicate constitution to bear? Yes, she is. And there, with the hankie poised, she waits. What's she waiting for? She's waiting for Nelofar or Shahin to divulge some intimacy—the source of their money, their real connection to Bo, an opening into which she might insert her proboscis and drain them of their precious life-giving mammon, but they, in turn, were waiting her out, nodding sympathetically back at her, and Bo saw that they were going to stall her until her wings melted and she fell right out of the sky, and he could have just dropped to his knees and mauled the toes of Shahin's calfskin brogues with his tongue, and Nelofar, oh, Nelofar, oh, spiced tits and mystery—

But what if it's too late? What if Daisy's already got what she needs and she's just digging in the turd pile to see what stinks?

My god. Look at these poor souls, Bo boomed. Waiting here dry as a bone and I'm just standing by like a drugstore Indian without even offering—champagne? French 75? A scotch? Old-fashioned?

Champagne would be lovely, Nelofar said.

I'll accompany you, Shahin said. Mrs. Walker? Anything for you?

Daisy held up her glass of white to decline. She tucked the hand-kerchief into her sleeve.

The two men lurched through the crowd to the bar.

Cagey old girl. Before you arrived, she was trying to suss out my bloodline, Shahin said.

She's a scourge, Bo said.

Insultingly direct. Something about talking to a brown person does seem to give these people the idea the boundaries of good taste are porous, Shahin said. And the look on your face! Charging over like a mother elephant to protect her calves. I was touched.

Jesus. No way I'd leave you alone with that one.

You have such little faith in us? Look at Nelofar. Like Talleyrand. She'll take that woman apart and leave her in pieces on the floor, Shahin said.

It was true that already Nelofar had Daisy on her back foot, flashing those porcelain dentures like fangs, and Bo felt another hot surge of lust.

No ill can befall me so long as she is by my side, Shahin said. But you know that. She's not the one you're worried about. You're worried what I might slip and offer up without so much as a finger's pressure?

Nonsense. Only trying to protect the investment, Bo said.

Ah well. In any case, misplaced concern, though I admire the energy you expend guarding *your* investment. I am sober as a judge, I promise. And when in this unfortunate state, I do know how to keep my mouth shut. Didn't I tell you about my exit interview? SAVAK had me in a chair for three days before they'd grant us visas and I can assure you they were slightly less civilized than dear old Daisy over there. I'm not a complete moron, you know, Shahin said, turning back to the bar to collect the scotch and champagne. And, Bo? If you want to shag my wife, just come out and ask. I know you Americans are pathologically afraid of voicing your urges, but it's just pitiful to watch you try to keep your tongue in your mouth.

With that, Bo's twenty-five-million-dollar long position in the West

Texas Intermediate crude market walked back to his wife to present her with the champagne flute he so elegantly cradled in his fingers. Shahin leaned in and spoke into her ear. She smiled broadly and raised her glass to Bo, diamond bracelet flickering at him like a thousand tongues. Goodness gracious, he thought. There's something to file away for a rainy day.

Dirty business, this, and gee, he felt terrific. Except the soul-sucking Beatles were still killing his party, hacking at its shins with their ice-cream sundae spoons, and he made haste for the hi-fi cabinet. *The Idiot* or *Lust for Life*? *Lust for Life*, of course. Ozone and hot aluminum when he opened the door. The needles tipping to George Harrison's guitar, barely even touching 100 watts. Pathetic. Bo hadn't paid some kid with bad skin in a Zeppelin T-shirt to build a system for him. He had sourced every item himself. Teac X-300 reel-to-reel direct from Tokyo. Two Audio Research EC-5 crossovers; Sansui amps and preamp; a TU-717 tuner; Bang & Olufsen Beogram turntable. He had two pairs of KLH Double Nine speakers, but those were for private listening. A party was a waste of their reproductive qualities. Arguably, a party was a bigger waste of the beasts from White Bear Lake he had running now, and which he'd taken delivery of only months earlier, Magneplanar Tympani IIIAs and a IIIA-W bass panel, speakers the size of room dividers, and that were, without question, the best money could buy, the Hope Diamond of speakers, the Holy Grail and the Ark of the fucking Covenant right there blowing divine wind into your ears. Too much for these cretins. But to hell with it, he was letting everyone listen to them because that's the type of guy he was. And George Harrison quim-toeing around the mulberry bush was no fucking test of the engineering behind a system like this.

A quick transition would be key. Silence, even silence signaling the death of the loathsome Beatles, would give the party time to think. You might as well turn the lights up and open all the windows. Like an empty glass or no one to talk to, silence stirred you from the shared dream, clapped a damper on the rhythm that propelled you from one conversation to the next, the upward flow of vibes, the expansiveness

that overtook you after the third drink and a bump of coke. Look upon
your kingdom, behold your subjects, how they move, their hair bouncing,
their bodies like leaves on a swift river. You cannot deny them sound,
even the wretched Beatles. God, now it's "Happiness Is a Warm Gun,"
though he could let it play through and spiral out, end of side A, switch
to Iggy then, everyone knows the album's all downhill after the first
side, it would be natural, a seamless shift, but he's got *Lust for Life* out
of its sleeve and Iggy's smiling out at him with those big goo-goo eyes
like Pat Boone, and god whatever became of Pat Boone, on the radio
in some hot moldy place by a lake where the moths laid themselves
flat against the screens at night like hieroglyphs and the frogs sang so
loud the air had texture. They'd been down South somewhere, the walls
and ceiling of the place knotty pine coaxing pareidolian visions as he
and his brothers lay in bed summoning animals, old hags, battleships,
long-limbed ball players, boobs, rockets, genitalia, and they'd lie there
in that hotbox of a house after lunch, imposed rest to keep them out of
the water so they wouldn't cramp up and drown, until set free to swim
and lie on the hot boards of the dock and watch the honey-colored
boats pull skiers back and forth in endless, lazy loops of the cove where
there was no chop because the smoothly sloping banks absorbed their
wakes with susurrous little splashes. Pat Boone's "Ain't That a Shame"
on the transistor radio all summer long, and the Fats Domino version on
the Negro stations, and they would switch back and forth and never not
be listening to it. Domino's was better—his really swung, and it was he
who converted them so that by the end of that July all they listened to was
WNKO. All night, jazz and gospel, the Soul Stirrers and Swan Silver-
tones, and R&B in the daytime, Little Richard, Chuck Berry, Fats.

"Happiness Is a Warm Gun" faded out and Bo hesitated, his hand
over the shelf of LPs, his finger seeking out Fats. Hell, why not, it was
his party. The needle tracked through the deep groove, the desert land
of dead wax, reached the end of its journey, died, and floated away.
Bo's fingertip bumped across the top of the albums. There. Tip, pinch,
pull. He heard the shush of the sleeve sliding out, a sound he couldn't
possibly have heard over the crowd but that he did, all the same, hear,

and there he held it, a temporal artifact—a record, ha!—encoded with his past, a time-travel machine. All he had to do was place it on the spindle and he would be transported to that summer, the one without his father, where he and his brothers and mother lived a light, gentle existence in a cabin by the water.

But not tonight. A more urgent need worked at his heart. He put Fats back on the shelf, laid on its side atop the rank and file. A voice shouted, Sounds, Vornado! and he responded with a middle finger directed at the heathen who might put demands on him in his time of reflection.

Because Bo knew that not one soul at his party had heard *Lust for Life* yet, and he desperately wanted to make sure that every time they ever heard the album again, they'd think of this night and his party. He knew the music was that good, and at the time, it was rare. Released September 1977, failed to chart in the U.S., buried under the re-release of Elvis's backlog so RCA could capitalize on the King's death, you couldn't pick up a copy at King Karol, couldn't find it at Bleecker Bob's. No one even knew *Lust for Life* existed until Bo played it for them, and therein lay the nucleus around which he had molded his entire life: the Sutor Mantellassis, the Joan Mitchell, the Magneplanars, the Iran oil deal, the R107 SL he kept on the island, his desire for any woman he'd never seen before, young, old, goddess, or goblin, the Patek Philippes, the Montblancs, the trips to Mustique, the standing army of acquaintances that filled seven Rolodexes. This party, this intimate gathering for five hundred. Displays of wealth and power? Sure, man. But wealth and power served a greater master: novelty.

Bo loved possibility. He was a hopeless romantic who saw limitless potential in every new thing he acquired. He couldn't help imagining his life transformed by the addition of new things—and so it had been, over and over again, each accumulation an adjustment. Just never enough. Boredom, that rarefied boredom known only to those who managed to achieve exactly what they'd set out to do, persisted. Make no bones, a charmed life is a dull life.

Bo slid the vinyl from its paper sheath and executed a gyroscopic flip, side one sunny-side up, spidered his hand beneath, checked the

pitch sensor, checked the amp volume, gave it some gas, and with
something like a giggle slotted the hole onto the spindle and released.
For a moment before the velvet surface caught, the record hung there
while the table executed glissade, and he got a quick thrill on the order
of seeing a Mustang doing a burnout, the self-annihilating explosion of
laying a good hit on a running back, a hard fuck in the daylight. Fuck,
yeah! he screamed and dropped the needle and the crackle came and
a deep breath later the kick drum started thumping, cymbal clanging,
the bass joined up alongside at the same pitch, the guitar picking up
the rhythm, and on and on for thirty bars, seventy seconds of setup, the
band lathering up and rinsing off like they're all drunk and aren't sure
they even want to play, but that rhythm keeps pumping along irresist-
ibly, a swinging tetrameter built on a kick drum floor tom Morse code,
and they can't leave it alone, they have to join in.

What could Bo know about the song except that he loved its dance-
hall jungle beat, that he loved Iggy Pop for being a profane presence in
the world? What more did he need to know? Did he need to know that
Pop and David Bowie wrote and recorded the song at Hansa Studios, a
stone's throw from Checkpoint Charlie? That Pop and Bowie, thrown
together in Berlin, settled in to watch *Starsky & Hutch* every Thursday
night on the Armed Forces Network, whose station identifier was a
pleasant rhythm of dits and das, a rhythm that Pop and Bowie passed
along to drummer Hunt Sales, who immediately recognized it as the
beat from the Supremes' "Can't Hurry Love," and cooked up a version
that sounded like a big-bore V8 running wide open on a cold, deserted
Indiana highway?

If he'd known any of this, would he have been somehow more rabid
for the song? Would the rest of the party, who had, incidentally, reacted
exactly as Bo had known they would, collectively trampolining, sloshing
their drinks all over the Afghan rugs and the calfskin sofas—would they
have felt any different? Probably not.

It didn't matter to my father, either, who mentioned none of it in
his book. But it matters to me, that military brat of a song, conceived at
AFN, delivered wet and squirmy on the front lines of the Cold War, its
birth certificate stamped in a country whose chief arms supplier during

both world wars, Krupp AG, had just sold a stake in its operations to the government of Iran.

A t their first meeting, in a booth at Studio 54, bubbles pumping out of tubes hidden in the ceiling, the music so loud it actually made champagne glasses shimmy across the tables, Shahin had yelled at Bo: I'll tell you a secret!

Bo opened his eyes, mouth, tipped back his head in a pose of open acceptance.

Pipeline management! Shahin yelled.

Bo flashed the thumbs-up, though he'd passed the threshold of aural paralysis about an hour back, when someone had fired an honest-to-god cast-iron naval cannon from the mezzanine at the twelve-foot Godzilla piñata gliding across the dance floor on urethane wheels, spooky as hell, Boom, smoke, paper everywhere, pharmaceutical-grade guts spilled all over the floor. Mob scene. Bo's ears had flatlined.

Three days later, they met again, this time at Neil's apartment on Park, in a living room with textured wallpaper and golden tassels on the brocade sofa pillows. If Shahin under the strobes had come off as a prick, Bo accepted that under normal light it was nothing more than standard Oxbridge snottery. Okay, so he'd eaten caviar out of some whore's cunt in Paris and he'd boxed up at university and beat off under his subfusc with the rest of them, let's get down to brass tacks, whaddyagot?

Shahin: The problem is *not* that the Shah will be deposed. He's an interchangeable part manufactured by your government. He failed to keep his own greed in check and he'll be overthrown. So be it. What will go with him, unfortunately, are the engineers managing the oil fields. The new regime will replace them with inexperienced engineers whose only qualifications are that they pray five times a day, and then we'll start to see real problems. Problems with extraction, problems with transport.

Okay, Bo said.

The oil won't dry up, but it will choke. My suggestion is to look away from Iran for profit. Look domestic. Look for profit in the expansion of the West Texas fields.

I appreciate the advice, but I can buy into the WTI market without you, Bo said.

Shahin shrugged and frowned in the French manner that said, Obviously, asshole.

All right, then, what? Bo said.

I have excellent connections in West Texas.

So do I, Bo said.

Excellent connections.

Bo laughed. Okay.

I know a man who knows everyone in West Texas and beyond.

Ah, Bo said, gears beginning to turn. Saudi?

He is Saudi, yes, Shahin said.

Aha.

He is currently partner in thirty-two ventures in West Texas.

Only thirty-two?

Thirty-two under the family name. There are more, you're correct.

How many?

Shahin shrugged again, looked at the ceiling. Fifty? he said. Seventy-five?

It was as though a stream of warm, fragrant oil had been poured over Bo's naked body. He struggled to control the muscles in his face, which were conspiring to set off a smile that would introduce the corners of his lips to his fucking eyebrows.

A partner of yours? Bo said.

Of sorts. We were up at Millfield together. And it is his opinion that American domestic production is set to rise. But I only tell you this as thanks for your time. I'm in shipping, what would I know about oil?

Right, Bo said. You're in shipping. He knew what was coming next, and he sat back and waited.

Shahin obliged, of course, cuing the origin story. My father, he said, was born into a feudal system and orphaned when he was ten. What happens to an orphan in Iran in 1920? He becomes a beggar. But my father was taken in by the caretaker at a mosque, a man named Parizad. He learned to read, he studied the Quran. He became a porter. By the time he was twenty, he had an army of porters working for him. After the British and Russians left in '46, his operations expanded, and after years of humble hard work he was in a position to take over some shipping routes in the Caspian. As you know, we now control three companies. Two overland, the other covering international waterways. To be frank, I'm having difficulty liquidating the companies, and every day my country moves a little closer to its inevitable fate. My family's money is staked in accounts outside the country—and that money is not money I can risk, you understand? That is money for unborn generations.

I understand.

I am an honest businessman, as my father was. My father cared for Parizad until the day he died. We are loyal. Until I am able to liquidate my companies, I need a partner who will—for lack of a better term—front me some cash. And for his risk, I'll pay back at a more-than-fair rate.

Gotcha, Bo said. And where do you plan to put the cash?

I'd like to make an investment in the West Texas fields, of course, Shahin said. I would never make a recommendation I'm not willing to take myself.

And what's my rate of return?

For this particular line of credit?

For *this particular* line of credit, yes.

Five percent and a percentage of the sale price of the shipping companies.

Gotcha, Bo said. He could get eight percent and a toaster at the Harlem Savings Bank. This was all expected. He'd walked into the room assuming the conversation was a front. The sale of the shipping companies—which would never happen—the absurdly low interest rate, all of it was stagecraft, polite misdirection. But because he's on his knees, he's going to make me come out and ask for it, Bo thought.

What more can I offer you? Shahin said. More than five percent?

Five isn't much.

Even in this market, Shahin said, the companies are worth thirty million. The assets alone would bring in fifteen. What do you want? Ten percent of the sale price?

What a performance, Bo thought. What about the Saudi? he said.

Sorry? Shahin said.

Good god, Bo thought. Can we stop fingering it and get to the good part?

What about your Saudi friend? He doesn't want to help you out with a little loan?

Oh no, not his line at all. He's a construction and oil man.

Got it, Bo said. What about I help you, you help me?

I see, Shahin said. With the Saudi.

And you can keep it at five percent on the loan, Bo said.

That's very generous, Shahin said. I believe I can arrange a very favorable introduction. Shahin paused, as if he were thinking about it, then added, I can *guarantee* a favorable introduction, in fact.

Bo knew better than to trust anyone who guaranteed anything, but he'd been on board since the moment Shahin had mentioned the Saudi. The shipping companies were a lost cause, who cared? The loan was nothing more than polite cover for what Shahin was actually offering: his services as a fixer.

And Bo was more than happy to pay twenty-five million dollars for a real and meaningful connection to Salem bin Laden. It wasn't that the guy was hard to get to. Holding his attention was another matter entirely.

7.

Despite Bo's prodigious dialing the night of the party, he never intended to call my mother and father. Neither did Jane. She had no desire to invite my father to a party intended to be enjoyable for the rest of her guests. Until my headfirst landing, the evening had passed normally in our apartment. We'd eaten, my father had disappeared into his study to work, my mother staked out the bright corner of the sofa with the quartered crossword page and her glasses perched on her nose. I had wandered around the apartment, looking out the windows at the snow, before finally setting up shop in the foyer. After a while, my father had come shambling in.

He was not an imposing man. His hair was weedy and he was a little chewed up around the earlobes, soft at the jowls and neck, suggestive of an English grandmother who put on pearls to walk to the end of the drive for the mail. A crosshatched, mottled span of flesh. Age had collected on him like a fine dust, yet his nose sprung as gracefully from his narrow face as a cliff diver launching into the air. The tangle of eyebrows overhanging his blue eyes was a promising start to old-man wilderness. The pot protruding from his midsection so contrasted with his otherwise skinny body that in profile he resembled a python digesting an antelope, and wasn't helped much by his usual mode of dress, unremarkable as it was, an adaptation of professorial comfort wear, corduroy and wool anchored by a pale blue oxford button-down shirt, that most rigid of styles which is defined by the care lavished on maintaining shabbiness and a sense of musty, subterranean lethargy. Physically, it was hard to say what distinguished him from thousands of other fifty-five-year-old Caucasian male New Yorkers; he was a caricaturist's final exam, a blank slate.

This will matter later: My father's memory was fine. He remembered what he was supposed to. His problem was that he had extra memories. He remembered things that hadn't happened, and he needed to repeat those things to other people. It wasn't an uncommon problem, and most people with extra memories are marginally productive members of society. Some go into sales, some into politics. Some become con artists. The rest become writers, which is what had happened to my father.

He worked in what had formerly been the pantry, bellied up to the elbow of two desks he'd wedged into an L against the back wall. He'd left up the shelves, rust-ringed from a century's worth of canned goods, now sagging a little under reference books and piles of old manuscripts. It was a closet, really, a space for a man who didn't like surprises. Between bouts of writing he haunted the apartment, floating from room to room silently, a man in a fog, acting like a fog.

In the foyer, heat whistled up through the floor grate. The parquet creaked when he crossed the threshold, but I didn't open my eyes. I was hanging upside down against the far wall, my blue school skirt a peeled banana skin over my torso. I was wearing blue leggings underneath, wrinkled at the knees. My small hands grasped two coat hooks, and I was trying to look as natural there as an umbrella. My toes were pointed at the ceiling and my hair just touched the walnut bench below. I'd emptied all the hooks and dumped the coats in a pile to the side of the bench to make room for my bat imitation.

Greetings, yogi, my father said.

I still didn't open my eyes. I'm watching stars, I said, the galactic firmament exploding on the backs of my eyelids. Also, I said, it's snowing.

On the stars? my father said.

Outside, Daddy. Outside it's snowing. The stars are shooting around.

You remind me of someone, he said.

I opened my eyes just a bit and observed him. I was used to being talked to this way and knew to wait for the punch line.

Yeah? I said, yawning out the word.

One of the popes. Pius the Twelfth. This was in 1958, my father said.

Were you alive then? I said.

I was, but you weren't.

I know I wasn't alive then.

Pope Pius had been kept awake for days and days by a strange ailment, and when he found himself unable to address the papal audience, he took to his bed.

And he finally went to sleep?

Nope. Couldn't sleep.

How come?

The strange ailment.

What's an ailment?

A sickness. He had a debilitating case of the hiccups.

What's debilitating?

Means he couldn't walk or talk or eat or sleep. He was sick from hiccups.

Hm, I said.

It's true. It's a documented case.

No he wasn't, I said. My eyes were wide open.

He made a motion to indicate that he was about to return to his office to locate supporting materials.

No! I said. Really? He couldn't stop?

Couldn't stop. And you know how they tried to cure him?

They tickled him, I said. They tickled him until he peed!

They should have. Instead they hung him upside down.

No they didn't, I shouted. They did? Did they?

They really did. They strapped him in and hung him like a bat.

And it cured him?

Nope, he said.

What happened?

He died.

Nooo, Daddy, no, he didn't! I was laughing, sputtering, gasping for air, my face flushed, my body shaking. The laugh transformed into a rasping sound that pitched up into a shriek as my fingers slipped. My head struck the bench before my father had even coiled to leap, my body crumpling as my hands scratched at the wood, twisted, unable to grip. My back ratcheted over the bench's lip. He managed then to dive for me, flat-out, making a play for a grounder, getting to me just in time to be of no assistance whatsoever. Kneeling on the floor, the rug a bulldog wrinkle beneath the bench, he gathered me up in his arms, and my first gulp of air gave me strength to land a fist on his cheek, a shot at the injustice of my fate, ejecting a lumpy silver crown from his molar.

Mah! he said.

The crown went skittering across the floor toward the heating grate, an ornate grille underneath the bench, which in the winter was hot as a waffle iron, a year-round consumer of marbles, pennies, walnuts, whatever the young residents of the Apelles found to feed clankingly to the furnaces.

Now it had got his crown. I hadn't meant to hit him, only to thrash against the embarrassment and the pain in my head, and I tried to restrain my sobs, fighting against my lungs, hitching for air in an attempt to silence myself so I could hear his silver tooth's plinking descent to the furnace. Struggling free, I wriggled across the floor and laid an ear close to the grate.

I can hear it, I said.

You hit me, he said—louder, he claimed later, than he'd meant to. But he hadn't meant to be gentle about it.

I curled up under the bench and started to cry again. I want Mommy, I wailed, covering my face and crying into the grate, my voice joining the murmur chorus living in the vents. Sometimes, in a coincidence of pneumatics and logistics, a wife on the seventh floor would hear her husband call, I'm home! only to find the foyer empty when she arrived bearing his tumbler of scotch, while a husband on the eleventh stood alone in his, raincoat draped over his arm, briefcase in hand, wondering where the hell his drink was.

Mothers on four adjacent floors snapped to attention.

Come here, kid, he said, pulling on my ankle. His hand was cold against the band of exposed skin between frilly white sock and blue cotton legging, and entirely encircled my ankle. I kicked as I slid across the parquet toward him.

You're going to burn your face off.

No, I'm not, I said. My chest was full of folded blankets. I sucked in a hitching breath.

Handkerchief, I heaved. Even at six, I was anything but a savage. Logical as an equation, I wouldn't sacrifice my dignity on the altar of self-pity, a characteristic my father claimed to admire. He extracted the handkerchief from his pocket and I took it from his hand. The cloth was embroidered on three corners with blue hearts, a gift from my mother, a coded message only three cryptologists in the world could ever have deciphered. Red thread ran from each corner and met at the center. The summer before, we'd stood at the vertex of Colorado, Utah, New Mexico, and Arizona beneath a sky the exact color of indigo she'd chosen for the hearts. We'd taken the train because my father had refused to fly.

I blew an oyster into it.

What happened? My mother had appeared silently behind him, crouching down, laying a hand on my head, the other on his shoulder.

Daddy made me fall down, I said.

Bad Dad, she said, pulling at my limbs. Your bones are still there. I don't see any blood. No blood, no Band-Aid.

The presence or absence of O negative was the yardstick by which my mother gauged the severity of virtually any accident, physical or emotional. Growing up with three brothers, she'd witnessed her share of gore. When she was a girl, nothing less than the exposed white of bone warranted her extended attention. Another trip to the ER. She'd shrug: Which moron this time? There would follow the ritual wrapping of the injured limb—her mother's domain—and bundling of injured party into a coat, my mother running through the house to turn off lights, everyone piling into the Studebaker while her father chewed his thumbnail, bored as a cabbie waiting for a cripple to drag himself in, the long drive into town, my mother jockeying for a waiting room seat that afforded a view into the ER, from which she might catch a glimpse of some action, awaiting arrival of the nurse who would take her brother back to the doctor who would flush and sew the wound or set the bone or both.

Her childhood home, the house itself, had borne the brunt of her brothers. It was a furniture mausoleum, decorated with cracked and glued lamps, smashed chairs reassembled hastily by the perpetrator, usually the oldest, whose addiction to mayhem was a shining example to his younger brothers. They were a Hydra of domestic destruction, and she, the youngest, was Athena observing from shore, usually left to her own devices except when a story had to hold together, and required the collusion of all the siblings, at which time she stepped in to weave her spell of conjunction.

She was no pushover, that girl, this woman. She cut waves like an oil tanker, diverted from her course by neither high seas nor marauders. But when I bled, she got very serious very quickly.

No blood, my father confirmed. Tooth went down the chute, though.

Show me, she said, peering into his mouth, venturing a finger.

Let me see, I said, struggling free from his embrace to gain a better sight line into his gaping maw.

Where? I said.

My mother pointed.

You have yellow teeth, Daddy.

Mawshes ah yehwoh behwee, he garbled around my mother's finger.

Let me see, I said, pulling at his shirt.

It's just a saying, my mother said. Daddy's belly is white as a whale's.

Hanks, he said.

Oh, lemme see lemme see! I said.

He would do anything to make me laugh. He wanted to give me a happy childhood. Moronic phrase, yet one he was unable to banish from his thoughts. It was a fantasy implanted in his head by guests on Carson who insisted that their childhood homes had been filled with laughter, an invention to put the audience at ease: See here, I've been content going way back, don't you worry about me. And the audience exhales, because it's nerve-racking, being responsible for the happiness of that guy in the spotlight, which, unless he tells you otherwise, depends entirely on your expressions of love for him. That's your job, to take care of the performer's feelings, to cradle him and caress him, to feed him your laughter and attention and make him feel okay.

So my father wanted me to have a happy childhood because it relieved him of the overwhelming desire to care for me? Perhaps.

It was true that I elicited from him a pure, aching compassion. He thought it possible that I was, for him, the origin of that very emotion, its first expression simultaneous to my birth, as though it were a rare tropical fruit he'd plucked from the tree and eaten while sitting on the forest floor, a sweeter, more elaborate flavor than he'd ever tasted from all the oranges and apples he'd mowed through in his life. He wanted me to laugh, perhaps, because he had no other gifts to give. He had darkness and introspection, a tendency to recoil from human contact. He had neuroses, cowardice, the nasty hangover of a past he couldn't shake. No natural feel for parenting, and at his age, little hope of learning. I was a grown woman by the time he got his arms around the task. He relied on simple rules, little orange flags in the misty landscape, but even as he trekked from one to the next he had no sense of up or down, north or south. No instinct for it, he thought, none at all. In art and argument he valued complexity, but when it came to me, his brain overflowed with monolithic, simplistic ideas: Spare the rod, spoil the child. Look before you leap. Haste makes waste. A happy childhood.

According to him, he was a bad parent, a notion bolstered by the prodigious ease with which my mother nurtured me. It was like playing Claudius opposite Olivier's Hamlet. He stuck to his lines and tried not to screw up the blocking. Simplicity. Consistency. Stay out of the way.

I had been just a newborn when my father had come to the conclusion that his own instincts were not to be trusted. Rocking me in my dark room one night, humming softly, he was overwhelmed by what could only properly be named a flood of emotion—not a single, identifiable feeling, but everything his heart was capable of throwing at him, a raging muddy river clogged with debris. He'd sobbed and held me as though I were his life buoy. Too much, he'd thought. It's just too much. Unsortable, uncontrollable. And how would he protect me if he was this weakened by love?

Ah yehwoh behwee, he again said around my mother's finger. I turned my head to hide my smile—I was not done with my accusatory tears. As I did, a spot of red appeared on my white shirt, above the school crest, at the clavicle. My parents both saw it and my mother ran her hand up my neck, her fingertips lightly touching the skin. I giggled and closed off access by clamping head to shoulder.

Honey, my mother said. She and my father were both looking for blood from the ear, of course, having been tempered to search out that cinematic signal of dire brain injury. Everyone bleeds from the ear or nose, a single trickle, before their eyes go glassy and they die. But it wasn't coming from the ear, and when I relaxed my clench, my mother canvassed my skull, pulling curtains of hair this way and that until she found the source, a split in the scalp, a wet mouth parted among the hairs at the crown of my head, darkly saturated, and a single stream running from the side. The wound was about three inches long. I, looking at the faces of my parents, suddenly realized something was wrong.

Just a cut, honey, she said. We should have a doctor look at this, she said to my father.

I have to go to the doctor? I said, clutching my mother's arm.

You don't want to bleed all over your uniform, do you?

I don't want to go to the doctor!

Look, look, my father said. I'll get a bandage for my mouth, he said, pulling back his lip to reveal the gap in his teeth. We'w mawch.

I don't want to match!

My mother pulled me close and pressed the handkerchief to the wound while I chanted that I didn't want to go to the doctor. Not now, not ever.

Let's get moving before we need skis, my mother said.

Right, my father said. What do we need? Boots? Boots. Do we need to take food? He went back down to his hands and knees, mumbling to himself about coats and umbrellas and gloves, bus routes, cabs.

Erwin, my mother said.

What? he said. I'm looking for her boots.

Erwin.

What? He looked back from beneath the bench. His rump was in the air and both of us were gazing at him with pity.

Oh. Oh, he said. He stood up. I should stay here, then.

It would probably be better if you stayed here, my mother said.

It's okay, Daddy, I said.

My mother called the pediatrician, but she got the service. She called her own doctor, then her ob-gyn. Because of the storm everyone had closed up early and made for Connecticut. My father was back on the floor, cross-legged, with me in his lap, his handkerchief's symbology flooded by a red lake.

What about Nachtman? he said.

I'm not calling Nachtman.

He did fine with this, my father said, tipping his chin at the crazed white scar traversing the webbing of his thumb, site of a self-inflicted knife wound he'd suffered trying to slice an apple for me.

He's not even a doctor! my mother said.

He's a doctor.

So he has a license now?

This is absurd. It's a piece of paper. His skills didn't evaporate when he emigrated.

His skills aren't going anywhere near her head, my mother said. She dialed another number. She waited an eternity before someone picked up.

Jane? she said. It's Sarah. Look, sorry. Oh really? Oh, how weird. So. No, no, it's not about that—no rush about that. It's— We have a little problem here. Hazel hit her head and I need someone to look at her, but— No, it's not serious. Yes. Exactly. Probably. No, she's sitting right here. No.

Honey, my mother said to me, do you feel like you're going to throw up? I shook my head. Dizzy? I shook my head again. No, no, neither. Yes, bleeding. Probably. Yes, probably. She looked in my direction. My head was on my father's shoulder, and I smiled weakly at her, resigned. That's the problem, she said, I can't get Foreman or anyone else and I wondered if we might stop by your place— Of course. Oh no, Jane, we'll just go to Roosevelt, then. That's no good. No, no, no. Are you sure? Really sure? Oh well, that might be fun. She raised her eyebrows at me. And if we need to go on to Roosevelt— Sure. Sure. Of course.

I'll see if he's up for it. Thank you, Jane. Thank you. We'll be up in a minute. Bye.

Vornados are having a party, my mother said after she'd hung up.

Tonight? my father said.

Right now. She said she was *just* about to call us.

I'm sure, my father said.

She said she'd look Hazel over and that we should all stay for the party. Erwin, they're having a *costume* party, my mother said and burst out laughing.

She actually said she was just about to call us? he said.

Spur-of-the-moment. They were just about to call.

My father shook his head and laughed, and then I started laughing, looking to him, then to my mother, for some clue why.

Now you're going to insist on coming with us, aren't you? my mother said.

Let me get my tux, my father said.

Daddy, you're coming, too? I said.

No, honey, said my mother. How to explain to me why it was funny? How much better it was to let me laugh alongside them, unencumbered by understanding, sounding my single note in their major key.

She actually invited me? my father said.

She did.

By name?

That asshole, I believe she said?

That's me.

I'll call if, you know. Anything, my mother said.

Anything at all, he said. He kissed my mother, kissed me, and slipped something into my hand. I knew what it was without looking, and he said, For good luck. It was the only time I can remember him parting with the hex nut he carried in his pocket, his talisman, a mechanical fixture whose intended use is to bind together, to stave off entropy and chaos, two forces he detected everywhere.

Part II

8.

In 1978, the tongue of land at the far eastern end of Long Island was home to the 773rd Radar Squadron of the United States Air Force, the Ronjo and Memory Motels, a trailer park out at Ditch Plains, a decent point break on the south side, and a voracious white-tailed deer population. Clusters of gray clapboard houses, battered by snow and ice in the winter, scoured by sand and sun in the summer. The red-roofed Coast Guard outpost just up the road from the Montauk Yacht Club, a ruin that played host to a few families on Sunday afternoons for lunch. The waters hadn't been fished to death, and a person with a boat could make a living.

There was speculation at the time that the Air Force had been taking advantage of the base's secluded location to conduct experiments on the population of Montauk (2,800). Unconventional psychological warfare, time travel, electromagnetism, invisibility. In 1978, it wouldn't have been impossible to fill most of the seats in the ballroom at the Montauk Yacht Club with members of the populace who claimed to have been abducted and forced to participate in those experiments.

On the Friday before the party at the Vornados' penthouse, I'd taken a train to Montauk with my parents. They'd kept me home from school and we'd caught a cab to Penn Station for the long ride out. For hours I'd been in stasis, suppressed to a near-narcoleptic state by the blurred rhythm that train windows impart on the world, but as we approached the station, the train slowed and the trees thinned to offer flashbulb views of Napeague Bay. Then the woods fell away entirely and there was the insinuation of a body of water to the south, Fort Pond, its presence marked by a void brighter than the snow. Even if you couldn't see it, you could feel the immense presence of the sea surrounding the place, but it was the infinite white ceiling of the sky, its sovereignty unbroken by office towers or billboards, that was unsettling to a child accustomed to the gray canyons of the city.

My father stepped down from the train first and reached up for me, and I fell forward into his outstretched arms for the short flight to the platform. My mother came down. My skin tightened in the cold. At the other end of the car, a lone passenger climbed aboard. A conductor's blue-capped head popped out, dipped back inside. The doors clicked shut and the train pulled out the way it had come in, terminus turned origin.

We stood on the platform setting down and picking up luggage, adjusting our coats and scarves. My father had his Olivetti case and a beaten leather valise, an artifact from his youth that I had stuffed with paper and colored pencils, assorted jewels, a plastic cup bearing the faded logo of the New York Yankees, and because the bag was also the permanent residence of a rock collection, two yo-yos, a Slinky, plastic plates, teacups, dollhouse furniture, hair bands, pennies, and a battered Etch A Sketch, it weighed almost as much as I did. I had made it as far as the apartment door before surrendering it to my father. He had a small gym bag, as well, containing his personal effects. My mother, in addition to her own bag, carried two more, one primarily stuffed with winter clothing for me, the other with board and card games. I was their only child; they were older parents; one might say they intended to treat me with great care, if not indulgence.

When my father looked at the sky, the gray, muscular shadowing of the clouds stretching toward the horizon, only the constant stitch of the power lines kept his sense of complete insignificance in check. It was nearly silent after the train had gone. A halyard tinged against the mast of a flagpole, the standard's fabric popping in the wind. Sound was swallowed up into the mass of the sky, and when he turned to say to my mother, There they are, his voice was carried away. She slipped her hand around his neck and pulled him to her ear and he repeated it, though she'd already seen.

Out in the lot, Jane Vornado was waving at us from behind the wheel of her Land Cruiser, its mint-green chassis spattered with mud and road salt. My mother and I climbed into the front and my father accordioned into the back, among fishing tackle, a flare kit, our luggage, and situated himself on a bench, atop a coil of marine rope. The vehicle smelled like gasoline and bilgewater. Jane took it easy out of the parking lot and ambled along at thirty-five, but even at that speed my father couldn't hear what was happening up front. The dash blowers didn't do much, and what little heat they did produce leaked out of the cab before making it to him. The whole thing rattled like a box of tools.

My father knew Sid Feeney would be there. The Feeneys owned the house next door, a white saltbox with a flagpole in the front yard. In the summer a ring of whitewashed rocks surrounded a bed of red, white, and blue flowers at the base. He supposed Feeney was out there at the first melt, touching up the rocks with a bucket and paintbrush, shimmying up the pole to polish the finial. Feeney wrote military histories, broadly researched hagiographies of Allied commanders that never failed to make the bestseller lists. He appeared never to have been troubled by a moral decision, which is to say that he knew inherently right from wrong and felt that it would be treasonous to question his self-assurance, installed as it had been by God Almighty himself. Feeney depressed the hell out of my father.

The tire treads sang on the pavement. Every pothole rattled his teeth, and when they plummeted from the pavement onto the dirt road that led to the house, he bashed his head against the steel roof.

Full of bile on most subjects, my father was especially sour about this setup. Supported by the pylon of their immense wealth, the Vornados rusticated on the weekends inside a full-scale reproduction of bygone days, playing out a fantasy of Life on the End, where they dried fish from the shed rafters and wore waxed canvas jackets, chopped wood, made venison stew, attacked the house's curling cedar shakes with antique shingling hatchets, at night slept under mounds of Hudson Bay blankets, refusing heat unless it came from a hot brick. They spoke of the land and sea as though they had bartered for their homestead with the Montaukett. It must have all come from a sense of guilt over their success, he supposed, a desire to do honor by the memory of their parents' struggles, or those of their grandparents, or whoever had come over in steerage and broken their backs on the Lower East Side for a dollar a week. Who, my mother asked, was he to judge? Just because they want to have a little fun on the weekends, their morality is out of whack? It's out of whack, he replied, because the Mercedes parked in the garage beneath the canoes *is* their morality. So that allows you to label them inauthentic? she said. This is what people do, isn't it, Erwin? They hang up one costume and put on another one.

Through the murky window of the Land Cruiser he saw, well, scenery: wilderness, snow, the wind-bent trees, a slice of the striated sky. The woods were thick on either side of the road, the spaces between pines stuffed with brush, spindly hardwoods struggling in the shade of towering hickories, an impassable landscape packed with eastern red cedars spouting billowing rolls of evergreen, one trunk spawning another, which split for another, and on and on. Even in the dead of winter the woods were as dense as a wall.

Once you had arrived on set, there was no way out. My father was to play the writer, the husband, the crank, the one with a fresh lump atop his skull to symbolize his spiritual injury.

A final spine-obliterating thud, and Jane ratcheted the brake. From the garage Bo Vornado approached the Land Cruiser, arms out, as if to embrace the vehicle itself. He moved through the world with an ease that my father imagined to be primarily the result of a healthy childhood, ruddy-cheeked, rough-and-tumble, football with brothers in the fall leaves, a hearty impertinence charming to teachers and girls alike, taking what he wanted when he wanted it, wanting for nothing. What he knew of Bo he arranged in a daisy chain that reduced the man to a manageable shape: varsity quarterback, student body president, matriculation at Harvard, Porcellian, elevation to toastmaster, reward of a desk at an investment firm. Taken under the wing of a managing director, he'd bidden his time, risen through the ranks, and, as prophesied, at the appointed hour slayed his mentor and appropriated his office and title. Then, bored by conquest, he'd struck out on his own. On principle, my father was opposed to Bo's existence, so anodyne, so well oiled, his entire life an unobstructed downhill run through fresh powder, yet he couldn't help liking him. Bo's masculinity had been so perfectly forged that it shielded him from any self-analysis of whatever failings lurked within his personality. He had, indeed, been raised to be a gentleman, charming, mindful of the needs of others, deferential to his elders, a steady arm on which a woman could lean. He'd never been in danger of displaying the syrupy, overly respectful attitude perfected by those boys who kept a sharp part in their hair, learned their catechism, and masturbated compulsively; he had, instead, a musky, mysterious air, that of a ram perched atop a mountain peak surveying his territory, and when he greeted my father with a hail-fellow-well-met embrace, my father's heart rose a little, as though they were old boarding school chums reunited after decades. There was no question in my father's mind that it was an embrace as practiced as a well-wrought wrestling hold, one designed to transmit authority and strength. Dominion. You are within my fold now, old boy, no harm shall befall you. It worked like magic.

Bo gathered up the bags—all of them, my father noticed, plus a couple of the boxes that had been knocking around the back of the vehicle, enough to crush an ox—and led the way inside, my mother and I trailing behind. My father had held on to his Olivetti case. Somewhere, Feeney's voice. An indistinguishable hum of words, then, Son of a bitch! rang out like a call to arms, and Bo's tattered laughter, and my mother's laughter—the betrayal!—and my father sensed that he, too, would have to enter the house now, the player called to stage, and so in he went, carrying the Olivetti case at his chest, braced for whatever might lie within.

Maestro! Feeney called, his mouth open wide enough to swallow my father whole, and came at him, right hand extended, palm as big as a broadaxe, a cigar smoldering in the left.

Hello, Sid, my father said.

You look like you need a scotch and a hooker, Feeney said.

Depends. You buying? my father said.

There he is, everyone! Ha ha ha! That's the spirit! Feeney roared.

God, look at him, my father thought. Like something out of Darwin's notebooks. That honker, the gaping mouth, those eyes bulging out like the view ports of the *Nautilus*—it was as though he had been conceived to consume as much of the world as possible. Extraneous elements like hair had been boiled away. His ears were pinned like shutters against the sides of his skull. He was nothing but sinew, the result of an inner engine that always ran at full capacity, burning more fuel than he had in reserve.

Feeney's wife, Carla, was a hummingbird at his elbow. Though my father had met her plenty of times, she never failed to surprise him. He was sure he'd never seen a smaller adult woman in his life who wasn't affected by dwarfism, an effect intensified by her apparent desire to vanish entirely behind her husband. What could explain the unfortunate combination of stature and timidity? It was too cruel a fate for the universe to have bestowed upon one person. Maybe, my father thought, silence is her weapon. Maybe the only one that works against a nuclear warhead of a man like Feeney.

Name, rank, and serial number, soldier! Feeney said. He always tried to get my father to cough up details about his time in the service, but my father never complied. Silent Death, Feeney called him. Surely, my father thought, Feeney had spent World War Two in some out-of-the-way post—Hawaii or a listening station in Greenland. No one who'd seen the front could be so pathologically gung-ho.

I'm going to try to get a little work done before we get wrecked, my father said.

A writer, Feeney said, is an addict whose drug gives him no joy but wastes his body and crushes his spirit. I can't recall who said that.

You, my father thought. You're the one who said that. He tugged some of the luggage away from Bo and headed upstairs. He knew his way to the bedroom, where he set up the Olivetti and pulled out his papers.

He had no intention of working. Once the desk was properly arranged, he positioned himself diagonally across the bed to signal that he'd been felled by an irresistible force. The silence and the light unweighted the air here; in the city, the air was fractious, stuffed with matter, and it insisted that he listen and record. It was a nuisance, he realized, as he always did when he was away from it, the city's false urgency. He closed his eyes and spiraled down quickly and dreamed he was in a swamp, chest-deep in water, pulling a boat by its bowline.

My mother called him from downstairs. It was dark, time for drinks, and he went into the bathroom and splashed water on his face, a performance intended to reimmerse him into the world of real things, but that was, in truth, only a means of delaying his entry into the audience downstairs. He told himself that wasn't the case, that the water was a baptism, a declaration of his intention to interact with his loved ones and his friends, and began the usual argument with himself over his own cowardice and inflexibility. A baptism? It was a dodge, but the problem was, which did he *believe* it to be? Both, but if a man can't decide what it means to put water on his face, what chance does he have in a room with Bo Vornado and Sid Feeney?

He went downstairs and took the drink waiting for him and touched me on the head and fielded the polite questions on the quality of his nap and the ribbing from Bo about sleeping on the job and Feeney's clunky barb about making a buck on his back, and my father laughed and shook his head at the tragedy of his own slothful disposition, saying with disbelief, I know, I know, and then, L'chaim! and dropped the first depth charge of the night, the first one always the most potent, the scotch sliding down his throat like a boy's fist stripping green leaves from a twig, and he was relieved, overjoyed, even, to feel the searing wash of the alcohol that would make him a tolerable dinner companion, one with no honor to defend, malleable opinions, a man who felt nothing but goodwill toward his fellow travelers.

The night tracked along the usual parabola, no acrobatics. They went through politics, money, art, real estate, things loosening up at the fourth bottle of wine, my father realizing by the fifth that even Feeney had softened when the man said he admired his own father for never, not even on his deathbed, asking god to ease his pain, and appeared to be choking back tears. Carla went home not long after dinner, leaving through the kitchen door with her wrist to her forehead. Around midnight my father made a slow, drunken ascent of the stairs to deposit an already-sleeping me into bed. He got me into my nightgown, put me under the cold covers, tucked the blanket around my body, smoothed my hair. In moments like those he felt that he was a father. The rest of the time he felt as though he'd been sent onto the ice without a stick or pads and told to take control of the puck.

Back downstairs he slumped onto the end of one of the sofas and put his feet up on the hearth. Bo dropped the needle on a record, dim but audible, and my father recognized it from years ago, Davis's trumpet retracing the lines scored in his memory, the apartment on West 77th, before he'd met my mother, before he'd published anything, when all he did was smoke and throw away what he wrote. Like paying an old friend a visit, recalling himself that way, and though there was conversation around him, he preferred the company of the past.

He, Bo, and Feeney were going fishing in the morning and Bo was outlining his strategy with a nonchalance meant to highlight his lack of obsession about the event, though to my father it seemed fairly obvious he'd been poring over depth charts and buying advice off the locals. Why else would he have said, Well, it's not like I've been poring over depth charts and buying advice off the locals? My father smiled at the ceiling.

What's funny? my mother said, shouldering him. His weight on the cushion had tipped her into his hip and he felt her thigh there against his and he felt the yawning within his body, an opening hunger for sex.

Nothing. Just listening.

She stay asleep when you put her down?

Out like Liston.

Didn't Liston take a dive?

I don't know what I'm talking about. Out like a sack of bricks. Down like a light.

Poet.

Watch your mouth.

There's a storm, Bo said, coming up the coast, but the fish can't feel it yet. They're nice and settled.

The music was good. My father was cataloguing the living room, dim, the lambent cone of orange from the fire, the dull reflection off brass handles and glazed picture frames. The saltbox couldn't have been laid out this way originally. They'd demolished walls, exposed beams, vaulted the ceiling, installed extra rooms to accommodate their modern appetite for space. But there was something more to it—an anachronistic solidity for a house of this age. The floors did not creak. The doors swung soundlessly on nickel-plated hinges. Their latches aligned precisely. Faucets delivered neat little columns of water and the cocks rotated with a whisper. The corners were perfectly squared. Even the kitchen knives were so sharp they fell through vegetables as though attracted to the cutting board by a magnetic force.

The music seemed louder now. Maybe just a loud passage. It was good but wrong for this full-scale diorama. Everything was just so. Did anything here have sentimental value to the Vornados? No family pictures, only black-and-white photos of trees, framed paintings of pastoral scenes. A set. Wasn't it a set? Even the cracked paint on the bookshelf, which held musty unread volumes in cloth bindings splashed with mildew, was the painstaking work of an artisan, one of the local eccentrics about whom the Vornados had a million stories. Were the books even real? Should he stick his hand into the fire and extract a glowing log to test the quality of the illusion?

This is a cognac ad, he said.

My mother studied his face. She knew this declarative tone. Salty, she said.

Fireside ambience, he said. Wool sweaters, loafers, amber liquid in heavy crystal. Hearty laughter and musings on contemporary life. The photographer would set up outside the windows over there.

Cut it out, she whispered. Feeney had been talking but now my father had everyone's attention. Bo and Jane's faces were open expressions of bemusement—they were waiting for him to turn the joke. Feeney was frowning as though he'd been distracted from some Clausewitz he'd been laboring to parse.

What's that, Saltwater? Feeney said.

My father ignored him and spoke to the air over their heads: The host's personality exudes a Caravaggiesque glow that illuminates the gathered friends' faces as they share intimacies and rest easy. What's that? The market's doing a swan dive? Babies freezing to death in China? They're *rioting* in the Bronx? Never mind all that! We're safe here behind the bulletproof fortifications of wealth and class.

He held up his fingers to frame the shot.

Jane tipped back her wineglass and took a sip, watching him over the foot.

I don't exclude myself, he said. I'm in the shot. I'm fully present. I'm enjoying the spoils of your labors. This place puts neurotics like me right at ease, like a warm glass of milk. It's a mind-control experiment. So much care put into the removal of uncertainty! Everything as predictable as a clock. We're the only thing left to chance. We're the only variables! Isn't that something? It's utterly precious and a perfect narcotic, to wit. Bo, I have to ask you, though. There's something about all this perfection that's a little emasculating, don't you think? Those perfectly flawed needlepoints in the bathroom? To have lavished such care on anything that doesn't require gun oil or have a gearbox? Either you're under your wife's thumb or you're a willing participant in this façade. Wait. Don't tell me it was all your idea.

Bo was relaxed, a tumbler balanced on his crossed knee. What a gas, he said to my mother.

Oh, he's just getting warmed up, she said.

Bo hadn't yet decided how he would react. Perhaps with the tolerant jocularity of a movie star pried from his dinner conversation by an ardent fan. Or perhaps he'd get up and smash the bastard's jaw.

Surely you must have realized that other men would ask these questions, my father said. I'm asking on behalf of these theoretical men, you understand? Because it's a lovely house. It's cozy as could be. It's just, I don't know, hard to identify the masculine presence.

Bo took a slug from his glass.

No offense, Jane, my father said.

She smirked at him and waved her hand. And there—it was all right. Bo had his answer. They'd take it as a badly delivered joke, this assassination. They'd blame it on his drinking.

But there is another possibility, my father said.

Erwin, honestly, my mother said.

Oh come on. What's the unexamined life? Here's the answer, in the form of a question. What if they've created this all explicitly to force these kinds of questions? What if they've done it all intentionally, just to attract the mockery of superior old bastards like myself? What if the façade isn't a mask to cover their insecurities but a medium for self-expression?

That's three, Bo said.

What?

That's three questions, Bo said.

So it is. Here's a fourth: What if you're a couple of Warhols? House as kitsch—your commitment to reproduction, it's a riff on the absurdity of the historical American house, the central lie of which is that there can be any history in a house that's only a hundred years old. America doesn't have a fucking history. Christ, go to Prague and they've got rats in the basement with more extensive family trees than the Kennedys. Here's what I want to know. How did you get them to do it? How'd you get the carpenters to overwork the floors just so? And all the handles? They're so carefully mean. Patinated, but with that shellacked permanence, like they're in amber. It's one thing to find an artisan who can age a piece of furniture, but to find one who can age it and then add the final step, so that the work itself is apparent in the final product, so that it displays its own artifice—that's real craftsmanship. That's what Jencks is talking about. True postmodernism. Am I taking this too far?

Oh, absolutely not, Bo said.

Good, because I'm quite serious. We're sitting in a piece of art here. This, all this, it's a commentary on those batty old Wasps who let their mansions come down around their ears because god forbid they should act like they care about *stuff*. Only new money cares about stuff. You had everything custom-made for this place, isn't that right? All the Chippendale stuff upstairs, that dining table? Made to order, distressed and faux-finished? You're the vanguard of an age of intentional inauthenticity! You're giving the finger to every white-shoe Princeton pseud who got it all from Mommy and Daddy. Fuck them! Fuck 'em well and right!

Christ, you're a piece of work, aren't you? Feeney said.

My father blinked. He realized everything he'd said had been directed at Feeney, trying to impress and destroy at the same time. He feared his friends' money and their confidence and their success and it was small, infinitesimally small, of him to malign them, even if by some miracle of inebriation it sounded to them like nothing more than a tone-deaf pseudo-academic roast. Small because he felt calm around them, yes, and that was a gift they gave him. He basked in the warm glow of the control they exerted over their lives, the opportunities that their money afforded them. He found comfort in their presence. But he was only here because he was added patina, and that was humiliating. He was here as author Erwin Saltwater, and he knew it because they tolerated him. Because Bo didn't slug him. Because Jane didn't tell him to shut the fuck up. He'd concocted the diatribe to thank them for their hospitality, to sing for his supper, to provide them a story they could tell their friends. Mission accomplished.

They'd moved on like it hadn't happened. Feeney was talking about the markets again. He talked like a flood sweeping through a village, in a chaotic rush of words that tore trees out by the roots and plucked houses off their foundations.

My mother turned to my father. Age of intentional inauthenticity? Been sitting on that one for a while, have you?

I suppose, he said. What is wrong with me?

Where would I even start? she said.

"Blue in Green" ended and Jane turned the record over. My father's eyes were closed. The needle popped, dropped into the groove, played a few bars of dust before the piano and the drums came sliding in like something out of a heist movie and Coltrane and Cannonball Adderley came in behind them, saxes crackling with spittle, and then Davis, restrained, creeping over the shoulders of his bandmates. "All Blues." My father let himself back into that old apartment on 77th. The landlord had installed his own mother in a top-floor unit one winter. Because he ran the boiler only enough to keep the pipes from freezing, she'd contracted pneumonia and died. That's how my father had heard it. He had trouble remembering her face. She was a black sweater and gray skirt, a column of dust planted in orthopedic shoes. She wheeled her supplies around in a squeaky folding grocery cart scrounged from a dumpster. She scrubbed the lobby floor on hands and knees, her phlebitic legs sticking out hideously like marshland maps cut and crossed by violet creeks and streams, the central rivers in cerulean. More than once he'd had to step over them to get to the stairs. Always mumbling to herself in Polish. My father could have spoken to her, but he hadn't. On weekdays she cleaned her son's other buildings. On Sundays, she cleaned the one where my father lived. Saturdays she went to synagogue. When her neighbor on the eighth floor had fallen ill, she'd made a pot of krupnik, wasn't that what someone had said? Things he'd heard after she was dead. She hadn't been old. Another thing he'd heard was that she'd been in the camps, but that she'd managed first to get her son on a train to Spain, then a boat to the U.S., and he'd grown up with his aunt and uncle on Long Island.

My father had lived on the second floor, in a studio with a mattress, his books, the Olivetti, and a portable record player. Some days he listened to "Blue in Green" three hundred times, at the tune's end his hand automatically reaching for the arm, fingers casually dropping the needle back at the beginning while their twins waited patiently atop the keys. This fine synchronization of body with machine rendered him calm enough to write, the repetition silencing the demon voices and tics that sabotaged his concentration.

That song was the score to his first book, a companion and an ally, and the Vornados had boiled it down to tar to patch holes in their conversations. The old woman was ingrained in the music, down in the grooves of his memory, her scrub brush, the swish of the brushes on the drum kit, her voice whining with the horn, with the sirens, the slamming of doors above and below, the concrete footfalls of his upstairs neighbors, the bass, the hissing of the radiators, the street, the snapping of the Lettera's typebars. How romantic it could be in retrospect. Why not also pretend that she might have been a beautiful woman before the war, a woman of culture? Of course she hadn't been.

Feeney was arguing that increased sales of nude pantyhose correlated with the increased availability of pornographic films. He was trying to get a rise out of the women, employing the genial lechery men used to compete with the detrimental effects of women's lib, the main of which, as any male of the species could tell you, was a complete loss of humor in the fairer sex. My father wanted to hear "Blue in Green" again, this time loud enough to drown out Feeney, but it wouldn't do to get up and flip the record over. Earlier, he might have had the right, but now he had to make an effort not to be such a grade-A prick. Instead he went and got another drink, waving the bottle, a peace offering, at everyone, who shook their heads no, and when he came back he sat on the other side of my mother, closer to Feeney and the Vornados, and when there was an opportunity, he apologized, bumblingly, with a convincing degree of sincerity that he felt at the time was genuine. Bo patted him on the leg and Jane waved him off again, just as she waved off everything, it seemed, that might impede the progress of her personal narrative.

My mother stitched the patterns in the bathrooms, Bo said. She loved Frost.

Jesus Christ, my father thought. She loved Frost. Frost! What a riot she must have been. I bet she threw herself down the staircase every Easter morning.

My father nodded. One of the greats, he said.

O n Saturday, at an hour so early the darkness was heavy as a slab of stone, the alarm clock by my parents' bed, conveniently set by Bo the day before, went off clangingly, prompting my father to thrash wildly in the direction of the noise, taking out an ashtray and a glass of water before he found the clock. My mother muttered something indecipherably profane and he dragged himself from the bed and into the black bathroom, where he and Doppler tried to hit the bowl. He picked his way downstairs. Bo and Feeney were already at the espresso machine, a chrome-piped contraption covered in pressure gauges, its chassis enameled in Ferrari rosso corsa. It was so early there was not even a pale line at the horizon.

The transistor radio on the windowsill was tuned to the local AM, which at that hour broadcast the time, temp, and NOAA forecast on a five-minute loop. In Bo's estimation, a good morning to be on the boat. Temperature in the teens. Nothing serious, atmospherically speaking. The storm was still making its way up the coast from the Carolinas but nothing to worry about today. None of them had slept more than three hours, and Bo's eyes felt like someone had attacked them with a melon baller.

Bo was a pioneer in the nascent world of leveraged buyouts, the spread in Montauk a minor facet in his crown. There was a castle in Ireland he had his eye on. A storage facility in Mahwah for his collection of buffalo hides. A separate facility on East 72nd Street for his paintings. Mountains of money: a phrase never far from his consciousness. He'd never felt a need to apologize for or curb his desires. If his confidence grated, that wasn't his fault any more than it was a tree's fault it provided shade.

He'd been chewing on my father's drunken rant from the night before. As another sign of my father's jealousy, it pleased him—it pleased him far more than all the obscene praise piled on him by men who wanted to fawn their way into his good graces. Bo understood that all men wanted what he had. His stuff, his power, his ability to ignore the problems that plagued their minds and forced them to tell themselves lies about their worth in the world. To Bo, my father was no different from the rest, except in the way he expressed his jealousy, which was honest, even soulful. Maybe this was how kings felt about their jesters: a fool was one whose disdain for the king's power was so pure that he could be trusted to tell the truth from time to time.

Doppio for you, Bo said, pushing a cup of espresso toward my father, who was still wobbly, unsure whether he'd slept or only rolled around the bed for a few hours searching for sleep, and he threw it back in one shot.

Vile, Feeney said. Americano for me.

We don't serve your kind, Bo said.

The hell, Feeney said.

Macchina italiana, speak no Americano, Bo said.

Goddamnit, Vornado. Just give me something with a set of balls on it.

This fine fellow passed out on the couch last night, Bo said to my father. Now I have to burn the thing. Bo slid an espresso cup across the counter. Doppio.

May you have only daughters, you son of a bitch, Feeney said.

Beware your half-wit sons, Bo said.

The way they talked, they could have been a pair of former college roommates, ever bound together by the barbed wire of competitive urges, surrogate brothers still capable of squabbling for hours over baseball stats. They spoke to each other in the tones of fraternal derision common to trading floors and golf clubhouses, fangs dulled just enough to allow them to sink their teeth into the other's hide without drawing any blood. But they'd known each other only a few years, since Bo and Jane had bought the house.

Still, my father wasn't convinced that the two weren't merely exceptionally skilled at wallpapering their contempt for each other. Feeney was the antipode to Vornado's swaggering gentleman, even now pounding the table like a piston as he made some point about how the cocksucking communist rebels in South America were driving up the price of coffee. My father doubted that the man had passed out on the sofa at all. Seemed more likely that he'd lain there, vampirical, his brain churning out conspiracy theories between fantasies of hand-to-hand combat with the Japs.

What my father hadn't yet hit on was Feeney and Bo's shared hunger, a Nietzschean impulse toward mastery. He would understand later. He was an observer on the edge of their kinship, though they didn't treat him as an outsider as much as a foreigner they'd come across in a bar, a sad sop who couldn't keep up with the slang and lifted his glass like a fruit, who for fun they kept pulling with them from one dive to the next. A mascot.

My father's only redeeming factor, by his own estimation, was that he could fish. He might be able to acquit himself on the boat. Maybe. He had fished muddy, sprawling waters as a boy, learning to thread jigs between the branches of the half-submerged trees where the bass hid on boiling summer days. Those slow chocolate rivers produced catfish as big as newborn calves, and they liked to flatten out and suction down into the sludge by the dam spillways. Towing them off the bottom was like hauling out a potbellied stove. He hadn't fished more than twice in the thirty years since he'd left home for college, yet he considered himself a fisherman, and when Bo suggested the outing, he'd agreed immediately, to my mother's vocal surprise.

He's talking about fishing on the open water, Erwin, she'd said. The ocean.

Where else would it be?

All right, Ahab. Just stay in the boat, okay?

Don't worry about me, he had said.

Of course, that was all she did.

There was a little light now. Down the white slope of the yard, Lake Montauk was a snow-feathered plane of ice. Bo's twenty-one-foot Boston Whaler, a fiberglass ballet slipper outfitted with a Mercury 175, was moored ten minutes away at the marine basin, where the commercial fishermen kept their vessels. He owned, in addition to the Whaler, a larger cruiser with an enclosed cabin, heat, a small fridge, but it was the naked, simple banana boat that he wanted for this excursion. Bo intended to take them deep, in search of blues, a probably quixotic expedition he was insisting on purely for the audacity of putting the other two through the Nordic hell of air so cold that spray from the bow would turn to ice pellets before it hit their foul-weather gear. Their boots would freeze in place on the deck. Their monofilament would sag with ice and lock up the reels. Should one of them be lucky enough to haul something out of the depths, they'd be treated to the spectacle of watching the fish freeze solid within a minute or two of landing on the deck. What sort of man was Bo? Like most men, one trapped by his idea of what he should be.

They drove through the dark to the harbor, again in the freezing, spine-shattering Land Cruiser, Feeney having insisted my father take the back bench so he'd have room to stretch his legs, though yet again he'd been pinned in by all the gear. Something still reeked. Bo backed down to the pier and started unloading. Everything my father carried down to the boat had to go back. Appreciate the help, Bo said, but you can leave the wet gear up there. Easier to get into it by the Cruiser. My father ended up standing guard by the vehicle while Feeney made trips back and forth, carefully selecting tackle boxes, rods, buckets, plastic containers in some preordained order that eluded my father, who moved to help at the apex of every trip only to have Feeney wave him off. No, no, get your beauty rest. Eventually Bo came thumping back up the pier and hopped in the driver's seat. He revved up the engine and popped it into gear before my father, leaning against the back, could react, and the Land Cruiser slipped out from beneath his hip, sending him sprawling onto the gravel.

Great shit! Feeney said. Always seeking the horizontal, aren't you, Saltwater? He offered a hand.

You think this is good, wait until we get out there, my father said.

You'll be fine, Feeney said.

He climbed the gravel track to the parking lot a few steps behind Feeney, who ascended in a sort of crouch. Near the lot, Feeney turned back to my father. My goddamn prostate. I'm either so jammed up I can't walk or it's leaking like a screen door.

My father nodded as though this information explained anything.

They got into the wet-weather gear, my father in a new set of rubber boots, rain bib, and foul-weather jacket, all in duckling yellow. Bo's bibs and boots were the same somber blue as Feeney's, scarred and caked in fish scales and blood. Feeney's jacket was dusky red, cracked at the elbows from age and exposure; Bo's was orange, with a Swedish flag patch on the left chest. It had been his companions' foul-weather gear he'd smelled in the back of the Land Rover, more powerful than the grease from the reels or the gasoline sloshing around in the jerricans. Mildew and seawater, rotting fish. A Precambrian sense of foreboding, that smell.

The sky to the east was fading to white, a peaceful dawn blooming, and the men's breath rolled from their mouths in long streams of vapor. Piles of dirty snow took shape at the edges of the lot. The security light flickered off.

All right, gentlemen, Bo said, slamming closed the rear hatch. They walked silently across the lot and down the slope to the pier. Bo boarded the boat first, then Feeney, carrying a battery under his arm, who momentarily summoned some dormant athleticism for the leap down, and then my father, who hesitated as he stepped, his boot levitating above the gap between the frosty dock and the white gunwale, while his brain ran a last-minute calculation, then overcompensating so that his foot shot forward, the wavy gum of his sole's heel catching the slick fiberglass just long enough to allow him to get his other foot atop the thin edge, where he tottered, Chaplain on the verge, juking and weaving, his boots squawking against the laminate. Bo's hand shot out and grabbed the front of his jacket and pulled my father down into the boat.

Mother of Christ, you weren't kidding, Feeney said.

Tide's running, Bo said, unmoved by the near overboarding. He'd turned his attention to securing the tackle boxes in a compartment below the center console. At the back of the boat, Feeney worked the battery into its compartment, strapped it down, affixed the leads, and scrambled back onto the dock, nimble as a mountain goat, to uncleat the ropes. Bo turned the key, trimmed the prop into the water, and fired up the engine, which chugged three times and then blasted alive with a cough of blue smoke. My father had moved to the bow, where he felt he might do the least damage, and Feeney tossed the bowline to him. He held the damp weight in his gloved hands and, not knowing what else to do, coiled it and stashed it in the cutaway along the inside wall.

All right? Feeney said, and Bo made a swirl with his finger. Feeney tossed the aft line into the boat and leapt in behind it as Bo clicked the throttle to reverse out of the mooring. They drifted gently back, parting the glassy water, and he clicked the lever forward. The prop dug in, gurgling, the water churning. As they swept out into the channel, Bo waved at my father and patted the gunwale next to him.

You don't want to be up there, he said.

My father complied.

Bo opened up the throttle at the mouth of the breakwaters. There was light enough to see the swells out before them, rolling gray seas not quite capping. Lacy tatters of foam rode the surface of the water. The boat commenced a gentle arc, heading northwest, directly into the wind, and my father, who'd dutifully glued himself to the gunwale, holding tight with his left hand, repositioned himself in a crouch, leaning forward as the bow rose up, grasping the rail on the pilot console with his right. Just past Shagwong Reef, the chop picked up, and when Bo speared the peak of a wave, spray exploded over the bow, splattering their jackets. Feeney caught the icy shower with a whoop. He was seated on a small shelf at the aft. My father noted that one bad bounce was all it would take to send Feeney flying overboard.

Bo at the wheel was some kind of orange-hooded Washington fording the Delaware. His orange glove was steady on the throttle as they dove into the valleys, climbed the rising faces, and sailed off the crests, the prop breaking free of the water, the engine whining like an Indy car's, before burying itself again in the froth when the hull smacked down against the surface. They were heading for the deep water of the Block Island Sound. If there were blues, that's where they would be. This was as close as Bo Vornado came to nervous, this single-minded focus driving him toward the fish he'd promised his guests would be there. He'd will them into existence if he had to. Nothing was fun unless there was a chase, but he wanted to stay cool around the older men, so he'd gotten up especially early and smoked a sausage of a joint in the garage.

My father lasted about five minutes before he felt it rising up in the back of his throat, that unmistakable tang in the spittle accumulating on his soft palate, the popping in his ears, the den of snakes in his gut. His jaw went slack and the base of his skull throbbed. Nothing but a full stop was going to save him. The wind in his face did nothing to the sweat oozing from his forehead but push it stinging into his eyes. Sweat was flowing down the small of his back. There was sweat between his toes. Sweat on his lips. His flesh felt as if it had shrunk and drawn tight as a cured hide. His organs had disintegrated into undulating liquids. His eyelashes fluttered. No, no, no, no, no.

Retroperistalsis began.

In 1944, my father was admitted to the U.S. Naval Convalescent Hospital in Santa Cruz, California. It was there that, on an afternoon pass, he'd taken a two-minute ride on the Giant Dipper, a wooden coaster at the boardwalk, conveniently located just across Beach Street from the hospital. As roller coasters go, it was about as wild as a Shetland pony, but my father's ride had been an adrenal Gettysburg, a real eyeball-peeler to the untold horrors his already unfriendly brain had waiting backstage, and he hadn't been able to shake the eschatological specter that had shadowed him after he'd climbed out of the cramped car, heart racing and palms wet, a sudden hangover crushing his temples. He started babbling about Hobbes and Dostoyevsky to his date, who capitalized on her opportunity to escape when he turned around to leer yet again at the carnival death trap flinging another group of suicidees against the crystal-blue sky. Something had cracked loose within him, hatched and emerged whole into the light of day. It was the thing that had put him in the hospital in the first place, diagnosed as malaise—an aristocrat's disease, a wilting of the spirit, an inability to sleep, treated with a Benzedrine/veronal dose pattern to reestablish the proper circadian rhythms—but now he saw that the thing had only been incubating, awaiting its monstrous rapture. He'd been insane to risk his life on that contraption. Even back on solid ground he winced as the wheels screamed and thunked behind him, the weathered wooden crosshatching creaking like a rope bridge over a gorge. It was the noise of imminent destruction, the terrible scream of an incoming munition. His eyes saw a changed world. Gulls hovering against the blue sky were agents of disease, the children's cries oscillating as the coaster whipped around a turn nothing more than civilization's death rattle. He had put his life in the hands of strangers for the sake of a quick thrill, to get the girl hot. What if some old carnie had half-assed his morning maintenance check, missed a loose assembly in the elbow of one of the oh-so-gentle sweeping banks, and though it had held for the first sixty-three rides of the day, a nut had been incrementally vibrating ever looser down the bolt's shaft, and finally, at ride number sixty-four, it spiraled free of the last micron of thread as the wheels clattered through the turn, the little hexagon of steel ricocheting down through the superstructure like a pachinko ball, and though good luck and friction had held the beams together, it had been my father's fate to be on the very next ride, the sixty-fifth, the one under which the crosstie had slipped, the rail distended, leaving the wheels of the leading car free to navigate the open air, and they all went plunging like a speared dragon to the boardwalk fifty feet below?

What if? What *if*? Of course the maintenance checks were half-assed!

Just because the roller coaster hadn't collapsed in a splintering, shredding implosion of wood and steel didn't mean it wasn't loaded with potential. He understood now. Every man-made structure was a collapsing machine, held in check only by the crews crisscrossing the beams and catwalks looking for cracks, banging on wires and listening for off-key responses. Architecture was nothing more than the art of creating things that fall down very, very slowly, so slowly that we might even forget the inevitability of decay.

The coaster had seven hundred thousand nails in it. Warehouses' worth of nuts and bolts. Millions of opportunities for the two eyes of the maintenance man to miss something. And how many mechanical elements had to fail at once to guarantee an accident? Two? Three? The potential combinations that led to mechanical failure were infinite. Therefore, infinite possible causes of death. To reverse the tape, an infinite number of non-failures had to occur every second of the day in order for my father to go on living.

He had never been known for his nerve. As a boy, he'd avoided swimming at the quarry, explorations of abandoned houses. He was quick to imagine the aftermath of a slip from atop a stone wall. He served as human ladder and, after boosting the last friend through a broken window, lookout, as they climbed out onto the roof of the Uniroyal warehouse, pretended to lose their balance again and again, tottering on one foot, windmilling their arms, while my father's breath caught every time he managed to bring his eyes up to see their black shoes and drooping socks, their pale white legs.

Putting himself in harm's way wasn't exhilarating, it was terrifying; hiking in the mountains with his father, he kept himself well back from the cliff's edge, so powerful was the call of the void. His head swam when his father, perched on a splinter of rock jutting over a thousand-foot drop, turned his back to the emptiness and called for his son to come on over and enjoy the view.

No, he'd say. No. He couldn't go to the edge because he couldn't trust himself *not* to jump. He wasn't suicidal, so why couldn't he trust himself? He trusted his present self—it was his future self, the one who lived five seconds from now, the one who stood at the edge of the cliff, whom he didn't trust. That future self had lived through a span, however brief, of unpredictable events. How could my father know what he might experience in those five seconds and how those experiences might shape his behavior? Why offer his future self the opportunity to jump? In every situation, the film raced forward to a dire outcome.

He spent the remainder of the afternoon lying flat on his back on the sand. Only there in the constant sun, the waves breaking predictably at his feet, did he feel calm enough to think.

The world was a slave to pressure and velocity, to the calculus of spinning rods and belts and gearwheels, to the transformation of circular motion into linear motion. All vacuum tubes, pipes, valves, flanges, whether taken individually or in system, as in an internal combustion engine, were potential bombs. Cars were nothing more than harnessed violence: beneath the hood, fan blades spun like saws, pistons fired, belts whipped by at blinding speed. The rotational force of the four Goodyears humming along at highway speed translated to potential destructive energy on par with a case of land mines, each wheel loaded for the moment of puncture when hunks of rubber would shear away, shattering windscreens to the rear, cars to the left and right inscribing twin-black sine curves across the tarmac as their drivers lost control, steel tonnage smashing into steel tonnage into concrete dividers, flying off overpasses, the helpless little meats inside pulverized. And what if an entire wheel disconnected, rim and all? He tried to calculate the stress placed on the shanks of the wheel studs, on the lug nuts holding the rim to the axle. How many thousands of pounds of pressure? And how many hands worked on an automobile production line? A hundred? Two hundred? Each set of hands was a new opportunity for a bolt to be over-torqued, under-torqued, mis-threaded—or, god help us, forgotten entirely.

An acute mental problem, unquestionably what was known to professionals in the field as a neurosis. He wasn't hallucinating, and he wasn't hearing voices. He simply couldn't stop his mind from compiling new ways to die.

Thirty-five years later his shrink, Dr. Asher Schiff, suggested that my father had *wanted* to die.

That doesn't compute, my father said. Not everything is a reversal. If I wanted to die, all I had to do was jump off the roof of the hospital. But I was *afraid* of dying.

Of course you were afraid of dying, Schiff said. Come on. Why can't you both fear and desire death? Are you a machine?

Because I wanted to live, full stop. A desire to die would have been easier to deal with. No conflict there. I jump off the roof.

And did you jump off the roof?

I did not jump off the roof.

Look, I say crazy things sometimes. I probably shouldn't even have started down this road with you, Schiff said.

This again, my father said.

Schiff had been on the pro tennis circuit before enrolling in the psych program at CUNY, and he had that ex-athlete's way of moving to avoid pain, every bend or stoop the sum of a careful calculation. Joints gone to hell, every ligament a bit too tight, every muscle on the verge of rupture, he usually sat draped over his leather chair, utterly slack unless movement was absolutely necessary. He had a big head that my father found comforting. His forehead had executed a sort of continental drift across the top of his skull and what hair he had left he kept stubble-length with an electric razor. He transmitted boundless waves of security and empathy. A cardigan over a button-down shirt, button collar, corduroys, big brown Earth shoes. My father had always assumed Schiff was good with children, and then, because Schiff had trained him well, he followed that assumption with a lengthy explication of why he wanted Schiff to be good with children, and whether or not he wished he were Schiff's child.

Schiff said, You fantasized that the bicycle you rode around the hospital grounds might suddenly become structurally unsound, snap in two, and spear you in the chest, is that correct?

And the inside of the thigh. Femoral artery, my father said.

And the roller coaster? You repeatedly returned to watch the very roller coaster that set the whole thing off?

Yes.

What do I know, but it sounds like you were looking for a way to die. Maybe hoping? Is hoping too strong a word here?

No, it's just the opposite. I never wanted to die. The fear tied me in knots. It made me a nonfunctioning human being.

Look, you want something from an old textbook? Say you've got a teenage boy who says he hates his mother. He storms out of the room whenever she walks in, won't speak to her, does everything in his power to stay as far away from her as possible. He's a raging asshole to her. When he does speak, he says vicious things. Every time she tries to give him a kiss on the cheek, he repels her. He drives her away at all costs. Why? His behavior tells a story. He doesn't understand it himself— here he is, pushing away the woman who has nurtured him for four-teen, fifteen years, a woman he wrote mash notes to when he was six. What's changed? Why would he behave this way? Because suddenly he has hard-ons for her. Her image invades his fantasies when he's jerking off. And what's worse, he's physically powerful enough to act on his desire. He has the equipment now, and for the first time in his life he's physically bigger than she is. He knows he could take her if he wanted her. And, oh boy, he does want her. Well, he doesn't have to have read *Oedipus* to know how *Oedipus* turns out.

I never had a thing for my mother, my father said.

Sure you did, but I was only offering an analogous illustration.

I think you got bored and wanted to talk about sex.

That's possible. Perhaps I got spooked and ran to sex because it counterbalances death? My point, if I even have one, is that an obsessive fear of death would be a natural reaction in a person experiencing an overwhelming desire to die. It's a reasonable response.

Oh come on. Everyone's afraid of death. It's our collective obsession with *not* dying that keeps us all alive, my father said.

It is?

Yes! Of course it is. You think everyone wants to die? Everyone's suicidal?

Yes.

You think everyone's suicidal?

Yes, Schiff said.

We need to switch chairs.

Now we're getting somewhere. You were insane. Yes or no? Schiff said.

No? said my father.

Wrong! But also right. Certainly no more insane than anyone else. In fact, I think you were expressing a completely sane reaction to your situation.

The roller coaster?

The war.

What war? I was at a resort! The hospital was the Casa del Rey! What was there to be afraid of at the Casa del Rey? Otters?

I don't know. Were you?

Was I what?

Were you afraid of the otters?

No! I wasn't afraid of the fucking otters!

Okay. Lemme write that down. Not afraid of otters.

And where were you stationed? my father said.

Would it be useful for you to know that?

Yes. Then I'd have an idea who I'm talking to here.

You know who you're talking to.

Tell me again, my father said.

I was with the Red One.

Ardennes.

Yes. We've been over this.

What were you, eighteen?

That's about right, Schiff said.

Then I must sound like a complete coward to you.

You sound like a man who suffered greatly during the war, and who's still suffering.

I helped write manuals, my father said. It doesn't hold a candle.

What was in the manuals?

Nothing. Instructions.

Survival manuals? Foxhole radio instructions?

No.

What, then?

Stupid instructional manuals. The point is, no one was trying to kill me. The 12th SS Panzers weren't lobbing shells in my general direction.

Where were your schoolmates? The boys who lived on your block. The ones you're always talking about.

European Theater. Pacific. Africa.

They were on the front lines.

Yes. Being killed on the front lines, my father said.

And you?

I've told you. Instructional manuals.

You persist in saying that as though it were some kind of despicable work.

It was.

Only to you, because you wished to die alongside your friends. And you felt that you betrayed them because you went right on living. Thus you created a world where at any moment a steam pipe might explode and crush your skull or a malfunctioning bicycle might spear your heart or a roller coaster might collapse and send you plummeting to your death. A dangerous world. And you still wish this dangerous world would harm you, to even things up.

Well, that's all behind me now.

When's the last time you rode an elevator?

They weren't my schoolmates, you know.

Your friends?

Yes.

Where did they go to school?

Well, you know, I went to private school and they went to public school. I was a dry old man and they were boys. Real boys. Boisterous and industrious. Like kids out of a *Life* photo essay. They were fearless. My job was to dream up the next stunt and watch them execute.

You were separate from them, an outsider.

Jesus, enough.

Only an observation.

Don't go shrink on me, okay?

So these boys were fearless?

Afraid of nothing, no one, and aware of the world. You know what the real difference is between private and public education in this country? It's not the money. Public school teaches you how to work the system. Private school teaches you to be the system. It's no different here than in England or Switzerland, or anywhere. You've been inducted into the family of power. Oh hullo, I'm Chas, pleased to meet you. I believe you prepped with my brother. Yes, Choat. Yes, yes, that's right—Tom Buchanan, he's my brother. And there you are, next thing you know you're at a goddamn family picnic on the estate lawn with Daisy and Jordan. Take away all that money and all that power, though, and you're a goner. You don't know how to do anything but shake hands and drop names. But a public school kid can get things done when the chips are down. He's got no family to depend on. *His* brother Tom probably owes half the guys on the block money. My friends from the neighborhood could walk into a bar seven thousand miles from home and when they walk out, they've got a place to stay, they've got tickets to the show, girlfriends, everyone wants to follow them to the next bar.

You think schooling was the difference between you and your friends from the neighborhood? Schiff said.

It's the reason I went into my precious branch of the service and they went into the infantry.

I see, Schiff said.

You know, they were funny, my father said. They made me laugh harder than I've ever laughed in my life. At eleven, twelve years old, they understood more than I ever will. Tell me Woody Allen would be funny if he'd grown up wealthy. Tell me he'd be funny if he'd gone to private school.

What the hell private school would have let in a Jew? said Schiff.

All right—tell me anyone who's funny who's gone to private school. Nobody, that's who. You have to know the truth to be funny.

And what's the truth? said Schiff.

That we're cannibals, said my father.

That kid—the one who falls down stairs on TV? Good-looking kid. Prep kid. Went to Riverdale.

I don't know who you're talking about, my father said.

You know, Woody Allen is only funny to goyim because he confirms your beliefs about us—we're neurotic, weak, sexually perverse, generally loathsome. But we think he's funny because he's really making fun of you morons.

See? Something for everyone.

Dangerfield's got better range, Schiff said.

You're a philistine.

I find his act enchanting.

He's a hack.

I never told you this, but I knew him a little bit, Schiff said. Smart cookie. Dark, thoughtful guy. You'd probably get along great with him.

Terrific. Let's have lunch.

Chevy Chase, Schiff said. That's his name.

Yeah. He's not funny.

You're more of an Andy Kaufman guy, I suppose.

Nah. Radner. Now, she's funny, my father said.

That thing she does—those spoof commercials. Jewess Jeans!

You don't have to be Jewish.

But it helps.

We should take this on the road. They'd love us in Peoria, my father said.

You they'd love. Me they'd nail to a cross.

Why do we always wind up here?

Because you're paying me to facilitate your delusional views about Jewish comedians, Schiff said.

Sometimes I lose track of who's delusional, said my father.

You know, that public school kid who walks into a bar walks out with new best friends only about half the time, Schiff said. The other half of the time he winds up getting the shit kicked out of him.

But he's not afraid to fight. He knows how to take a punch.

Because his father taught him how.

Oh come on. What are we talking about here?

We're just talking. I have a theory. Want to hear a theory?

Is it going to hurt? said my father.

Of course it's going to hurt. Now, listen. Americans are obsessed with renewal. What's our number one sales pitch to the downtrodden masses? A fresh start! A shot at reinvention. Adopt a new identity, become someone unrecognizable to the hicks back in the ancestral village. What was the Boston Tea Party? A costume ball. What is politics? A stage play. Actors playing politicians playing gods. That's why there are so many steps on the Capitol building. A stage high enough for the whole country to see. Everyone's playing dress-up. We know we're being told fictions, yet we continue to watch, reacting with outrage when our gods behave like humans. It's our role to yearn for them to do good deeds, and we're thrilled when they don't. You don't see the French impeaching anyone for spying on the other party. Good god, they'd impeach d'Estaing if they found out he *wasn't* spying on the Gaullists. The French have made an art form of complication, and what did *our* most famous homegrown philosopher say? Simply, simplify.

I hear he kept a radio under his cot.

It's a fool's philosophy. You cannot simplify yourself. You are complex, infinitely complex. Like everyone, you contain multitudes, you're a warehouse of selves, innumerable versions of you. When you talk to me, you're pretending to be my clever patient. When you're talking to Sarah, you're pretending to be a distracted husband who wants to get back to his manuscript. When you were in the Army, you were a file clerk? A copy editor? Come on. And now you're pretending to be a comedy expert.

And who are you pretending to be?

Your therapist, I guess.

You need to work on your accent.

Lemme write that down.

Keep at it.

What was in the manuals? Schiff said.

Instructions.

That's time. See you next week.

His knees quavered and he went down in the narrow channel between the console and the hull wall, his gloved hands vainly groping for purchase. Oh god. The boat flew over the top of another wave and the deck fell out from under him. Feeney hooted with glee from aft, the deck rose back up against my father's body, and the dark thought materialized that if he could muster the strength to throw himself overboard, he could drown within minutes and it would all be over. He gave up trying to reach for the cutaways where the rods were stored. He was sliding around like a dead fish on the icy deck, getting the hell beat out of him every time the boat crested a wave, driven on by Bo, who was really feeling the weed, hadn't noticed my father's predicament until he careened across the deck and came to rest momentarily against his boot. But what could he do? Now they were out on the open water, and Bo wasn't going to cut power, not in chop like this—you had to beat it back with velocity, that was the only way to conquer rough seas. Every time my father hit the deck, he groaned so loudly that Feeney could hear him over the drone of the engine; he had lost control of his body and had resigned himself to whatever expulsive force chose to visit itself upon him. Then he felt a weight on his back, pinning him to the deck; he managed to twist his head to the side and saw that it was Bo, who had stomped on him as he might have a potato chip bag tumbling around in a backyard twirler.

Hold still or you're going to bounce overboard, Bo yelled into the wind.

My father moaned. He curled his arms beneath his face and remained secure beneath Bo's boot until they reached the deep water of the sound, where all those blues were allegedly schooling in the depths. Bo throttled back. The sun was a hard ball of ice just over the horizon.

Bo set the engine to idle and released my father.

Sorry about that, he said. There's no cure out here for what you've got except to grab your sack and pray.

My father barely heard him. He was still facedown, a puddle of water licking at his cheek. His ears were popping.

Let's do it, Feeney said, planting his foot between my father's spread legs so that he could reach the rods. You'll acclimate, Salty. Get yourself up where you can see the horizon. That'll do ya.

My father groaned and moved one of his fingers to signal his assent.

It was another white day, the sky washed clean of color, with a decent wind whipping across the water. The boat rocked gently as the rollers marched beneath it, a pendulum ticking out a dirge. It rose and fell, and my father rose and fell with it. He felt it with his every cell. Eventually he managed to drag himself into a sitting position—cheers from his boatmates—and lodge his chin on the gunwale while they rigged their lines on the other side.

Punishment comes slow but harsh, my father thought. So much to pay for. He opened his mouth and let forth an eruption of vomit that slid over the gunwale, down the fiberglass hull, and into the water.

9.

Back at the house, beneath a headboard as darkly ornate as a Gothic altar, I was asleep in the enormous bed, a bed so large that my presence barely disturbed the expanse of its surface, enveloped in the cocoon of heat sleeping children spin around themselves, curled beneath a gray wool blanket, heavy, a layer of warm lead; when I moved, it did not move. My small face a pebble on the pillow. I was dreaming that our black-and-white cat, Slade, was creeping along a high beam traversing the span of a barn, and I was below him, my arms extended to catch him should he fall. Dust hung in a wedge of sunlight, cinematic. Slade, who in waking life had never displayed the courage to venture farther than the threshold of the apartment door, was exhibiting unusual daring, and when I suddenly found myself on the beam with him, transported there by dream physics, I took his tail. I knew Slade would lead me to the other side. Instead—horror—he leapt, spreading his limbs like a flying squirrel, and we plummeted before planing out inches above the packed dirt floor, accelerating through the open barn doors, arcing upward in a graceful climb, the green hills flattening out beneath us. Good boy, Slade, good boy!

Over the countryside, over the square hats of high buildings, past dark factory stacks oozing smoke, and down over suburban neighborhoods, each yard a perfect green cube bounded by a high, white wooden fence. Slade set down on the sidewalk in front of a white clapboard house. Tail high, he trotted down the walkway and slipped inside. I chased after him. It was dim inside, a warren of narrow corridors, and off the corridors, small rooms. In one room a boy sat on a bed all alone. The room had been turned inside out—chairs faced the wall, a standing mirror showed off its plywood back. A man entered and began to spank the boy. I ran out. I woke up.

I was not disturbed by what I'd dreamed, but I had no desire to close my eyes and return to that house. I was fully conscious in seconds, that great trick made possible by the porous membrane between a child's dreaming and waking life, and in that blink of time I became aware of the weight of the blanket pinning me to the bed, and I drew my feet up and propelled myself out through the top of the pocket my body had formed in the covers. I stood straight up on the pillow and surveyed the room, then clapped my legs together and dropped bottom-first onto the pillow like a pile driver, the bed's ancient timbers shuddering and clacking, before flipping over on my belly for the blind drop to the floor. I was supposed to be quiet. A child up early can have a house to herself if only she is quiet. I lowered myself down a millimeter at a time until my socked feet touched rag rug and I released the mattress.

Though I slept there, I was an interloper on the second floor, where my parents slept in the other guest bedroom, where Jane and Bo slept at the end of a long hall, where the atmosphere was saturated with evaporated sounds, loosened belt buckles and bathroom faucets, the bumping of shoes, hinges, squeaks and thumps and muffled voices, commonplace noises made mysterious by a closed bedroom door. There was a bathroom off the hall, and other doors leading to more bedrooms. I went downstairs, careful to tread lightly on the steps. In the kitchen I felt the cold granite floor through my socks, a wide, living chill radiating upward into my feet, a pleasing contrast to the warmth of the bed. No one was around, but I saw the coffee cups on the counter and knew that adults had been there before me. Bo, my father, and Mr. Feeney had gone fishing. The fireplace was a cold, black square. There were wine bottles and beer bottles on the hearth. The room smelled good, like charred logs.

Behind the sofa was a chest of toys, but it contained nothing of interest. Old wooden trucks with strings attached, a few cloth dolls with yellow yarn hair, a set of jacks with a rubber ball that had turned to stone. I'd already been through the desk drawers and the cabinets beneath the bookshelves. The house was like the gymnasium at school, large and empty, concealing nothing. The drawers had nothing in them except pads of paper and pens. It was like a dollhouse, too, in that way, lacking the proper distribution of the detritus that accumulates in places where real people live, and I had rightly deduced that I was to proceed with care. This was not a place for children. My own suitcase of toys was upstairs but didn't interest me, either.

There was one thing in the living room, a *Nutcracker* soldier with red gums and white teeth whose head popped off to reveal a hollow interior that emanated a thick purple scent, the dregs of candy, perhaps, though I did not connect the pleasure I took in inhaling the soldier's empty body to what might have been but what was at that moment there to smell. I felt no need to sift through an imagined past, no need to unearth the source of my pleasure. The possibility of stealing the soldier had not yet formed in my mind but would later that day.

Through a pair of doors with large glass panes there was a sunporch, brilliant with light, and I entered and breathed on the glass and drew faces in the condensation. The world outside was white. The dream was with me still, the parts where I'd flown with Slade over forests and hills, houses with white plumes of smoke rising from their chimneys, and I exhaled again on the glass and drew curves and loops, linked proto-infinity symbols that flowered across the surface until my finger reached the edge of the condensation and, like a skater catching a blade at the edge of the pond, snagged and tripped on the dry glass. I mashed my finger against the cold surface. Parts turned yellow-white and parts turned red, and I flipped it over and looked at my fingerprint, which was flat and white, freeze-pickled. Against my philtrum the flesh was smooth, cold. I stayed at the glass for a while, pressing, touching my finger to my lips. Usually when my mother and I went away, my father stayed home and fed Slade, but because my father was with us this time, my mother said she'd left enough food in the bowl for Slade to eat until he exploded. In my mind I replayed the image of Slade bursting open. I'd been doing it all weekend. His legs would shoot out and his fur would undulate in sharp waves, as if he'd been electrocuted, and then there'd be a cracking sound like a balloon breaking and a ball of smoke and Slade would be gone. It worried me and made me giggle every time I thought about it.

The snow-crusted yard. The driveway, a gray cicatrice that disappeared into the woods. Jane there, pushing a wheelbarrow on the driveway, and when she saw me at the window she set it down on its skids and waved two work-gloved hands. I waved back. Jane mimed digging with a shovel, waved again, and lifted the wheelbarrow handles. I liked Jane.

The sun had found a gap in the trees and transformed the seamless white yard into a ragged moonscape, pockmarked and cratered, and arcing through it, evidence of Mrs. Feeney's journey from the kitchen door to the property line the night before. I looked for a long time at the footprints, not knowing or caring, of course, whose they were, and I watched the trees swaying in the wind. The chuffing scrape of Jane's shovel was far off, a rhythm, and I observed with a clarity of vision sought by poets, discovered by those few for whom the physical world can become, with great concentration, nothing but itself, free of the influence of art and metaphor, those palimpsests we lay atop the chaos of existence in the name of order and explanation. The trees were trees and the snow snow, and the footprints footprints, and I did not question the meaning of these things.

IO.

The lone adult in the house was upstairs, still asleep, dreaming of a marathon. My mother had reached the final leg and the course had led the runners into an office building. She was out ahead, alone, her shoes thumping down the carpeted hall. She made the right-hand turn onto the straightaway, saw the banner draped from the acoustical tiles, cheering fans lining the walls, and then another runner blew past her, blond hair streaming, tan legs striding with equine grace, that familiar narrow ass flexing in her blue nylon shorts. It was Jane, and she crossed the line first, arms aloft.

My mother woke up and thought, Well, that's a little on the nose.

She extended a foot from under the blankets to test the air before stretching out one arm to retrieve her nightclothes, a pair of long johns and an old blue T-shirt and a pair of wool socks, which were draped variously over the bedside table and a wicker-seat chair that she now looked at with some suspicion, after my father's fireside assessment of the house.

Had he jumped on her in the night? She didn't remember getting in bed naked, but she'd been bombed. No, they hadn't. You don't sleep through that, but she checked for crust between her legs, just to be sure. The air in the room was frigid, but the vent was blowing, which meant that Jane was up and had turned on the heat, a concession to the weaker constitutions of her guests. It annoyed the hell out of my mother, this insistence that they sleep in subfreezing temperatures. She loved Jane, but good god, she was from California and had conjured this New England puritanism out of thin air. She talked as if the landscape commanded it of her.

Thrift and responsibility. Tight straps, she thought, that Jane was using to keep herself from flying apart. When they'd met nearly thirty years earlier, Jane was the girl from Modesto who as a joke had kept a framed photo of her prize 4-H pig in their dorm room, who had ached through the long northeastern winters, fleeing campus at the end of every May for bright Capitola, three months in a swimsuit, bonfires, reading Rilke on the beach, screwing around with surfers under the pier.

She'd had no fascination for the seafaring life, no lobster pot at the foot of her bed. She hadn't been the sort that went around promoting *Moby-Dick* as the cure for twentieth-century ills. What, my mother wondered, did it matter? No one was the sum of her parts. It all went askew. So what was it that was so annoying about Jane's manufactured fidelity to this house and the grim ghosts who haunted its rafters? She was a grown woman and she could do as she pleased. She could do as she pleased, but Erwin had been right. It grated, all of it.

Through the window my mother watched Jane in her big Wellingtons slopping around in the driveway with the wheelbarrow full of gravel, her Kreeger & Sons coat open and flapping in the wind, like Hepburn out there with her hair piled atop her head, a crown awarded for her inexhaustible dedication to ending the scourge of potholes. Did Jane take adulthood more seriously, was that it? Had she simply done it better, with more foresight and more alacrity? They'd both left girlhood far behind. Their futures were as predictable as anyone else's. At least they were neck and neck on that one. They'd crossed the dividing line. When you stopped believing yourself to be beyond the grasp of death, you became an adult. And if that didn't make you want to pretend to be someone else, what would?

Yet Jane never mentioned suffering any of the questions that ate my mother up, the nightmare-inducing inadequacies, the fear of fraudulence and certain failure that riddled her existence. Jane was, after all, a doctor. Perhaps, having taken her dose of medical-grade confidence, there wasn't much room left for questions. But that wasn't it. For god's sake, she'd been one of only two women in her class at med school. She'd been confident at eighteen and she was confident now, and really, my mother thought, that was the momentous accomplishment; plenty of fools were confident simply because they didn't know any better, but Jane was capable of introspection. She was well equipped to delve into the dark questions that haunted her existence. The question was, when had she ever found need to? Perhaps Jane was some sort of statistical anomaly, a person who never bet wrong and had avoided all the corrosive mistakes that had caused my mother to question her own ability to navigate the world, much less pass along any useful information to me. But wasn't that the definition of a safe life, the avoidance of failure? Weren't we to believe that failure shapes character? Well, so does success.

Maybe this could all be part of the pitch.

Erwin said they were pseuds. Usually my mother didn't bother arguing with him. The standard low-grade sniping she had to put up with in order to get him out of the house. And it's not like she disagreed, not entirely, but weren't she and Erwin huge pseuds, too? Wasn't everyone? My father, by his own admission, was just playing at being a writer all day; who was she but a woman playing painter? The difference was, he'd been rewarded financially and she hadn't.

You didn't do it yourself. It wasn't all your own fault. It was the people who surrounded you who truly made the playacting possible. The older she got, the less convincing she found her own performance, yet every year her students became more reverent. If they were buying it, maybe she should, too. So she kept showing up in a turtleneck and suede boots, waving her glasses around like she knew what the hell she was talking about, and they kept packing into the studio three days a week. Inexplicable. It seemed possible that they were getting younger, too, as if they were trapped together in a time-space continuum anomaly, infinitely receding from each other. Before she knew it she'd be a hundred years old, waving her cane at a roomful of crying babies.

She wondered, though, wriggling to get her socks on underneath the covers, what it was all about, my father's, and her own, aversion to cracks in the façade. Why did they expect so much of their friends?

Life was flux, a swirl of cellular degradation and regeneration. To demand consistency of a person's character, then, contradicted our most basic biological state. Why did it grate so when Jane and Bo smiled beatifically across their faux-wormwood table at their guests? Was it because their feelings were fake? No! They believed. They ratified their feelings by believing they felt them. They believed every word they spoke, they believed every fish they pulled out of the sea, every nail they hammered, every vegetable they harvested, every fire they built. Yes, it was a stage play, and they were playing characters. But it worked backward. Jane and Bo were constructing outer lives that might confer some meaning upon their inner lives. They had made themselves into exactly who they wanted to be. And wasn't that commendable?

Wasn't it? Why did it make her sick?

And who are you, she asked herself, optima, the all-knowing judge of what is fake and real? Nah, just a casual observer, uncommitted, unspoiled. Pretty much perfect.

Are you going to do this or not?

Socks on, long johns hitched up, she stretched in the light. The blanket fell away from her torso and she drew a sharp breath when the cold hit her bare skin. She pulled the shirt on and swung her legs out of the bed. There's something about the light here that cleans you out, doesn't it? It's the refection off the snow, the gonging whiteness pouring in through the windows like an awkward teenage boy who's everywhere at once, thrashing around the room in search of something important he's lost—a guitar pick or a condom that's slipped between the wall and the dresser. It's assertive, this light, she thought, insistent and irritating, but you still want it all over you.

Goddamn, she said out loud in greeting to the day, a solvent to break down the noise in her head and start fresh.

Shivering bathroom ablutions, freezing toilet seat, robe, downstairs for coffee. Is she going to do it dressed like this? Yes. While the men are out.

She'd shown Jane and Bo the new series of paintings for the first time a month earlier. Jane had been back to look again, alone, a good sign, and my mother hadn't mentioned it to either of them since. These things took patience and delicacy. But sometimes a push. Just a nudge. My father's rant might have helped—by insulting their taste, he might have rattled Jane just a little, just enough to give her something to think about, and if either she or Bo had been suspicious about my mother's motivations for dragging him out to Montauk for the weekend, he'd taken care of that. She had something to apologize about now, a way into Jane's inner sanctum.

II.

After emptying his guts over the side of the Boston Whaler, my father found his attitude greatly improved, his body cleansed. The air on his face was rejuvenative. It was almost as if he'd expelled the sense of dread along with the rest of the contents of his stomach. He sat up and slowly got to his feet. Without any commentary, Bo put a rod in his hand, baited the hooks, and pointed at the water. My father took a moment to get the heft of the rod before whipping the tackle in a soaring arc, hitting the water about fifty yards away, prompting Feeney to utter a grunt of approval. It was a nice rod, responsive at the tip, solid against his hip, the fiberglass transmitting the pull of the current, the pull of the weights. He had tugged the rod tip upward to get a feel for the weight of the leader and for the water itself, and the water had pulled back once, more sharply a second time. He hauled back on the rod, and the line went taut, vibrating as it sliced the water.

You're goddamn kidding me, Feeney said.

My father's fingers dropped to the reel, and he leaned back to take in some line, dipped the tip, spun the crank a couple of revolutions. Nothing huge on the other end, he thought. Then it dove with furious strength, and he thought for a moment the line might not hold, but he got to the drag in time, let it sprint. When the tension eased, he hauled back, watched the tip bow down against the fish's next powerful run for the deep, and his frozen fingers fumbled for the drag. He let more line spin out. The tension in the rod relented and he held steady, waiting to see how far the fish could go. The fish had only paused, and now it ran hard, plowing deeper into the cold waters, diving for the seafloor, it seemed, and my father waited. Neither Bo nor Feeney spoke, though they were both watching. The line was fizzing off the reel, and just when he thought he would have to take a chance and lock down the drag, the fish relented. My father pulled, both hands anchored high. He got the rod vertical, dropped the tip, reeled like mad, pulled again.

There you go, Bo said quietly.

He dragged the fish up from the black depths that way, heaving, reeling, heaving, reeling, until it emerged into a depth where the striated sunlight broke across its big yellow eye and something activated within its brain and it went on another run, this time not straight down but at an angle before turning directly at them and shooting beneath the boat, the line going slack, then emitting a twang as it tightened against the hull. My father opened up the drag just in time, surrendering a hundred yards of line in the time it took to stumble over the center console to the starboard side, Bo ducking as the rod came whistling over his head.

Get him up close and I'll stick the son of a bitch, Feeney said.

My father was weakening, his arms cramping. He hadn't been at it very long, maybe three minutes, and the fish was on a wild tear now, heading back out, the line trailing out directly behind it, and it was pulling like a tractor. My father once again locked down the drag, trying to break the fish's will, and he leaned back against the console to rest. There would be no relief for his arms, though, short of releasing the rod and letting it skate across the water. He held on, his fingers frozen, sweat stinging his eyes, the muscles in his forearms searing, until the fish had given up. Life and life and, just like that, death. He reeled a couple of times, tentatively, and wasn't even sure there was still anything on the other end of the line, so easily did the line glide back through the eyelets and onto the spool. A little jolt confirmed that the fish was there, but it had depleted its stores, and all he had to do was drag the carcass back through the water. He continued to pull back line and just as he felt the fish should be rising through the surface, another convulsion stabbed his arms, and the fish went banging away, a final desperate surge as it fought to loose the hook from its jaw, before breaking the surface of the water with a wild thrashing animosity that my father felt in every fiber of his body. The fish was big, a single flexing muscle, a raw, elegant distillation of strength.

My father was a little mesmerized by the sight of the animal, until then nothing but a dark force beneath the water, in a sense nothing more than an exertion of his imagination, and he recoiled when the single steel tooth of the gaff swung down and pierced the fish's flank. Feeney gathered the fish on board, its blood running pink onto the deck, and Bo leaned over and cracked it on the head twice with a wooden mallet, and the fight was over.

Nice fish, Bo said.

Big son of a bitch, Feeney said.

They can pull, can't they? Bo said.

A little bit, my father said.

The fish was sleek, robust, its porcelain belly darkening to virescent gray on the sides, and across its back, mottled greenish yellow. It had a perfect mermaid's tail. The mouth was rimmed with wicked-looking teeth, and its dorsal fin was an elegant fan that receded in an arc like a schooner sail. It lay there, freezing to the waffle pattern on the deck, while the men stood looking down with their hands on their hips.

That one had only been the start. He'd pulled out another one as big as the first, then an even larger one, while Bo and Feeney had plashed their bait into the water with not even a single strike between them. My father's recovery had a warming effect on all three of them, and Feeney's verbal jabs landed differently afterward. He was less solicitous of my father, throwing harder, sharper. Bo was pleased—that he'd caught nothing himself didn't matter. He was like a grandmother presiding over a groaning Thanksgiving table, delighted by her own cooking and her family's appetite. For Bo, stoned and focused, it had been a righteous experience to watch the man battle those fish. It relieved him of his embarrassment for my father, whose success as a writer meant nothing to him, and though the next day he wouldn't be able to quite recall exactly why, the feeling of warmth didn't entirely disappear, and he was thankful for it. This was the way men won other men over: not by defeating them but by making them witnesses to the triumph of inner resources. My father had risen above his limitations to become, for a moment, a hero.

Those were the fillets my father had dropped without ceremony into the frying pan on the night of the blizzard, my mother and I upstairs at the party, my father's choice of prep quite intentionally in direct contravention of Bo's solemn instructions to marinate each in a four-hour milk bath before grilling them. Or you could do it right and smoke them, Bo had said. You can just bring them up to me and I'll do them for you. I have this Finnish smoker—no one else has one. Just bring them up to me.

My father had grimaced and nodded amicably. There is nothing as unmovable as the opinion of the amateur authority, and nothing so irritating as the inevitable condescension with which he delivers it.

My father's revenge: He had lit the stove burner, dropped some butter into the iron skillet, and tossed the fish in fresh from the fridge. As an afterthought, he dug a Pyrex lid out of the drawer and clamped it on top to contain the splatter. He wandered back into his office to turn off the lamp, but sat down, just for a moment, to read the last thing he'd written, and that had been the end of the fish. When the acrid smoke reached his nostrils, he was penciling in some anatomical details in his description of the Buddha's first sexual experience. Wouldn't the low-hanging earlobes play some role? Aren't they inherently erotic, those loose, tender flaps of flesh, just hanging there, scrotiform? How could Yashodara's virginal lips *not* close around them in a suckling embrace? Or perhaps they were but normal earlobes until Sid met Yash and all the pulling . . .

He hated that book, incidentally, his comedy about the life of Buddha. He was packing it with choice hippie bait like, *Only by looking away shall you see what is before you,* and *Trust not the eye alone, for it is but a single instrument with which to navigate the world.* It was a way out, this dive he was taking, a book not merely dumb but offensively stupid. And so far, so good. In a way, he reveled in its stagnant reek, page after page of sewage.

He had already written three painfully intellectual novels, books full of linguistic backflips and sly tricks that did a decent job of papering over his failure to locate the truth. They were smart and soulless. Fortunately for him, no one was watching. Then his fourth, *Slingshot*, inexplicably made the bestseller lists. Somehow, without intending to, he'd written a story with universal appeal, a gripping thriller about a mild-mannered Polish man's daring escape from the Nazis. Reviews appeared lauding his paradigm-shifting approach to the genre. A studio optioned the film rights. His back catalogue started selling. My father's life was thrown into chaos. On the downtown M11 he'd seen people reading the book, apparently enjoying it, and twice on the uptown he'd been approached and asked if he was the writer Saltwater. (Who? he'd replied.) He'd gone on Dick Cavett's show and lied as much as possible, and had enjoyed seeing up close Cavett's superhuman ability to feign interest in whatever pabulum he coughed up. Profile writers showed up and he lied about everything that couldn't be fact-checked—his process, his inspiration, his intentions as an author. He'd attended an endless stream of parties. When he had tried to avoid them, his publisher threatened him by saying that if he didn't feel up to taking a cab across town, maybe he'd prefer a European tour. So he went to the parties, and it was there that he honed his imitation of the author of *Slingshot*, a Saltwater as fictional as any of the characters in the book, a haughty, irascible bastard, rough to reporters, an inveterate drunk. There was no sign of his paranoia, none of the convulsive terror that consumed him upon entering an elevator car or at the sight of an airplane, none of his towering fear of other people.

He netted enough from the movie deal to buy the apartment in the Apelles. Not just any apartment—one so large he and my mother had never found a purpose for the fifth bedroom, which remained empty, like an artist's painstaking reconstruction of an unoccupied room on display for some downtown gallery, a commentary on America and manifest destiny or process or a piece of anti-art. It was chilly in the winter, stuffy in the summer, smelled of damp plaster, a featureless white space with two windows in the wall. As far as my father was concerned, it was just an empty room. Tabitha, our cleaning woman, said it had weird energy.

How right she was. It's where I sleep now.

Maybe the room was a metaphor for something, an empty chamber in my father's soul or a symbol for some piece of the writing machinery that had gone missing, because after *Slingshot* he'd dried up. He couldn't believe that he'd fallen prey to so clichéd a trap, but there it was, day after day, a blank page in the Olivetti. Time passed. Deposits of soot and dust gathered in the crease where the rubber rollers met the page and were buried underneath something more permanent, something granular. For so long he'd been misunderstood. For so long he'd been able to hide behind prose rubbed smooth as an aluminum wing, words flashing bright as seraphim. His books were fireworks, lights and noise and smoke and the next morning, an empty sky. But five million readers in twenty-two languages had screwed it up for him, or he'd screwed it up for himself, he wasn't sure which, and he'd been forced to fashion the new Saltwater, one who might survive the public glare. It shouldn't have surprised him that his invention had fallen prey to the great myth of writer's block. The invention was, after all, a hack.

Why was it so important to be misunderstood? I know now that anyone concealing a secret, however small, wishes to divulge it. Secrets will fight their way to the surface, as a splinter wedged deep in the ball of the hand will eventually surface, forced out by the generative forces of the body. My father was caught between his desire to divulge and his desire to conceal. While he could contain his secret, however, as he had for nearly thirty years, his books were falsehoods, and he deserved his obscurity. He'd unwittingly done something honest in *Slingshot*, though. He'd divulged some of himself. And that meant the thing was close to the surface. It was going to emerge. He could feel it.

So he drank. He wept with his head in my mother's lap. He behaved badly at parties. He wasted days writing pseudonymous columns for small-town newspapers upstate. (His writer's block was never bad enough that he couldn't pen a screed.) For a while he'd pedaled an exercise bike for five hours a day while watching TV. Here and there he got into fights with critics in the letters sections of various reviews, and one night, swollen with fury at a windbag who'd called his characters *nothing more than Freudian archetypes*, he'd impregnated my mother. My conception, a complication. First he couldn't write another novel, and now this.

Schiff, his therapist, had suggested that the pregnancy might reconfirm his ability to create something.

Gimme a break, my father said. I write something, I get paid. A baby's nothing but a deficit! A bum shook his cup at me the other day and I started laughing at him. I laughed right in his face. Do you have any idea what a baby costs?

Schiff, father of three, raised his chin.

Anyway, I still can't write.

But my impending birth had at least compelled him back to his desk, and he sweated it out for a month, sitting again at the blank page, forcing his fingers onto the keys. Taking them off, looking at the ceiling, sighing, fingering the keys again, eyes on the page, back to the ceiling. He blew away the grit at the roller wheels. New deposits accumulated. The chair's thick steel spring squawked when he shifted to relieve his mortified glutes.

At the desk he wore an odd look on his face, that of a partygoer cornered by an inveterate blowhard. Eight hours a day, that's how he sat, his face screwed into a hopeful wince, waiting for silence to shut up so he could get a word in edgewise. One afternoon the light bulb on his desk popped and the windowless little space snapped into darkness. He sat, unmoving, for an hour. A mouse scraped at the lath in the wall. The dark persisted. The mouse came out and poked around at the baseboards. My father sat and he waited and nothing happened. He changed the light bulb and he sat in the light and nothing happened.

Back from the widow's walk? my mother would say when he emerged at the end of another day. Somehow instead of infuriating him, her unwillingness to engage his despair calmed him. She looked different.

Patches of melanin were darkening her cheeks. Her hair was thicker. She was dusky. She was expanding. So I sit and nothing happens, he thought, so what? So I never get back to it. So what?

And then, with no preamble, no attention to phase of moon or alignment of sign, on a day like any other day, he'd begun to write. His fingers had moved, and what had come out had been bad, absolutely terrible. He'd smashed out a first chapter, knowing all along it was garbage, something the critics would hate, something the fans whose letters compared him to Beckett, the ones who sent him their own work in over-taped manila envelopes, would hate. It would be a wilted disappointment to the preening young magazine editors who had found *Slingshot* to be *so compelling*, a warm dose of schadenfreude for the academics who'd invited him to headline symposiums and sniped about his unworthiness while he was barely out of earshot. A signal to the intellectually fashionable that, right on schedule, it was time to toss *S-shot* and return Cortázar to his rightful place on the coffee table.

Its terribleness sent the juice roaring through his veins. This was resurrection through failure. He would write something so stupid that Rod McKuen and Richard Bach would get in a fistfight over who got to pen the cover blurb.

Oh, make no mistake, this was a guaranteed bestseller he was working on, an insipid fantasy that required nothing of the reader but a willingness to lie back and be buried in waves of warm pluff. This was a book that would take over airport kiosks and bus stop placards. Oh yes, he'd found a new way to evade the truth. The old Saltwater had cashed out, flown south, phoned it in, flushed his talents, and shat the bed. This was the new Saltwater, the grand, sweeping generalist; this was the crater-faced vampire who sneered at cameras and poured beer on Mailer's head; the one who'd thrown a chair at Pynchon, who'd snagged it midair and thrown it right back.

God, what glorious bullshit.

That was how it had started, his way out. By the night of the blizzard, he'd been at it seven years. The only surprise had been how difficult it was to write a bad book, because not only was there the problem of writing the bad book, he had to do so while inhabiting the invented Saltwater who would dare undertake so cynical a task. Soldier on, good soldier.

When my mother had called from the Vornados' penthouse that night to ask him if he wanted to come up, he'd assumed she'd asked only out of a sense of irony. The last place he wanted to be was a party. Must be a good one if she was still there, though. Or maybe she had found someone to pitch her latest series to. Maybe she did want him there. He should go up, put on the Saltwater show, help her beat the carpets to see if any money fell out, but . . .

But he was hungry, so he'd thrown the fish on the stove.

A predictable slapstick. My father flailing around the kitchen. Fire, water, brown steam, a window flung open, the blizzard sweeping in, smoke carousing, my father cursing the weather, the fish, the pan, the heat, the cold, flapping dish towel, cupped palms scooping at the smog, which, due to the equilibrium created by the wind blowing in and the heat attempting to pour out through the window, only swirled and eddied in place for a moment until the wind direction shifted and the smoke vanished, as if sucked into the vacuum of space. He slammed closed the window, dug out a plastic bag from beneath the sink, one with a yellow smiley face on it, and chipped the charred remains loose with the spatula. Somehow they still reeked of brine.

Getting rid of the fish should have been simple enough. The trash chute down to the incinerator was in a shared vestibule immediately outside the kitchen, but when he opened the door, he was greeted, to his great annoyance, by a Christmas tree. It had been wedged into the garbage chute in a manner that resembled the hasty and incomplete disposal of a murder victim, and protruded a good four feet from the wall, the trunk conspicuously addressing Turk Brunn's service door. The floor was thick with brown needles except for a spotless wedge of gray concrete before that same door, the effect of a foot arcing wiper-style, as if to attempt to conceal a person's involvement in an unneighborly act of Christmas tree disposal.

He tugged on the trunk but the tree didn't budge. He looked down at the plastic bag in his hand, Have a Nice Day, and sighed.

There was protocol for situations like this one: a handwritten note on one of the ecru notecards readily available from the tables in any of the Apelles' seventy-two elevator bays for the express purpose of communicating minor grievances, a format embraced at the turn of the century by the Wasp scions who'd first inhabited the building, a tangible projection of the building's high-minded ethos, a sort of marketing campaign promoting civil discourse. But my father opted for a more direct approach. He wedged himself between the trunk and the door and tapped lightly, just a single knuckle, a courteous Hello there, don't mean to bother. Eliciting no response, he tapped harder, and harder, adding knuckles, pausing to listen for a response, until he was pounding with his fist, bashing the metal as if it had done him a mortal wrong. Nothing. He pounded some more, and then he put his face in the seam where the door met the jamb and he said in a ponderous whisper, I know you're in there, Turk. I know you're in there. I know you're in there. And then he pounded some more, until the head of Hastings Sebenlist, the stockbroker who lived in 14F, emerged from the door to my father's right, bald, wrinkled as a thumb knuckle. His reading glasses were perched on his nose, and over the tops of the lenses, Sebenlist's and my father's eyes met. Sebenlist's eyes went to the tree, back to my father. Soft music streamed out of Sebenlist's apartment, and he raised his hands in lamentation, though whether it was directed at my father or the tree was unclear, before ducking back inside.

Sebenlist knew trouble when he saw it. My father's trouble with Turk, though, was not some long-standing feud, not the deep, geological accretion of anger that piled up over years of neighborly friction. She'd babysat for me, cradled me in her arms and sung me to sleep. True, an arrangement fostered almost entirely by my mother, but he hadn't objected. After I had gotten a little older, Turk would let me rummage around in her storage room, and we'd have tea. My father liked Turk, didn't he? She'd read his books, and not only that, she treated him as though he belonged to that order of writers he wished to belong to.

Sometimes he'd have a cigarette with her in the vestibule and they'd gripe about their latest shared outrage, the Knicks or macrobiotics or Tom Wolfe.

Why, then, oh why, was he trying to knock down her door? Because of the elevator. Because now, in order to throw out the fish, he'd have to take the elevator. And for my father, few modern conveniences were more terrifying.

12.

It was rumored that Turk had acquired a foreign exchange student from some sweltering Oriental backwater where the plant-based diet and nonexistent child labor laws made sure that no one got bigger than an average American ten-year-old. Had anyone ever laid eyes on the exchange student? Perhaps. Fleetingly. All anyone knew for sure was that he was small. Service Swensen, the talkies actress and self-appointed hall monitor who lived in 14A, claimed she had seen him, but, her cataracted peephole eye lacking the ability to tell one Chinaman from the next, she had, in fact, misidentified a delivery boy from Grand Szechuan, the kitchen of which fed fully half the Apelles on Friday nights and had a lock on a quarter of the residents most other nights of the week, and whose employees were as common in the hallways as the residents themselves. Service, who spent much of her day with that cloudy eye pressed to the brass plate in her door, spooning peanut butter into her toothless mouth, had, in fact, on numerous occasions seen the exchange student, our friend Tanawat Kongkatitum, but in every instance assumed him to be a Grand Szechuan delivery boy. For the record, Tanawat was six feet tall.

Turk's history and my own are a tangle of confluence and coincidence. She was our neighbor, of course, and still is. She was not, as my father claimed in one of the many confabulations he visited on me when I was a girl, Turkish, and though she laughed along with the stories of Ottoman conquest he told me about her, her name was short for Turlough, itself an Anglicized bastardization of Toirdhealbhach, after the blind Irish harper, a national hero, a name chosen by Turk's German parents in a post–Great War attempt to shield their child from the misanthropy they expected to be visited upon her by her American classmates.

Turk was plenty American, having emigrated in utero, in the aftermath of the Kaiser's fall, born red white and blue in 1920 (a smack on der Hintern cleared up the blue). Brothers Seamus and Teddy arrived in '22 and '24. Turk's father, formerly a professor of Eastern languages in Bonn, had established a successful language school in Manhattan, then expanded to Boston, Philadelphia, and Washington, the last leading to a lucrative government contract training diplomatic attachés heading to the territories. In the late 1920s, the Brunn Institute for Linguistic and Cultural Advancement was the height of intellectual fashion in New York, offering exotic languages such as Hindi, Japanese, Tibetan, Basque, Maa, and Dinka, taught by native speakers who administered pronunciation drills while wearing native dress, and it was not unusual to find classrooms packed on Friday evenings with flappers and swells, who after class would catch a drink and practice the dirty Mandarin phrases they'd been able to extract from their teacher before diving into the oily night. (Lie la zhoo ta ma da!) The schools survived the thirties by floating along on meager government contracts, and when war broke out in Europe, Roosevelt's Department of State enlisted Turk's father to increase the readiness of the diplomatic corps. Then the world fell apart and the diplomats were replaced by recruits from the newly formed Office of Strategic Services.

That's where our family histories first crossed, when my father enrolled in a class to brush up on Polish slang.

Turk and her two younger brothers spent the war unencumbered by concerns more dire than canned pineapple shortages. She cruised through college, picked up master's degrees in anthropology and sociology, and enrolled in a doctoral program at Columbia (the family business: her unfinished dissertation was titled "Twentieth-century linguistic transformation of the Bahau Dayak"). By the early 1960s, Turk was a familiar face in the West Village bars where NYU professors took their latest conquests, where everyone was arguing politics, high as kites, throwing poses, doing their best impersonations of credible sources.

Who was she to that crowd? A dyke, a cipher, perpetual ABD, here and there auditing a class at the New School, versed in Schopenhauer and Friedman but bored by both, someone who always picked up the check and always went home alone. She smoked with her cigarette wedged tightly into the webbing of her index and middle fingers, and she wore dungarees and a leather jacket, which once led an empress dowager at the Apelles to remark in a public whisper that Turk might as well have been a dockworker. Turk volleyed back that given the spread of the old hag's ass, she must herself be a welcome sight down at Pier 12.

Her concerns didn't include the opinions of others; she detested those papery souls who attested at every opportunity that they couldn't care less what people thought of them. Wouldn't you be disappointed to know how seldom they do? she'd say. She was herself steadfast in her determination never to defer to the opinion of strangers or friends.

She didn't need anyone, which worked like a magnet on both sexes. The lunatic fringe, poets, actors, the hip-pocket revolutionaries, bored housewives slumming it in the Village, the three-piece wool and steel-rim crowd looking for a girl and a room, the doe-eyed professors dreaming of Paris. She threaded her way in and out of them all.

By the time Turk was in her mid-forties, she was the lone resident of the sprawling apartment at the Apelles. Her mother had died and her father had been packed off to an institution in the Berkshires, suffering from a strange, possibly self-induced mania that caused him first to speak in tongues and then not at all.

Lazlo. Dear Lazlo. Because his strange story is essential to my strange story, I must tell you about him. Turk's father, born Lazlo Friedrich Krupp, unraveled in 1961. At the time of his de facto resignation from his post at the Brunn Institute for Linguistics and Cultural Advancement and his commitment to the decidedly less gabby Pickering Institute for Psychiatric Care, there had been no signs of illness, no frailty beyond a hitch in his stride (bone spur, heel) that required a walking stick, and he'd continued to work quite happily until his collapse, precipitated by an unexplained physical event. One night Turk had come home late, peeked in on him at his desk, where, still wearing his Koss SP/3 headphones, he appeared to have nestled down for a nap, and she'd gone to her room to get out of her rain-wet clothes before she returned to his study to rouse him.

If he'd suffered a heart attack or a stroke, it was certainly one of the more genteel in medical history, as he was arranged in the manner of a chem major catching a few winks in his carrel, head atop neatly folded arms. The rain was trickling down the bow window, projecting colloidal shadows that drained up the back of Lazlo's tweed suit coat, through the gossamer atop his head, wiggling like tadpoles across the various texts spread out before him, through the glass jar of pencils, across stacks of tape reels, the gray tape decks, the row of books barricading the far side of the desk, over the sill, before meeting again at the glass their progenitors. She'd not been at his desk in several weeks, and it was hard to ignore the unusual symmetry of the items atop it.

Her father had bisected the space so that on the right were Urdu texts: academic papers, brochures, recipes, maps, and notebooks filled with glossaries, phrases, grammatical rules. A couple of primers on the German language for the ambitious speaker of Urdu. On the left were German texts on Urdu. On both sides were translations of original texts into the correlative language. The collected poems of Khawaja Haider Ali Aatish in both tongues. A two-volume original and translation of *Baḥrul faṣāhat*, Najmul Ghani's treatise on versification. *Also sprach Zarathustra* (زرنُشت بقول) and a twelve-volume set of Goethe (گوئٹے volumes 1–15). What was here was there and what was there, here.

In the background, the two Grundig TK 45 suitcase reel-to-reel tape decks, friendly-looking fellows: each one had two big spools for eyes and a set of push-button teeth along the bottom. The left was slaved to the right with a bit of wire so that they would start and stop simultaneously, controlled by the playback buttons on the right-hand unit. RCA cables fed into a Y-connector that had been modified so that the right tape deck played only in the headphones' right ear cup, and the left deck played only in the left.

When Turk found him, the decks had spun out their reels and the flopping tails of tape were spanking the heads at about fifty bpm. As mentioned, her father looked to be snoozing peacefully, and she reached over him and turned them off, unalarmed. Not a light sleeper, it usually took him a while to come around, and after some gentle nudges Turk finally gripped him by the shoulders and gave him a coconut-tree shake. Pale, a distant look in his eye, he rose, tapped his chest, and said something that sounded like, Obligartiamo essa boulxin plang qualz.

Turk, considering the options available to her father—Esperanto, Italian, Chinese, German, Dutch, Schweizerdeutsch, Wallisertiitsch, Creole, Persian, De Gammon—all of which he spoke on a conversational level, all of which she thought she might have heard within the miasmic tones he'd uttered, not to mention hints of a couple of others with which he had a passing familiarity—a touch of Gullah or Hokkienese?—answered as she'd always done, speaking only some Bornean tongues and a couple of the more pedestrian Romance languages herself: ¿Que?

He obliged, even in his diminished state attempting, as always, to teach by example, and, under the impression he was repeating himself, slowly drawing out the words so she might make some sense of their construction; to his alarm, what came out of his mouth bore no resemblance to what he'd said before. Stung. in. tr'amal. eng. er. wayeh! he said. His fingers walked over his lips, as if to identify the strange source of these splatter paintings. Turk was now alarmed.

A stroke, she thought. He's obviously had a stroke.

The Brunns were not a particularly affectionate family—reunifications after extended absences had always unfolded like middle school dances, no one sure where to put their heads, their hands, their—dear god—their bodies, the advances and retreats comical if not for the desperate tang of anxiety, the frozen, apologetic rictuses, all in the name of a simple embrace—and Turk found herself patting her father down, as if searching for a weapon, her hands tattooing the length of his arms, legs, torso, though she wasn't sure why. Perhaps for the same reason Peter insisted on touching the wound in Jesus's side. A person who loses his lingual ability does suddenly transform into an alien being, profoundly unknowable.

It was a few weeks after her father had been installed within the taupe and avocado confines of the Pickering Institute, his own macaronic limbo, before she could approach the tapes. They stood in four neat towers on his desk, each slender BASF box identified with a letter, A–Z, each one preceded by (U) for Urdu or (D) for German. She knew nothing about what he'd been working on, and he had by then become a monolith, speechless and nearly motionless (his writing, before he froze up, was just as bad as his talking: given a pencil, he moved it, but imperceptibly, taking an entire day to form a cursive *I*), thus he wasn't much help. She suspected that he had been developing a course of home study that would allow the Brunn Institute to capitalize on all the stereo equipment coming onto the market.

The setup on his desk was easy enough to figure out. She put on the headphones and began with the tapes that were still loaded on the machines. She rewound the spools, but she was in no hurry to depress the START key, and her finger rested atop the smooth white cube until she felt she'd amply prepared to receive the secrets of what had derailed her father. Physically, he'd been fine after the attack. The doctors allowed that it was possible, if undiagnosable to the standards of modern medicine, that he'd suffered a mild stroke, which accounted for his aphasia. At first he'd appeared capable of understanding when spoken to in English or German, though he responded with gibberish. After a week he seemed to have lost his ability to comprehend any form of communication and he'd sunk into a depressive state, sitting silent as a stone in his wheelchair. Small groups of teachers from the Brunn Institute were brought in to see if he'd respond to any of the forty-five languages offered at the school. If they made sense to him, he didn't, or couldn't, show it—and by the end of the month he exhibited signs of distress (rapid breathing, eye-rolling) unless he was facing a featureless white wall.

Turk might as well have been sitting in front of a pair of guillotines. She detected in the machines' stillness a predator's coiled study of its prey, though eventually she swallowed, threw back her shoulders, and pressed the key. The spools began to turn. Test tones hummed a three-dash ditty at 220-440-220, synchronous in the right and left headphones, followed by a few seconds of tape hiss, and two voices began speaking, Urdu on the right, German on the left. Men's voices, evenly matched in pitch and tone, identical in volume, similar in their cadence, though not matched word-for-word. In the gaps she could make out specific tones in Urdu, or pick up a word or two in German. She pulled the right cup away from her ear and listened to the German. It was Nietzsche. *Zarathustra*'s prologue. She put the Urdu back to her ear and removed the German side. She listened to the rolling song of the Urdu, picking out Zartosht here and there before replacing the German cup, closing her eyes, and linking her fingers over her belly.

Comprehension was a pinball shooting back and forth between two bumpers, impossible to catch, impossible to control, and she eventually found a space between her head and the window, somewhere over the desk, into which she could focus her mind, a place that allowed her to hear without listening, as if she were a child sleeping in the backseat, catching splashes of her parents' conversation from the front mixed with the buffeting of an open window, the crescendo of a car blowing by in the opposite lane. A mellow, passive state of existence. The tapes ran for nearly an hour and Turk scarcely moved. Her mind wandered, tripping over memories that had been buried for years, odd sequences of images—a field of corn, a box of donuts, a curl of black hair on a white sheet, a fence, a newsstand, a pencil sharpener, the face of a woman she'd loved—and she'd recoil, reintegrate with the physical world, she'd feel the interlocking web of her fingers, the prickle of the rug beneath her feet, her eyelids bursting bright red, spotty, dark, and she'd slip back into another sequence, and the languages would rise up in her head and fall away, and she wondered what her father had heard, what difficulty he must have had in throwing his supremely analytical mind forward, away from cognition, from linguistic structure, identification of proclitics, the intricacies of transliteration . . .

She'd begun to wonder if he had embarked on a deliberate act of self-abnegation, an attempt to reach a state of divine blankness, a slippery, liquid emptiness, endless and featureless, an ethereal water, if that's even what it was, not the angular, assertive stuff we have on earth, when the tapes stopped. She opened her eyes and reached up to remove the headphones, aware of a slight spatial distortion, a little blurring of vision, and the knuckles of her right hand bumped the plastic headphone cup before her fingers found purchase. She'd just set them down on the desk when she was overtaken by a wave of nausea. A burst of air rose up from her stomach like a weather balloon and exited as hoarse and resonant as a bullfrog's call. She tumbled out of the chair, head spinning. A gyro had broken loose inside her skull. No matter which way she rolled, she was falling ass over teakettle. The floor was the ceiling, gravity in revolt. She grabbed a leg of the desk and held on for dear life, moaning, burping, moaning, burping. When her bowels turned to lava, she dragged herself across the floor toward the bathroom and climbed into the tub.

In the process of tumbling in, her foot caught the shower curtain and the whole assembly came down with a hollow clang, the rod cracking her on the head as she struggled to get her pants off before the liquid came bursting forth. When it came, boy did it come, rushing for the exit with the ungodly reek of death, her anus a searing ring of copper from which shot a fiery glop, and she tore away the curtain, groped for the shower lever and its blessed stream of rain, the cold water baptizing her while the shit streamed around her calves and heels, her body heaving like a bellows, her mind a—well, what was it? It was not the usual catacomb of dim, lizard thoughts that accompany extreme physical discomfort. Dizzy, yes, but the dizziness was pure, not dancing with its usual half-wit, pusillanimous partner, the *physical*, the one who made a career of stepping on toes and droning in complaint with rotten breath about the temperature and the humidity in the ballroom. Somehow her mind was quiet, at a remove from her body, and after the expulsive forces relented and she'd pulled herself vertical bit by bit, a one-woman revival of the evolutionary chart, tested her balance, her legs shaking jellies, her hands sleep-weak, and after having shifted the lever to send some warm water running over her quivering frame, soaping up when she felt she was capable, afterward wrapping up in a

robe and towel, shuffling to the kitchen where she rolled small balls of
Wonder Bread and with trepidation lay the host to dissolve atop her
tongue—after all that, she recalled that during the worst of it her mind
had been like a TV with bad reception, displaying crackle and snow,
nothing more. No stranger to the effects of amphetamines, ephedrine,
barbiturates, marijuana, mescaline, she couldn't say that this feeling of
simple blankness and disengagement was in the same family. All the
white-clear spirituality imposed on a peyote trip came from external
interpretation after the fact. But the deep blankness she'd experienced
was self-generated.

She handled the tapes with delicacy on subsequent visits to her father's audio lab, listening for only a few minutes at a time, and thus
avoided violent reactions while still getting to bask in the warm dawn
light that poured through her every cell, vaporizing the smoggy film
that had built up on the portals connecting her physical and spiritual
selves. With the blankness came some minor spatial disorientation that
disappeared as quickly as taking a couple of deep breaths, some esoph-
ageal tremblors behind her sternum.

A new side effect appeared after a couple of weeks, discovered when
she'd gone directly to the kitchen to make a grocery list after remov-
ing the headphones and her hand had been frozen, the graphite stuck
on the notepad's blue anchor line, as though it were a curb the pencil
couldn't hop, unable to initiate the *g* in *grapes*. Like the kid's game of
trying to force two magnetic dipoles to kiss, letters repelled one another, and when she finally roused the muscles in her hands from their
glacial sleep, what they produced looked like a man-o'-war, tentacles
trailing beneath the surface, a cartoonist's shot at Sanskrit.

What had happened to her father? Perhaps he'd shorted out his
Broca's area, fried Wernicke's to a crisp. If medical science would clas-
sify what happened as a stroke, so be it—he'd induced a stroke. In a case
like Lazlo Brunn's, diagnosis is a trip around the Monopoly board. Is it
treatable? No? Roll again. Call it Bronze John or dropsy or the screws, if
you can't reverse the tapes and pour his brain back into his ear, you can
say he's got the clap or whatever and it won't change a thing. She visited
him every week, and told him about her voyages with his recordings. If

he meant to warn her away from them, he gave no outward indication. He gave no indication that he knew she existed. He'd blown the popsicle stand and left a scarecrow leaning on the counter.

It was during one of her visits to see him that her apartment had been burgled. As far as Turk could figure, they had penetrated the Apelles' defenses peacefully, probably disguised in the slacks and clip-ons favored by city pipe and wire inspectors, entered 14D by picking the service door, or the front door (impossible to tell, so thorough was their erasure), and removed the tapes, the notebooks, the texts, the headphones, and the decks, which conveniently came built into their own stylish black leather suitcases with chrome clasps. They took the pencils and the paper clips, the rubber bands and Pelikan jars (blue, black, indigo), the letter openers, the wax seal bearing the yin yang, and they took the ring bearing Lazlo's father's seal, FFK. They took the fountain pens. The ball of twine, the matches, the cigarettes, ashtray, a tidy packet of identification papers he'd carried with him from Germany, and an accordion-fold series of sepia babes secreted in a snuff box. They took the ancient business cards Lazlo had ordered at the print shop on East 3rd in 1925, the curlicues of his name like flying pennants atop the stolid serifs of the Brunn Institute for Linguistics and Cultural Advancement, 271 W 20th Street, BALDWIN 5741. They did *their* part to reverse his condition, returning his desk, if not his brain, to a preterite state, wiping it clean of wax drippings, ash, dust, fingerprints. If they touched anything else in the apartment, Turk didn't notice. The extreme care taken to denude the desk signaled to her that not only would the police be of no help, but that this was one of those true crime situations in which alerting the authorities would precipitate a blindfolded van ride to an undisclosed location. She knew about her father's work for the U.S. government during the war, knew that spycraft had been of more than passing interest to him in the ensuing years, and suspected that his study had been visited by members of whatever acronymic group was paying him to research the efficacy of binaural language acquisition. They'd no doubt dropped in on him at Pickering, but she knew better than to ask the staff there for a clue. They'd have been paid well to shake their heads at her and pause before answering, No, no, nothing that I can recall, why do you ask?

The tape decks turned up in Caracas a few years later, in a standard concrete holding cell otherwise outfitted with one high-intensity lamp, one wooden table, one restraint chair. By 1971, a form of binaural erasure had become commonplace at the Canadian black sites charged with reeducation of American double agents and the occasional Soviet defector. In 1973 the methodology briefly found its way into a language lab at Denison University, the result of a conversation between an ex-spook and an enterprising college professor at an airport bar in Madrid, both men down in the dumps on account of it being Super Bowl Sunday and every TV in the whole damn place being tuned to a Montserrat Caballé concert, which led them to overindulge on kalimotxo, the spook to overshare a little bit, the professor to mishear a little bit, and the brief hospitalization the following fall of four Spanish 101 students for dizziness and disorientation. As application and methodology underwent refinement through the late twentieth century (audio engineers at DARPA caught Lazlo's pie-pan toss and flipped it back with hyzer), it shed its sinister overtones and for a brief shining moment showed potential as a means of erasing intrusive memories after battlefield trauma. Funding was diverted after 2001, however, into projects designed to create more battlefield trauma.

Turk changed the apartment locks and closed the door to her father's study. Her mother had died the previous Christmas (pneumonia contracted doing charity work), and once Lazlo had been declared legally incompetent, her brothers, Seamus and Teddy, sold the language school and the three siblings divided their parents' remaining holdings. Turk got the apartment, sizable deposits to her accounts, and closets full of evening gowns, tuxedos, shelves of high heels, drawers of undergarments, socks, garters, watches, jewelry, banker's boxes of files, photo albums, yellowing notepads, a hundred pounds of letters, some bound in twine, some by rubber band, some with ribbons. Artifacts of an earthly existence. Her father had not touched his dead wife's things. Thus she inherited the tangible absence of both parents all at once and, being a good Brunn, immediately set to categorizing and organizing. Her father's office at the language school arrived in fifty boxes, mostly books. She'd gone through the lot of it within a week, working daily from dawn until midnight. The personal effects took a month. Turk held on to the books, the pots and pans, the furniture, papers. A solitary sentimental gesture, she kept her father's wristwatch, a Technos Atomium, and wore it every day. The jewelry she unloaded in the Diamond District. Everything else went to the incinerator or to the Catholic church on 82nd. And then she was alone.

Turk, who at the time knew nothing of her father's origins except that he refused to talk about the shattering loss of his family during World War I or his and Magda's nearly instant immigration to the United States, had no more reason to suspect that her father was a Krupp than the king of England. Lazlo had been meticulous in his destruction of all physical evidence connecting him to his family, who were, when he and Magda decided to bug out in 1919, very much alive and well and hard at work on the fatherland's illegal rearmament and military reindustrialization. He engaged a forger in Bonn to produce new birth certificates, transforming him and Magda into Brunns; his property was sold off through an intermediary to raise funds for their new life. If not exactly a cakewalk, an unexceptional series of events in the postwar haze, when regulations weren't much more than smoke rising off the once-reliably thorny bureaucracy that had gone kaput with the rest of the empire. Lazlo burned photos, letters, diplomas. In Berlin, death certificates for L and M Krupp were drawn up and archived (he was KIA; she starved to death during the British blockade), a final act of erasure before the freshly minted Brunns hopped a train to Antwerp and from there a steamer to New York.

It was after committing her father to Pickering that Turk, just a liberated gal looking for a way to tame her wild despair, underwent a reinvention of her own. No torched documents, no new name, no transoceanic voyage, her ride on the IND Eighth Ave line down to that MacDougal Street basement was no less transformative. She hadn't been searching for a new self or a new line of work. She was looking only for a little relief, and there was nothing like the loving embrace of the creaking leather straps to help you let go of the feeling you're responsible for every living thing on the planet. Turk tried it once, got intrigued, became a regular, her tastes expanded, and before long she was on the other side of the dungeon, rigging her own subs. When the bondage market exploded in the early '70s (Vietnam plus Nixon times Vatican II equals), she put out her shingle.

Twenty years later, Turk was running a well-regarded dungeon, but trend lines were down. The internet was wrecking everything, and she was forced to pivot to a new experiential tableau. She was no dummy. She subscribed to *Red Herring* and *Inc.* She was hip to the innovate-or-die ethos.

What she came up with was something like an emotional amusement park, a menu of scenes that would appeal to the varied tastes of her client base. She began testing different complications: hostage situation, verbally abusive parent, bank holdup, little scenarios she could set up and run within the confines of the dungeon. Clients were enthusiastic, but there wasn't much repeat business. The complications were novelties. They lacked soul.

She kept working on it. Each new complication was a step further down the path. After a year of R&D, she chartered a 727 and sold tickets for a hijacking complication. Fifty-seven participants paid $8,500 each. Seven paid a $1,500 booster that got them a pistol-whipping from the Libyan hijackers. A female client fought back and they took her in the galley and raped her ($2,000). On subsequent hops, Turk added a bareback fee of another $2,500 (pre-complication testing included), but the whole thing got out of hand. Too many clients were signing up for slashings, whippings, and rapes, men and women in equal numbers, and everyone was enjoying it all a little too much—the rapists, the victims, the other passengers. It didn't sit right with Turk. She was a capitalist, but she'd begun to think of her business as a gallery of sorts. She wanted her product to mean something. She didn't want clients who were paying to be entertained. She wanted clients who were paying to be *moved*. She could see the entertainment parabola arcing back to the dungeon, and her business was no longer in the dungeon.

She spiked the plane complication and came up with a clever gas station complication in which a participant, working behind the counter, might or might not experience a brutal robbery customized to his or her psychological profile. She jacked the price up into the five figures. The uncertainty was the selling point—it was luxury in the extreme, tying on that blue bib and waiting all weekend on a stool for the holdup man to come through the door. You waited and you waited, and he didn't come. He never came. So wait a minute—you're telling me you spent all weekend in a shithole south of Albuquerque, sweeping scorpions out of the john, watching dust devils hop the highway, and nothing happened? And it cost how much? That's exquisite, sign me up!

She had run the complication for five different clients before she sent in a crew with guns. How, you might ask, did she keep getting people to pay for the experience of doing nothing?

Look, it's a fact: There's a subset of the wealthy who love to get ripped off. I suppose it's not far removed from the SM binary of powerful businessman by day, gimp by night. Because the U.S. dollar no longer activates their jolly glands, they have to come up with new forms of currency. And the gold standard, the crown jewel, the one thing that will get everyone to shut up, gather 'round, and pay attention, is a good story. They're all chasing stories. And good stories are always about failure. The more humiliating the failure, the better. You met Mick Jagger on Mustique? Yeah, well, he went down on my wife in a bathroom at the White House, and I was outside holding his coat. Let me tell you how it happened.

Turk understood that if the complication was a guaranteed rip-off, they'd line up to take two. They couldn't *not* tell their friends. There was a waiting list. But it troubled her because there it was again, a complication turned into entertainment.

So she mixed things up to invert the inversion. She sent in the gunmen. On the day of that fateful complication, the man behind the counter, who had graced the covers of alumni magazines of Yale (undergrad), Stanford (business), a son of the Mississippi Delta who had slept in the Lincoln Bedroom, was at the time the lone Black man in the lily-white field of dot-com billionaires. The gunmen wrenched him over the counter by the collar of his Ascot Chang and sent him through the plate-glass window headfirst (sugar glass, of course, safety being priority one). They dragged him across the parking lot by his heels, secured a noose around his neck, bound his arms and legs, and tossed him into the scarred bed of a Ford F-150. Drove long enough for him to get an eyeball full of the inked 88s and iron crosses. Impressed upon him their violent intentions, in case he had not understood, by invoking the terminologies of slavery and invisibility. Pressed the blades of their knives to his crotch. Waved around a flare gun and made clear their willingness to use it to clear his sinus passages. Pulled into a field, pitched him over the side of the truck, threw the length of rope over a high branch, and began to hoist him up.

He felt the rope bite in.

The final act would always be a problem. You couldn't kill the clients, even if that's what they wanted, but without the threat of death, the complication was only playacting. It was the dungeon all over again, welts on the thighs, sore nipples, a bruise or two, puffy eyes and a snotty nose followed up with a cool-down cuddle in the safe room. No one died on a Saint Andrew's Cross. The client always remained in control. When it was all over, the staples came out neat as you please, the blood was swabbed away, the contusions healed, and the pain relieved your psychic agony for a while.

That was the spiritual divide Turk had to cross. She had to withhold the safety word. The new model was creation of a fresh wound atop the old one. Not healing, but crippling, destroying, laying waste to the psyche and breaking the heart. Leaving the participant in significantly worse shape than when he'd come in.

The noose was hemp, tested and retested for elasticity and tensile strength across a range of humidity and temperature fluctuations, and doctored at a point four feet above the knot to break within two seconds of supporting the participant's full weight of 197 pounds. (He'd been weighed in a comprehensive fashion, once during the pre-complication medical evaluation, once before entering the convenience store, and his stool behind the counter was situated atop a pressure plate. Pre-assault adjustments were made to the rope to accommodate variations due to sweating, eating, excreting.)

When they kicked the box out from under him, the rope performed flawlessly and, complication having ended promptly at the moment that the final fiber unraveled, the skinheads caught him and lowered him gently to the packed, dusty earth, untied him, removed the noose, and offered cool water, terry-cloth wipes, and a fresh change of clothes. A Mercedes van arrived to ferry him back to the hotel where he could shower and, at his leisure, proceed to his jet for the trip to SQL.

Was he pleased with the service he'd received? He was listed as a reference by eight subsequent participants. He declined the exit interviews (one immediately following the experience, one forty-five days later, a more reflective array of questions), which led Turk to breach protocol and contact him directly. She'd taken him further than she'd ever taken anyone. She was worried about him, and more than a little guilty. He politely declined all her attempts to speak with him, and initially she thought she'd pushed it too far. But as new clients arrived on his reference, she reconsidered her evaluation. Given his psychological profile, she decided that it had been a success no greater or lesser than any other—her reaction, her attempt to get him to talk, had become an extension of his complication, nothing more than continued attempts to exploit and brutalize a man whose race ensured that he was brutalized every day of his life. Why, then, had he paid for a complication and specifically requested that, in the event that a violent episode was part of the complication, he be the victim of a hate crime? Pointless to speculate. He wanted to conquer his fears. He felt guilt for his success while so many others suffered and failed. He was suicidal. He was consumed with self-loathing. He was a history buff. An adrenaline junkie. A quiet man with secrets. Yes. No. Pointless to speculate.

I believe that's when she began to consider the design of the holistic complication, one that would continue to run long after the client had gone home. A complication that began before the client ever signed up. The complication that didn't even require the client to sign up, and took place without her knowledge.

When the tech bubble burst, the NorCal line of revenue dipped, but by then Turk had enough deposit-paid clients on the waiting list to project steady income for five years. She tweaked the lineup. Complications that mirrored contemporary fears had the deepest spiritual impact. Most sought-after: school shootings, terrorist bombings, earthquakes. Each one possible to replicate in a controlled environment, and Turk by then had hired an FX adviser, a couple of former Navy guys who knew their way around weaponry and explosives, a few psychologists who helped her tailor the experience for each participant, a few retired set builders from Silvercup. A legal team on retainer.

She made an interesting discovery along the way: complete realism wasn't a must. Some clients wanted to be aware of the artifice concealing the art, and each participant's tolerance for simulacrum was figured into the complication.

Some folks could close their eyes and lose themselves in a dream. Some wanted full-body contact. I was one of those who washed up at her feet after the great spiritual realignment of September 2001. There were millions of us on the island, on hands and knees outside McHale's at two in the afternoon, getting into fistfights in movie theaters, screaming matches in the checkout line, packing the synagogues, breaking down the doors of churches, lying wild-eyed and clenched in our dark apartments, listening to the radiators click, our eyes dragging us by our faces out of bed at the bleached whine of a LaGuardia-bound jet bisecting the sky above Fifth Avenue, the Strike Eagle engines screwing the air up and down the Hudson, ever watchful of the contrail scribes at thirty-five thousand feet, ears ever attuned to the howling sirens, awaiting copycat attacks, topping off the acid ache in our throats with a little more vodka. The smell of char emanating from the cavity could jump you any time you were south of 14th Street, and sometimes it crept right up to my doorstep, way uptown, took the elevator up, let itself in, and curled up next to me in bed. Desperately seeking: website capable of accurate wind direction predictions.

Did we have seasons that year? Do you remember?

You enter Turk's place of business through an apartment building on Broadway. Buzz 1B/Borromeo, give your name. Electrical click and door swings into the narrow Lysoled lobby. Cracked terra-cotta floor, chipped marble fascia, the yawning mouths of mailboxes, yellowed scrollwork at the ceiling. Go around the back of the staircase to the basement door, a U-turn, and descend into the orificial reek of wet buckets and rotten vegetable matter, at the far end down another disintegrating set of concrete stairs, through the iron door, into the catacomb, the length of the corridor lit with bare bulbs like droplets of light melting from the pipes overhead. You're under the street now, a part of the chthonic circuitry of the city, a part of the flaking plaster, the soot, the curling paint, the decay, the mold, the grease, the rust. At the far end of the tunnel is another door. Press the button, look up at the camera, wait for the buzz. Open, enter, down another set of stairs. You're in the Apelles subbasement.

A few years after Vik disappeared, on the advice of a widow who laughed and told me all I had to do to wake up was walk across the street, I arrived with vomit on my breath, my vision frosted, sleepless, some sort of wraithlike thing that might show up in a photograph as an unexplained greenish glow.

What do they do for you? I'd asked Eden.

They put you inside, she said.

There were no normal conversations then. We still talked in a weird, ethereal code, the parameters of reality undefined, in gestures that raised the hair on our necks, always asleep, always awake, like an eastbound wind meeting a westbound wind over a rotten Jersey marshland clogged with garbage, destroyed cars, decaying marine life. We behaved like ghosts because that's what we wanted to be. We ran into ourselves everywhere—at the OCME, counseling meetings, grocery store, cemetery. I saw myself in kids, husbands, wives, fathers, mothers, all down the line, the solidification, as though we'd undergone a geological process by which we'd sobbed ourselves dry and had turned to granite. A single stupid word chiseled into each of us: Why?

Eden's face was still a medium for the sorrow that had been inscribed there by such a wickedly heavy hand, but something was off.

Somehow she was alive again; there was an illicit flare to her nostrils, as though she was carrying a great secret. Indeed she was. She was a 9/11 widow who'd regained her substantial nature. It was almost as though she could move her body again.

They put you inside what? I said.

Inside the building. But it's specific to you. To what you need.

Cognitive therapy? I said.

No, she said. There's nothing therapeutic about it.

Sign me up, I said. Do they yell at you about what a piece of shit you are? I'd pay five hundred an hour for that.

They might, she said, wincing.

Ohhh, I said. It's—

No. Well, I think they have the equipment, if that's what works for you . . . but that's not really their main line of business.

Can you just fucking tell me what it is? Is it Fight Club?

It's Fight Club, she said.

Fight Club's for little boys, I said. What are we talking about here?

It depends. There are a lot of variables. What they did for me isn't what they'll do for you. Unless that's what you want. It's bespoke.

Oh, perfect, I said.

I'm fucking this up, she said. It's not bespoke. Everyone who goes gets something different. And they *will* figure out what you want. You can be honest or lie but if you lie you'll probably just have to keep going back, so it's cheaper to be honest.

Honest about what?

About everything. Everything. There's a question about, you know, what's your greatest fear or something. It's more subtle, but that's what they're after. And I gave them the usual bullshit at first, you know, like, What have I got to be afraid of at this point? Nothing scares me now except my own face. And this woman, she's a shrink, she writes that down and goes on with the rest of the questionnaire and then at the end she says, Would you like to die? As in, If you would like to die right now I can make that happen for you.

She what?

This woman, if I'd said yes, I would like to die, she would have, I don't know, shot me right there, pulled out a needle, whatever. I knew it like I know my own name. She was totally calm about it. It was an adult conversation and we both knew exactly what she meant. The way a doctor tells you it's stage four and you're terminal. She let me know that *she* knew I'd already weighed the options and could make a perfectly informed decision.

And you said?

I said, No, thank you, not today. And she said, What, then, is your greatest fear? And I was like, All right, I get it. I understand. And we talked some more and finally I said: I'm afraid that he's not dead. I'm afraid that he's still out there.

Okay. Right.

And she says, Good. We can work with that. And they did.

What do you mean? I said.

I mean they worked with that.

They made a hologram of him?

Jesus, Hazel. They applied the information I'd given them, and . . .

And what?

They built a complication for me. They call them complications. They built his office. His desk, where he sat, what he saw out the window. And I got to sit in his chair and look in the drawers and look out the windows—I guess they were screens or something, but they were hi-def, and I didn't see the same boat twice on the river. There was the bullpen, you know, the traders, and the analysts, Bloomberg terminals, TVs on the walls. I mean, they pulled out all the stops. And they said to me, you know, Now sit in his chair, and become him. Take your time, as much time as you need, and when you feel comfortable, allow yourself to occupy his body. And so I did. I watched the boats on the river, and a helicopter went by, and when I was ready I said, I'm ready, and the phone rang, and it was Tyrone Flint on the other end, because he was talking to Tyrone Flint when the plane hit. Because Tyrone Flint reported to me himself—the guy who insisted that I meet him in Central Park, face-to-face, do you remember that?

I remember.

And I'd told them this, they're very thorough, and I say, Hello? and there's Tyrone Flint on the phone about some cross-border lease agreement that was tied up in legal. And, you know, he called before nine deliberately to miss Stephen. He wanted to dump a message on voice mail. So I say, Ready, and the phone rings, and it's, Oh, Stephen! I didn't think you'd— Tyrone Flint at Crutchfield Alliance here!

And the time on the phone is 8:45, so I have sixty seconds, give or take. I have questions, of course. But he won't shut up. I don't think it was a recording, but he didn't let me get a word in edgewise. And he kept calling me Stephen.

Do you think it was really him?

Who knows. They seem to have the ability to— I don't know. They seem committed to providing good service.

And?

And then it's 8:46. And everything turns into a furnace. The whole office—like a volcano. The walls are gone. Vanished. The desks flew up, the TVs exploded, the fire ate everything. Everyone was on fire. The black smoke. Everything exploded.

What do you mean *exploded*?

It—everything. Not just the TVs. I screamed and got under the desk. The floor moved, I could feel the concussion in my chest. My eardrums felt like they were shredding.

But the fire and the—how did you survive?

The fire didn't come into Stephen's office.

They protected you.

Apparently what I told them was that I wanted everyone in the office to die except Stephen.

You told them you were afraid he hadn't died.

Yes.

So they . . . interpret?

They have ways of figuring out what you really want, Eden said. And then they leave you to it.

Turk had turned operations over to her staff years earlier, but for me she was front and center, met me right there in the lobby. White-glove service. I don't recall being surprised to see her there, the only addition to the jeans and button-down shirt she wore every day a blue shawl, an attempt to appear matronly. I'd known her my entire life, of course. I'd assumed she was independently wealthy. We were neighbors, but what can you really know about anybody? Every so often she would come tapping at the service door. Spare some milk, have any sugar? When there was a blackout, I'd check on her if she didn't check on me and Vik first.

As I emerged from the cryptoporticus, she took my arm and walked me through the marble lobby to her office in the back. The lobby looks the same today as it did then. Standard corporate scenery. Glass, marble, tasteful gray twill sofas that have never hosted a set of buttocks. When I asked Turk why she hadn't extended the corporate façade all the way out, she explained that it was of particular importance that participants remember they were underground, down with the rats and ancient creeks. Anyway, she said, leaning in to me, do you have any idea what it would cost to waterproof that tunnel?

Good Turk.

Her team constructed a complication for me that put me right back in the same office space Eden had watched erupt in flame. Vik's office, after all, had been right next to Stephen's. But I wanted some changes. I wanted to be out there in the bullpen when the flames swept through. I wanted the place to disintegrate around me. Wanted the ceiling to collapse. I wanted to be buried in rubble.

On the appointed day, they sent a car to deliver me to the compound upstate, on the Wallkill River. They layered me in Nomex, full hood, breathing apparatus, forty pounds of shielding, ushered me onto the office floor, where I stood among my husband's colleagues—professional stuntmen and -women, I now know—variously hammering at their keyboards, or sucking on coffee cups with a foot on the file cabinet, or watching the news, and there was this one guy who had a phone to his ear, nodding, scribbling on a pad, and it was he who got my attention because I wanted to know what he was writing (gibberish, doodling interlocking benzene rings, or had he so committed himself to the role that he had collected research on deals the firm would have been tracking that morning and was jotting from memory so that I, the participant, might in some way benefit from his method approach?). I stood against the back wall in my green EOD suit, peering out through the acrylic visor at the scenery, and there above the windows (Eden was right, what a view!) were the LED clocks for London, Singapore, Tokyo, Frankfurt, Buenos Aires, Shanghai, Milan, New York, and it was 8:42, by my request, and when I said, Ready, into the hands-free, the colons on the LEDs began to flash and I prepared to die. I'd spent a month under the supervision of a psychologist, but when it was showtime I didn't feel like I was Vik or myself or an all-seeing eyeball. I felt like I was a stranger to us both, someone who'd paid an outrageous sum of money to participate in an outrageous stunt in the name of distraction. I felt crass and dishonest and utterly American.

I had a long four minutes to consider the implications of what I'd undertaken, the fiction I was creating, the familiar sense of life at a remove from life. I had time to consider the presence of Albert Caldwell within me—yes, still there, always there—either directing me toward or away from the truth from his frozen little cave, I couldn't tell which, I could never know, my existence being a dictatorship of ignorance, and at the mark, the windows erupted and fire stormed through the space, a rolling, rippling flood of plasma, incinerating carpet and paper, carbonizing the ceiling tiles, roaring like river rapids, exerting an unexpected force, a physical force—what had I expected, seaweed lapping at my legs, lambs licking at lilacs, *tongues* of flame and all that? Certainly not this godlike presence crushing me from all sides, reducing, suffocating, combusting within me. The flaming analysts had all dropped safely into the subspace through trapdoors, and when the ceiling collapsed, my puckering throat sucked at the deoxygenated atmosphere, even though the EOD suit had been reinforced with a carbon-fiber cage so that I was wearing, in essence, a protective refrigerator, and the O_2 was flowing normally.

The crushing panic was only my neurons hurtling along ahead of the physical sensation, playing the odds, and as I lay pinned beneath the rubble, panting, stinging sweat searing my lips, the screech of steel girders shearing from their mounts piped into my headset, rebar screaming as it knotted and broke, I recalled my training and opened my eyes so that I might take in the same darkness as Vik, had he been there. Had he been there and had he survived the initial impact. A tiny flame danced around in the little pocket of rubble before my eyes, gobbling up oxygen that, had Vik been trapped there, could have sustained him for just a few seconds more. A bright red combustion thread crawled across a wafer of ceiling tile wedged against my helmet. Soon that light, too, flickered and dimmed and died. The rubble shifted now and then, and I watched and breathed and listened.

As Eden predicted, the complication did nothing to make me feel better. It didn't do anything except fill me with the desire to do it again. On subsequent runs I refused everyone's advice and insisted on getting exactly what I wanted. It pleased me to think I was screwing with their system, forcing them to rethink their omniscient attitude. I was really going to put them through the ringer. There weren't going to be any surprises, oh no, not like Eden's complication. I knew exactly what I wanted.

I was being, of course, as predictable as a sunset. I paid to do it again. I had insurance money, and the brokerage accounts had rebounded, so why not? Why not blow it all playing with fire? I should have been suspicious; Turk was giving me too much leeway, wasn't she? Letting me control every aspect of the complication. I was supposed to be getting what I needed, not what I wanted. I said I wanted to be convinced of the existence of reality as it had been explained to me. I had been told that Vik died in Tower One, and I didn't believe it. Put me in the office so that I might believe, I said. Turk didn't put up a strenuous argument. The staff psychologist went along, too. Maybe, I thought, it just so happened that what I wanted and what I needed were one and the same.

So I stood again in the EOD suit, waiting to be convinced that my husband had been burned, pulverized, vaporized. I was cooked and crushed and I still didn't believe it.

Turk listened to my list of complaints, where the complication had failed to mimic reality, where it had failed metaphorically, why I wanted it louder, hotter, with the smell of smoldering steel. She made notes and passed them along to the designers. I was pleased to be in control of something.

My complication had little to do with what was happening within the firebox, but I couldn't have possibly comprehended that at the time.

All the pre-launch histrionics, all my insistence on maintaining control, asserting my agency: that was the real complication, the site of my transubstantiation. She let me run the fireball complication six times in total. I got friendly with the staff. We made slight modifications. After the third performance I no longer needed the office, the actors, the soundtrack. Just the fire and the collapse. I really thought I was making some progress. *On my own terms*, as they say. By the end, we were down to bare concrete and a wire frame to support the ceiling, no more vid-screen windows, and Jerome, an ex-chemist who'd worked at ILM before Turk hired him away, casually mentioned that for about a tenth of what I was paying, he could shoot me with a flamethrower and drop some reinforced asbestos tiling from a rig, and it would only take about an hour to set up. I didn't hear sarcasm, but kindness; I felt encouraged that he understood. He saw that I was narrowing the scope of my research, and that as I gathered more information I was discarding superfluous elements of the set. Reality was collapsing beneath the symbolic. As I moved toward the truth, ornamentation was a distraction. Jerome was an excellent actor.

The firebox was not without its merits. It was there, buried beneath the ceiling, watching the flames eat the world, that I brought myself into focus. There, just for an instant, the paper-doll cutouts (me:me) aligned and my borders felt clear, definitive. For a moment I could believe that Vik had died.

In the end, a complication is nothing more than the practical application of a philosophy that substitutes one accepted reality for another. Suppose you have a computer. You exchange its hard drive for another, identical drive. The inputs processed by the identical drive are no different. Maybe there are slight improvements in processing speed; or maybe it's a little slower. But nothing you'd really notice. Arguably, data flowing through the new drive undergoes a spiritual alteration, affecting every letter and number you type, every image you save, but are such things visible to the naked eye? And do they even matter, if you're not looking for them? What if someone switches the hard drive without telling you?

A complication is not an escape, but an adjustment. Not an awakening, but a deeper, clarified slumber. It's both the well and the bucket. Perhaps you drown or quench your thirst. Nothing changes or you might benefit from the placebo effect. We're not Scientology, we're not Freemasons or Figure Sevens. We are simply a conduit.

For a few months Turk and I saw a lot of each other. The thicket of sorrow that made my morning walk from the bedroom to the bathroom a bloody, grievous ordeal parted in places to allow me passage. Food went down without lodging on that shelf in my throat quite as often. I might have indicated to my counselors that I'd been sleeping better.

Around that time, Turk started making noises about getting old, about hoping to wind down the business. She talked about it casually, dropped hints, led me to the lake and waited for me to drink. When I asked to buy in as a partner, I thought it was my own idea. I suggested training with her for several years, and then, if all went well, I'd buy her out entirely when she was ready to pack it in.

You can pad my coffin with the money, she said.

In three years she'll be one hundred. My contribution to the business has been minimal, mostly operational streamlining, some low-watt whisper campaigns after the '08 crash to drum up business. Hire good people and get out of their way, that's my motto. Everything will be fine after I'm gone.

Through our Silicon Valley clients we became beta testers for all the latest virtual gear, and now most of the complications play out while the participant reclines on padded mohair in an aromatic room equipped with surround sound and synchronous temperature controls. Certain complications, of course, require full-body participation, and for those setups we maintain the complex upstate.

The ethos hasn't changed: Not what you want, but what you need.

My own education in the dungeon was, Turk felt, essential to a complete understanding of her business. To understand what it's become you have to understand where it started, she said.

These days we don't get much call for the leather and rubber, but occasionally I open up the cells, pull the sheets off the saltires and stockades, oil the chains. They're all older clients who've been rummaging around in the past, looking for the key to a door that won't unlock. If, as I'm whipping them, they peer back over the welts rising across their sagging skin (moisturize first or it tears like paper), I can see they're searching, listening to each lash, mind focused, hoping to catch the ignition of a single dendrite, dim for all those years, because sometimes it only takes the one and, presto, you've got it, you're back, you're rising off the surface of the earth with a nuke jammed in your crotch, old Slim Pickens run in reverse, out of the carnage of the lived life back into your mom's bomb bay, and the mouth says, More, More! and within reason, okay, but where else can a person go? How far back into the nothingness do you really want to travel? Yes, I'll do what I can to help, of course. I'll create a rhythm with the strokes, an exit through which they can be reborn, deborn, vaporized.

Those souls who still need a stranger's hand, the presence of a sentient life force in the room, I'll admit I have a soft spot for them, and I'm the only one who caters to their needs because it makes zero financial sense to keep a domme on staff, and a reasonably priced freelancer—well, you get what you pay for there, mostly NYU and Columbia kids who are *working through something*, don't have the stomach for skin contact, and otherwise don't have the proper practical experience. It's one client every couple of months. So I get into the gear and sweat a little. Keeps me in touch with our roots. Am I *working through something* myself? Of course I am.

I've accepted that, just as I lived first in my father's book, I now live in a construction fashioned by Turk, my very own personal complication. I was not graced with this knowledge via a broiling cumulonimbus extending a luminous finger to tap me on the crown of my head. No wizened African American man on the bus turned and spoke to me in metaphors. So how could I *realize* I am completely enmeshed in a complication, a full-scale operation that has no end, a supreme act of love, the sort of love that makes real the interlocking nature of everything in the universe, the visible, mystical, intellectual, farcical, organic, mechanical? I *realized* nothing. I *realize* nothing even now. Yet I have no doubt she set in motion a great mystery that has begun to unravel, and the mystery is part of the complication, just as the complication is itself part of the complication. Cue the music, full-cast soft-shoe to that old favorite, "I Know That You Know That I Know That You Know That I Know That...," jazz hands, heel spin, scissor, scissor, sliiiideee. I have my delusions, and perhaps I've lived strangely, but I've lived. My granite soul has cracked and the question inscribed there has crumbled.

13.

Back to 1978. Tanawat Kongkatitum was the grandson of Lazlo's third employee, Sasithorn, a Thai linguist who, while studying at Columbia, pulled rent teaching at the Brunn Institute. Now his grandson, Tanawat, aka Hiwatt, had himself matriculated Columbia to study chemistry and was occupying one of Turk's empty bedrooms. Turk didn't mind the company, and Hiwatt's father sent rent money via Western Union every month, which Turk, who didn't need it, turned over to the boy, who didn't need it, either, since he also had an account at Chemical Bank that magically replenished itself whenever the balance dropped below $10,000. The rent money went primarily to Times Square peep shows.

Turk was ethically opposed to moral advice, and any dead-of-the-night thoughts she might have had about warning Hiwatt away from Times Square always vaporized in the light of morning. There was no judgment at the breakfast table, where she sat in an ancient terry-cloth bathrobe, crunching on toasted Roman Meal with butter, 1010 WINS droning from the transistor on the windowsill over the sink while rumpled Tanawat compared—not without eloquence—the skills of employees of Show World, Satisfaction Emporium, and Peep-o-Rama, the Harvard-Yale-Princeton of jerk-off joints.

Every few weeks, she traded him a couple of twenties for a lid of Oaxacan Red, a strain he'd introduced to her after securing a hookup his first week on campus. It wasn't that pot was particularly hard to come by, but since the previous May, when her dealer graduated and loaded up his Fiat for medical school in Ann Arbor, the stuff she'd been able to lay hands on was just a cut above what she could liberate from her own spice rack. She kept the stash in a golden box shaped like a single cell of honeycomb, adorned at the edge with two bees made of onyx and yellow sapphire, a gift from her father on her thirtieth birthday.

Her after-dinner routine was invariable: she cued up some Grand Funk Railroad, propped her feet on the ottoman, and blazed a fat doobie, which was exactly what she was doing the night of the blizzard, the only difference being that Hiwatt, usually engaged by 10:00 p.m. in a masturbatory revel on 43rd Street, had been turned back by the ferocity of the storm and now occupied the sofa opposite her, his own propped-up feet smaller, woolen mirrors of her bare ones. His big toe protruded from a hole in the left sock, and he was wiggling it back and forth mesmerizingly. Turk was watching with interest. There was something heartbreaking about a boy with a hole in his sock, and though she considered herself anything but matronly, she worried about the kid's well-being. Sure, it was the weed talking, but her heart went out to him, so far from home, in winter, all alone except for live girls doing finger shows.

The phone was ringing but neither of them moved.

Take it off, she said, pointing at the offending article.

He retracted his toe, then, as it reappeared from the hole, said, Mothra emerges from her cocoon and warms her wings. Wiggle wiggle.

Take it off and I'll ... mend it. They were swimming through syrupy air, and after what might have been ten minutes or an hour, the sock arrived in Turk's hand and she set out for her brother Seamus's former bedroom, the de facto storage shed that was home to an assortment of steamer trunks, her mother's foot-pump Singer, stacks of sheet music, old tax forms, a set of dining room chairs, disintegrating linens, and somewhere inside the little rolltop desk at which her brother had done his sums, a sewing kit in a blue velvet bag.

The room was at the farthest end of the hallway, rarely visited, an expedition into her childhood, and it took ages for her to navigate the

Sarab floor runner, her cannabinoid receptors having transformed the patterns thereupon into a down escalator she was trying to ascend.

The phone was ringing again.

She was sucking wind by the time she got to the door, yet when she opened it she summoned enough air to push out a full-throated, Hiwatt! that brought him running, if unsteadily. He kept nosing into the wall like a balsa-wood glider that had its wings trimmed wrong, and thought it would be proper to announce, as one must, as surely as the sky is blue and cats meow, This is some good shit! But he was outthinking himself two-to-one, and felt pointedly that he'd already revealed too much of himself to Turk, upon whom he'd developed an if-not-quite-debilitating then definitely goo-goo-level crush, and the utterance of that particular cliché would bring into stark light the creaky apparatus of his altered state, thereby throwing into question the intimacy they'd shared earlier that evening when they'd rapped about their families and Turk's memories of Hiwatt's grandfather and her own doubts about the efficacy of her upbringing. He worried because, of course, there is the question of authenticity that lurks around any confessions or intimacies shared while on drugs, since in an altered state one can no longer be considered oneself, but some other, uninhibited, even alien, person. He worried his brain into somersaults over it.

Hiwatt was a passionate guy, strong on desire, weak on restraint, a connoisseur of inhibition when it came to the game of exposing himself, whether physically or spiritually. He had certain needs, one of which was to experience the struggle between shame and the desire to share himself with strangers, a little saga that played out every time he entered the booth, unbuttoned his jeans, and began to masturbate, separated by only a pane of glass from the naked girl oozing around in front of him. His excitement relied entirely on being observed. Classic exhibitionist. He would have preferred that his observer be clothed, but he hadn't yet been able to bring himself to offer any of the dancers money to put her clothes back on, feeling that it might cross a line of perversion that not even the official live girls at Show World would put up with. He had shared this concern with Turk, and she, given her own line of work having a bead on the full spectrum of New York's rarest fetishes, had shrugged. What's the harm in asking? she'd said. It seemed to have no effect on Turk when he talked about the girls and how quickly and explosively he ejaculated on the matte-black wall beneath the window. She listened, nodding, sipping from her coffee, offering no indication that she admired his courage at all. Perhaps she had no inhibitions of her own, he thought.

Hiwatt was, at the tender age of eighteen, primarily interested in re-creating a lost relationship, specifically the one he'd shared with his nanny, who since his birth had performed all the functions of mother and, after he'd reached puberty, the physical functions of a girlfriend, to a point. She let him feel but never see, and she stroked him off most nights before bed, with a bored, distant look on her face that Hiwatt would forever seek from his sexual partners, followed by praise for the velocity and quantity of his ejaculations. The nanny saw nothing out of the ordinary in their ritual, no more shameful than scrubbing his ears in the bath, proving yet again that, begun early enough, practiced often enough, anything can achieve the splendiferous normalcy of oatmeal.

The silhouettes didn't line up, but it was close enough. Turk reminded him of his nanny at the hairline, a Transylvanian peak that announced itself when she pulled her graying hair into a ponytail, and sometimes if he squinted he could, at a distance, make it all fit. That Turk gave no indication she meant to care for him in the only way that would cure his homesickness was no deterrence. He'd understood that he'd have to convince her; New York was not the same as home. Here, he would have to express his manhood.

Commenting on the goodness of the shit did not, therefore, align with his master plan to project himself as a cool, enterprising, and altogether responsible, if horny, young man worthy of her attentions, and by the time he'd completed his spectacularly uncool journey to the end of the hall, he'd decided to say nothing at all. When he saw what was inside the room, he blurted out, Oh my word! then, as a corrective, Shit! an overreach, and as a corrective to that, Gee-dog! which was followed by a groan of despair, the realization that his spirit was weak, his mind weaker, and he'd be alone forever. Good shit, indeed.

Gee-dog is right, Turk said.

Before them lay an eleven-foot-seven-inch Scots pine. A mystery conceived and solved in the same moment. The tree, not unfamiliar to either of them, was still wearing its ornaments and lights, tinsel draping sweetly from its brittle branches. It was on its side; specifically, it was canted at about thirty degrees as a result of the crown's contact with the far wall, bending up now like a creepy curled finger, in any case positioned to indicate that it had been carelessly discarded and left to disintegrate all over boxes and chairs and the rolltop desk Turk had set out for in the first place. The stump had oozed a little resin onto Turk's sewing machine.

There was disappointment in her voice, her first genuine expression of that emotion in the six months Hiwatt had lived with her.

I truly thought it had gone over the balcony, Hiwatt said, affecting the Commonwealth tone he employed when he required authority in the face of authority. He pondered the tree, stroking his chin. How on earth? he said. He kept stroking his chin because it felt wonderful.

It didn't climb back in the window, now, did it? Turk said.

Most definitely not, Hiwatt answered, still stroking his chin.

It was February 6. At the end of December, Turk had taken her annual trip to St. John, leaving Hiwatt alone in the apartment through New Year's. Having no children of her own and lending no credence to anecdotal evidence about the expansive sense of social charity that overcomes a young person left home unsupervised for longer than a day, she hadn't issued ground rules. She was no fool, but she wasn't the enemy of fun, either, and when she returned on the evening of January 1, tan, hungover, bearing a bruise or two from her own revels, she set up a pot of coffee and asked Hiwatt to join her at the kitchen table.

Get up to anything fun? she said.

I did! he replied with a lush gargle of a laugh. Hiwatt was doing his straight-backed, good-breeding routine that could sometimes cross the line into fawning maître d', which actually relaxed Turk a hair, as he only put on the college interview voice when he was nervous. Plus, he was stoned out of his gourd. He went on: I hosted a splendid party, what I can remember of it. I was told an African prince attended, but I can't imagine he wouldn't have had more attractive options.

I'm always sweeping them out of the corners after my parties, Turk said.

Hiwatt nodded as if chewing on a piece of particularly interesting information.

I'm sure you were a charming host, Turk said.

I am. It's a well-known fact.

So, everything seems to be in place, Turk said.

Yes.

So where's all the carnage? Surely all the furniture's been replaced, or something.

There was one minor incident.

Yes. Where's the tree?

Of course you know! You did fail to mention the ceremony before you left, though, Hiwatt said.

Which, now?

The—the what do you call it?—the ritual.

Did I?

We counted down the final minute of the year, as is customary, yes? And then my guests gathered at the windows overlooking the courtyard, as there was a commotion outside.

They called us over. I was very drunk, but I made it in time to see a few of the trees. I had not been told about this practice, though it was, in its way, elegant.

Everyone was throwing their trees off their balconies, Turk said.

Yes, the trees, raining down into the courtyard and all the men in their tuxedos and the women in their evening gloves—quite elegant, you know, throwing their champagne flutes after the trees, Hiwatt said.

It's been a while since I've seen that.

A building tradition, I assumed? We felt compelled—my guests felt compelled—I was, as they say, plowed by then, ha ha—to join in. I was apparently unable to contribute in a meaningful way and my classmates carried me to the sofa, where I awoke only this very afternoon. Shoeless and wearing a feather boa!

So your friends tossed the tree out the window, Turk said.

I can only assume that is the case. The Christmas tree is gone, ergo . . . I'm truly sorry, Miss Turk. I should have waited for your return?

No, no, Turk said. It's just strange. No one's done that for years.

We acted properly, I believe, in the spirit of the season? Perhaps next year you can stay in the city for New Year's?

Perhaps, Turk said.

Oh, and there was something else, but . . . It's strange—it's the alcohol. I'm not used to it. Give me a bowl of hash any day . . .

Turk waited for a couple of beats, then said, Something happened?

Oh yes. I can't say exactly. I believe something happened. There was a Russian student here, and I believe my classmates—no, some friends of theirs, perhaps—it was very crowded, a smash hit of a party . . . Hiwatt, smiling faintly, drifted off into a recollection of the night's grandeur.

What about the Russian? Turk said.

Oh yes! He arrived wearing a tuxedo! Isn't that funny? And his hair was black, and like an explosion, an atomic bomb. I don't know who invited him, but he was very demanding, ordering everyone around. He repeatedly called me boy, even after I made clear that I was the host. Strange fellow. There were so many people here I didn't know.

Turk looked around the kitchen, out through the door into the dining room. Not a picture askew, not a bowl out of place.

Then, later, I was on my back, on the sofa, perhaps even then shoeless, and the Russian fellow was being held aloft, like this, you see, on everyone's hands? He was kicking and twisting, and everyone was laughing at his predicament. They were moving toward the balcony—the doors were open and the curtains were streaming inward quite beautifully on the wind, and everyone was shouting over the music. Their faces were so bright and the girls were all flushed, the backs of their arms splotchy and red, as if they'd been exercising vigorously.

And what was this Russian boy saying?

As I recall, he was shouting, as well, though with Russians it can be hard to tell whether they're shouting or just speaking in that imperious manner of theirs—anyway, he was making noises as they approached the balcony doors. Some of the boys were wearing skirts! I've just remembered this. Isn't that funny, how these images drift in and out?

What happened to him?

Obviously, I believe they intended to carry him to the balcony, you know, to pitch him out like a Christmas tree.

To pretend to throw him over. To frighten him.

To frighten him, yes. Or, perhaps, to throw him down to the courtyard with the trees. Hiwatt shrugged and went on. I've seen instances of this sort of behavior. Crowds can be very excitable. Generally speaking, one can expect a crowd to behave badly.

I assume no harm came to the boy, since I didn't come home to an apartment full of cops, Turk said.

If only I could say for sure. I fell asleep.

Turk went to the window and peered down into the courtyard.

And the tree? The tree went out before or after the Russian?

After? No, before. It's hard to remember what happened, in what order.

We should call one of your friends to get the story, don't you think?

That's a splendid idea, Hiwatt said, but neither of them made a move for the phone.

What else did they throw out? Turk said.

Hiwatt smiled, his lips peeling back to expose the perfect arches of his white teeth. I'm terribly sorry, Miss Turk, he said. There was one other thing.

Turk raised an eyebrow at him.

Yes, I regret to inform you that your big earthen bowl, for the cheese—the, ah—what do you call it—the heavy one you put over the fire?

The fondue pot?

Yes. I regret to inform you that I have not been able to locate it.

Turk fell back in her chair as if she'd been punched in the chest. She threw her arms over her head and shrieked. Savages!

Hiwatt giggled.

Out the window? Turk said.

No doubt out the window, Hiwatt said, whistling.

Wish I'd been here, said Turk.

There was a somber air to Turk and Hiwatt's work. Branches came off in their hands, cracking sharply, shedding waves of brown needles that disappeared into crevices to await a distant, yet unborn great-niece or -nephew, onto whom someday would fall the task of conducting the posthumous cleaning of Great Aunt T's apartment.

Maybe, if we conduct a thorough enough search, we'll uncover the Russian, Turk said.

A mummy, Hiwatt said.

Hiwatt, did you actually have a party?

Oh, I'm certain I did.

You weren't here alone, eating pills?

That's possible. All things are possible, are they not? Without corroborating evidence, who could say whether there might or might not have been a party? Perhaps even both. A party and not a party! Perhaps at this very moment in a parallel universe, we are not cleaning up a Christmas tree!

Lucky us, Turk said.

Silently, with the singular focus of the deeply stoned, in blissful harmonic coordination, they wrapped each ornament in crepe paper and stacked them in cardboard boxes; floated tinsel into paper Zabar's bags; crammed the lights into little shoebox coffins to be buried in a closet for another year.

We could burn it, Turk said when they were finished.

Even in his altered state, Hiwatt knew this was a bad idea.

Too large for the fireplace, he said.

Ah.

We'll call one of the servants, yes? Hiwatt said.

Tanawat, they're employees of the building. They're unionized.

So should we not call the unionized employee-servants of the building to carry away the tree?

No. Yes. Yes, we should call them, but . . . be respectful.

Am I not respectful? Hiwatt said, genuinely wounded by the implication that his behavior could be interpreted any other way.

On occasion you reveal the royal aspects of your upbringing.

I am far from royalty, I assure you. The blood connection is on my mother's side, and fairly distant.

Turk got up to call the lobby, but when she dialed, no one answered. She tapped on the switch hook, tried again, no answer.

It's late, Turk said. He's probably in the basement playing cards, she said. After a long draught of pot-fueled contemplation she said, We'll do it ourselves.

Pardon?

Grab a branch. A sturdy one.

As you wish, miss.

They managed to work the tree loose and get it through the doorway, taking out a few hallway pictures and upending a console table in the process, and leaving a massacre of needles in their wake. They grunted and heaved the thing through the apartment, claiming a few more victims—a set of jade figurines, a small flower vase—and arrived at the service door soaked in sweat.

What's that smell? Turk said when they opened the service door.

A fire. A cooking fire, Hiwatt said, testing the air. That is undoubtedly burning fish.

All right, tallyho! Turk said, giving the tree a shove out the door.

They managed to get about seven linear feet of the tree into the trash chute before it jammed. Hiwatt climbed onto the trunk and, bracing his hands on the ceiling, jumped up and down in an attempt to break it, but succeeded only in stabbing himself in the legs with the branches and sending a shower of needles to the floor. He executed a precarious dismount and stood squinting at the tree as though it had deliberately defied him.

Stop smelling your hands, Turk said, and get in here. With her bare foot she swept at the detritus on her doorstep while Hiwatt tiptoed past her.

We can't leave it like this, she said.

Oh, absolutely not, Hiwatt called from the sofa, where he was lighting up another joint. Turk backed into the apartment and joined him. Before long, she had embarked on an inventory of the bones of her hand while Hiwatt was sketching up a revolutionary theory of hydrodynamics on the back of an envelope, a schematic composed of blocks and circles to indicate sluices and valves, each connected by double and triple integrals signifying water. The tree was long forgotten. The phone was ringing again.

B y the time my father came upon the tree, Hiwatt had left for the Vornados' party and Turk was passed out on the sofa.

To my father, the tree was a deliberate act of sabotage. He thought: This is exactly how it begins. This is step one.

Having banged on Turk's service door long enough to stir Hastings Sebenlist from his burrow a second time, my father relented. He and his bag of burned fish went back into our apartment and out the front door, intent on the little tray of notecards by the elevators. A dozen blue Bics were in a leather dice cup on the table opposite the elevators, and he fell into one of the antique armchairs to compose a complaint, which, according to custom, he would slide under the perpetrator's door.

He wanted to keep it simple, but he couldn't find the right tone. *Very disappointing* had a colonial tang to it, an air of self-pity and saccharine innocence in the face of a crumbling social order, like some sop with a pince-nez watching his Rhodesian manor burn while the natives sharpened their spears behind him, and *Unsurprising* wasn't much better, only more American in its sarcastic attempt to stave off the expression of any real feeling. Same for *Shocker*.

The fish reeked.

Fuckface made an appearance, but this was Turk, after all, no need to turn on a flamethrower, and the word looked silly just lying there on the notecard like a cat lounging in a doorway, anyway. He shifted into full drafting mode, filling cards front and back like a middle school toilet stall, until the stinking bag at his feet and the slowly dawning recognition of the absurdity of the project combined to produce *Have a Nice*

Day, which he underlined twice and propped up against the flower vase behind the stack of cards.

He'd only been stalling for time. Now he stood before the elevator call button, his moment of reckoning. He examined the doors, above them the fleur-de-lis in its radiant garden of numbers, and he considered the blizzard, the potential for a power outage. Under perfect conditions, he was, at best, a wary passenger. Under current conditions, he was scared stiff. It hardly mattered that he was intimately familiar with this particular elevator, assembled in Toledo, Ohio, a Haughton Elevonics updated with Schindler parts, as he always paid to accompany the inspectors on their twice-yearly look-sees, the most recent of which had taken place on September 17, 1977, with Andrzej Kaczynski of the New York Department of Buildings, who'd had some stories to tell about the days of occupation, though my father hadn't volunteered any particulars about his time in Poland except to say that he'd seen some of the countryside, and who my father trusted as much as he trusted any of the inspectors, which is to say zero. He had a special flashlight for the job, a Kel-Lite 5 cell, known to the NYPD as the persuader, and while the inspector did his cursory scan of the hoistway and pit, my father lit up the shackle ties and the rail blocks, the pulleys and ropes, squinting through the distance as though trying to decipher graffiti high on the wall of a paleolithic cave. He of course had the paranoiac's keen eye for signs of wear and tear on the steel cables, which the inspectors disconcertingly referred to as rope, and which at the Apelles was eight-strand, superior in tensile strength to the perfectly acceptable six-strand—or so you would think. Oh god, the lectures he could deliver on von Mises stress and friction coefficients on drive and deflector sheaves, the immense pressures that could cause the rope strands to score the channel, which would in turn abrade the individual wires, causing deeper scoring, more abrasion, until the strands unfurled one by one, edging toward the inevitable catastrophic failure. So, ultimately, did you want lithe, low-coefficient six- or burly eight-strand? Well, there was a lecture for that, too. He understood in equal detail the safety features of modern elevators, the emergency brakes that made it impossible for a car to careen unheeded to the floor of the shaft, yet that knowledge did nothing to assuage his fears. He believed in extraordinary coincidences. A probabilistic number could be assigned to the likelihood that a pulley would fail at exactly the same time the safety features would fail. The probability might be small, but it existed, and its existence alone was enough to give him the raging palps. He not only believed in extraordinary coincidences, he expected them to be catastrophic. Not only would the engine fall off the jet, it could coincide with the failure of the other three engines under whose power the plane could easily have gotten home. And once you were thinking that way, why not expect the simultaneous failure of the wings, the avionics, the fuel lines? What was stopping the plane from turning into a ball of flame halfway through an otherwise uneventful flight?

That's how my father walked through the world, waiting for the subterranean steam pipes beneath his feet to rupture at exactly the same time an air conditioner slipped loose from its mooring twenty stories up. Every time he ventured out of the apartment he was confronted by new ways to die. An elevator was a coffin on wires.

Sometimes, under the right circumstances (proper lighting, endorphin levels, barometric pressure, etc.), he could overpower his fears, but that night the storm was one variable too many.

Stage one had been the Christmas tree. An innocuous domestic abnormality, but one that funneled him into: stage two, in which he is forced to take the elevator, where he is trapped when the storm conspires to engage: stage three, power loss. And if those three most unlikely events transpired, what was to keep the cables from snapping, and what was to keep the governor and emergency brakes from failing?

It was the problem of excess imagination, of possibility carrying as much weight as reality. My father had lived there for ten years, and he was religious about using only one passenger elevator, his Haughton Elevonics updated with Schindler parts. He knew its wobbles and clanks, its shimmy at the sixth floor. So slavish was he in his devotion to that elevator that he didn't even know the names of the doormen stationed in the other three lobbies, each one situated at the elbow of each block-long run of apartments. For that matter, he wouldn't have recognized residents of the other wings of the building. His realm was the fourteenth floor, the West End side, apartments A through F, the outer limits extending just around the corner to 14G, on the other side of the elevator.

Everything beyond was tundra. He might offer a tense, arm-crossed elevator greeting to a few members of the vertical brotherhood who occupied the apartment lines above and below him, but by and large he lived in a world of his own making, into which few were allowed to enter, and out of which he rarely ventured.

No doubt about it: He was nuts. But on the whole, no more nuts than, say, a woman who, upon finding herself in an empty elevator, seizes the opportunity to ball up her cardigan, jam her face into it, and scream all the way to the lobby. People do all sorts of things, and in his line of work, an overactive imagination was hardly a handicap.

My father sighed, gave the bag a twist, and made for the stairwell door.

14.

In the early days of the twentieth century, residents of the Apelles marked holiday celebrations with the defenestration of champagne flutes, dessert plates, hurricane glasses, whatever was lying around on the sideboard. Anything that made a satisfying pop on the cobblestones of the interior courtyard was fair game. What fun! Less festive, but worth noting: Twice, in episodes separated by twenty-five years, the industrialist Alexander Flagg played bombardier with dining room chairs, both times targeting men he suspected of staining his wife's honor. Both times, building management levied heavy fines.

The first Christmas tree was jettisoned by a freshly discharged Army Air Corps lieutenant in the early hours of New Year's 1946, and although the building's management board frowned on what they wrote up as a dangerous act of impertinence, they assigned a token fine of only a halfpenny, as they, like the young pilot, were feeling buoyed at the time. Though the lieutenant was merely happy to have survived the shooting galleries of the Pacific theater, the board was, to a man, ecstatic over the recent atomic annihilation of hundreds of thousands of Japanese civilians, which had set off a sustained market rally, which pleased the bankers among them, and had opened up new territory into which to expand American factories and export American goods, which pleased the industrialists among them.

Residents interpreted the halfpenny fine imposed on the lieutenant as an implicit blessing, and the next New Year's Eve, as fireworks flowered over the Hudson River, a cascade of trees showered the courtyard. The residents, however, had been mistaken. The board, detecting folly, imposed a ten-dollar fine on each tree. They intended to shut this business down just as they'd have shut down a labor union or a socialist revolution.

The residents, who were themselves mostly bankers and industrialists, reacted as the wealthy always have. Their indignity stoked, they retrenched and carried on behaving just as they pleased. When New Year's 1948 rolled around, even more residents took part in the tree toss. Alexander Flagg, an enemy of regulation in any form, purchased a second tree and had his butler affix a banner that read:

COMPLIMENTS OF ALEXANDER B. FLAGG, ESQ

Duly provoked, the board announced new fines for the following year. One hundred dollars per tree (today about an even thousand, adjusted for inflation). For New Year's 1949, Alexander Flagg tossed three.

Residents of the Apelles, riding the postwar wave of prosperity curling majestically down an infinite American shore, obviously enjoyed burning up their cash. They were aroused by the thought of being so careless with an instrument that so much of the world was dying for want of. Every year the fines increased, and every year the trees kept flying. But as much as they enjoyed throwing money out the window, they were not entirely without conscience, and in 1955 a proposal was brought before the board by Magda Brunn, Turk's mother, to put the fines to good use for the poor of New York City. The board, its ranks of aged curmudgeons having been thinned somewhat by infirmity and death, had among its new members some more progressively minded men who managed to push the proposal through in 1956. By then it was part of the fun to affix embroidered identification banners to the trees, and the board's Xmas fine slush fund was edging close to $100,000. Quite a tradition.

Magda Brunn was put in charge of establishing the charitable organization that would dispense funds to the indigent, and she did a fine job—so fine, in fact, that the organization, known as the Apelles Fund, branched out after only three years of existence and began taking donations from all over the city. On the way out of Bonwit's or Macy's with your Christmas gifts, you dropped a coin into a little plastic castle with red plastic flags flying from the turrets, and your donation sponsored after-school programs in the Bronx, soup kitchens in the Bowery, summer camps, single mothers.

Magda died on December 27, 1960, having spent every day post-Thanksgiving soliciting donations for the fund outside Barney's. Pneumonia. Even though she wasn't around to ring the little silver triangle anymore, the fund kept going strong.

Over the years, apartments changed hands and the tree-toss lost steam. By 1978, no one was throwing much of anything out the window due to liability concerns, but everyone in the building still made nice donations to the Apelles Fund.

For instance, the year of the blizzard party, Bo and Jane Vornado had donated ten thousand dollars. They were also cochairs of the fund, which is in part why they had such huge Rolodexes. Almost everyone at the party except for me, Vik, and Albert Caldwell had donated that year. Even Shahin and Nelofar Jahanbani had chipped in a thousand.

While I was in the bedroom with Albert Caldwell, my mother was chatting up the Jahanbanis. Sales were not her strong suit, but Neil Ford had been talking her up while she studied the backs of her hands and smiled sideways, and the Iranians were urbane and seemed interested, so she was doing her best to come off as cool but not too cool. She didn't know that the Jahanbanis were looking to stash money anywhere they could before the U.S. government could get its greasy palms all over it, but to be fair, their motivations were not exclusively financial. Neither were Neil Ford's. All four of them were, like most people, aswirl with contradiction, their shifting desires constantly reshuffling their intentions. They were, each one of them, cunning, benevolent, fighting back their kindest impulses with guns firing self-interest. They overruled their basest instincts for no reason other than human decency. They were angels, they were selfish pigs. They were just people trying to have a conversation. At the time, my mother's overriding desire was to do something about the nagging feeling that she wasn't a very good painter, which, unbeknownst to her, meshed nicely with Neil's intention to get her into bed. He also intended to help his clients hide their money. He kept calling her a visionary. And he meant it. The Jahanbanis were as interested as people could be in art they'd never seen. They were all trying to do the right thing, up to a point. It was a Mexican standoff where everyone was trying to serve everyone else a cream pie.

When my mother died a few years ago, she and Neil had been living in Salerno, Italy, in a medieval house high on the side of a mountain. From inside she could see the bay and the shipping channels, the small cloister windows having been stretched to accommodate a more modern field of vision, and in every room the light was spectacular, but she had stopped painting, and those beautiful stone walls were not hung with her paintings, or anyone else's. She had an herb garden, three orange trees. On the east side of the house were neat rows of olive trees. Goats roamed the slopes, their little neck bells clanking. She was bitter, ashamed of her work, unable to separate herself from her most famous painting. Publicly, she had chosen to avail herself of the artist's credo, which states that once a work leaves the studio, the artist no longer has any claim to its interpretation or use. Thus, if *Satellite*, purchased by Shahin Jahanbani a week after they met at the party, was later gifted to his partner Salem bin Laden, and if Salem, in turn, made a gift of it to his brother, Osama, she could frown and say, It ceased to be mine long, long ago. But she didn't believe that. In her estimation, she'd as good as killed her own son-in-law.

Osama was a horse guy, not an art guy, and once in his possession the painting had gone straight to a warehouse in Riyadh, where it stayed until his Saudi citizenship was revoked in 1994, whereupon it was shipped to a warehouse in Dubai, then to Switzerland before being sold.

In the interim, Salem, a passable guitarist who, once they got to know each other, liked to jam with Bo Vornado whenever he was in New York on business, flew his ultralight into a high-voltage wire and that was the end of him. The bin Laden patriarch, Mohammed, had died in a plane crash, too. It's just a coincidence, a point of intersection, just as it's a coincidence that at the same time Vik was delivering Albert Caldwell to the room where I was sleeping, my mother was delivering into the stream of commerce a painting that would fund the aeronautical training of Mohamed Atta, who plunged American Airlines flight 11 like a broadsword into Tower One.

Before it was destroyed, *Satellite* found its way back to the Apelles. It was Bo Vornado who bought it at auction in 1998, a sort of dim-witted gift for Jane, who had for years agonized over whether my mother would have stayed at the party that night trying to sell it to the Jahanbanis if only she'd agreed to buy it instead, friendship be damned. Bo paid two hundred thousand dollars, not including commission and tax, to Sotheby's, which cut a check to a shell corporation established by François Genoud, the Swiss banker who represented Third Reich interests after the war and later established the Banque Commerciale Arabe in Lausanne, which laundered money for the PLO and other anti-Israel groups. Thus one might argue that it was actually Bo's money, not the painting, that sent Atta to flight school. When government investigations after 9/11 exposed the painting's chain of ownership, Bo burned it and dumped the ashes in the Atlantic. He retired not long after, and he and Jane moved permanently to their house in Montauk.

Albert Caldwell would have pointed out that my mother and Bo hadn't acted with malicious intent, therefore couldn't possibly have been held responsible, but it was exactly her own passivity that so distressed my mother. By her art, she had been made into an instrument of Vik's destruction, a dupe, a member of the same club as the flight instructors who'd trained the al-Qaeda crews, the government agents who'd missed clues, the desk agent at the Portland airport who dismissed his suspicions about Atta and his accomplice Abdulaziz al-Omari, the captain and first officer of the flight that transported the men from Portland to Boston, where they boarded the 767, which had been assembled by workers at Boeing in Everett, Washington, whose livelihoods owed a debt to Senator Henry Jackson, who'd lobbied for the plant's construction way back in 1966, who owed his position of power to the voters who elected him, and on and on.

The party. People who'd eaten downers were all over the penthouse in various states of crumple and drape, chins slick with drool; the upper-eaters were all over the place, too, but like a band of rhesus monkeys, and they wouldn't shut up, and were responsible, it turned out, for one hundred percent of the damage done to the apartment's bathrooms and bedrooms. It was a subset of the speed freaks, a few cranked-up former residents of the Apelles, who decided that the building's most spirited and dearly departed ritual should be revived without delay. When they threw open the terrace doors, the storm welcomed itself into the living room, snow plastering Franklin the bartender, and a great insane greeting, something between a groan and a whoop, rose from the crowd, each individual reacting uniquely to the blizzard conditions as a result of the aforementioned intemperate approach to the intake of psychopharmaceuticals and alcohol. Pandemonium at the doorway, as if an air lock had been sprung and suddenly everyone was flying out into space. There were tornadoes of snow on the terrace. Thunder rumbling across the shrouded sky. Everyone pitched their drinks into the white void over West End. A pause, and then a man in a tiger costume hoisted a wooden chair aloft and hurled it over the edge. It arced gracefully down until the wind blew it into the building's façade at the tenth floor, where it caught an outcropping, ricocheted, and went into a tight spin before vanishing into the swirling snow.

Bombs away, baby! cried a white man dressed like Jimi Hendrix. Another chair went over the edge.

It all went—the rest of the chairs, the table. The crowd cheered every time something new disappeared over the parapet. The twin concrete planters, leaden with frozen earth, required teamwork, two guys each, and after they'd wrestled them onto the top of the railing, the crowd counted down from ten and over they went, synchronized sumo divers. On the way down, a percussive crack as one took out a gargoyle on the eighth floor. Holy shit! several someones cried, not unhappily. This marked a turning point in the exercise, the moment at which their exultation in the freedom of flight was eclipsed by the joy of destruction. In a corner of the terrace was a French café table, a little wire job, and some iron chairs. They were passed forward, hand over hand, floating across the top of the crowd like leaves on a river, the revelers closest to the edge simply handing them along to the blizzard. Down, down, down.

Short of Bo's Finnish smoker, they emptied the terrace of everything that wasn't bolted down. A couple of guys were itching to rip off the doors or dismantle the crosshatched wooden pergola down at the other end of the terrace, already heaving in the wind. They eyed the smoker. But they held off. Maybe they'd satisfied their urges. Maybe they'd decided to call it quits before they killed someone. Maybe they'd decided that whoever was going to cut Bo and Jane a check in the morning was already in hock for enough as it was. Okay, okay. Enough. We're not savages, after all.

And it was then that Sid Feeney appeared on the living room threshold, having field-humped Albert Caldwell from the bedroom where he'd found the sick son of a bitch naked on the bed next to me, holding my hand, mere seconds from committing an act of perversion that Feeney had himself repeatedly been subjected to as a child, though he'd never spoken of it to a soul, an act of perversion that had left him with an undetectable internal injury that had led to a lifelong struggle with malfunctioning reproductive equipment, and a surely not unrelated pear-sized prostate—the very prostate that had sent him on a quest for an unoccupied bathroom in which to relieve himself, the urgency of the situation reaching critical levels as he frantically crab-walked door to door, the ticking bomb in his gut clicking ever closer to detonation even as he gobbled up eyefuls of the same orgiastic scenery Vik had, shouting mangled encouragements he'd picked up on visits to brothels in Bangkok and Kyoto, before trying to bulldog his way into the hallway bathroom, which had attracted even more participants since Vik's visit, Feeney going in low and fast not for fun but for relief, that sweet expulsive release, rebuffed due to space limitations despite his insistence that it'd just take a goddamn minute, his feverish worry swelling as the pressure in his pelvis increased, leading to his decision to utilize the next amphora or Ming vase that swung into view, hell, any old receptacle into which he could coax out the dribble that would, over an agonizing stretch during which it was not uncommon for him to get through a liberal sampling of J. P. Sousa's greatest hits, reduce the searing pain in his abdomen by increments so subtle as to render the process of urination a kind of cosmic joke. It was in search of such a receptacle that he burst into the bedroom where I was asleep.

I've been told that once incarcerated, when time was available at a discount and reflection was encouraged as a means of reducing recidivism, Feeney claimed to have given the matter a great deal of thought and arrived at the conclusion that his actions had been redemptive. He expressed amazement that his own life—an old creased map he'd hardly even bothered to consult anymore—could have surprised him so. By his reckoning, it was his own weekly childhood buggering by the next-door neighbor that had saved my life. All the suffering and shame had served a goddamn purpose, after all! How intricate and unknowable, he would say, is the universe that God hath wrought!

Like many a God-fearing man, Sid Feeney's interpretative powers were governed by the desperately optimistic belief that there's got to be a brighter day just around the corner. Well, Sid Feeney found his, and I suppose that's worth something.

The first thing Feeney had done was punch Albert in the face. That got no reaction, so Feeney grabbed Albert by the neck. It was then that I began to wake from the strange dream, a dream about a flood, that Albert had invaded.

Feeney's bladder had gone ahead and begun to empty itself when he'd hoisted Albert up onto his shoulders, an enuretic saddle forming along the inseam of his khakis. When I opened my eyes, Feeney was already at the door. Albert was naked, draped over his shoulders like a sack of rice but, being wider than both a bag of rice and the doorway, suffering the comic trope of having his head slammed repeatedly against the doorframe. Eventually Feeney prevailed and muscled him through. I trailed after them, pulled out of the room by the thread that connected me to Albert, a weird sense of familiarity, locked together by his presence in my dream. Through the smoky foyer, vortices swirling off Albert's protruding buttocks, past the Joan Mitchell, toward the wash of music. The crowd parted.

I witnessed Sid Feeney's crazed path across the dance floor. In the living room, the wind tearing through the terrace doors had cleared the smoke, and the snow had created a white runway that he mounted as though summiting a mountain peak. His legs stabbed forward and he was yelling. I couldn't make out the words over the percussive force of the music blowing through my body, but learned later that he was issuing the Roman war cry, *Barritus*. Sid Feeney was a maniac. Of course no one tried to stop him. What were they going to stop him from doing? Who could have imagined? No one touched Feeney, but a few slapped Albert's naked rear as he passed because, you know, what a riot.

Once Sid Feeney was on the terrace, he went directly to the parapet and threw Albert Caldwell over.

He'd done it with a dipping, shrugging movement, as though Albert were, in fact, only a sack of rice destined for its spot in a general store display. He just tipped his shoulders and down Albert went. It was his composure, I think, that blinded everyone, causing those very people who'd seen him commit a murder, those people who'd been standing right next to him, to question the trustworthiness of their own senses. He was so cool about it, how could they square what they'd thought they'd seen with what had actually happened? Obviously what they *thought* they'd seen was some kind of illusion, or a hallucination. It was simply not possible. He'd thrown a . . . bag of something, right? What the hell was it? Sack of sand? Was it some sort of mannequin? A sex doll? What a gas! Feeney walked back inside to the bar table, where old Franklin, standing with his back to the terrace, had seen nothing, and in his long-suffering way leaned in to hear Feeney's order.

No one looked over the edge. Once Feeney had his glass of whiskey in hand, he crossed the living room, where the dancing had stopped and little constellations of eyeballs had formed to stare at him. He took a seat on the sofa, where his bladder continued to leak. He was about seventy-five feet from the terrace doors, and the crowd outside, like exiles amassed on the deck of their escape vessel, was frozen, staring in at him as though he manned the cannon on the cruiser that had tracked them, the one who could sink them or allow them to slip into the fog and escape.

About thirty people on the terrace had witnessed him throw Albert over the parapet. Another hundred had stepped aside when he'd zagged through the living room. They'd seen him carry a person—a torso, arms, a head of white hair, the pickled feet, the sad little cuttlefish dangling between those scrawny legs—across the room and onto the terrace, only to return without the person.

Sid Feeney had once lived at the Apelles, before the West Side turned into a communo-miscegenist freak show and he'd fled across the park to the East Side. He was familiar with the tradition that had led to the genesis of the Apelles Fund. He'd sent his check that year, enough to keep Jane Vornado off his back.

So when he yelled, *I made my goddamn donation! I'm entitled!* surely more than a few of those within earshot would have gotten the reference if they'd been able to hear anything over the music. Would they have even thought it was a crazy thing to say?

Worth noting: observing a murder while scrambled on quaaludes doesn't make one a reliable witness, and if the shock sobered the crowd up, they collectively dove right into their pockets for another dose. Before long, the witnesses had shaken the whole scene off like a bad dream, which was how most of them described it to themselves the next day: a bad dream, a thing too weird, too unbelievable, to have actually happened. Those who got pinned down by New York's finest were all, you know, somewhere else in the apartment, or looking the other way, or were embarrassed to say they had no memory at all of the party. You know how it is. But that night, staring at Feeney, wetting himself over there on the sofa with his drink on his knee, they knew it had happened, every one of them, because no one joked about it, and no one turned to a neighbor and said, Hey, did you see that? Without speaking, they collectively agreed to an alternative reality. It's a common occurrence, more common than we might think. Silence alters the past.

No one at the party called the police. No one jumped on Sid Feeney and pinned him to the floor. No one freaked out and ran around the room pulling out her hair and ululating. No one fainted. One by one, people drifted in from the terrace. The constellations broke apart. People started swaying again, almost like dancing. Their arms moved as though they were shoveling dirt into a narrow channel of shared memory. All was forgotten. Except by me.

Part III

15.

He was in a hospital. There was water to the south. Albert's eyes felt like oblong, distended cones straining against his eyelids, the cornea aching against the tender conjunctiva like a hatchling working at the shell. They wanted out, they wanted to see! Oh, deny not the sweet delight of oculism! But deny he did, clenching tightly as he lay in the bed listening to the clicking wall clock and timing his breathing to the second hand in approximation of a sleeper's respiration. In, hold hold, out, hold hold. In, hold hold, out, hold hold. The nurse was still there. What in Satan's fiery red hell was she doing?

Polishing her nails? He'd never known a nurse to do anything more than the absolute minimum required. Needle in, needle out, roll, cover, and tuck. Their smug polyester hips and square shoes, the stern architecture of their caps. Where were those romantic nurses of the Great War, plump, young, and dimpled, so eager to subsume their own desires to the recovery and carnal repair of the wounded soldier? Of course, not even the most patriotic example would be able to bring herself to minister to Albert's sallow flesh. He remembered what it was to be young; to have no awareness of one's body as anything other than an instrument of pleasure. He hadn't lost that memory. To be old was to be an encyclopedia of the plights of the flesh, lord of a crumbling manor. It made you zealous in your adherence to those routines that, when performed in the proper order, might reduce your pain one-tenth of one percent. Constant awareness of your own decrepitude. How many times had he been in and out of the hospital over the last ten years? Five? Ten? Prostate, heart, colon, an iron triangle of ailments, each one a subtraction of pleasure: a good orgasm, a good walk, a good shit, all gone. Leakage, palpitations, fear of the outside, depression.

What in Satan's fiery red hell was she doing? He heard the soft rustle of polyester, an inhalation strumming the harps of her nasal cavity. Slowly he lifted his eyelids, just enough to peer through his eyelashes' dewy prisms at the penumbra of her shoulders as she stood at the window, her back to him, arms crossed as if to warm herself, her fingers clasping the backs of her arms. Christ's sake, she was watching the snow fall? He waited until she dropped her hands and smoothed her uniform. By the time she'd turned toward him, his eyes were closed and he was a vision of peace.

The nurse squeak-rustled nearer, past him, out the door. Hermetic swoosh, latch snapping into strike plate. He waited thirty ticks of the clock before attempting to lever himself out of the bed. Once he'd gotten his feet on the floor, he made his way across the linoleum to peek through the crosshatched glass. The angle was bad for a full sweep of the hall, and he cracked the door for a better look. They never left you alone for long. He'd have to be quick about it. To the right, the hall was clear to the elevator bank. To the left was the nurses' station, and though he could hear their voices, they came from somewhere else, down the corridor, around the corner. Satisfied with his chances, he removed the gown, located his pants, shirt, and shoes, dressed, and crept out. He did not bother with the buttons on his sleeves.

All his life, he'd relied on logic to survive. On the playground, scrawny Alfie had been able to demoralize bigger kids with his argumentative powers. That hadn't stopped the beatings, and often enough invited them, but he secured his intellectual superiority early, and it became his source of power. In court he was an assassin, logic his dagger. He argued with an otherworldly calm that unhinged opposing counsel—the more devastating the argument, the more beatific his countenance. It wasn't a strategy, one of those synthetic plays lawyers trot out to woo jurors. It was genuine. The more decisive the blow he'd dealt, the dreamier the look in his eyes. And he'd won, and won, and won, piling up a record of dominance that made him not only rich but deeply feared. Nothing in his life suffused him with the warmth he felt constructing a perfect stone wall of argument. In those days, his mind had been so supple he could recall every legal argument he'd ever made, each one a dark line traversing the Irish countryside, the full effect like a Mondrian scored into the rolling green, the interplay of precedent and analysis, policy and proof, arguments intersecting and reinforcing one another. A grand construction, a life's work, from his first, in Constitutional Law with Professor Haggerty, 1923, to the last, New York State Supreme Court, 1971. Logic had been a reliable companion, a guide with whom he had been unafraid to wander the darkness. It had been his only comfort. And what more did he need? The capacity for reason was the only measure of a man.

Now his reason was failing him, or, more precisely, he was failing it, failing to abide by its tenets. He was on iffy terms with cause and effect. To wit, his failure to consider the weather's ability to foul up his suicide plan. The plan itself—that Goldbergian construction of fake emergency call, ambulance as escape vehicle, his decision to invite himself into yet another prison from which he'd have to engineer a break—was testament to the cracked, weedy ruin of his logic.

However, at the moment, his adrenal glands were streaming heavy doses of spirit-elevating hormones, and he felt sharp again, electrified. As I sift through the history of his mind, his brief visit to Roosevelt is a bright atomic spike on the dull flatline of his last year, a landmark I can use to orient myself. As familiar as I am with his inner workings, even I sometimes get lost in the wasteland.

He felt it powerfully, the resurgence of his logic, a crackling essence that he'd thought was gone forever, evaporated like the angel's share. It marshaled his intelligence into a clear, cold liquid that coursed through him, an unstoppable natural force. He felt like he'd pinned a witness on cross. It has been so long. Oh god, the clarity, just this side of madness.

Down the hall he found a janitor's closet, and inside, a heavy canvas coat hanging on a peg, a knitted cap sticking out of the grease-blacked mouth of one pocket. He pulled on the coat, flipped up the collar, tugged the hat low over his brow, and practically floated to the elevator.

At that late hour, the old man in the enormous coat found decent cover among the other passengers—orderlies, insomniac patients in paper shoes, interns, blurry-faced attendings who'd been pulled from their warm beds. No one gave him a second look.

The doors opened and Albert got off. On the other side of the lobby, an eager young fact-checker from WPIX named Bobby, elevated to on-air correspondent for the night, armed with a mic and a winning attitude, was conducting man-on-the-street interviews, playing goalie at the revolving doors: And what's your name, ma'am? And are you a patient? Have you thought about how you'll get home? Have you ever *seeeeen* weather like this in New York?

At first Albert felt a flash of recognition, a remnant from days when news crews parried their silver microphones at him as he loomed over the city from atop the steps at 60 Centre. They're here for me? he thought. Damnit, why? Remember, damnit. The confusion that followed (so much for all that adrenalized logic) had a familiar shape, as though he'd awoken in a dim hotel room, unable to recall in the dark where he was—he thinks first of home, no, he's somewhere else, turns on the lights, a hotel room, there's my suit on the door, it's freezing in here, it's Chicago. Albert stood now at the edge of the light, casting about the lobby for the clue that would retract the tumblers locking tight his mind just enough to crack the door, let in a breath of air. But no.

Like bald tires spinning on ice. Unable to catch his breath. The obvious one: thrusting, thrusting away like a damn piston, but no release.

No, honestly, it wasn't like any of those things. This defeat, this inability to catch the tail of whatever thought was eluding him, was excruciatingly nothing except itself. The loneliness of being adrift in his own mind, urging his brain to catch, like an engine on a cold morning. No, not that, either. An empty white room? How else am I to explain his predicament, where one moment there is sanity and understanding and in the next it's been vaporized? Funerals are for the living; these metaphors are for my own comfort.

He took stock. Evidence on and around his person suggested that he intended to exit the building. A sequence of events initiated by a former he, the one who got on the elevator, a lost self. He stepped forward, falling in closely behind an orderly pushing an empty wheelchair, borrowing the man's momentum, matching the pace of his footfall on the marble floor, shrugging off ambitious young Bobby as he reached for his arm, the wailing siren, Sir, sir, sir. The orderly swung to the side and parked the wheelchair, and Albert, caught in the no-man's-land between exit and eager young reporter, Sir! lunged at the crossbar on the revolving door, which, frozen in place, wasn't budging until, Sir! on the other side of the door came two men whose added effort, Sir! cracked loose the icy seal and with all of them leaning against the grindstone at once, there was the sweet luffing pop of the weather strips as they brushed the glass cylinder, Sir! Sir! hissing advancement, the wind battering him as he emerged on the snow-washed brick. Bobby pounced on the new arrivals, a pair like a circus bear and his handler, No, no interviews, the older, smaller one said, but Bobby persisted until the bigger of the two, holding a towel to his forehead, screamed, Getthafuckoutta-myway loud enough to rouse even the deepest sleepers draped over the lobby chairs, and he and his handler were allowed to proceed to the desk while Bobby was left spinning his microphone by its cord and eyeballing the lobby for the old and weak.

Out in the blowing snow, Albert looked for a cab, but the arcing drive down to the street was empty. Albert thought: Satan's fiery red hell. And with that, his memory recovered enough ground for him to orient himself. Southward, south to the water.

The coat was heavy but the wind cut right into it, and he huddled behind a concrete pillar. What was he supposed to do, walk from here? If so, which direction? All he saw were dim outlines and snow.

Remarkably, his grandson, the impetus for this entire escapade, had been absent from his thoughts since he'd placed the phone call that set in motion his creaky machine, as if a final settlement had been agreed upon and his accounts, so long out of balance, had been paid in full. As he cowered from the wind, a strange thought bloomed, perhaps unfolding to fill the space vacated by the boy. Strange, because it was the first time he'd considered the question of who would maintain the memory of the boy's death once he was gone. He'd written down none of his thoughts on the matter. He couldn't remember having told anyone about what had happened. Shouldn't he have? Shouldn't he have ensured that his own memorial would be one of unabashed hatred, that someone would daily think of him with scorn? He was, after all, responsible for the boy's death. Architect and contractor for the gallows, knotter of the noose.

Did he think these things or did I? Perhaps none of these thoughts crossed the transom of Albert's conscious mind—they existed, I promise, within him, I'm sure of it, but as to the question of when I became aware of them, that's a little like attempting to mark the moment one's eyes become adjusted to darkness. Outlines, gradations. How long have the objects slowly coming into focus been there? A second? A minute? Decades?

So I've poured some of my own ink into the waters of his mind. But I only want to be fair. It's true that I long for an impartial ear, and can only ask as much of you as Albert did of me.

He was about to start walking when a Checker cab crept around the curve. Albert waited motionless in the lee of the pillar while the driver got out, shoulders up around his ears, and danced over the icy concrete to the back door, where he helped out an old woman in slippers. Her terry-cloth housecoat hung below the hem of her black overcoat, whipping around her shins as she shuffled into the hospital on the driver's arm.

Albert's first step sent him slipping and pinwheeling across an icy patch but he caught his balance on the other side and shuffled around the front end toward the driver's door. The wind pushed at him as he made his way around the big chrome bumper, the coat filling like a spinnaker, and he held on as well as he could to the car's cold wet hood, working his way back until his fingers found the seam of the door. He pulled it open, got in, struggled it closed. A cigarette was smoking in the ashtray, and Albert opened a crease in the window and pushed it out, where it stuck against the wet glass.

Albert had not driven a car in a decade. Like all New Yorkers, he prided himself on his poor driving skills and the rarity with which he needed to employ them. Even when he'd driven the Coupe de Ville every weekend on Long Island, he'd never felt at one with the machine, not in the way of a man who'd come of age with his elbow out the window, wrist on the wheel, who'd learned to smoke sitting on the hood, had his first misaligned sexual experiences in a backseat. He'd come along too early and too poor. As if bringing himself physically closer to the machine might correct for his lack of experience, he'd always driven with the seat dumped forward, body hugging the wheel. He accelerated in pulses, the car surging forward like a rowboat, the children in the back lurching in time, while in the passenger seat Sydney perpetually kept her hand on his knee in an attempt to smooth their progress. He yelled when he drove. From the moment he slid the key into the ignition, he was locked in battle with the goddamn idiots populating the roadways, the unpredictable decelerators, the nervous Nellies, those with liberal signaling habits. Old men in hats were dependable targets. It's not a wagon train! he'd growl if anyone rode his bumper. As soon as he parked and got out, he settled. The farther he was from the detestable Cadillac, the better. When he kicked the tires, and he often did, he did so with the intention of inflicting pain. Nothing in the world quite so brazenly represented his inability to master the subtleties of mechanical control. His partners zapped around the island in Alfa Romeos and MGs, in the manner of exiled Russian counts, behavior he found wholly inappropriate for men of their fiduciary responsibilities. The legal profession was a service industry, not a beauty pageant. He hated those cars.

He was especially unqualified, then, to handle two tons of Checker Marathon in a snowstorm. Not all that quick off the line in normal conditions, on the snowpack the cab's handling was decidedly slicker and it sluiced around the curving hospital driveway like a pinball out of the shooter lane, crashed into the street, the front bumper gouging into the snow, tagging the pavement with a shriek. To avoid plowing into the cars on the opposite curb Albert cranked the wheel like a helmsman in a gale, narrowly avoided that disaster, and bounded off pulsingly up powdery Columbus.

The cabbie came out of the hospital's revolving door just in time to see his car disappearing up the avenue, rooster tails spraying from the back tires. Typical. You try to do a nice thing. You take somebody's grammy to the hospital in the middle of the storm of the decade, and some punk boosts your ride. Thanks a fucking lot, New York.

16.

By then the snow had erased the city. On West End, just outside the Apelles, the wind was whipping a NO PARKING sign like it was a fighter getting worked in the corner of the ring. Snow covered the streets, and the streets covered the pipes, the tunnels, the conduits, the corridors, the ancient veins of the city ferrying transmissions telephonic and electric, the steam, the words and water and waste, ever excavated and re-entombed by Con Ed hardhats. Traffic lights jounced around on their guy wires. Streetlights burned like quasars, tinting the white surface of the roadway tangerine, painting the flakes as they shot by. This snow did not twinkle or float. It crashed down. This storm meant to do harm to the earth, to obscure the land and all who walked upon it. It had silenced the mechanical thrum of the city, the grating metal and the horns and the incessant wail of sirens that proscribed its functional limits more than any boundary on a map. No cars out except for the ones crash-landed and abandoned at drunken angles to the glacial curbs. Even that ambient hum, the background noise audible on the quietest corners of residential streets in the dead of a summer night, beneath the air conditioners, beneath the distant hum of traffic on the FDR, the machinery inside the island that kept it inflated and breathing, a sound like air rushing through a canyon, even that noise was gone. People? Only a few. The city had been swept clean.

One of those people was my father. At shortly after midnight (twenty-one degrees, sustained winds from the northwest at around twenty-eight knots, gusting to fifty) he emerged from the Apelles. He had picked up a leather jacket from the apartment to wear over his enormous wool sweater, gray, with red and blue snowflakes encircling the midsection. The sweater was itself as thick as a coat, a Scottish invention capable of warding off anything gale force on up, and was such a tight fit inside the leather jacket that the two created a sort of vacuum seal against the elements. The furry edge hung below the bottom of the jacket, and the rolled neck extended so high that it made a scarf superfluous. He was also wearing wool pants, his writing pants, the seat nearly obliterated, and he was holding in his right hand the plastic bag containing the stinking, charred remains of the bluefish fillets.

The bag was snapping around like a ferocious little dog straining at its leash. The round yellow face on one side was a familiar hieroglyph commanding the user to Have a Nice Day!, hardly despotic but offering little choice in the matter, and fell into a common category of menacing American commands, along with Enjoy! and Smile! and Have Fun!, all of which rankled my father acutely with their insistence that he attain a lighter state of being, pronto. Having performed upon the bag the same inquiry he would have leveled at any other communication (being the sort of person whose mental filter trapped everything, everything, from legal disclaimers to the hierarchy of movie credits to the endless stream of advertising tag lines pounding on him every time he left the apartment, which he subjected to analysis normally reserved for exegeses of poems), he'd determined that in this case he was being commanded (by whom? God? Mother? McCann Erickson?) to experience a sublime joy, something like a hundred simultaneous orgasms—no, even more, the endorphin flood that soaks the brainpan at the moment of death. This required him to feel not just orgasmic joy but Death Joy. The happiness that surpasses all happiness. Not bad for a slogan bashed out by a speed-balled copywriter at a Madison Avenue shop, picking through embers of his own dying life force for some flickering memory of joy, riffling through images from those months camping in Big Sur after graduation, where he'd dropped acid with his friends and achieved a state of ecstasy that manifested, like really manifested, projecting him upward on a beam of light, up above the trees, above the clouds, into space so that he could observe the complete blue marble herself, whence he inhaled all of America, the clouds and sun, viewed the top of every citizen's beautiful unique head, from sea to shining sea, each one as perfect as a pin, before coming down, experiencing a hunger as wide as the plains, hopping in the VW, driving out of the forest to buy supplies and experiencing the aura of that girl behind the counter, the one whose eyes blew right through him, and who ten years later still haunted his memory, who had said to him when he pushed open the screen door to leave, Have a nice day, baby.

Normally my father wouldn't have been caught dead carrying such a bag. He usually tried to sidestep the transubstantiation that rendered human beings billboards for all manner of capitalist sub-philosophies, philosophies of consumption he couldn't even understand, ideas that made people meaningless except as ambulant advertising, but he'd been distracted by the smoke and the fire and the fish, and the distraction had almost turned him into a normal person who could simply grope around under the sink, grab a bag, and go.

So, while he hadn't quite been able to ignore the yellow face, he hadn't balled it up and whipped it into the trash in favor of a plain brown paper bag, which was, he'd always thought, his personal analogue in the world of bags: plain, square, liable to fall apart in the rain. He'd dropped the fish into the plastic bag as though he were not a man who could be thrown into a spiral of rage by an insipid piece of graphic art commanding him to alter his behavior.

Waist-deep drifts had blown in against the foundations of buildings on the east side of the street, the snow packing in alleys, on the cross streets turning brownstone stoops into ramps, but where my father was standing, just outside the arched west entrance to the Apelles, maintenance—on this lonesome night a crew of one, long-suffering Sandor—had been working his way nonstop around the building, the footprint of which filled an entire city block, salting and shoveling, re-salting, reshoveling, a task my father quickly classified as the philosophical equal of suspension bridge painting, those crews who spent their entire working lives yo-yoing back and forth across the same ironwork span. He supposed that for any given worker, which side was considered the starting point was a personal matter, one that depended entirely on which direction the crew was moving on that particular guy's first day on the job, so that painting crews all over the world must be divided into two factions, those who considered *this* side the start and *that* side the finish and those who considered *that* side the start and *this* side the finish, and surely they spent their professional lives in joking competition with the opposing faction while feeling just a touch more fraternal toward those in their own faction, heightened no doubt by the natural ease with which weekend bowling or pétanque or calcio squads were divided up according to faction, and perhaps it even came to influence which side of the bridge a worker chose to live on (a preference for *this* side because, between you and me, who wants to live on *that* side? I mean, sure, they're regular slobs like the rest of us, but come on), which undoubtedly could lead to dissimilar political views, conscription into opposing militia factions when civil skirmishes broke out, and so on. And he wondered, of course, with all those internal pressures how the crews could be trusted to do even a halfway decent job of scraping the bird guano and applying the anti-corrosive paint to the exposed structure of the bridge. The answer, of course, was that they couldn't, and there you had it.

Sandor, normally a retiring, thoughtful fellow himself, might have been driven to violence had he known that while he was aggravating his angina and adding to his collection of slipped disks, my father was watching him as if he were a zoo animal. Already he was going to rain hellfire down on the rest of the night crew for this. They all lived in the Bronx and had fled for home when the mayor's office announced that nonessential government services were closing down. All except Sandor. Double overtime wasn't going to buy him a new spine.

Sandor turned the corner onto 78th, and though my father had intended to pitch the bag of burned fish onto the four-foot wedge of ice and snow at the curb and hightail it back inside, it was hard not to notice that the street had become an alien thing, and he wondered at the silence, as out of place as a panther in this Upper West Side neighborhood. Before him the air was a curtain of undulating white and within the folds he saw a dark movement—another person. The figure was about three blocks away, advancing slowly, steadily forging north.

The figure passed into an orange cone of light, out of it, into another one, as if fixed on a strip of celluloid advancing a single frame at a time.

Heavy wet flakes clung to my father's face and eyelashes, and he pawed at them with his free hand, but there was no way to see clearly. The wind had parted his hair in a neat line down the back of his head, snow packing into the seam like caulk. He squinted. He curled the fingers of his hand into a tube and brought it to his eye. He still couldn't see.

No music, no delivery truck loading decks slamming against the concrete. No buses heaving into gear. Wind. Rattling street signs. Somewhere to the east, a snowplow clattering over the pavement. God, was it quiet. When was it, my father wondered, that we became frightened of silence? When he was a boy, his father had come home after work and had sat in a rocking chair by the window, pondering, sometimes smoking, the chair creaking back and forth while his children fanned out across the room to read. No one spoke. No one turned on the radio. It was quiet enough to hear the contraction of the timbers releasing the day's heat into the cool dusk. Quiet enough to hear the tobacco crackle in his father's pipe. When he was a child, the ability to hold his tongue, not to blurt out the answer, to keep thoughts to himself—these were pact and signal of adulthood, of a thoughtful nature, ideals to which he aspired and from which he sometimes wondered if he'd ever escaped.

There was the stillness that would fall across the crowd at a Yankees game, a fog, a lull born not from anticipation for the next pitch, but of shared contentment, it seemed, a silence that had once been as natural as a cloud drifting in front of the sun but that was now obviously a source of anxiety for management, who viewed the absence of overt displays of happiness a sign that at any moment the crowd might descend into a state of mass reflection from which they would never recover. Steinbrenner had marshaled his troops to attack silence with the dipsy plonking of "I'm a Yankee Doodle Dandy" on the electric organ, or canned chants over the PA, as though quiet were a pernicious creature who'd wandered onto the field and had to be exterminated with great prejudice.

Oh hell. What bullshit. Baseball, last stop on the double-decker tour of great American propagandas, right after *Life* magazine and gap-toothed soda jerks and Bobby Kennedy's jaw. He wasn't in that line of work anymore. Great American somethings were behind him. Of course, there was no greater American something than always-charming, ruby-lipped, plump-assed mass appeal, whose wretched acquaintance he'd made all too well with *Slingshot.* Nope, nope, hold the watery beer and false hope, thanks anyway. Interiority? Self-examination? Even that had become a noise-making enterprise, primal screamers yelling into their own vertiginous hollows. Theater, all of it. You want to be left alone? It's a downright guarantee if you slip back down the mineshaft of your own navel again, Salty.

Over his own brain's dissonance, my father heard an engine revving, rising, too, over the wind and the distant sound of the plow, and he turned in time to see a Checker cab drifting around the corner of 79th, tires ripping up the graupel. The driver had the nose pointed more or less in the right direction, that is, south, but the cab was sliding intently eastward across the width of West End, toward the shoulder-high snowbank behind which my father was standing. He caught a glimpse of white hair, hands cranking at the wheel. Engine gunning, the cab continued to drift to port until the whitewalls caught for a moment and the car lurched forward, but alas, they only held to the next slick patch, where the slide recommenced, and it was then that my father's adrenal glands awoke to the insistent banging at their door, and they basically flipped over the bed, chair, and everything else in the room scrambling to see what the hell was going on, which shot some voltage into his sympathetic nervous system, as it had been lazing around just downstairs but now everyone was up and they were throwing open the windows and sticking out their heads, and all at once he had become a black hole, sucking in snow, air, car, howl of wind, cast of streetlight, the sort of distracted wonder with which he'd been watching the night suddenly frozen in place, as was he, his legs having turned to concrete, braced for impact, his muscles taut, sphincter locked down, his jaw a sprung bear trap. The cab kept coming, sliding elegantly, like a dancer emitting a spiritual code, its frictionless progress penetrating into my father, the buildings, the falling snow, the light posts, projecting inevitability in the way that only the elephantine in motion can. In a category headlined by tidal waves and mushroom clouds a taxi is only a footnote, but it nonetheless shares the same operational principles of irreversibility and the blind, objective destruction of anything lying in its path.

My father's teeth were bared and he'd stopped breathing. His eyes clamped shut and his brain fired a monstrously pedestrian message of utter surrender: an image of the fish that had brought him to the spot on which he was about to perish. Throw the bag! Throw the bag at the cab! his brain told his body. Of course his arm did not move. He was helpless, about to meet his end in the manner he'd always imagined. The taxi kept coming, floating across the surface, drawing ever closer, growing larger and larger until it broadsided the snowbank with an exquisite boom, a shattering noise that resonated up through the concrete and snow, into his feet, setting his organs ashudder.

By exactly the type of coincidence that my father didn't believe possible, between the cab and him, frozen deep within the snowbank, was a row of newspaper boxes encased in ice, each one bolted to the sidewalk so no one could boost them, and to which a winter's worth of trash bags, cardboard, and ripped-out plasterboard panels had all attached to form a substructure as solid as concrete, so that instead of blowing through the pile of snow and making a red blotch of my father, the ton and a half of inevitability sprung up on its creaking shocks and came thudding back down, wheels spinning madly, and shot directly at a Chevrolet Caprice marooned near the corner of 78th. The violent tearing sound of the big aluminum bumper gouging the snowbank ricocheted off the buildings on either side of the canyon.

The cab shot right, away from the snowbank, clipping the Caprice's bumper and swerving into the intersection, where a berm created by crisscrossing snowplows loomed twice the height of the cab. It plunged through the pile like a football team storming the field, the snow exploding in a shower of festive chunks.

Its engine revving and retreating, pulsing, one might say, it then ran two blurry stoplights before sliding into a right turn, in the direction of Riverside, headed the wrong way down a one-way street. The sound of the engine faded and there was nothing left but wind and clanging street signs.

Mother of Christ, my father whispered.

He could see down the sidewalk that the dark figure was still closing the distance. It appeared that he was carrying something on his back.

Lightning flashed and thunder rolled across the sky.

17.

anny was pulling a double because Dolan, the night man, hadn't been able to get across the bridge, and he'd been praying for a respite from the couples who'd been showing up all night for the Vornados' party, though up to that point never more than a few at a time, traipsing into the lobby as though their arrivals had been timed by a precise randomization equation, completely unpredictable, making it impossible to catch a wink, but finally there'd been a lull and he'd been able to tuck his chin and close his eyes just long enough to zone out. He wasn't even bothering to call up, anyway. No one was answering. If Chewbacca walked in, it was PH1, enjoy the party. He might as well be asleep. He lifted an eyelid just in time to see my father heading out the lobby doors, the faint smell of charred fish lingering behind him.

When Manny heard the muffled whump of the cab hitting the snowbank, he sat up on his stool. He thought about it for a while, arguing with himself about whether Mr. Saltwater might be involved, and whether it was his responsibility to check on him if he was, and he was still arguing with himself when he pulled on his overcoat, slipped the rain rubber over his hat, and went out. Resigned but nonchalant. Like to check that the pavers had been sufficiently salted.

He watched my father through the spike-topped gate, closed and locked tight at all times, and, like its twin on the opposite side of the courtyard, adorned with curlicues, stylized smoke buoying APELLES in a golden rainbow. A door-shaped gate within the gate allowed residents in and out, and Manny pulled it open and stepped through, the iron clanging behind him. He noted that my father did not turn in his direction. Manny knew he had heard the gate, and something about my father's arrogant posture reminded him of a lieutenant he'd served under whose perverse interest in the suffering of others, the godlike detachment from the world and its inhabitants, had earned him the unrelenting hatred of his troops. In late 1971, that man, a Lieutenant Spitz, had been standing atop a wall of sandbags watching a stream of villagers, worldly possessions strapped to their backs, traverse the access road beyond the base perimeter. His disdain for the Vietnamese was well known, and though he'd arrived green as a gooseberry, he had a million names for the locals: jungle bugs, slicks, slants, zipperheads, squats, squints, treads, quans, poons, TPs—toilet paper or target practice, no one knew which—besides the standard dink, duck, gook, sloat, Charlie. They poured out of his mouth like runoff from a storm pipe, as though before shipping out he'd made a list and was working his way through it. It was too obvious an attempt to win the approval of his men, and he was an embarrassment to them.

According to Spitz, the villagers who lived near the base were paddy niggers. Manny's platoon had a good sergeant who'd suggested to the lieutenant that he might want to deescalate the rhetoric a hair, but Spitz, who took all advice as a challenge to his authority, stepped it up and deployed the term in the presence of all races of troop, holding the eye of any Black soldier who might take issue. He managed to further distinguish himself by displays of piety, praying aloud in the mess, engaging Christian leadership initiatives around the camp, holding meetings Wednesday nights to read passages from the scripture. In his spare time he got blow jobs from the girls who hung around the gate. Manny had his opinions just like everyone else, but he minded his own business. He followed orders and adhered to the military code of behavior. The lieutenant was too much personality for Manny, too often proclaiming what he was or wasn't to actually be anything at all.

Paddy niggers, Spitz had said from his perch on the sandbags, shaking his head every so often at their primitive stupidity. The previous night's shelling had finished their rice fields once and for all. Their animals had been shot, blown up, or appropriated long ago, and their village itself had been reduced to a seam of mud that reeked from the base's latrine runoff. Where in hell they think they're going? the lieutenant wondered aloud.

No one, least of all Manny, called up to him, Hey, boss man, look sharp! as he stood like an olive drab Statue of Liberty atop the escarpment, tracking the villagers through his Nash-Kelvinators. A decent lieutenant never would have been up there in the first place, wearing his collar bars, no less, but there he was, scanning to see if his hooch boy was bugging out, and if half the men were praying that a VC sniper was dialing in on his forehead, the other half weren't going to take the high road and hold it against them.

All the same, they jumped when the binoculars exploded, at the thudding sound of the slug crashing through glass and plastic, the flying black wedges of plastic and metal and the gray and pink spray of his head webbed out all over the bags behind him, and after he'd begun to fall, there'd been the crack of the rifle rolling across the red, white, and blue side of the valley. Someone had mailed that shot from a long, long way off. Down on the access road, the villagers hit the deck.

Manny had peered through an embrasure and seen the villagers lying in the road, mounds of gear atop their backs. American tracers were flying over them but not a one moved. He didn't understand them when they spoke at him, always in a frenzy, always shouting, always desperate, and though his heart went out, what could he do? He was scared shitless, too. A few of them who provided goods and services were allowed in and out of camp, but Manny didn't want anything to do with them. Seemed like bad luck. The lieutenant had let them tidy his tent and service his needs, and yep, sure enough, look how that turned out.

After Spitz got killed, command flew in another cardboard cutout to replace him; clueless, but at least the new one washed his own fatigues and didn't fraternize with the locals. Manny's tour was up by the time that lieutenant was killed.

Mr. Saltwater might have been there, he was thinking. Manny recognized the sickness hanging about him, the ineffable detachment. There were rumors about the man, of course, that he'd been Army intelligence or CIA. Manny knew better than to believe chatter from the tenants, but you could get a bead from the old ladies who dressed up and put on hats just for the ride down to the mailboxes. They'd been around. They knew things. Mr. Saltwater's wife was nice enough. The kid was polite. Deliveries of books, mostly. Pizza on Sunday night. When spoken to, Manny nodded or shook his head, as appropriate. He was himself affable, didn't know nothing about nothing, except that from where he stood, Saltwater was an odd bird. Fair tipper, though Madam appeared to handle that end of the business. No one would ever accuse Saltwater of wearing out the finish on the front desk. Manny classified him the same as everyone else who lived in the building. Standard New York grade-A nutjob.

Mr. Saltwater, sir? Manny called into the howling wind, the snow clotting on his coat.

My father turned his head slightly, but his eyes remained locked on the figure in the distance.

Sir, anything happen out here?

Nope, my father said.

Uh-huh, Manny said. If there's anything I can help you with, you'll let me know?

Absolutely, my father said. He reached over and gave the doorman's woolen arm a squeeze. I'm alive! he added.

Very good, sir.

There's an issue with the chute on fourteen. Brunn, my father said. I had to get these fish out of the apartment. I did a real number on them. Had to get them out of the building.

Yes, sir, I can take that down to the incinerator for you ... Manny didn't bother to finish. It was February, the dead cord of winter wrapped tight around a dark matrix, ice atop snow atop ice atop snow, and they were standing in a blizzard. What the hell was he standing in a blizzard for?

Why don't we just pitch the bag, Manny said, and get back inside?

Roger that, my father said. He casually tossed the bag toward the street. The wind spiked it into the snowbank.

For all Manny cared, my father could stand in the snow until he froze to death, as long as he went across the street to do it. But standing on the sidewalk in front of the Apelles, my father had made it a financial issue for Manny. If something were to happen—and it would, even in a blizzard, it would, god help him, that would be his luck, wouldn't it, at best Mr. Saltwater would only get mugged, mugged by the only mugger out in the whole city, and a man like him would probably fight back, which all the libertarian types did, which would guarantee blood, which would find its way back to Manny's hands, his neglect having resulted in a tenant's beating, and there's only so much the union can do in a situation like that—Manny would be culpable, so he, too, would have to stand in the snow and wind freezing his ass off until this nutjob decided to conclude his meditation, or whatever he was doing. Assault might be the least of Manny's worries. My father, it occurred to him, was the type who might die from exposure because he got lost in his own head.

The streetlights were horizontal. Manny was losing contact with his toes and ears. He clamped his teeth together and bounced on the balls of his feet.

My father wasn't much better off. After the initial blaze of heat that came in the moments after the incident with the taxi, his trapezius had clinched tight against his neck, an ammoniac ache transmitting up to his skull and down the trapdoor to his spine. He was snorting vigilantly to counteract the copious streams of snot escaping his nostrils, and his jaw was set in concrete.

Waiting for someone? Manny said.

No, not in so many words, my father said.

Probably someone coming to the party, Manny said, tipping his chin at the figure down the block.

Some nut. I don't know, my father said.

The day before, my father had caught the first train home from Montauk, leaving my mother and me to snowshoe and skate with the Vornados. We were going to have fun. He'd thought he'd better get out before it was too late.

On the subway from Penn Station, a blind man had come tapping into his nearly empty car and had pitched a finely cadenced oration delivered in oaken tones that carried cleanly from one end of the car to the other, touching on his personal journey as a man, his failures and struggles, the temporal nature of existence, before landing on the emotional appeal for whatever a kind soul might be able to spare. The change in his cup had rattled as he'd walked, and he'd paused directly in front of my father, facing the wrong way, which my father assumed was intended to sell his state of terrible existential loneliness, a nice piece of stagecraft to underscore the fact that not only was he a blind beggar, but he was bad at it, miles more pitiable than your run-of-the-mill retinopathic pencil salesman. But it had backfired. He'd overcooked it. This wasn't the Peoria Playhouse, kiddo. If only he'd shuffled a few feet farther down the car, canted himself at a diagonal—no, it was too pathetic by half. My father looked at the man's shoes, disintegrating brogues held together with twine, the pants and coats in triplicate . . . and he felt a pang, and then he thought what he always thought, which was, what difference did it make if the guy was president of the con artists union? Who the hell would choose to live this way? Was it really so impossible to believe that the man was blind? If my father said nothing, and if no other passenger verbally identified himself—a likely scenario, as the only other passengers were a couple of winos sleeping it off and a solo passenger at the far end of the car—then for all the blind man knew he was floating in space, shaking his cup at the galactic void. What if he'd stopped in front of my father not to sell it but because he was hopelessly wretched at begging, so wretched that he had been relegated to roaming these wretched tunnels, addressing empty cars, rattling his cup at empty seats? No, my father thought, it couldn't be a con. His spirit couldn't take it if it was a con.

Genuine blindness, then. And what a relief, because my father was then freed of his fear of making eye contact, which was what all the mental acrobatics had been about in the first place, because even after all these years guilt was writhing around inside him, down beneath all the dead skin encasing his soul. Sure, the city was a bathypelagic zone, but the company line—that he had to protect his own tender heart with a thick callus—was bullshit. The truth was, he couldn't give because he couldn't take on the man's burden, not even for a second, and if he looked him square in his fake blind eye, he'd have to help. My father was already carrying too much.

The IRT screeched northward, lights flickering, and the blind man moved on, tap-tapping, pausing at the sour scent of the drunks, giving the cup a cursory shake, passing on. As the train neared 66th the other passenger at the far end stood up, just as the blind man positioned himself in the same exit, facing into the car, giving no indication that he intended to disembark. The other passenger was well dressed, wool coat, hair parted crisply, polished oxfords. He positioned himself directly in front of the blind man. Even from fifty feet away my father heard clearly what the man said: Get the fuck out of my way, you blind fuck.

The man looked down the car at my father. For commiseration, or to stoke my father's outrage—either way, seeking acknowledgment that he'd meted out some of the casual abuse that kept the city lubricated, but my father refused to look away from his own reflection in the opposite window. The poor bastard must get it a hundred times a day, he thought, his insufferable life made worse every time he mustered the strength to shake the cup.

But, then, really, don't get sentimental. Which of the men was more deserving of pity? Which was blameless and which one's mortal soul in jeopardy? Surely the beggar had earned his seat in heaven. Would Jesus extend his kindness only to the halt and lame? Wouldn't a truly benevolent savior go to the ends of the earth to recover the powerful evildoer who has strayed so much farther from His grace? Furthermore, he thought, which one of these men might be Jesus in disguise, come to the door in the dead of night, a frightful visitor asking for a place to lay his head?

And then my father wished he, too, could tell the awful blind beggar to fuck off, just for being so perfectly weak, ruined, so utterly blameless.

He said nothing. He was not an active participant in the drama of the world. A bit player, at best. But those bit players are not to be discounted—where was almighty Christ without the soldiers who erected the cross and nailed him to it? He'd be sitting on his crossbeam atop Golgotha tossing pebbles at the vultures, waiting for someone to make him the savior of the world, that's where. Whose sacrifice was greater? Jesus gave up his life, briefly. But the soldiers who nailed him up sacrificed their eternal souls. Just like the Jews who had sent him to his death in the first place: forever reviled, symbols of callous humanity, the lost, the unsaved. Without them, Jesus would have died of old age, arthritic, a little nostalgic for his fiery youth.

My father knew his role in that play. He'd have stood by the side of the road and watched as Jesus passed by in his crown of thorns and then he'd have gone home to scratch onto parchment what he'd seen. Watcher, voyeur, a receiver open to all channels, dutifully taking the world's transcription, a living, breathing skein gulping down the rank matter of life, distending, bulging, and when he couldn't swell anymore, shitting it out onto the page. It was a task he took very seriously, staying out of the light. He'd made his own soul insignificant, an afterthought in a corner of limbo so that he could filter the lives of others like a baleen inhaling krill. A watcher. Because when he took part in the pageant he became dangerous, a weapon. He had done it once before, and it had made him a murderer.

So what had he done after witnessing that act of cruelty on the train? He'd ridden on to 72nd, gotten off, climbed out of the ground on the icy half-moon tracks scored into the frozen stairs, up to the bright frigid morning, onto the deserted sidewalk, past the cabs idling here and there, plumes of white streaming from their tailpipes, past the steel cellar hatch doors winged open at the grocer's on 73rd where a guy in a butcher's apron was pitching down the cardboard boxes piled in slumping towers at his side, and my father had swollen a little more with every step, vacuuming up the smorgasbord, and he turned and walked under the Apelles' arch, crossed the courtyard, into the lobby, past O'Halloran, the weekend man, without so much as a nod, and gone up to the apartment, shedding suitcases, boots, gloves, socks, and hat behind him in a bread-crumb trail that led into the pantry, where he banged at the Olivetti for three hours before he felt he'd unburdened himself sufficiently.

Writing down was emptying, yes, but there was no bright moment of relief signaling the end. The writing went on, unresolved, and would go on until he was dead. How else could a person make sense of the world and its inhabitants? He didn't understand people who didn't fear oblivion, people content to exist and then leave behind nothing more than a headstone. Every book he wrote was, of course, a faltering attempt to understand those very same people.

And here was another of those mysteries, a prime example, this beast plodding ever closer to my father through the blizzard. Oh, how cute, thought my father, my very own Christ, laden down beneath his cross, disgorged by the city, another chance for me to redeem myself. Hooray. Perhaps I could throw down my coat to line the poor soul's way. And what monstrosity could this city offer up by way of a savior? A Frankenstein cobbled together from a murder victim's severed limbs, a brain from an East Village shooting gallery OD, a waterlogged heart from a concrete-shoed Sicilian?

Whatever messenger the city had sent, it was now approaching 78th Street, only a half block away, coming fully into focus in the orange snow-strewn light, not a monster at all, a natural being, a creation like all nature's creatures, a being brought to life by the conjunction of sperm and egg, an existence. Another Christ figure just like all the rest.

Manny got a bad vibe from this guy. He wasn't coming for the Vornado party, not with whatever the hell he had strapped to his back. And no one in his right mind would be out on a night like this, not unless he was coming to the party. Anyone who was, this angry weather would just stir up the blood. Manny looked over his shoulder, just to check.

My father, to his credit, was wondering if the guy was one of those who had the collective psychosis that infects cities after a war has done its erasing act. You saw it everywhere in New York. On every corner, the ever-tensed sternomastoids, the blood-red eyes of the berserker, teeth ground to stumps, lips soldered into a single angry band of wire, waiting for you on the bus, on the train, in the alley, in the empty lobby, on the deserted stretch of sidewalk, in the stairwell, coming through your windows at night, consumed by a ravaging hunger. For what? Is it a deficiency of compassion that leads us to this, my father wondered, the way a lack of vitamin D makes the bones brittle? The city was starving, and it reeked of ketosis. Broke, smoldering, a gigantic ashen heart. The Skulls, the Nomads, the Savage Samurais roaming the night, bellies rumbling, the kids, everywhere the kids, roaming, always on the move, Central Park, Riverside, tagging trains, boosting anything that wasn't tied down, Hey, mister, hey, mister, the most feared words in the city. A punch, a crack on the head with a Fanta bottle and the waffle sole of a Chuck in the ribs for good measure, maybe a blackjack or brass knuckles, a quick jab from a ghost that opened your head like an overripe melon. Spread your cash around, stow some in your jock, some in your sock. Keys an awl in your fist. Look crazy. Look poor. Never carry more than one grocery bag at a time. Don't be old. Don't be young. Don't be slow. Travel in packs. Don't fight back. Don't look anyone in the eye. If spoken to, get your head down and hustle for the light. If grabbed, submit. If confronted with a knife, monitor your bowel and surrender your wallet. Never widen your eyes, never cry or shake. You're a teller window, compliant and efficient. If a gun, pray and obey. It will all be over soon.

And if you're serious about survival, if you have the means and you're ready to adopt the only truly pragmatic solution, you'll board yourself up in your apartment and avail yourself of the city's delivery apparatus, the protection of doormen, hired cars.

You'll never have to set foot outside again.

But the emissaries of violence weren't what kept my father up at night. He'd seen worse. He was terrified of the benign. Those who blundered along happily, those too loose with their own fear of the end, those who substituted good luck for ontology. The average schmuck who didn't keep his tools clean and slept off his hangover behind the boilers.

So Schiff had told him that this obsession with death was a yearning for death, but that felt a little transparent, just a cheap inversion. What help was it? My father maintained his routines, attended to his checklists, guarded his talisman, which did help keep the fears in their cages. He hadn't always been this way.

He had trouble managing risk and all humans were risks. Machines were risky because they required maintenance performed by humans, humans who might never have to entrust their lives to the proper function of those very machines they were charged with maintaining. Mechanics didn't drive the cars they worked on. Carnies didn't ride the roller coasters. Airplane mechanics? Dear god. Elevator technicians? *Technicians?*

Boarding a train was an act of faith. Riding in an automobile driven by anyone he had known for fewer than twenty years could bring on hyperventilation. Airplanes, of course, were out of the question. They hadn't always been, but by the time I was in high school, they were off the menu.

Mr. Saltwater? Manny said. He was hopping around, puffing into his cupped hands.

You're absolutely right. I know, I know, my father said.

Great. Let's pack it in, sir.

Manny, who would be out on a night like this?

Manny stared back at him and smirked.

My father made a coughing sound that approximated a laugh.

Mr. Saltwater?

Yes?

Sir, do you think you might enjoy watching the gentleman there through your window?

I have considered that, my father answered. But I can't watch him like I'm a god peering down from above. I need to be in it. Human contact. An attempt to—to connect.

Uh-huh, Manny said.

The figure, meanwhile, was no longer a figure but a man. He was carrying a dining room table on his back, and as he closed the distance, features were beginning to emerge, like photo paper submerged in emulsifier.

I can't in good conscience leave you out here by yourself, Mr. Saltwater.

Well, that's thoughtful, but I'll be fine.

All due respect, but I'm freezing my ass off and I can't leave you by yourself, so if you want to tête-à-tête with the abominable whatever there—Manny tipped his head and shrugged—you're gonna have to make it worth my while. Otherwise, we're both going inside and you can throw ticker tape out your window, for all I care. Sir.

Done, Manny. Consider it done. My wallet is upstairs.

Really worth my while, Mr. Saltwater. If I come down with something and have to call in—

I'll take care of it, Manny. Don't worry. And look at this. You've got a front-row seat to the human condition here.

I take the 3 train every day, sir. I'm all full up on human condition.

Sure, my father said.

The man was wearing leather ankle boots, the kind that zipped on the side, and he'd stuffed the cuffs of his polyester pants into his snow-crusted tube socks. Balls of freeze hung from his beard. The wool cap and scarf had disappeared beneath clinging white, and plumes of smoke blasted from his mouth as his legs stabbed forward. His coat was wet with snow, the brown fabric splotched with darker brown, creating a camouflage pattern where the water had soaked in. Buttons were entombed in plaques of ice. On his back, an ornate oak dining table, which he'd inverted and was carrying like the carcass of an animal, had developed its very own snowdrift.

Mister Universe, Manny said.

Mhmm, my father said.

At a distance of about ten feet, the man stopped and gingerly straightened his torso, the table sliding down until the back edge slipped into the snow with a *shush*.

Wedged beneath the front half of the table, the top resting against his back, hands on his knees, he ran his eyes over my father, and then Manny, who was dancing in place, then back at my father. The man's tongue flicked at the corners of his frozen mouth. He repositioned himself slightly forward, bending deeper, dropping his elbows to the shelves of his thighs, like a linebacker, fingers clasped loosely.

My father was consuming him, assessing and recording. The man's eyes were sunken into his skull, shielded by a protruding brow. There was something familiar about him. It never was the eyes that one examined, not really, but the tender flesh around them. All eyes are the same, my father reckoned, marbles stamped out by the celestial organ machine and dropped into their sockets, sacks of vitreous humor for collecting reflections, light and dark—and how, in a place like New York, can the darkness not spread throughout the body, infecting every system until the person is nothing more than a miniature city himself, gray, covered with weedy spalls? That's what shows up in the bags beneath the eyes, the wet canvas sag of the upper lid.

The man's tightly trimmed beard, the mask of the frostbitten and hypoxic Everest climber, his icy, swollen cheeks, lips chapped to the consistency of beef jerky. My father felt the overwhelming need to greet him as one who'd completed a spiritual journey of vast proportions. He wanted to strike the right tone, jocular but respectful. After all, it was not every day—

Enjoying the show? the man said.

Who's that? Manny said. He took a step closer.

Manny? the man said.

Who's there? Manny said.

It's John Caldwell, the man said.

Ho shit, Manny said under his breath. Get out from under there, Mister Caldwell, he said, taking hold of the top edge of the table.

My father reconciled the face before him with Albert's. So this was the son.

Appreciate it, John said to Manny. He planted his hands in the small of his back and arched.

Mister Caldwell, said Manny. Far out. Did someone call you?

Can you believe someone threw this away? John said. Left it on the curb at 72nd. It's solid oak. You put in two weeks of work and it's as good as new. You see those barley-twist legs? A real craftsman built this. Probably not a drop of glue. All dovetails and dowels. What kind of sicko throws away something as beautiful as this?

Mr. Caldwell, if no one's called—

Good eye, my father said.

Thank you, said John.

Erwin Saltwater, my father said, holding out his hand.

Pleasure, John said. You live in there?

Mister Saltwater's upstairs from your father, Manny said, which is what I wanted to ask you about.

What about?

I figured someone would have tried to call you. But if you've been out.

What about? John said.

Your father. They took him out on a stretcher a couple of hours ago.

A stretcher? my father said.

Yes, sir, Manny said. Mister Caldwell, sir, do you want to step inside for a minute? You can use the phone.

Oh, that's perfect. That's just perfect. What happened? John said.

Possible heart attack? Manny said. They weren't sure.

That bastard. Did anyone call Fil?

Lines are down, Manny said.

What about the girl who stays with him? John said.

I believe he fired her, sir.

Oh for Christ—so no one went with him?

No, sir.

Where's the girl—what's her name?

Erica, sir. Like I said, I don't think she's working for your father anymore, Manny said.

And Fil knows? Tracy knows?

Mister Caldwell, you got me. Lines are down everywhere. If you want to try yourself . . . Manny shrugged at the building.

You're Albert's *son*, my father said.

John looked at my father with unrestrained annoyance.

Manny, tell us again. Spell it out slowly? my father said.

I got no idea, honestly. Ambulance came, I took them up, they rolled him out on a stretcher. He was awake. That's a good thing, right? Maybe he fell? Hip?

He didn't fall, my father said.

Whatever you say, Mister Saltwater.

We've got to go to the hospital, my father said.

John made an effort to look around as if he hadn't heard, as if his mind were somewhere else. What about this? he said, thumping the table. I'm not just leaving it out here where someone can take it.

That don't seem real likely, sir, Manny said.

You don't think so? John said.

We could put it in the package room, Manny said. Temporarily.

Temporarily, John said. Should I leave a deposit?

No, sir, Manny said.

Okay, then, John said.

The men converged on the table, tipping it onto its feet and taking up positions on either end, John and my father on one, Manny on the other.

Ready? John said.

They lifted, my father and Manny grunting identical expletives as the weight hit their arms, and they shuffle-tripped over to the archway, scowling against the wind, the unbalanced division of labor setting them in opposition to one another, working their way through the gate like a drunk trying to find a keyhole. Somehow they got through without doing too much damage to themselves or the table, and they set it down with a unified groan so Manny could wedge the lobby doors. A couple came in behind them and he waved them up to the Vornados' place.

A screeching, thudding passage through the lobby into the package room, the table coming in like an overweight cargo plane splattering itself all over a dirt runway in Burma. Manny extricated himself and assumed a post-wind-sprint stance by his desk, knees locked, elbows locked, huffing at the floor, while John slouched greaser-style against the lobby wall, a trespasser in the building where he'd grown up. He was watching the elevator, unable to shake the premonition that his mother would at any moment charge through the doors, eyes narrow, finger apoint, lashing him for his unacceptable behavior toward his father, his only father, the man who put a roof over his head, food on his plate, clothes on his back, never asking for his thanks, never asking for more than a moment of his time. Her strong mezzo filling his head like a gas. She'd been dead only a few years, and as his fine-lined memories of her had receded, John's recollections had become charcoal sketches, thick, impressionistic strokes that imposed moods on her, and which had less and less to do with the vital expression of her inner being than with his expression of himself through her.

My father was watching him from the package room doorway. John was dripping like a cat pulled out of a drainpipe.

You look like you got into it with a brick wall, my father said.

John held up his scraped-up hand, the knuckles brown with dried blood, and said, Minor altercation.

Albert's son, my father thought. You want to use our phone, towel, whatever you need, my father said. The words fell like lead pellets from his mouth.

Hm, thanks, John said, I'll call from down here. That okay, Manny?

Sure, Mister Caldwell. Desk phone or the one by the service elevator?

Doesn't matter. Where'd they take him? John said.

Roosevelt. I'll get the number, Manny said, disappearing behind the desk for the yellow pages.

Suit yourself, my father said.

You're new, John said.

Sorry? my father said.

You didn't live here when I was a kid.

I guess we've been here seven, eight years, my father said.

Hm, John said.

Your father's been here since—

'Forty-five. You know him?

I do, my father said.

Then you know he is a man who finds all aspects of the species equally detestable.

Well, said my father, he does have strong opinions.

Manny held out the phone to John, who took it without turning away from my father.

Albert Caldwell, John said into the mouthpiece. Yes, a patient.

That familiar imperiousness. No hello, no need for the polite how-do-you-do that weaker men deployed to get things done. He was Caldwell's son, there was no doubt about it.

My father knew how this little drama would unfold. John wasn't going to get far with that attitude. Depending on her disposition and how deep into her shift she was, the switchboard operator might decide to transfer him to the lounge, where, at this hour, the phone would ring fifty times before a groggy intern picked it up; or, stale joke, she might send him to the morgue; or she might simply put him on hold while she paddled her coffee with the rough wooden stick that was somehow meant to serve as a minimalist spoon, as though a chair might just as well be a nail, a car a cup of gasoline, a flower a grain of sand. It made no sense, none of it: why she sat in a windowless room, her head plugged into the knobby wall, why her legs throbbed, every second of the day a new manifestation of the never-ending aggravations foisted upon her by an uncaring god. Eventually she would disconnect the call. He'd call back, only to be flatly denied access to his father, the operator inventing a hospital regulation about calling hours, and he'd demand to speak to an administrator, someone he'd know by name, a family friend. He'd threaten her job.

But that wasn't how it was going at all. He wasn't his father, not exactly, then. John was speaking calmly into the mouthpiece. Please, yes? Yes, I'll wait.

So he can't help the ingrained habits, the domineering attitude, but he's not a perfect replica.

Do you mean in a different part of the hospital? John said.

. . .

Who saw him last?

. . .

Well, can I talk to someone who does?

. . .

John dropped the mouthpiece below his dripping beard and said, They lost him.

He said it the way a person might declare the corkscrew or pliers to be missing, with a hint of pique, a flat atonal lack of commitment to genuine concern. After another minute, John said, Thank you, and passed the handset back to Manny. He crossed his arms and studied his feet, all too aware that he was under observation. The presence of the other two men had forced John to react in a way that made it impossible for him to discern whether the news had moved his heart to concern or urgency.

How far's Roosevelt? he said to the floor.

Thirty blocks? Manny said.

Thirty, my father confirmed.

All right, then, John said.

And back he went into the blizzard.

18.

John was only thirty-one but already showed signs of ticking around the eyes, the sympathetic droop of the lids you see in social workers and the clergy. His skin was pale, in some places almost transparent, the blue veins beneath his collarbone glowing through, and since graduating high school he'd worn a beard to cover his acne scars. He was fussy about it. He wasn't interested in looking like Grizzly Adams. He aspired to project urbanity. On the occasion of his winning a vocal competition in the Catskills several years earlier, a part-time critic at the *Kerhonkson Reporter* had described him as being in possession of a "sort of diamond in the rough face." His hairline was in retreat, which he'd accepted as the price of adulthood.

John had made two stops that night before arriving at the Apelles. Like everything he did, they had been attempts at forgetting that his son was dead. He had stopped first at the Cosmic Diner, a place he'd never taken his little boy and that he therefore hoped would not spring any memory traps on him. Anyone else would have gone to a bar, but John did not drink. His father drank, and that was reason enough for John not to. The second stop had been a movie theater that specialized in erasing time.

For the record, the bulbs in John's brain were fine. He had just the right number, and they turned off and on when they were supposed to. His bulbs' efficient reliability caused problems, however, since what he needed most in the world was to forget the death of his little boy, so he might have benefited from some faulty wiring or burned-out bulbs. But what he had instead was a perfectly functioning device for playing back his recording of a tragedy.

Four years had passed since he'd been inside the Cosmic, and when he'd entered he'd recognized a few of the waiters, and one of them recognized him, too, and didn't seem to care that he'd taken up a four-top for the better part of the afternoon. John had been avoiding his eye, but when things calmed down the waiter sauntered over.

So you finally come for the job? the waiter asked, arms crossed over his profound chest. He wore a white shirt and black vest stained with a palette of soups and pastes, and transmitted the impatience of a professional forced to deal with amateurs all day long.

Where do I sign? John said.

Nikos, the waiter said, extending his hand.

Nikos, John said. I remember.

I tell you something, Nikos said. These guys . . . He shot the kitchen a forlorn look and stroked his white mustache, movements that invoked a spectrum of ancient disappointments that somehow encompassed brutal winters and rotten harvests, deaths at sea, generations living in the disfavor of the gods. It's been a while, my friend. You've been in prison, no?

John shook his head.

Ran off with a woman?

Something like that, John said.

You finished school?

All done.

So finally now you come to work for us? the waiter said, jabbing John in the shoulder.

When he was at Juilliard, John had talked with this waiter sometimes, late-night, the place populated by old men in overcoats nursing cups of coffee, old women reading the *Times* with a magnifying glass.

These guys, the waiter said again. He slid into the booth across from John and leaned across the table. I tell you, he whispered. These guys. He can't fire them, you know? Good luck if you *do* want to work here.

John raised his eyebrows. The owner, who occupied a stool by the door, his girth running over the sides of the seat like warm dough, spent his day ringing up checks and intermittently yelling at the staff, rousing himself only for shuffling trips to the head, didn't strike John as the type who'd think twice about firing his own mother, much less his kitchen staff. That wasn't the point. This waiter wanted to vent his spleen, divulge the same complaints he laid on anyone he got into a corner, John suspected. He was about to deliver a conspiracy, and all conspiracies were the same: conceived in fear, nourished with jealousy and spite. All Nikos wanted from John was a little collusion, a sign that he, a fellow white man, had also suffered as a result of the special treatment the Negroes, the coloreds, the whatever-they're-called-this-week got. How about a little compassion, a nod of agreement at the injustice? John set his face to regard the waiter without malice, but with no hint of understanding.

They come down from Harlem, the waiter said quietly, splaying out his fingers on the tabletop. First he hire only one. But then another, and another. And now they're a gang. If he try to get rid of one, he has a riot on his hands. The whole restaurant, burned. You see what they did in the Bronx, right?

John tipped back his head to indicate that he'd listened with an impartial ear, a judge on the bench.

The Black Panthers are everywhere, the waiter whispered, holding up his fist. You understand?

John sipped his drink.

I tell you one thing. He fire them right now, maybe no problem. Those people can't stand cold, so no protests. I don't make this up. It's evolution, it's scientific. This climate is all wrong for them. Survival of the fittest. They're too easy to spot in the snow.

Nikos stopped talking and looked at John. He waited.

Finally John said, So how long have they worked here?

Nikos said, Twenty, twenty-five years. So you see my point, yes?

I suppose, John said.

The waiter leaned back in his seat and wiped his hands on the towel slung over his shoulder. You got a job? he said.

Trademark office, John said.

The waiter nodded. You still sing?

Here and there. Maybe a summer tour. Festivals.

So, the trademark office?

Just temporary until I get a role.

To keep the mind occupied, the waiter said.

Something like that.

No? Don't occupy your mind?

It's fine.

You don't like it, you come work here, Nikos said.

What a joy that would be, John thought.

How's family? Your wife is happy?

Yep, John lied. You know. Marriage.

Nikos smiled, exposing two rows of perfect popcorn kernels.

You lost your ring, Nikos said.

She's pregnant, actually, John said. He and his wife had split up. She was not pregnant, at least not that he knew of. He hadn't seen her in three years.

Congratulations, my friend! the waiter said, clasping John's hand in his own.

Any day now, John said, nodding, smiling.

I'm sorry, now I've forgotten your name, John said, still holding the waiter's hand.

Nikos.

Thank you, Nikos, John said, sliding out of his seat without releasing Nikos's hand, making it impossible for Nikos not to get up from his seat, too. It was an old trick he'd seen his father use, and he was surprised at how well it worked, as though he'd pulled an antique flintlock pistol out of its velvet case and it had fired a round straight and true.

I get you a refill, Nikos said, heading off to the fountain with the red plastic cup in his hand, his shoes crunching on the salt-caked floor.

John had worked at Patents & Trademarks off and on over the years, checking and cross-referencing files. Practically the entire research staff was singers. It paid by the hour. You set your own schedule. John preferred the emptiness of the place at night to the day-shift company of other singers, who were incapable of talking about anything but contests and auditions, whining about the undeserving and talentless who'd stolen their roles, the rest of the sad sad story. If not for the storm, he'd be on his way there soon.

Nikos was coming back. The way he held the cup at eye level, as though fording a chest-high stream, reminded John of a child. How old was Nikos? Cup met table with a slosh, which he dispatched with a single stroke of his towel.

I see your father all the time, Nikos said.

Oh, John said.

He comes for breakfast. Pretty girl with him.

Yeah.

She sits over there, though, and he sits over here. A real gentleman.

She's his helper.

A nice girl, Erica. She's been coming in since she was . . . Nikos held his palm out at table height.

Sure. She's a nice girl, John said.

For years she came in with her grandmother. Always helping out with the old ones.

Yes, John said.

But for a week or so now I don't see them. Usually every morning but Mondays. But I think I haven't seen them for a week. They finally run off together?

John smiled.

No, of course not, Nikos said. They don't even sit in the same booth! But your father, he is okay?

He's fine, John said. I'm sure he's fine.

I think he has a touch of . . . Nikos tapped his head and frowned. Happens to the old. Happens to all of us.

I think I'll check out the movie, John said, pointing at the TV on a wall mount near the kitchen slot. He straightened up to his full five feet nine and three-quarters inches. He was rabid about those three-quarters of an inch. It was bad enough being a lyric tenor sharing the stage with basses who could play tackle for the Giants.

Even still, Nikos had to look up at him. John shook his hand for the third time that afternoon.

All right, then, Nikos said.

All right, John said, and dropped back into the booth. Nikos went back to the wait station, and John sipped his Dr Pepper and watched the promo for a Vincent Price flick on *The 4:30 Movie.*

The trailer faded and one of the regulars shouted, Sound! The counterman, without looking up from his story in the *Post*, reached above his head to the volume knob with the assurance of a pilot setting a toggle switch on the ceiling panel. The Weather 7 graphic faded to the meteorologist, a comb-over in a turtleneck, blazer, plaid pants. He slid his flock of cardboard snowflakes and clouds across the magnetized map, pulled up some more from down south, then more from the north. Pivoting to a second map, he swept his arms across the greater metropolitan area, conjuring the storm. A cloud fell off and clattered faintly on the studio floor. He liberally exercised his right to bestow *massive* upon every noun he uttered. Massive storm. Massive fronts colliding. Massive snowfall. Twenty inches in New York. Thirty in Boston. Massive drifts. Massive tides! P. T. Barnum pitching meteorological disaster.

John closed his eyes to the miraculous banality of the world, the flat world on the black-and-white screen, the pointlessness of prediction. Massive, massive. Apocalypse and destruction. A hysterical troll two inches high trapped in a brown box, a herald of electric prophesy. A day was marked by the accumulation of dread. It drove him like a spike into the earth. In the morning he got out of bed and felt it plinking at his skull like rain. By the time he fell asleep, it was a sledgehammer. Maybe tomorrow he could allow himself to be crushed, maybe tomorrow he could give up.

He decided to stay for the beginning of the movie, and gathered up his coat and scarf and hat and dumped them onto a swivel stool nearer the TV. The counterman shifted down the counter like a great hairy animal grudgingly making room in his den, sliding his paper with his thick forearms, cutting his eyes, sizing up the intruder who dared trespass his habitat. John went back to retrieve his glass from the table. Returned, he settled in and lifted his face to the Sylvania screen.

The counterman closed his paper, and reordered its pages with the

The Blizzard Party

care of a priest arranging his vestments. I'll leave the sound on for you, he said, lingering, inviting a smart-ass remark, but John said nothing.

Sure, you could get stabbed to death in broad daylight in your apartment lobby, but it was the incessant attitude that really killed you. The endless stream of commentary that piled up inside his head, glop clogging all the drains, the never-ending frustration of being in the way, of everyone else being in your way, of never being first, of telling yourself you're all right with the elbow in your back but not with the boot on your toe. Remarks, always with the remarks. Some bitch in a fur flinging open a shop door and charging headfirst into the oncoming throng, expecting the sea to part before her glory. A cigar-chewing slob sprawled over the steps, gruntingly ceding passage with a You're Welcome. On the subway, old women in pillbox hats, embalmed and powdered, motionless, then inexplicably viperous. High school kids whose faces were already closed for business. Not a spark of light anywhere. Everyone an enemy. Most days John wanted to kill someone; rarely did a day pass that he didn't expect to be killed himself. He had not been bothered by these things before his son died.

His heart was a fist. It took nothing to set him off. A subway turnstile eating his token. Some cabbie cutting a corner too close to where he was standing. The kids slouching all over everything, cigarettes tucked behind an ear, blocking the sidewalk, clogging things up for sport, just like everyone else jockeying for a little attention, poor babies. Cry me a fucking river.

He hated wiseass countermen with shellacked hair and dirty white T-shirts, toothpicks rolling across the craggy range of their misbegotten dentation, a fading tattoo of a pair of tits as doleful as Dopey's eyes on one forearm. Yet John didn't rise to the bait. Not today. He wished to be anywhere but New York. To fall into a battle with the counterman, to have the standard-issue verbal altercation over this little patch of real estate, would be a leap into the abyss, confirmation that the city existed right now, that it was within him, and today he didn't have room for it.

A flashbulb memory, sitting on the hot sand with his sisters at the Cape. The shore was a sheet of dark, ovoid stones, the water so cold that going in had been a heroic act. He was small, and Fil and Tracy had held his hands, and he'd entered the shallows between them, gingerly, and he'd stopped when the sharp cold bit into his thighs, he'd leaned back like a dog against its leash, and they'd let him go back to the beach while they waded deeper and deeper into the dark water. It had been in a bay. There had been no waves. The stones had warmed in the sun and the heat wobbled around him and he kept his legs on the towel. Where had their parents been? Fil and Tracy came back with hard skin—cold, rigid, and rough under his fingers. They'd lain flat on the stones and he smelled their wet towels steaming beneath them.

Because he couldn't excise or beat to death the part of him that time-traveled, he had settled on this establishment, a hermetically sealed capsule buried during an earlier life. His memory went everywhere with him, that was the problem. In his wallet was a photograph he hadn't looked at in three years. At first he'd thought when the memory had faded he might look at it. He imagined looking at it, holding it by its scalloped white edges, and though he didn't weep anymore when he thought of it, the memory hadn't faded a shade. Nope, it had done just the opposite, it had expanded, covering the landscape in every direction.

Could he stay here all night if he got his head straight? It was a good stool he was on, that's what Bronson would say, a good stool, and the movie would be good, and that would get him through until dinnertime.

Be a man. A man with balls and a spine. Pull yourself together.

Hey, the counterman said, eyes fixed on John. He'd been trying to get John's attention for some time. John turned away from the opening strains of *The Pit and the Pendulum*. The counterman stood up straight and hooked a thumb through his leather belt while with the other he stroked his stubbled cheek as though he'd just woken up.

You gunna order or what? the counterman said, pacing the words as if reading from a cue card.

Dr Pepper, John said, tipping his cup.

We got Mr. Pibb.

John looked back at him, down at the glass of Dr Pepper he'd been working on for the last hour. Some toast, he said.

Wheat white rye.

Rye, John said. Through the cutout, John saw Nikos palling around with the line cook.

The counterman called it, hojack whiskey down, and went back to smoothing his paper. He shook his head, whether at John or some indignity contained in the *Post*, it was hard to tell, and really there was no difference.

John pulled out his plastic pouch of Sir Walter Raleigh and his pipe, a bruyère so smooth it could have been poured from a pitcher, a richly figured barrel with a line as graceful as *La Maja Desnuda*'s hip. So he'd been told by the guy who'd sold it to him. One eye still on the movie, he folded a paper napkin several times until it was firm as a pool table bumper. He held it all together by pinning one corner to the counter with his thumb. Then he rapped the bowl of the pipe against the bumper, each whack dislodging a spray of carbonized tobacco.

Hey, buddy? the counterman said.

John continued unabated, his face an expression of most genuine perplexity, as if to comprehend this request would require that he speak a foreign tongue, and intended to antagonize so completely the counterman that there could be no other possible reaction than violence.

You wanna knock it off?

The pipe hovered by John's ear. In the kitchen, a patty sizzled under the cook's steak weight. John brought down his arm, cracking his pipe against the counter with an extra snap of the wrist.

And so it was. Three hundred pounds of Bronx-born fury lunged at John, who slid back off his stool, pipe and tobacco in hand, as if to avoid a spreading spill on the counter, one that in this case was swiping at him with a hairy arm while making sounds that, although unrecognizable as postlapsarian language, were nonetheless wholly comprehensible to everyone in the diner. Blood would be spilled. John recognized it, too, and while his assassin was still beached atop the counter, roaring, perhaps overdoing it, for what is rage but a release, and who doesn't enjoy it *just a little*, John, gripping the pipe with his left hand, closed his right into a fist and crouched down, just out of reach. From there he slowly, with excruciating truculence, erected his middle finger, held it there like an exclamation point, still as the sun in the desert sky. The counterman made an epic swipe, a game-winning pitch that John evaded by scrambling backward over the salted floor, his left hand, holding the pipe, coming down hard behind him, and a sharp sting of pain shot up his arm as his knuckles smashed into the serrated surface of the salted floor, a stunning flash of agony. He instinctively retracted his hand and went tumbling sideways.

The counterman was having his own difficulties with gravity. The violence of his grab for John had unseated his considerable mass from the counter, and he was in a nosedive, but with his arm crossed over his chest, which meant he couldn't break his fall, and his forehead hit the floor with a crack. His eyes blew open and he went silent. John, still scrambling, crashed into a table, its pedestal rivets groaning, managed to get a hand on his coat, then sprung to his feet and made for the door, shoulder down in case there were any heroes between him and escape.

Inverted, motionless, the counterman was wedged between two stools, breathing onto the filthy linoleum, his toes resting on the counter. A dim light glowed deep within the cave of his brain, a fire tended by two of his hairy ancestors whose shadows were thrown in monstrous relief onto the ceiling as the quartzite in the walls flickered. They were plotting against a third hairy ancestor, the one who stood outside the cave counting his chattel. Murder. The counterman needed to murder someone good, but who? Then, out candle, out, a blank.

For that moment after his brain got smacked silly against the forewall of his skull, there was quiet. He was not transported to happier days. No first kiss or Wonderwheel rides, no recollection of the hot tarmac at San Francisco International, where he smelled the salty bay and got down on his knees and kissed the concrete slab, unfreezing blood that had been frozen tight in his veins for the year he was stationed in Truong Lam. When he hit the floor, he remembered nothing; he became a rolling blankness, a deep, briny Arctic channel.

In the seconds following a sudden act of public violence, paralysis often strikes bystanders, and it was only to pay bravado its due that John had dropped his shoulder as he ran for the door. The waiters, in no hurry to put themselves in the path of trouble, couldn't have backed up any faster if he'd been waving around a pistol. The owner, whose mushroomed girth prohibited him from a livelier reaction, swung his fleshy arm in John's direction, clearing the checkout counter of the mint dish and check spike, a crack, tinkle, and clatter to accompany the shrieking of the door's aluminum frame against the salty jamb as John charged onto the sidewalk in a spy's karate crouch.

It was dark, the street clogged with cabs, exhaust, steam pumping out of manhole covers, pedestrians exhaling plumes of white. John zagged through the crowd to the curb and, keeping watch on the door, buttoned up his coat, clapped his hat on his head, and carefully wrapped up his neck. If he was meant to be killed by the savage counterman, he would perish with a warm neck. A cold body led to constricted cords, caused tension everywhere that threw off the tone and turned a vibrato into a warble. Even worse, obviously, was illness—a cold, an oozing sinus, congestion, god help him, bronchitis. Breath control vanished. The limbs became leaden, the diaphragm weak, the bellows clogged, the sound cut off at the tap. Singer muted.

A thought whipped past as if on a stock ticker: Go back and fight. Be a man. Fight. He stepped toward the diner and saw the waiters tending to the counterman, whom they'd comforted into a booth. It was not big enough to contain his sprawling mass, his lolling head. The counterman was facing away from the window, and John moved yet closer to the glass and watched as Nikos applied a bag of ice while another waiter planted pats of reassurance on the man's back, broad as a Volkswagen. He would have ripped my head off, John thought.

A man and a woman, the woman in a long cashmere coat, her shoulders padded with snow, passed John on their way into the diner. They were just inside when they saw the huddle at the booth, and they turned right around and left.

Nikos glanced back at the door, and saw John through the glass, the nice young man with manners, peering in at him, his face desolate. Why would he behave this way? Every day Nikos watched customers flow in and out, mostly regulars, dependable people. A boy disappears for years. He returns and . . . this. Who could explain such behavior? He lifted his arm from the counterman's back and shooed John away, the same threatless gesture his father had employed to rid his café of the poor boys who begged five lepta coins from the customers back in Patras. Such a life, here in this stupid filthy flat city. Such a life, that he should find himself here, working in this place, nursing the broken head of this maniac.

A normal person, having incited a stranger to murderous rage, having possibly broken some part of his own hand in the process, might find his own thoughts to be as thrashingly wild as a flock of geese frightened into flight, but John, forged in a Caldwell-brand furnace, was tempered to resist chaos. He had it to thank for his controlled performances—he never missed a cue, never botched his blocking. His body was under control. He kept his voice under control, no matter the venue. But it had turned out that audiences wanted a wild man, not a record player.

He inhaled a sharp bellyful of February, his face a Kabuki mask. He waved farewell to Nikos, and as he did, he realized that for a few minutes he'd forgotten his son.

He walked south on Broadway. A flotilla of gray cloud was dragging across the jagged reef of high-rises. Wind barreled down the avenue, bending the saplings planted in the center divider, and John sank deeper into his collar. Northbound, southbound, the avenue was awash in hazy taillights, red dots and dashes transmitting an endless, meaningless telegram.

His chest was tingling and his blood was flying around inside his limbs. A man must maintain dominion over himself. His appearance is his calling card. Things his father said.

What would it feel like, he wondered, to grab the wrist of anyone who sat across from him—even Nikos—and pull that person to him in a tight embrace? How great the gift of another person's attention, how unthinkably loving. He'd gone the wrong way with the counterman, but he'd had his attention, just for a moment.

John ducked into a tobacconist's, not his usual. The man behind the counter, his pilled brown sweater zipped up to his chin, strands of white plastered to his shiny scalp, was yelling into the phone, And, and, and you think you have time to wait for the next goddamn thing to just fall into your goddamn lap, like you have all the goddamn time in the world? . . . You'll see what *happens*? How can you say that?

The shop was one of those miraculous closets that occupied gaps between the city's plusher retail offerings, with only enough room inside for a counter along one wall and a corresponding corridor wide enough for a single customer. The tobacco was under glass, and stacked to the ceiling on shelves behind the register; cartons of cigarettes were stacked high on the counter and to the ceiling on shelves behind John. From somewhere among the boxes a transistor radio played Ravel. The owner yelled, I'll call ya back!

Never work with the public, had been Albert's advice to John. The old man had got that much right.

Evening, John said.

The man raised his considerable eyebrows without uttering a sound.

Sir Walter Raleigh Aromatic in a pouch, John said.

John heard the glass door slide, and the man's arm appeared in the case at knee-level, felt around for the blue pouch, his eyes on the ceiling, upper lip curled slightly, the face of a doctor conducting a digital probe.

A sharp medicine, the man said.

I suppose, John said, opening his wallet.

A physician for all diseases and miseries, the man added, standing, stabbing at the cash register's gray keys.

John held out the money.

Sir Raleigh's final words, addressed to the axe that separated his head from his shoulders, the man said, taking the money, stabbing the keys again, the cash drawer shooting into his gut.

Is that so? John said.

A poet to the end, the man said.

This was the problem with people, John thought. They were always springing traps to make you listen, but they never listened in turn, like a preacher in a pulpit.

You don't say, John said.

Ya, the shopkeeper said, waiting. When John only stared dumbly back at him, the man relented and dropped the money into his hand. This pleased John, to have broken him, and sympathy surged up to fill the empty space annoyance had vacated. What did this old man have but his little brown box of a store and someone to yell at on the phone? Why spoil his fun? And where else did John have to be, and who else did he have to talk to? But he couldn't think of how to make it right, and he dropped the change into his pants pocket, slipped the pouch of tobacco into his coat, and said, Good night. The man's finger was already in the phone's rotary wheel. Didn't matter whose ear he was chewing, as long as someone was forced to listen. Up crept a bitter snarl into John's throat, a wild desire to tell the old man to shut the fuck up for once in his life. What a pain in the ass he must be to his family, alternately barking disapproval and dispensing unsolicited lectures on subjects useless and obscure. Cuts of tobacco, biographies of colonial governors, the history of the Tariff Act. If he's so goddamn smart, what's he doing running a smoke shop? Brains didn't get you very far, not in this world, did they, pal?

John paused at the door and took his time arranging his scarf. All he needed was to catch the old man out, all he needed was a touch of spark to tinder and he could give the guy a piece of his mind. He'd be doing the world a favor. He listened to the rip and burr of the wheel as the man dialed. This city was a petty tyrant's paradise, its citizens ever open to assault from distemperate delivery guys and short-fused butchers, the asinine ministrations of bagel shop proprietors.

He couldn't linger any longer. In or out.

Louise? Louise? Put your mother on, the shopkeeper said.

John was ready. The speech was writing itself. The man's accent—Louweese? Louweese?—was an assault, the conversion of an innocent wisp of a word into a boot-clad lout.

John had struggled in diction class with Edith Braun, the German octogenarian who taught from a nubby green recliner, perspective rendering her face the same size as the oblong soles of her size-four feet, the student forced to sing directly at that oval trinity because Braun was deaf and corrected pronunciation by eye. John's exercises for her were abominations, his mouth a flopping mess, and he'd drilled hours a day to adopt a stage voice that was part Olivier, part machine, and in the end wholly unnatural. He'd become, in the process, as intolerant as Braun of imperfect pronunciation.

Hello? Nora, is that you, love?

The word thumped John in the chest. *Love,* rolled flat as dough. He glared through the glass door. February, whore of a month. This weather, the city's punishment for glib April, when the sidewalks flooded with people concussed by the air and sun, incapable of walking a straight line, dumbly following their noses toward the new grass in Sheep Meadow, the Great Lawn. February was when everything died. Even January offered up empty blue skies, but February was a dark, Norse month of ice and cold.

Hold on, the man said into the phone. Do you need something, captain?

John raised his hand no and went out. The new snow fringed the dirt around the skinny black tree trunks, frosted the manhole covers, telephone booths, clung loosely to black-coated shoulders and the crowns of men's hats. Unless he looked into the streetlights he couldn't see it coming down, but he knew it was there. He pulled his collar tight and turned downtown.

19.

Sal Fumoso ran only one film a day at the decommissioned Penn Yards YMCA. He spliced reels and taped them end to end in a single continuous loop that ran on a platter system, like a celluloid cat's cradle. You could watch an entire film six, seven times in a sitting. No intermissions. What minuscule profit he might have scraped together was eaten up by the endless boxes of carbon arc lamps needed to keep the projector lit for ten hours straight. Only mechanical malfunction put a stop to the proceedings, and even then, like audiophiles who shushed everyone else in the room to listen to the pre-song pops and crackles on some beloved LP, his customers watched the darkness as avidly as the light. They considered him an artist, the old YMCA his studio.

Sal had been the projectionist at the Japanese Gardens until he'd gotten drummed out of the Local 306 for repeatedly supporting outliers during officer elections, candidates who were not really leadership material, guys who thought that John Berger was, like, the man, and who advocated for lectures before, during, and after the showing of movies. He'd appealed to the International and spent most of his settlement on a used DP70 and sound system. What was left he gave a sailmaker in Port Jeff to cut him a screen, which he installed in the abandoned YMCA, rent $10 a month. With the rest he bought boxes of bulbs. He showed whatever he could lay his hands on.

He was drawn to this work by a youthful experience (file under

Abduction, Alien), not so much a trauma that needed *working through* as an event that he likened to being taken backstage at a production of life itself, and the whole reason he believed it was necessary to untie time from its frame and let it flap free in the whistling breeze.

If his method of showing films amounted to an ethos, it was this: After multiple viewings, even the worst film would become sublime. Same as when a child repeats a word until it becomes a clot of alien sounds, the film has to break loose from its prison of meaning. After five consecutive viewings, metaphor loosens and slips off like a snake-skin, revealing the clean unadorned weirdness of the world beneath the imagined dream. No longer does artifice conceal art. Art reveals artifice. Actors grasp at their chests, emoting death throes while silently cursing craft table tacos; stuntmen tumble off roofs into well-worn crash bags. Knives plunge into themselves, no longer piercing the pearlescent flesh of the showering beauty while her wounds squirt the sweetest Iowa corn syrup. Patrons of Cinema West embarked on an intentional attempt to view not the artificial but the actual, to reach a state of communion with the actors on the screen, not with their characters.

This was film as projectionists saw film, the daily cycle of the early bird special followed by the matinee and then the two and four o'clock shows, then the date crowd. Projectionists were forced to watch: they could not look away, timing the cuts from one reel to the next, checking focus. They loved *A Clockwork Orange* for the method of Alex's rehabilitation. Why, then, did they come to Sal's? To watch, finally, the full loop, to complete the revolution, and complete it again, and again. It was the breaks that soured the commercial experience, the artless previews and dancing tubs of popcorn, and the gray screen, the void between shows, the audience chattering blithely in their seats, stupid-faced, warming up their coughs, testing the creak of their chairs.

And what happened after days of uninterrupted viewing? Take the Gill-man from *Creature from the Black Lagoon*. Standard zoomorphic substitute for the adolescent male whose happy childhood has, thanks to puberty, given way to disenfranchisement, anger, fear, whose only desire is to touch a girl and relieve himself of the ignominy of solitude. Submerged in the depths of the Black Lagoon, the wretched aquatic monster lurks, so far beneath the bronzed girl on the boat. She enters the water, and from his nest on the lagoon floor, the creature looks up and sees an angel flying above him, soaring beyond his mortal reach, yet he dares swim upward, extending his webbed monstrosity of a palm toward her foot. Oh, Grendel, oh, Icarus, oh, Elephant Man—mustn't we feel sympathy for this poor, sublime fool who only wants something more than himself? Who is this outcast but us?

Yet, watch again, and then again, and again. Note the staggering, unsteady gait of the aquatic monster as it tries to navigate the terrestrial world. You see that it is so like your own staggering passage through the world. Watch again, however, and you will come to recognize that the monster's gait is a mechanical issue, the result of stuffing a man into a rubber suit that chafes at the crotch, rips the hair from his legs, boils him in the sun, drowns him in his own sweat. The suffering is not metaphorical. Ben Chapman, the man in the suit, suffers for all to see. The story is about *his* imprisonment. Do you choose to see, or will you continue to look away? And if you choose to see, what then? Could you begin to see the transparent world, the truth?

Or *Psycho*. After five loops, the rise and fall of Norman's knife loses its fury, the stabbing as becalmed and as predictable as water dripping from a flower petal. Meaning peels away like a label from a bottle. Image surrenders its authority, reverts to its ephemeral origins, shadow and light. Watch again. The images change again and become memories. Watch again. They become secrets, stories related in strictest confidence, then confessions, then, finally, a crushing banality, a fact from which you can't turn away, no matter how bored. Truth emerges, and becomes, always, boring. But like monks at meditation, Sal's audience strained to transform boredom into a sublime calm, an effortless state of existence.

And that was why John, first taken to Cinema West by a Juilliard classmate, a trumpet player who liked to eat red devils and settle in for the cycle, visited that night: to join the disciples who sublimated themselves to the great flickering modern god, lord light, while their high priest at his pulpit, monitoring the take-up sprocket, the focusing knob, the racking knob, tending to the splice and tape, conducted worship with his whirring machine. Those poor slobs, those agents of a new age of light and screen, maybe they were onto something.

Their temple was a dingy brick outpost amid a wide, flat waste of black earth crisscrossed by arcing railroad tracks, peppered with piles of scrap metal and creosote-soaked ties, electrical cabinets looted for their copper wire. A sad collection of former trees held up a latticework of power lines. Abandoned freight cars, like caskets awaiting the gravedigger's backhoe, peeked out from the tunnel at the north end.

Yet on that night the snow was smothering it all, obscuring the tracks, burying the elevated Miller Highway that passed over the yard (a more recent addition than the YMCA, which had sacrificed its roof to the roadway's substructure), and by the water the jagged black pilings and disintegrated piers were outlined in white, almost glowing against the river.

John had walked south from the tobacco shop, humming Tamino's aria from *The Magic Flute*, the tempo a little hot to match his pace, thoughtlessly looping from coda back to the opening bars. The snow had picked up, and the wind was cutting into his coat. His injured hand, the skin split at the knuckles of his first and second fingers, across the transverse metacarpal ligaments, notable because during neither of his hospital visits later that night would he avail himself of medical services, was mercifully numb from the cold.

When John reached the exposed overlook of Freedom Place, the Hudson lobbed pillars of snow at him, possessed, it seemed, of an animal intelligence intent on driving him back where he'd come from. The long iron stairway down to the yard was ramped with snow, and he held fast to the frozen railing with his good hand, skiing the descent. At the bottom, a tin signal shed was peeling apart in the wind.

Once inside the YMCA, he shuddered off the snow and slipped between the thick curtains hung in the library vestibule. Up the mezzanine stairs, he held out three dollar bills, awaiting the flashlight beam from the cutout in the booth. Beam lit the bills. Sal's hand emerged and took two. Nothing new tonight. John knew not to speak to Sal. He descended the stairs. He knew not to tombstone anyone, not to lean in and ask what was showing. Simple courtesies, house rules. The sacred observances.

He took some satisfaction from adherence to these shibboleths, the same satisfaction his father had once taken at restaurants where he was welcomed warmly, seated expediently, attended to with precision. One earned one's place of value, his father believed, by understanding what was expected of him—not politesse or, worse, friendliness, but adherence to the standards that defined a gentleman. If a plate of food failed to satisfy Albert's expectations, he sent it back; it would have been disrespectful to the chef, he explained to his son, to accept substandard fare. What were they, women, falling all over themselves out of fear some stranger might dislike them? How was anyone supposed to know how to act if they weren't all playing by the same rules? This was the compact, broken at the risk of sacrificing civilization, a precious concept each man carried within him when he went forth into the world. Like explorers into the heart of Africa, said Albert.

Like Jameson? John said, seventeen at the time.

That's a point of contention and you know it, Albert said.

I read the diaries, John said. What's the point of contention?

That goddamn school, his father said around a load of pommes frites. Jameson, he said, sacrificed his own legacy when he purchased that girl's life. And he did it so no man need ever again go through the trial of watching such a thing. Why else would he have made a visual record of the event? He was an observer. He never touched the girl! You can't apply the standards of the modern age to that benighted era.

He bought her for six handkerchiefs and watched them carve her into pieces, John said. How much would you sell Fil and Tracy for?

How do you think her life would have turned out in a place where the tribal elder would sell her for six handkerchiefs? said Albert. Hm? Do you think this was a place where she would marry and raise children and spend her afternoons drinking iced tea in front of the television? She didn't even put up a fight. She knew her fate. She might even have been exalted for it.

Like we can trust Jameson's story, anyway, John said.

Albert put down his fork. Civilization is tectonic plates heaving against one another, he said. Glaciers carving valleys. Vast, collective movements. Individual lives are ground up and forgotten in an instant. These things unavoidably exceed the understanding of a teenager.

Not all teenagers, John said.

All teenagers, Albert said with a laugh. They were talking about the war now. It was a slow, murky river of disagreement from which flowed the tributary arguments that had come to define their relationship. Albert had forbidden John from enlisting though he agreed that there was no substitute for the lessons learned in war. It cooled a man's impulses, made him less susceptible to the trifles that plagued weaker men, more perfectly oriented him to succeed in the world. If he survived. But what of those whose bodies survived but whose minds didn't? Albert's first apartment in New York, 1931, had been in the West Seventies, and if he craned his head out the window and looked west across the rail yard (the same rail yard where John sat at that very moment in 1978) he could see the squatters colony called Camp Thomas Paine. The camp had been populated by forgotten soldiers of the 1917 war. They kept the pathways swept clean and ran the camp with a semblance of military order, but it was unmistakably a place for the lunatic and socially unfit. There was the outcome as likely as death: survival in name alone. No, not for his son. John could locate his sense of purpose without the war. A fair trade in exchange for not having to risk getting his head blown off.

I'm a pacifist now, John said.

A wise indulgence, Albert said.

Better a pacifist than a coward, John said.

Wait until you have a family of your own. Then you'll see what cowardice is, Albert said, forking steak into his mouth.

Albert Caldwell was not one to be caught in the tectonic meat grinder. He lived as though he'd created an extra dimension beyond time and space, one that enabled him to stand out from the dull grain of the city like a chess piece atop an empty board. Over time John recognized his father's godliness as the true seat of their disagreement.

Fifteen years later, the father's omniscience was as secure as ever.

Whether John was buying apples or on an audition or in bed with a woman, his father was there, peering over his glasses, judging, praising, chastising, casting aspersions, opining on the quality of his son's choices, from clothes to bus route to meal to mate. So present was the old man's voice that John rarely had a thought that didn't lead to an internal dialogue with his father.

John lit his pipe. He'd recognized the movie immediately. *The French Connection.* Has Hackman ever *not* worn a raincoat? Does he have some kind of contractual thing with London Fog? It's a short man's solution, of course, a way to elongate the torso, but in Hackman's case it just looks like he's a perv. No, wait. This isn't *The French Connection.* It's *The Conversation.* Oh hell. The only thing good about it is the first scene. The whole film's a gimmick. A theory with a movie built around it. A movie made to convince everyone that the director is an artist, that's what it is. A showpiece. There's no story, and the whole premise is based on a misunderstanding. A cheap, stupid idea. John kept flexing his hand to irritate the skin over the knuckles, each one a fat baked ham about to split open.

He'd moved into a sublet after she left. Out of a misguided sense of hope that she'd return, he'd held on to the lease at their apartment, though he couldn't bear to stay there anymore, not after what had happened. The sublet was a studio so claustrophobic that it might have been the cabin of a sailboat with a single hazy porthole at the bow. It was at the top of a set of comically narrow and crooked stairs, a dark, snaking flight of risers that could have been carved into sandstone in some prehistoric cliff dwelling. Climbing them predisposed him to the queasiness that overtook him when he was inside.

Even now it made him sick, a tapping at the back of his throat, when he pictured it, the crooked plywood cabinets, the daybed piled with deflated pillows of various sizes, the spindle-legged desk the color of eggnog, the single wobbly dining chair with a ripped wicker seat, the stuffed chintz chair with greasy armrests. The fireplace had been jammed full of cardboard boxes of clothes, not his. The gap between daybed and chintz chair was just wide enough to allow passage to the filthy window, through which it was sometimes possible to assemble an approximate sense of the weather. Candlesticks encrusted with dusty wax were fused to the air conditioner casing. The kitchen was four squares of linoleum, an oven that whanged into the refrigerator when he opened it. Inside were shoes, not his. The bathroom was wedged in behind the kitchen. Heavy porcelain fixtures, H&C, a standing waste, crumbling grout and crooked tiles and a tub streaked ochre. The little casement window operated by a rusty crank. It was in the ancient ruin of a sink that he threw up every morning, exhausted, his body a sack of wet bones he willed into a standing position long enough for him to complete the expulsive ritual. Then he went back to bed and lay there for another hour of sweaty recriminations. He saw her everywhere, and he saw his boy everywhere. Through a crowd on Columbus, getting on a bus, the two of them holding hands.

He'd stayed in the sublet for months, though he couldn't afford rent on both places. Some nights he would wander up Broadway and over on 83rd to their building, take the elevator to the eighth floor, walk to the door, position his key. There was an empty apartment on the other side of the door, but he would imagine that she was inside, alone, and he was aware that he'd pushed his own loneliness into the spotlight, and that he was grieving then for himself more than for his son or his marriage. He was not inexorably drawn to the apartment. The door did not exert a magnetic force on him. So, then, why was he there? To test his broken spirit, of course, but why test it in this way, standing there at the door *performing* his grief—not real grief but a pantomime grief that existed alongside his actual grief, like a pool of gravy under a grisly, cold slab of meat. He was audience and actor when he stood at the door, imagining that she was inside, standing on the other side of the door, listening. What would he do if he were to unlock the door and find her there? He would enter. She would beg him to reconcile. She would fall to her knees, her cheeks wet with tears, throw her arms around his legs, and wail into his pants leg, Please please please, and the apartment would be in disarray, her clothes flung over the backs of chairs, bras on the floor, the sink piled with dishes, the white glow of the television in the bedroom, a damp towel reeking of mildew lumped on the sofa, empty bottles of wine; the nest of a broken woman. He would refuse her.

And there the fantasy would fall apart, not because he'd reached satisfaction but because of his own embarrassment. How could he play this game when he should have been mourning his boy? How could he miss her when the boy was gone forever? Defeated by his own spinelessness, he'd leave and walk south to Cinema West.

The Conversation. You don't know who you're tangling with! the guy with the mustache was yelling. Harry Caul. That was Hackman's name in this one. John chewed on the stem of his pipe while he watched. He crossed his legs the way he pleased, in the manner of the French café patron, the way a schoolboy never should because it was how women sat, and in defying his father's ancient instructions he felt a bit more like an adult. The soundtrack crackled at the high end, and echoed eerily, as most of the chairs were empty. There were voices in the stairwell, beyond the vestibule, loud enough to gain the interest of one of the moviegoers sitting nearest John. His chair creaked when he looked back into the dark. Outside, the wind was howling.

In the sublet John would watch *Hawaii Five-O* and Archie Bunker reruns on channel 11 until the station sign-off, and then he'd twist the UHF knob until he found a movie to watch while he tried to masturbate. He barely slept, and when he did, it was the sleep of an animal on the jungle floor. Too exhausted to make use of his sleeplessness, he lay in the white glow of the TV and felt shitty. There was a telephone that never rang. He had begun to go bald.

There were voices outside the library, odd because no one who wanted to be allowed in would dare speak above a whisper.

He relit his pipe, the wheel rasping against the flint, sparking, the flame bowing down to worship the bowl when he drew. This conceit in movies that every gesture, every word had power and meaning, this absurd convention of *moments*, moments that changed lives, moments in which irreversible decisions were made, ultimatums delivered and enforced. Anyone who lived that way would die of exhaustion. He only wanted peace from the never-ending skid of emotional engagement. When life becomes a series of interconnected dramatic events, you can't think straight, and that was his whole problem. He couldn't eat an orange without thinking of their last trip to Florida, or of standing beside her at the kitchen counter, cutting an orange with the red plastic-handled knife she'd bought on Bowery, without the voice of his father commenting on the weakness of remembering those things. Buy a box of macaroni and he was at their last Christmas dinner, when they'd been fighting, burned the bird to a crisp and had to make do with what was in the cabinet. Every graffiti-tagged wall was an illuminated manuscript, a record of their every trip down the sidewalk together. The city was two filmstrips that had been laid atop one another, present and past, both projected onto the screen simultaneously. And in every shot, the little boy.

He'd given Bronwyn's well-being more consideration in the time since they'd split up than he ever did while they were together. Her friends had turned against him, and he had flipped the switch that allowed him to hate them back. They had no idea what she was like.

Months after he'd moved out, months after he'd last seen her, he would put on a shirt that had been laundered ten times since, and there on the cuff, tickling his hand, a long blond hair, hers. Undoubtedly hers. Off to the bathroom to puke in the sink. He could not imagine her without imagining the boy. So there were three filmstrips. Past, present, and the boy.

The voices outside were actually only one voice, a spice importer named Bonny Patel who rented some upstairs office space from Sal, and who sometimes drifted down to chat with his landlord in quiet British English, hanging around if an old black-and-white was on the bill. He was a Cary Grant fan. There was a gentleness about Bonny, an insistence on ascertaining the well-being of whoever he was speaking to. He had so perfected the art of concealing himself behind questions that invariably his conversant was left feeling invigorated by Bonny's attentions, but wondering who, exactly, he'd divulged himself to.

Usually he wore a double-breasted suit open to allow his not-insubstantial belly to breathe, his shirt open at the collar, a pair of English monk straps. When he spoke, he did so with his hands, moving them in a deliberate, artful fashion that irritated Sal, who, to be fair, would have been equally irritated had Bonny stood with his hands in his pockets or had he lacked hands entirely. Sal's end of the conversation usually consisted of dry air punctured by throat-clearings.

In the hallway Bonny was calling Sal's name. He didn't stop calling when he entered the library, feeling his way toward the spiral stairs. Sal's head popped out of the booth.

Bonny, what the hell? he said in a whisper that was itself an act of violence.

Where is Vikram? Bonny said.

How should I know? Sal said.

You have not seen him?

No!

Bonny climbed the iron stairs that led to the mezzanine, a clanging, squealing ascent, and once he'd cleared the top his heavy footfall shook the floorboards as he hurried around to the projector booth.

Something has happened to him, Bonny said. He left hours ago. I'm sure something has happened to him. He's been robbed, beaten by one of these gangs.

The man sitting in front of John leaned back and said, See there? I knew it was about money.

I haven't seen him, Sal said.

Please, we must search for him. Please, the lights, Bonny said.

Be quiet, Sal said. He slipped through the booth's door. Sal was, on a good day, a jagged personality, one of those raw, vibrating nerves who took over corner tables upstairs at the Fairway by spreading around their small rubber-band-bound notebooks, a solitary creature whose every public act was intended to ensure the uninterrupted continuation of his seclusion. When confronted with the vicissitudes that tore up the lives of other people, Sal didn't have much to offer in the way of compassion. His was a limited menu, one that offered only bland, starchy fare and subsistence portions.

He left before dark, Bonny said.

What do you want me to do about it? Sal said.

He is lost in the snow. I'm sure he's been robbed. Beaten. I called the bank and there is no answer.

No shit. Banks closed hours ago. Bonny, it's simple. He went home, Sal said.

He is not home, Bonny shouted, eliciting some noises from the audience. He directed himself to the dark mass below. I will pay you. Just one hour of your time. I will pay each of you to search for my boy. Help me find my boy, and then you can return to your movie.

Shhhh! went a chorus of voices.

Money, said the man in front of John. Always money.

John, in the second row from the back, had turned around to look up at the voices on the mezzanine.

Bonny tried again. Only an hour and I will pay and feed you all!

No one responded this time. Standard determination: engaging with a nut only encourages him.

Christ almighty, you keep it down or I'll throw you bodily out of here, Sal said.

Bonny then committed an act of sacrilege. On the wall just to the side of where they stood were the rockers that controlled the library lights, and he reached out and mashed his hand against them. Ten banks of fluorescent tubing flickered on above the audience, who en masse turned around in their chairs to squint up at the perpetrator of this inhumane act. They were a motley bunch, patchy goatees and combovers, brown and orange sweaters straining at the gut, clutching smoldering cigarettes and potato chip bags, their eyebrows working against the sudden onslaught of light, the overall effect not unlike that of a squad of cockroaches caught on midnight patrol out in the expanse of the kitchen floor, their antennae dipping this way and that, reeling at the shock of exposure.

I will pay you! Good money! He is just a boy. You must have some compassion in your hearts? He is only thirteen years old!

But Bonny must have seen that he was pleading with the mewling faces of a nursery, fat cheeks and drooling mouths, black eyes open wide but unseeing. He was at that moment as alone as he'd ever been in his adopted country, an alien among aliens, searingly afraid that his boy, born and raised here, was well on his way to becoming one of these bloated, weak American creatures, which was exactly why he was lost in the snow, having fallen prey to one of the gangs that roamed Riverside Park.

Sal reached for the lights, but Bonny caught his wrist. I beg you.

You're about to lose that hand, Sal said, trying to wrench his arm free, but Bonny's unwavering strength suggested a different outcome. You call the police? Sal said.

The police? The police do nothing, Bonny said. Call the police? Am I mad?

Your, ah, what, community, then?

What community? You are my community! Bonny yelled.

Sal was at his wit's end. You check the hospitals? he said, and, finally released, cut the lights.

Pardon me? Bonny said.

If the hospital's no good, you check the morgue. If he's not home and he's not here and he's not at the hospital—

Bonny stared through the dark into Sal's face, unbelieving.

I've got paying customers here.

My son!

This is my place of business. This my place of business! My business is to show film, not run search parties.

Twenty dollars a man! Bonny said.

Not for sale! shouted the Marxist in front of John.

Sal put his hands on Bonny's shoulders and began to turn him toward the stairs.

You know my son. He's a good boy. A paying customer, Bonny said.

I can't do anything for you.

John almost offered his help. How different things might have been if only he had. But he reconsidered. As far as he could make out, the boy had seized the opportunity to escape, however briefly, the watchful eye of his loving jailer.

Sal marched him down the mezzanine stairs, across the back of the library, and out through the blackout curtain. Bonny's voice beseeched the audience from outside, rising over the soundtrack: You have children of your own, do you not? Are you not the fathers of children? And if your children went missing in the night? In a storm like this? Would you not do everything in your power to save them? Would you not?

There was not one man in the audience who had a child. Not one.

John went back to the movie and his pipe, the soundtrack rising and falling. His attention drifted, then snapped back to the whirring spin of professional eavesdropper Hackman rewinding a tape of the fateful conversation, the recording revealing its layers as Hackman carefully adjusted the levels on his machines, drum noise lifting away like balloons, exposing the central line of dialogue, *He'd kill us if he got the chance.* Right, right. Stupid premise. John's mind returned to Bonny, and the more he thought about the man's hysterics, the more he disliked him. Yet as he thought about the exchange and his own reaction, he began to worry that it had not been his reaction at all, but his father's reaction. It was his father who would hate another man for committing the sin of vulnerability. His father had no use for a person who couldn't protect his own and looked to other men to solve his problems. These were the men his father had served every day of his professional life. Wealthy, vulnerable men, heads of corporations, unable to fend for themselves when they found themselves caught in the vise of the legal system. He hated them all.

John stayed until the end, and then watched another showing, then another. More after that? He had no idea how many, or what time it was when he decided to leave, only that the desire to stay unraveled within him slowly, after he'd become an inhabitant of the movie, after he'd been shaken loose of his own convictions and feelings and had taken up those of the actors. The only way to mark passage of time at Cinema West was to keep track of how many beginnings you'd watched, and he hadn't. The man with the lost son was forgotten. Briefly, his own lost son was forgotten. He was fully immersed in the movie now, eager for certain parts to arrive. The sonic baffling of the opening scene, sure, but other parts, too. The woman in the green dress, the bus rides. It's genius, John thought. The acting is genius. The directing is genius. The editing is genius. It's nothing less than the human condition in full. The mime, the raincoat, the frosted glass, everything opaque, a haze, everything unspoken, everything misunderstood. Harry Caul, an unborn baby experiencing the world only by pressing his ear to the wall of the womb. Exactly, exactly. *Sons of bitches! Those smart-asses! Who the hell do they think they're tangling with?*

When he left he exited into snow dense as a fog, the wind off the river tearing at his coat and scarf, and he immediately felt whitewashed, cleansed by the astringent precipitation and the wind thumping his back, pushing him toward the city. For a lesser mortal, the stairs might have been a problem, as they'd been completely obliterated by the snow, but he dug in his toes and climbed slowly up to the street. Clear of the rail yard, he turned to look down at the old YMCA but could not see it through the whiteout.

From a deep brownstone porch across the street, well enough protected from the storm and wearing the best snow boots and parka a doting father could buy, Vikram Patel watched John hoist himself up the iron staircase. Vik was out in the storm for no reason other than he was thirteen and subject to the same urges that had driven his father to leave Mahuva in 1961, that same intense curiosity and fearless embrace of solitude. Vik had been back to the office and, finding it empty—Bonny'd had no choice but to set out on his own in search of Vik—assumed his father had left for home. He knew he should do the same, but the empty city beckoned to him. On this night, New York as barren as a desert, he only wanted to survey the storm, snag some samples for himself, examine them under the portable microscope he'd brought with him. He wrote poetry when he was thirteen; maybe he wrote one about that night. I never thought to ask. Sweet boy, my Vik, my vanished husband.

20.

By order of the freshly anointed Mayor Koch, Vik had spent most of the day hanging out with Bonny. New York public schools had closed early, and while his father slept off a long night haggling at the dock warehouses, Vik spent the afternoon in the office double-checking his father's entries into the cloth-bound rokat khata and jama nakal, zeroing out the previous month's nutmeg, cinnamon, fennel, cloves, tamarind, turmeric, pepper, and chili sales. December was always good, then January like a cliff, but they'd done okay. Once he'd squared everything, he stamped the checks and nudged his father, snoring on the settee by the heater, into a state of near-consciousness.

Sign, Pita, he said, dangling pen, deposit slip, and checks. Bonny, without sitting up, cracked his lids to allow the barest sliver of light, and scratched the pen across the checks. His eyes closed and he patted his boy on the arm.

Going to the bank, Vik said.

Bonny raised his hand, his gold pinkie ring glinting, and was asleep before it fell back to his belly. Vik zipped everything into the pouch, clicked the little padlock, and slipped it inside his coat. He went down the stairs, past the blackout curtain over the entrance to the library, the piano theme from *The Conversation* lilting out.

It was nearly dark outside even though it was not yet four o'clock. Feathery snow was dipping around in the air, and the sky was baggy, foil and slate. Even though he knew the banks were probably closed along with the schools and the office buildings and everything else, he had to get outside, out of the pickled air of the office where his father had been asleep all day and where the soundtrack from Sal's film would soon be drifting through the wall at a volume just loud enough to distract him from his reading. He was a good kid, ever attendant to the letter of the law. He would try to deposit the checks, but he was also a teenage boy with an ulterior motive. In his other pocket was a Hensoldt Wetzlar Tami pocket edition microscope, a square of black velvet, and a penlight. Extra Rayovacs for the flashlight.

The Chemical branch was on 72nd, five minutes' walk. A typed notice on letterhead was taped inside the glass:

CLOSED DUE TO STORM

Beneath that, a rectangle of cardboard, dual hole-punched by a pencil, suspended from a length of string, declared in heavy black Sharpie:

<u>CLOSED</u>

So he roamed. He had pocket money. He saw two movies, *The Bad News Bears Go to Japan* and *Coma*. He ate dinner at the Cosmic: meat loaf, mashed potatoes, cubed vegetables, a grape Fanta. He stole glances at the bandaged counterman, who had gone back to his post and was doing his woozy best to stay on his feet after his dustup with John a few hours earlier.

Afterward, Vik rambled some more, down to Columbus Circle, along Central Park South to the Plaza, up Fifth a bit, east on 60th, back down, west on 58th, proscribing a Keanesian pattern of loops and reversals along the southern rim of the park before heading west, for once unconcerned by the vigorous beatings normally awaiting any loner who passed the kids from the Amsterdam Houses and the Lincoln Towers. They were out as usual, but too busy pelting cars with snowballs to bother with him.

By the time he returned to the edge of Penn Yards, his father had already left on his own wild-eyed expedition, the search for Vik that had begun so ignominiously at Cinema West. That father and son didn't cross paths was just another cruel coincidence on a night full of them. Vik picked a brownstone just east of the yard, one whose windows were dark, climbed the stoop, and tucked himself into the lee side of the porch.

From his pocket he took the Tami, a black and silver cylinder that, collapsed into its protective cup, fit neatly in the palm of a hand and might have been mistaken for a candle snuffer. It was German-manufactured, an artifact from the 1920s that fifty years later remained a coveted item among botanists doing deep fieldwork. Vik was enormously proud of the scope. It had been the first-place award, middle-grade division, 1977 New York State Science Fair, for his experiment tracking Brownian motion in smoke cells.

He cleared a protected corner of the porch of snow, unscrewed the Tami's hood, and set it down next to the velvet to allow them to equalize to the air temperature.

The blizzard howled off the river, its shoulders down, plowing through the open air above the rail yard. Yet when Vik told me about that night, he never mentioned being cold. He never mentioned the stinging slap of precipitation against his face. When he talked about it, it sounded as if that night he'd gone into a trance, a sort of spiritual snow blindness. I have my suspicions but he insisted he wasn't stoned. The only thing he mentioned about the weather was that the rail yard was concealed by a variegated wall of snow undulating in the air—his words, not mine. His presence in the blizzard was an act of poetic import, an experience of the same rare clarity I was about to lose, his vision unencumbered by linguistic blinders. The night was transient, not a future page in the brief history of his life. He had no way to record the snowflakes he observed, no camera, no sketchbook. He intended only to catch them on the velvet bed, observe their structure up close, perhaps report back to his science teacher that among the needles and prisms he'd spotted some stellar dendrites, a signal that cloud temperature and humidity were oscillating, a sort of exciting phenomenon to observe from down among the terrans, picking through the diamonds coughed up by the heavenly volcanoes.

And when a figure emerged from the old YMCA, a black blur within the snow globe, and climbed the stairs up to Freedom Place, Vik embraced the poetic visitation he'd been waiting for all along, some untamed, untranslatable figure emerging from the wastes, a welcome mystery. Odd, since he knew the crowd at Sal's, the cross-eyed weirdos who stashed tacos in their coat pockets and on a good day exuded all the personality of wet plaster, and he must have known that whoever had decided to trek home through the blizzard could only be an exemplar of that homuncular brotherhood, yet he watched the man cross the yard, slowly ascend the iron stairs, and pass directly in front of his bivouac in the shadowed portico of the brownstone.

Before the man turned onto West End he stopped and looked up at the brownstone. He shielded his eyes. Vik raised a hand in greeting, but the man didn't wave back. He tucked his head and turned north onto West End.

Vik collapsed the Tami and followed him. When the man stopped at 72nd and West End to dig into a snowbank, Vik hung back, a detective shadowing his perp. When the man lifted a table—a full-sized dining table!—onto his back and continued up West End, Vik maintained tail discipline, keeping a block's distance. His gaspingly lonely adolescent brain was filling out the man's résumé to fit the form he so desperately sought. A rambler, a stranger in a city of strangers, a quiet outlaw, one whose cutting insights sought a receptive and finely tuned ear, which Vik happened to have two of.

But Vik got too close. John Caldwell was, after all, a New Yorker born and bred, eyes in the back of his head, and he'd already had one run-in that night. It's not that John feared for his physical well-being. He knew the kid on his six was the missing boy. But he'd already done him one favor by leaving him alone. Now he'd gotten himself into some kind of lost-puppy situation, and John had already made his decision, back there at Cinema West. Around 75th Street, he ditched the table, spun toward Vik, and charged. Not a jog or a slippery trudge through the snow, but a full-tilt attack-speed charge. He was waving his arms and yelling, and Vik fled through the intersection before cutting toward Riverside Park. He didn't slow down when he hit the waist-deep snow that covered the open field between Riverside and the Hudson. Vik crossed the park, fighting the drifts until he saw nothing but icy river in front him.

He crouched against a tree by the river, roughed up by the wind, bummed out. And it was there that he encountered his second Caldwell of the night, making passage through the blizzard, leaning into the driving wind as he picked his way along the railing that was intended to keep pedestrians from falling into the Hudson.

21.

At grade, the average American walks a mile in about twenty minutes, at a speed just a hair over three miles per hour, and an average American heart prefers to beat about seventy-five times a minute. Between the two exists a proportional, rhythmic relationship. You ask most people in the city and they'll tell you the average New Yorker covers a block a minute (and then they'll qualify it with, Not avenue blocks, obviously). But the average New Yorker in truth walks twenty blocks, or one mile, in fifteen minutes, at an average speed of four miles per hour, more like one-point-three blocks a minute. How do we account for that extra point-three? Okay, New Yorkers are on-the-go, unstoppable, undaunted by all manner of street-level effluvia that might cause the heartiest Topekan to retch and reach for the Lysol. However, it's when we consider the myriad obstacles that confront a pedestrian in this city that the extra point-three gets really mysterious.

Even by a conservative factoring of waiting times at crosswalks, crowd density, sidewalk blockages caused by incidentals like vegetable pallets, stroller phalanxes, the old and infirm, flying wedges of tourists, bike messengers, construction fencing incursions, scaffolding, dumpsters, and the insane who walk in front of you pulling ooda-loop maneuvers on the widest stretches of unpopulated pavement, telepathically predicting your every countermove, the average New York pedestrian burns five to seven minutes over the course of a twenty-block transit jagging, zigging, charting a path that consists more of diversions than adherence to any single bearing, to say nothing of the decelerations required, occasional near-dead stops (though, notably, never actually stopping, always shuffling left, right, jockeying, inching ever farther into the street at a DO NOT WALK signal, timing a gap to shoot). After all that, what could account for the point-three? Is it possible the average unencumbered, obstacle-free New Yorker actually walks an average of six miles an hour, which is in most corners of the world considered a decent pace for a jog? It's the only possible explanation. New Yorkers, weaned on smog, tilted ever forward into the oncoming barrage of whatever, living in fear of the faster whoever coming up from behind, have developed bigger hearts than the steadfast Topekan, their sinus rhythm/leg-speed ratios increasing to the point that they're basically running even though it looks like they're walking.

When John Caldwell left the Apelles for Roosevelt Hospital, he knew he'd be walking. The MTA had stabled the Broadway local at the Inwood depot, silent and dark. The buses were long gone. Taxis, with the exception of the one that had nearly killed my father, had evaporated. Roosevelt was twenty blocks south, a mile.

My father, compelled by fears about his own elbows-deep relationship with whatever was going on vis-à-vis Albert Caldwell, insisted on going with John, and they agreed—first thing first, according to the law applied to a group of two or more men on an excursion of any effort and distance: establish travel time in as expedient a manner as possible—that they would be at the hospital by 1:00 a.m. Strictly speaking, it didn't matter what time they got there. It was a hospital, after all, it wasn't going to close. But as the unacquainted do when forced into close proximity, they had seized on that minor point of procedure with the single-minded focus of a pair of physicists on an equation binge.

Once they'd agreed that they'd be there by 1:00, they settled into silence. My father, not normally given to conversation anyway, but definitely predisposed to worrisome thoughts, was occupied by a real behemoth. He was thinking that he, of all the people in the world, he was the one who could have stopped Albert. To put it another way (the way his ghastly brain did), my father was the one who had facilitated whatever fate had befallen Albert.

And he wasn't entirely wrong. It was his nature to stay out of the fray, but he'd known about Albert's plan—he'd been aware of the existence of a plan, at least—and despite that natural tendency to avoid participation at all costs, he'd been instrumental in bringing Albert to the point of executing that plan. And the execution was taking a different shape than what he'd imagined. Why would he ever have thought Albert intended to go quietly? None of it made much sense—if he'd tried with pills at home, why had he called an ambulance? If he had wanted to OD at the hospital, why had he disappeared? Whatever form my father thought it would take, the reality of the old man's suicide now fully asserted itself on his psyche. He felt as though his blood had been drained and replaced with mercury. That's why, when John had tried to set out on his own, my father insisted on accompanying him, and had been keeping pace alongside him, a self-appointed minder charged with ensuring his safe passage.

They'd gone another two blocks when John turned to him and said, Really. If you're doing this to keep me company, don't.

I have my reasons, my father said—shouted, actually, over the gusting wind. They both were shouting.

This is family business.

I can go a different way if you prefer, my father said.

Suit yourself, John said.

They passed the next ten or so blocks in silence. At every cross street the wind bullied them from the sides, the snow plastering them like buckshot. My father barely noticed. At 1:01 a.m., he followed John through the revolving door at Roosevelt.

The sanitary warmth enveloped him and he set to brushing off the drifts that had piled up in his jacket's every crevice and crystallized little arctic kingdoms in his hair, rivulets retreating around the ovoid arch of his ear and down his neck. A skirt of beaded ice clung to the lower edge of his sweater, resisting all efforts to remove it, glinting wetly, flaunting its snotty tenacity. He yanked at one wet crystal and succeeded only in ripping out a flag of gray wool.

My father was ashamed at where his thoughts had gone. Albert had made sure to protect him, hadn't he? He'd sworn to my father's safety, legally speaking. Hadn't that been an essential aspect of his participation? He should have insisted on seeing the letter, but he'd taken Albert's word.

The lobby was full of strandees sprawled over the modular furniture. A security guard leaned against a pillar, gazing across the lobby at his reflection in the plate-glass window. His arms were crossed and his cap was tipped back on his head. A toothpick slid from one corner of his mouth to the other and back. Black pro-grade shoes. Off-duty cop. Did a cop ever put his hands in his pockets? Thumbs in belt or arms crossed, done and done.

At the opposite end of the lobby was a vending nook, the lintel helpfully labeled VENDING, inside which was a soda machine, a snack machine, and a coffee dispenser, backlit COFFEE emanating little brown wavelets. My father felt the familiar twang in his chest, a twinge of weakness in his knees. The potential energy within the soda machine, a mammoth, a Vendo V-528, was on the order of fifty thousand psi. That took into account only the Coke cans, none of the machine's refrigeration mechanisms, none of the Freon, the pressurized tubing. My father's brain immediately offered up at least three ways to initiate a chain reaction culminating in the simultaneous explosion of five hundred cans of soda, a wide dispersion shrapnel profile that would result in a +50 percent casualty rate. And then there was the coffee dispenser, a huge brown cabinet filled with spaghetti towers of copper tubing, heaters, cisterns of pressurized, scalding water, which made the Coke machine look like a Molotov cocktail next to an ICBM.

John was at the information desk, playing the role of concerned son, decisive and forthright. The woman he was addressing, a battle-hardened veteran, gave no indication that she intended to help or even acknowledge his presence.

My father is a patient here. I'm told he's gone missing.

The woman said nothing.

Is there an administrator I can speak to?

She adjusted her glasses, cat-eyes on a silver chain. Her hair was salty gray and fell in long kinky strands down over her shoulders.

I need to find my father, John said, louder this time. The security guard moved his head with such turtle-like dispassion that it seemed possible he was reacting not to John but to some unrelated thought that coincidentally occurred at the same time.

Hello?

I'm not deaf, the woman said. She produced a clipboard with a pen attached by a chain made of miniature silver balls. As she handed them to him, the pen made a dive for the floor, the chain thrushing against the edge of the clipboard.

I'm not signing in, John said, groping blindly for the pen, down there somewhere, oscillating. Not a patient.

You said your father is a patient. Fill out the form. Relative's name, pertinent information.

And then?

And then? she said. Then you bring it back, dummy.

John looked around, hoping to engage the sympathies of a witness.

My father took a step closer, but not close enough to cross the threshold of that particular theater of the absurd.

Not here, the woman said when John began to fill out the form atop the desk. She gestured languidly at the waiting area, which at the moment resembled a bus station. John walked in the opposite direction, toward the vending machines, and my father followed.

Jesus, what a performance, John said. They sat down on a ledge by the window.

My father had his eye on the machines. He was about fifteen feet from them. He swiveled until he was looking at the plate glass. He put his nose close to it, and shielded his eyes from the light, creating a viewfinder through which to see outside. The snow was peach.

You're worried? my father said to the glass.

He's fine. Wherever he is, he's fine.

Where do you think he is?

No idea. Maybe he needed to make a phone call. Maybe he got hungry, John said.

You think he went out for an egg roll?

Maybe.

I suppose you could threaten to sue them if something happens to him, my father said.

Exactly why there's no point in trying to figure out where he went. Their problem, not mine.

John worked through the form, then took the clipboard back to the counter.

So? my father said when he'd returned.

So I wait.

You're not worried.

We've established that.

You want to go poke around the halls or something? my father said.

John shrugged.

This, my father said. Pretending you don't care.

I do care.

What happened to your hand?

Nothing, John said. I slipped. John looked at the ceiling and said, I've read your books.

You haven't read my books. No one's read my books. And the last one doesn't count.

I didn't read the last one.

Which ones, then? my father said.

El El Narrows. The Horseshoe Crab. The one about the shipping company.

Plover, my father said.

Yeah, *Plover*.

You didn't read *Plover*. No one read *Plover*. Why would you do that?

Suicidal, I guess.

They were assigned for a class.

Nope. All on my lonesome. Your books are witness to the blasphemies of the twentieth century, John said.

What is that? Jacket copy?

Absolutely. I read the jacket copy. I read them inside and out.

But you didn't bother with *Slingshot*.

I'll get around to it after everyone else is done. Library's only got twelve copies.

Your father never mentioned that you'd read them.

When did he mention me at all, is the question.

Only when things were going wrong.

Yeah. You going to write him into your next book? John said.

He'd probably sue me if I did, my father said.

He's a blasphemy of the twentieth century if ever there was one.

Which is why you don't care what happens to him? my father said.

John worked his pinkie nail around the bowl of his pipe, a gesture of consideration, and as he did, he was struck by what a performance it was, like everything else he did. How well do you know my father?

I know him well enough.

So you might understand that who he is now is just a sharper version of who he's been his whole life. It's like he's gained superpowers. He's broken the bonds of mortality. This disappearing act? Just a new and improved way to torture the family.

I see.

Let me guess how you met. Co-op board run-in? Nothing makes him happier than putting the screws to someone in the name of due diligence.

No, not exactly.

You some kind of friend? John said.

I'm not sure, my father said. We had a standing appointment to meet every Monday.

A drinking buddy.

Not really.

John studied my father's face. What, getting his affairs in order?

In a sense.

In what sense?

My father drew up inside his enormous sweater, exhaled, examined his palms. In the sense that I was his proctor. I gave him a memory test.

You're a shrink, too?

No. He just needed someone dependable. Someone with nothing better to do. I just read him questions. A machine could have done it.

A memory test.

He'd written it up himself. He said he'd consulted some neurologists. Some psychologists.

Never mentioned a word about it to me, John said.

You know, he did talk about you from time to time, my father said.

In glowing terms, I'm sure. Strange that he never talks about you.

I doubt I count for much in his universe. I've only known him a few years. Now that I think about it, I suppose we did first meet because of the co-op board. I had to get his approval to fix the plumbing in our bathroom.

He gave you a hard time?

A little grief. But rubber-stamped it. I expected more trouble given that we're right on top of him.

Directly upstairs?

That's right.

So you bought your place from the Mellins?

Yes, my father said.

You know the KGB designed the vent work in that building, John said. Used to be that I could lie in bed and hear every single thing Cynthia said. What a piece of work she was. Her bedroom was right over mine. She cried herself to sleep every night. This is when we were both teenagers. I mean, it scarred me. You could hear everything.

Hm, my father said.

Do you know what she does now? John said. She lives in Afghanistan and exports rugs.

One way to make scratch, my father said.

She's a millionaire. She lives in a castle. An actual castle, a medieval stronghold. She's got connections everywhere. Embassies, Afghan government, she knows everyone. She's got fixers, she's in with the banks. What a piece of work. They must have blown a million dollars on therapy for her.

That which does not kill us, I guess.

Yeah. Strange my father never mentioned you. He talks about your kid enough.

Does he? my father said.

Hazel, right?

The one and only, my father said.

She's got potential, according to him. You know how he is, always scouting for self-reliance. He can tell you who's going to be a bum, just from looking into the crib. It's very scientific. Cynthia? Right from the start, there was no hope for her. You want to turn out like Cynthia Mellin? he'd say, and this was when I was, you know, a kid. How the hell had she turned out? She was eight!

And what's his prediction for Hazel? my father said.

World domination, of course. He says she has a skeptical eye. I don't even know what that means.

Means she's from Manhattan, I suppose.

Condolences, John said.

He told me you two hadn't talked in years, my father said.

Probably not the only fabrication he laid on you, John said.

He told me you lived up the street and that you hadn't talked in years.

True and false, John said. I go by to see him once a month, John said. Maybe we don't talk all that much, but I go. It's like being in a waiting room. Toughing it out until we get the bad news. Maybe we watch a game or something. He was never much of a sports fan and he can't keep track of who's who on the field, anyway. We sit there and watch the game and every two minutes it's, Who's that? Who's got the ball now? Who's that in red? Who's that in white? If he's not soused, we have the carousel conversation. He asks me about my wife, and I tell him she's not my wife anymore, then he tells me Fil and Tracy are saints, which is just teeing up for telling me about what pieces of shit their husbands are, then he goes on about Nixon for a while, then Carter, then he asks me about my wife, so I tell him again, and we're back to Fil and Tracy being saints and their husbands being pieces of shit. Those boys figured it out years ago. *They're* the ones who haven't laid eyes on him in years.

He's an uncompromising critic, my father said.

An uncompromising critic? Are you kidding? He's an asshole.

Arguably, his behavior owes something to his condition.

It's a sieve, his condition, John said. It's clarified him. This test you gave him. How'd it work?

My father paused to consider the legal jeopardy he might be putting himself in, then considered the fact that he deserved his fate. Names and dates, he said. I'd ask him—you know, I'd ask him for the date of an event, and he'd tell me.

Clinical as ever. Of course he'd enlist a near stranger. Did he give you his bank account numbers, too?

He wanted an impartial judge. Someone who wouldn't give him hints.

Jesus, what a stonehearted— He really said he never saw me?

He's not well.

How many times do I have to say this? He's no different than he ever was.

That's a convenient thing to believe, my father said. Keeps the fires burning, but it can't be strictly true, can it?

John detected the challenge in my father's voice, and at that moment recognized that my father felt some warmth toward Albert.

I'd wager that by any standard, he's the same man he's always been, John said. Eats at the same diner every day. Talks about the same damn things he always talked about. His core hasn't been affected a bit.

Well, now you're talking about the soul, my father said. That's above my pay grade.

How often? John asked.

Sorry? my father said.

To the shrink. You.

Oh, my father said, laughing. Three. Three sessions a week.

That's the spirit. Don't let them get you in there every day. It's not *your* day job. Five days a week and you'll never get cured.

Let's say I'm in semi-retirement, then.

Your idea or the shrink's?

To go to three a week? Mine.

Bravo. He's dependent on you, not the other way around. Just make that your mantra and you'll survive.

Spoken like an old pro.

Trained courtesy of the Albert Caldwell Foundation for Assholic Children. John tugged at his scarf. So how'd he do?

My shrink?

My old man. On the test.

Some weeks better than others. The last couple of times, though. Not so great.

He's still sharp in a lot of ways, you know, he knows how to cover, John said.

I know.

Have you noticed he'll get polite when he doesn't know what you're talking about? Nice change of pace. So maybe there's an upside.

How old are you? my father said.

Thirty-one.

He moves like an old man, my father thought, especially when he talks about Albert.

My father said, When I agreed to proctor the evaluation, he gave me a packet of mimeographed sheets and a letter. He told me to hold on to the letter until he failed the test. So I did. Then, last Monday, he failed it, so I went upstairs to my place and got the letter. I don't know what it said, but he told me we were done.

Done as in don't come back?

Yes, my father said.

Hm. Mostly dates of naval battles, I assume, the questions?

Family dates. Other highlights. But mostly family.

Like what?

What year he made partner. What year he got married. That sort of thing.

What other family questions? John said.

Names. Dates of birth.

Date of death?

My father blinked. Yes. Of course. That was the only question that mattered.

How long has this been going on?

About a year. I'm a quarter through the stack of mimeos. I don't know if that meant he thought he'd last longer.

You know the important dates.

I suppose.

Okay. So at this point you're a more reliable family historian than my father.

If an encyclopedia's better than a novel, maybe.

And what's the most important date? John asked. If there was any challenge in his voice, my father didn't hear it. He heard only genuine curiosity.

The day your son died, my father said.

An important question.

Yes, my father said. When I said it was the only one that mattered, I mean it was the only one that mattered. None of the other questions counted toward the final score.

Only the last one.

And he never missed it?

No.

Not until the last time?

That's right.

So that letter, John said.

Instructions to himself, I suppose, my father said, and he understood that John had reached the same conclusion, the only possible conclusion, and he watched the younger man with apprehension. What had he done?

I'm sorry, my father said quietly, as though he couldn't bring himself to speak so useless a sentence.

That's what they say. John cleared his throat.

How could any person survive it? my father thought. If you're young, maybe you have a chance, by the grace of ignorance. You're young and you think, Maybe I can go on, maybe I can persevere and fight my way out of the grief, and by some accident of memory if I live long enough the images will fade and . . . But of course you can't. This is a thing that's inscribed on your bones. An old man knows you can't.

He thought it was his fault, my father said.

I know, John said. So you think he's trying to make amends?

In his way.

It's too late for him to do the honorable thing, John said.

I don't know that honor has anything to do with it, my father said.

He was three and a half, John said. He tipped onto his left haunch and reached around to his back pocket. Oh god, no, thought my father.

He looked at the vending machines and tried to will them to explode. Please, god, no. John took out his wallet and flipped it open, dipped his fingers inside, and extracted the photo, the one that he himself could not bear to look at. He held it up so my father could see it. Among the limited benefits of my father's solitary profession was a conviction, arrived at through years of probing the dark matter within himself, that a person with a story always wants to tell it.

It was a benefit because, as uncomfortable as other people made him, as soon as he realized everyone else was dying to blab, he never had to do anything but ask questions. It was amazing what people would tell you. No matter how sorrowful, no matter how shameful, all stories lie in wait of a sympathetic ear. But he didn't want to hear this story.

The mechanism my father engaged to keep from bursting into tears was complex. He tried to summon up the vampire Saltwater, the one who sucked at the ripe neck of humanity in the name of fiction, but he wouldn't rise. That character, so familiar, had no place here. There was nothing sinister about lending John his ear, nothing parasitic about one person listening to another, enacting the old communion that had kept humanity glued together for millennia. When would he let go of this idea of himself as a menacing force? The job was certainly easier if he only pretended to shoulder the burden, but in the end he took the burden anyway, no matter what he told himself, not because he was a saint but because he was nothing more than a man who could not resist the ache of empathy.

We were in Florida, John said.

My father wanted to bolt. He had to get out of there.

My mother and father had a place down on the Gulf, John said, and we were all there together. My sisters and their families. My wife. Our little boy.

My father stayed put.

22.

He knew the story. He'd heard it two years earlier, a glass of Cragganmore in his hand, which he had, midway through, put down out of respect for Albert, who was gripping his own two-handed, fingers laced tight. My father had felt that the act of cradling his own drink, as if in the expectation that he might be moved to sip from it in response to a ribald comment or in a moment of contemplation, conveyed a sort of casual hope, an expectation of entertainments to come. Yet any deviation from the gruesome tale Albert was relaying was inconceivable. So he'd set his glass down on the coffee table, a monstrous mistake, one he recognized almost immediately, and his eyes fell back again and again, gazing at it with increasing urgency, thirsting for a gulp of erasure, but unable to make himself pick it up.

In 1963, Albert had purchased a house in Sarasota. Four bedrooms, pool, a wedge of private beachfront, a low, long modernist slash set into the white sand with palm trees for shade and bougainvillea crawling along the fence. It was penicillin for the gray New York winter.

I bought it for Sydney, Albert said. So I told myself. We'd taken a vacation down there, just the two of us, winter of '62. Had quite a time. We were like kids again. I had an agent on the phone the day after we flew home. Signed the papers in April. A little temperance on my part might have been in order, but it was as if I were under the influence of some kind of drug. Only time in my life I've let passion get the best of me.

We enjoyed that house immensely. When there was no moon, it was as dark as pitch, and the frogs sang all night. Like paradise. The winter of '73, John and his wife had been there for a few days, and their boy was with them, of course. He was three, quite a talker. And at the age where they collect absolutely everything. He had his little pail filled with shells and dead bugs, scraps of plastic, whatever he came across. He could barely carry the damn thing by Tuesday. It was a Tuesday when Tracy and Filomena got there with their families. I can't remember my own name sometimes but I can tell you it was a Tuesday.

Albert was affectless. His voice didn't waver. The story came out of his mouth as evenly as a kite string unspooling into the sky. Why would I expect histrionics? my father thought. These things happen every day.

As if to answer him, Albert said, Normal Tuesday. That's the bitch of it, of course. There's a pleasant breeze, and the pleasant breeze doesn't stop blowing. The palm trees keep swaying, the waves keep breaking. You hear the cars out on the road, and of course the people inside are carrying on with their lives as if nothing has happened. Their day is a normal day. Go to the beach, take a nap, make a sandwich. And for a moment or two, you yourself don't know that anything has changed. The event has taken place, yet you still occupy your happy place among the unwitting.

There was no signal, no sign. I don't believe in omens, Albert said. Convenient answers to thorny questions.

My father nodded.

Everything that's gone wrong with this country boils down to convenience. And the first convenience is superstition, Albert said.

He paused to consider the clock on the mantel.

This will all go, he said. I'll lose all of it. The ability to reason, the ability to make a convincing argument. I've seen it. It all goes, and it goes in a horror. At the end you're just holes for food to go in and out of.

He paused again to look at the clock.

It was boiling out. We had the air on and the doors were closed. We were inside, he said, just on the other side of the sliding glass doors. Fil had made a recording of John at some festival or another, and she'd put it on the reel-to-reel. Fil was very supportive of his singing. She and Tracy were his protectors, his biggest fans, of course, as older sisters will be. And there's John, in the middle of this, like a king on his throne. Now, you lose sight of your child, you don't hear him playing, you wonder where he is, don't you? You wonder where your child is. Wouldn't you wonder where your child is?

I suppose so, my father said.

That clock, Albert said.

My father turned to look at it.

It was a gift, but I can't remember who it was from. Now, I focus my mind on retaining the details of that day and I still have them. He tapped the side of his head. Not for long, though. Not for long.

A death certificate, he said, requires classical precision. It puts one in the mind of those little monks at their desks, toiling over their Latin manuscripts, don't you think? Wet-drowning. Asphyxia. The language, I'm talking about. This is an area that would appeal to you, I'd think.

My father made a plaintive gesture.

I went to the—to see the body. I went to the. Goddamnit. Good poets read medical texts and good doctors read poetry. Isn't that so? Isn't that what they say?

Sounds plausible, my father said.

Plausible, Albert sniffed. Indeed. A plausible thing to say. I won't mind losing the proper names for things, not as long as I can still imagine the thing itself. You're not one of those neoliberal bed wetters who believes that without the word to describe it, the thing evaporates? Disciple of high priest Chomsky? You're not a member of that faction, are you?

Oh, I don't think so, my father said.

Yes, I wouldn't have taken you for one of those. The conceptual—that's what worries me. I'll lose the abstractions and I won't even know what I've lost. I saw this happen to my father. At first you can't call up the words for things. That's just forgetting someone's name. You can still carry on a conversation. The name is lost in the clouds, so what? But losing time—my father's comprehension of time vanished and just like that, he was an empty body. His ability to remember numbers, gone. Ability to *understand* numbers, gone. Once that went, he was a different

man. Really quite something. At first all the grudges and the old ha-
treds that were the fiber of his being rose to the surface. He was a holy
terror for a year or so. And then they fell away. Just vanished. He lost
all shame. He was an open book, guileless, like a child. A completely
different man.

Morgue. Morgue. I forgot it for a moment there, but now I've found
it. Signal of what's to come. But that's all it is. A signal. Not a crippling
symptom, not yet. Your parents are both dead?

My father was taken by surprise. Sorry? he said.

Your mother and father? Dead?

My father saw the clear outline of the litigator across from him.
Yes, he said.

And you've not lost a child of your own?

No.

You grieved for your parents?

Yes, I did. Of course I did.

Can you imagine that grief expanded to encompass the known
world, so that no part of the world, no building, no act, no mountain,
no facet of language or scientific fact, is not consumed within that grief?

My father held Albert's gaze.

Sound plausible? Albert said. Now I have your attention, don't I?
Well, there you have it. Nothing, absolutely nothing, lures your eye
away from the dead child. I was ten feet away. A pane of glass. A sliding
glass door. The house was mine. The swimming pool was mine. It was
as much my fault as anyone's. More my fault, in fact.

My father started to speak.

Let's skip the attempts to convince me otherwise, all right? Albert
said. Let's be men about this.

My father raised his right hand in surrender. He still couldn't pick
up his drink. Why was that?

I will not, Albert said, enter into the state of blissful ignorance that
ate up my father at the end of his life. I refuse. If there is moral recti-
tude left in this world, it exists in the form of action. Any fool can speak.
Anyone can make a claim. My compact with my family, and with my
grandson, does not allow me to absolve myself of my role in his death.

From here on out, my sole function on this planet is to live as long as possible with his memory, and with the memory of that day. When I can no longer remember it, I am done.

You've been diagnosed? my father asked.

I have.

There must be drugs.

None. Nothing reverses the deterioration. I knew this already. I didn't need a doctor to tell me.

But isn't it possible that you're under the influence of that deterioration already?

Of course. But I've been to Hopkins, I've seen psychologists at Columbia and City. I have affidavits—signed and notarized—confirming that I am of sound mind. Minor memory impairment. All done under the auspices of drawing up a final edition of my will, of course.

Ah, my father said.

In my father, Albert said, it took a decade. A slow, degrading march through a swamp that became deeper and deeper until it had closed over his head. The old bastard deserved worse still, but it wasn't pleasant. He fell apart like an old house. A shutter came unhinged here, the foundation cracked there. They say there is no standard progression. It can be quite swift. But it seems that nature prefers to drag it out. In my case, too many variables to make an accurate prediction, they tell me. They're obviously worried if they get it wrong I'll slap them with a malpractice suit. But two years. I heard from all of them, at one point or another, two years, so I know they've identified a common marker, even if they're too careful to stake their bank accounts on it. They did, however, put their good names behind my current state of sanity.

Two years, my father said.

A death sentence.

And you're—your state of mind . . . my father said.

Am I frightened? Yes, yes, it comes with the territory. Here's the thing, Erwin. You're trustworthy, at least as trustworthy as any man can be. More to the point, you have no reason to wish me any harm.

Well, I don't suppose so, my father said. I have the feeling you're about to tell me why I should think otherwise.

No. Beyond the occasional glass of scotch, we are unconnected. We're acquaintances, wouldn't you say?

That's accurate, my father said.

I wouldn't think of asking your assistance if I couldn't offer something of equal value in return.

Have you asked me for assistance? my father said.

I am about to.

Aha, my father said. He eyed his drink.

I don't mean to sound melodramatic, but our secrets shape us, Albert said. They give us form. Without them, we'd be perfect, smooth creatures. Angels, or something like them. But it's by these distensions that we identify ourselves. By the time you're my age, you're bulging with secrets. And the odd thing is, we desire nothing quite so much as to divulge our secrets. We *want* to give away the very things that make us individuals. I've never reached a satisfactory conclusion as to why. Do you have any idea?

My father didn't have to think about it, though he made a face that communicated that he was thinking on it, when in fact he was thinking not on Albert's conundrum but on the larger question of why Albert, the pragmatist's pragmatist, had suddenly thrown a philosophical proof onto the table. My father had, of course, spent decades thinking on the very matter of what we kept to ourselves and what we didn't. He couldn't have agreed more with Albert's assessment of the human predicament.

In most cases, it's a selfish morality that keeps us from divulging them, my father said. A fear of losing our moral rank in the eyes of those people whose opinions we value.

That's not a bad thought, Albert said. I've never believed morality to be anything more than a trap to save us from our worst impulses—and a badly designed trap, at that. It's nothing more than weights and balances, each life assigned poundage, and the heavyweight always wins. Christ himself, the prince of morality, salvation of all mankind, could have been talked out of it under the right circumstances. Tack Mother Mary up there on the cross and tell the Son of Man to recant if he wants his mommy down. How could a moral man refuse? So your argument is interesting, but I think there's more to it than mere morality. The urge to protect a secret is self-preservation. We lose ourselves when we lose our secrets. The wonder of it, from where I'm sitting, is that I don't have to know what your secret is, for example, to use it against you. All I have to do is let you know that I recognize its presence within you.

You recognize its presence within me? my father said.

Hm, Albert said. Most people want to live in a state of suspension, a balance between concealing and divulging, because it's when we're out of balance that we experience . . . problems.

My father nodded and said, That seems—

Plausible? Albert said, hacking out a laugh.

Yes, plausible, my father said.

Thus, we conceal this and divulge that, constantly trying to find the right balance. The whole of Western culture is built on secrets. What's the church but a pharmacy selling the sickness around back and the cure out front? What a relief the thief feels when he finally confesses the crime! We need to conceal first so that later we might divulge, do you see? Who was Dorian Gray but a man who merely delayed the inevitable confession? We crave confession—and we crave everyone else's secrets, too. Surely in your line of work you know this to be true. What's a novelist but a man who turns loose his private thoughts in a public arena?

I suppose that's one interpretation, my father said.

Or is a novelist a man intent on throwing a blanket over his most private thoughts? All right, a different profession, then: psychiatry. I have spent a mint on psychiatric care for my children. Who knows what they've told those hacks? The girls swear it's life-altering. They've even suggested that I try it. Can you imagine me—me?—on a couch, divulging my secrets to some little man in glasses with a notebook in his lap? I'm too old to excise my essential nature. I am the shape of those unspeakable things I've done, and I do not, at this late stage, have any desire to change that shape. I've explained my reasoning. My obligation is to remain static. My obligation to my grandson.

I understand, my father said.

I imagine you are familiar with the practice of psychiatry.

I am.

Has it changed *your* life? Albert said.

Come on. That's how children talk, my father said. At best—at best—it allows you to admit your own secrets to yourself.

So you're on speaking terms with your secrets.

I have them around for poker every Thursday.

Hm, Albert said. You confess those secrets to your psychiatrist?

My father's eyes narrowed ever so slightly. Psychologist. No. Not all. Not a terribly effective therapy, I'd say.

He's not there for gossip, my father said.

Does it do the job, though? Does it protect you from the fears that keep you from crossing the street alone? What about the elevators? Does it protect you from those?

My father finally picked up his drink.

Even if I didn't see you out there, Albert said, gesturing toward the window, cowering at the street corner like some mental patient who's afraid winged lions are about to swoop down from the sky, I'd know. Your deformity is obvious.

None of us live in a state of grace, Albert.

You'll get no argument from me there. Come on, now, have another drink. Have I offended you in some way? Certainly you don't think your phobias are some sort of secret. God, man, you practically wear them on a sign around your neck. You're a wreck of a human being, Erwin.

And I can't argue with that, my father said.

I'm no different, Albert said. At least you might get better. I'll only get worse. My condition will turn me into a drooling idiot. Which leads me to my proposal. I would like to chart its progression. In exchange for your help, I think we can make productive use of my condition. I believe I might be able to help you with whatever dreadful thing has made you into . . . this.

By all means, don't spare my feelings, my father said.

Whatever transgression you've locked up within yourself, it's turned you into a creeping bug of a man. What if I could help you shake it loose? Give it a shove and see what happens to it in the light of day?

You're a charmer, Albert. But what if there's no mystery? Maybe there's nothing more than good old child abuse at the root of my problems.

No, Albert said in a tone without menace. No, it's not that. You're suffering for your own actions. You've done something terrible.

My father did not answer him.

Have you ever considered what it would be like to speak that shameful secret aloud to another person?

I don't need the sales pitch, my father said. What is it you want me to do?

I'd prefer that this be an equitable arrangement.

I'll consider your offer. But tell me what you want me to do for you.

I'd like you to administer a test. Once a week.

To chart the progression of the disease, my father said.

Correct.

Your daughters can't do it?

I don't want my family involved. They'd either be feeding me the answers or weeping uncontrollably. They wouldn't be able to help themselves. I need an impartial judge. And, frankly, you don't seem like you have any trouble keeping things to yourself. Your—whatever you call them. Phobias. Neuroses. They're all the evidence I need. In return, as payment, I'd like to suggest that as my memory fails, I might serve as your confessor. At a time of your choosing, you can speak your secrets to me, in whatever detail you like. And you'll be assured that I'll have forgotten them by the time you've gotten home.

It's a novel idea, my father said.

I'm told it's liberating, relieving oneself of the burden, Erwin.

You're selling me the cure?

I haven't spent my life in courtrooms without learning a thing or two about a man's conscience.

No one's ever accused me of having one of those, my father said. Why don't you have a neurologist administer the test?

A neurologist would want clinical justification, and they'd just put me in front of some standardized test, anyway. More importantly, a neurologist would inform my family, and that can't be allowed.

And why don't you just write up a multiple-choice test and grade it yourself?

You don't think that's my preference?

So?

Have you listened to anything I've said? When the mind starts to go—when it's hurtling downhill faster than I can run—I won't be able to keep the schedule. I won't remember to stay within the time limits. I don't trust that I'll even remember to do it in the first place. I need an interrogator.

I see, said my father.

I am your way out, Albert said. I will be the bottomless hole you can pitch your transgressions into. You can confess the sin without confessing the sin.

Why don't I just go down to the coma ward and tell a vegetable? my father said.

You know that won't work, Albert said. You need a living, breathing, conscious human being to react. You need the *reaction*. If I am horrified, if I am shocked by the depths of your depravity, then you'll know you've told the truth. You'll have dug right down to the root.

I'd rather you just give me a six-pack and thank me for my time.

That's an option. But out of balance.

Because you need commitment that goes beyond my desire to do a good deed.

Yes.

And once you've reached a state of incapacitation and I tell you all my little secrets, then what?

Not complete incapacitation. Incipient incapacitation. When I reach the cusp of forgetting my grandson's death and my role in it, that's where we end.

And then what? my father said.

Then your work will be done. The weekly tests will end.

For Christ's sake, Albert. And *then* what?

Then I'll shuffle off this mortal coil. Clear enough? You'll be legally protected, if that's what you're worried about. If I behave in an unusual manner after the evaluation period ends, you'll have nothing to concern yourself about. You'll have done nothing more than proctor a test.

Oh, for Christ's sake, Albert. You can't be serious.

Albert shrugged. Arguably, it's the only sane decision available to me. And you have the stomach for this sort of thing. I know that much, he said.

My father looked back at him.

Generally, you hear that boys aren't a gentle species, Albert said. Girls are more perceptive, even when they're small. You know this. Your daughter's a sharp one. But my grandson didn't fit the mold. He was small—even for a little boy, he was small. And he was gentle. I don't know that he would have been able to make his way in the world. You worry about children when they show no inclination toward cruelty, don't you? You think, How will they survive? We had little talks, he and I, about dolphins and starfish. His very existence was steeped in innocence. For me to do less than attend to his memory in this way . . . I might as well piss on his grave.

Albert said, At the very end, after *he* became an innocent, my father went through one final transformation. He became an animal. Raving, calling out to phantoms, throwing punches at anyone who came near him, and two seconds later wailing like a lost lamb, holding his arms out, begging for us to embrace him. Save me, he'd cry. Save me! Then, just before he died, he became peaceful. The demons vacated his sorry corpus and left behind nothing but an empty sack.

I understood, eventually, that all along he had been concealing wild terrors of the mind. Some kind of waking nightmare, fighting to understand what before him was real. It was night; he slept; he woke; it was night again. Or was it? Surely divisions between day and night dissolved. His existence made as much sense as in a dream. He had no past and no future. There was a dinner roll on the plate, and then there was not. Had he eaten it? His wife was by his side, and then she was not. Where was his wife? Who was she, for that matter? His own being was mutable, a pappus pushed this way and that by the breeze, rising and falling, a being of immaterial lightness, an observer without sentience. I know what the end holds, Albert said. Oh yes.

Until the very end, Albert worked to maintain his ability to slip in and out of that day in Florida, and he experienced his memory of it with unusual lucidity. He heard the water that ran up over the coping in sloshing jolts and hit the concrete with a chirping sizzle. He smelled the billowing chlorine and the concrete. The wind that day was onshore, holding back the gnats, but the horseflies had come in powerful numbers and there were a couple of their finely figured bodies floating near the skimmer port. Tad, Tracy's husband, was in the water. Through the glass he had seen the distended shape refracted on the surface and shot through the sliding door. His drink, iced tea, was on the counter where he had left it. That was his way, controlled, steady even in the nexus of a storm. He had been a football player at North Carolina, a massive man, the embodiment of everything John was not and so desperately wished to be. Useless miracle, Tad had trained as a paramedic in the off-season.

Tad's mass had set the water rolling over the coping, where it was in rhythmic recoil by the time Albert, with the rest of the family, emerged, the concrete dark, the humid sear of hot chlorine everywhere. Tad had the boy clutched to his chest and he was plowing through the water toward the steps. He emerged from the pool, the water shredding in white channels around his legs. Tad could tell by the way the boy's weight dragged through the water there was nothing to be done. That knowledge didn't slow him because it was not a conscious thought—it was something he knew as he knew his own body's balance point, and he was not aware that he was struggling against his own animal under- standing as he laid the boy down on the concrete and put his mouth on the boy's mouth, pinched the boy's nose with pressure enough to close the nostrils, but gently because, again, without conscious thought, Tad meant not to cause the little boy any pain.

Albert had cultivated the ability to become Tad. That is, he could imagine himself in Tad's body, his lips on the boy's, the fear and anguish in his massive chest. He could inhabit in the same way, as in a dream, Tracy, Sydney, John, Fil, her husband, Skinner, their daughter, Beatrice. He could inhabit the boy's mother. The boy. The boy, mesmerized by the strange skin of the water, the winking reflection of the sun. A horse-fly riding the surface, and his frustration at not being able to reach the insect as it flicked its wings, his arm stretching, knees on rough concrete, the enclosure of the water as he tipped in and sank. The weird, not-unbeautiful moment of descent. Then the larynx snapping shut, the heart still beating normally, the brain, unperturbed, dawdling for a few more seconds. Then panic, a child's panic, which is not fear of death but fear of separation from his mother, and he cries Mama, the water flooding into the esophagus, forcing the larynx into spasm, the trachea sealing off, oxygen level dwindling, the painful astringency of inhaling chlorinated water, the larynx pulling down yet more water, great gulps of water, the little hands seeking purchase, grasping at the cool liquid, thrashing, finding nothing to hold on to but water until it is over, his life is over. The boy hangs there, suspended above the bottom of the pool, and no one sees him. His blond hair spreads in a corona around his head. The surface of the water is smooth. The spirit leaves the body, and the body becomes a place as serene as deep space, and as cold and airless, a place of acute absence.

For Albert, it was a sharper punishment to plunge into the memory chest of the grieving mother, to sit in the discord of her inner sanctum, to hear nothing but the accumulated voices of the world's every farewell echoing off the walls. At battlefronts, on train platforms, beneath hotel awnings, in airports, at prison gates, at hospital beds, across courtrooms, at gravesides. They resonated endlessly in languages known and unknown, Xhosa mixing with Giligudi, an Irish fisherman's watery cry as he is pulled to the bottom of the North Atlantic, the Chinese miner's to his family, scribbled on a cigarette package after the cave-in, the slave's grievous, unspoken farewell to her children at the auction block. And not all tragedies. In balance and provocation, the tossed-off seeya as a roommate leaves for class, a see-you-in-a-minute run to the corner for cigarettes and milk, the paratrooper's truncated Geroniii— as he hurtles away from the jumpmaster.

They mock her, Albert thinks, these farewells, all of the.. ... It's torture. There's a keening beneath the collective din, an.. ...at's her voice. She, after all, could not say farewell, becaus⟨ the b⟩ ⟨e⟩ver left. He was right there, wasn't he, right beside her chair, arranging his stuffed animals in a row, speaking through them the concerns of his day. But no, he was not there. She'd failed to watch over her own son. Until the day of her own death she will call out that animal wail. Awake, asleep, she will never be without the sense that she's left it undone, that the most essential part of herself is lost, drifting, stranded on an ice floe carried out to sea on the tide. A cliché? They exist to make horrors like this comprehensible.

Bronwyn was a good girl, trustworthy, and lost in the way of all Californians who abandoned that coast's optimism for the great soldiering-on of the granite-willed East. She and John had gotten married in July 1968. She had a broad, substantial face that Albert liked. He approved of her shapely body, sharp mind, the unadorned beauty that wasn't exactly innocence, but related. He saw what attracted John—the same thing that had attracted him to Sydney. Neither of them put up with any bullshit, and he could see that Bron kept John in check. He was erratic, an easy mark for provocateurs, a peculiar and dangerous characteristic for a New Yorker to possess. When introduced to Bron, Albert had recognized the iron will immediately. They carry it in their shoulders, women like that. There was a drunkard father back in California, or a dead mother, a brood left to fend for itself, something along those lines, and Bron would have been their protector. As it turned out, neither death nor drink had shaped the girl—it was the other thing, success, a father who had worked hard, provided for his family, prospered, and a mother who commanded equal respect, and exuded a sunniness that seemed to endlessly billow up from within her. Albert was as stupidly misled about his daughter-in-law as he was about his own son. It was a father-in-law's hopeless enchantment with the girl who he feels is at least in part his own, part daughter, part lover, and who, in turn, should adore him back.

Her family was physically imposing. That was what you noticed first. When Albert and Sydney had taken the Breckenridges up on their offer to spend Christmas at their home on the Russian River, Albert felt as though he'd walked into a hallucination. The house, built from the ground up by Bron's father and her brothers, was scaled to their maple-sized frames. The kitchen counter hit Albert high on the rib cage; Sydney, attempting to safely deliver a plate into the depths of the industrial-sized porcelain sink, had to stand on her tiptoes. The stairs were something from an acid trip, and although the furniture had been purchased in the world of standard sizes, the beds, four-posters built from wood cut on the property, each post a tree itself, bark intact, required visiting mortals to use step stools. Getting down in the dark for a midnight piss was a dangling, toe-waggling descent over the cliff's edge. The bed was itself easily large enough to host a family of five. The damn robes were on hooks six and a half feet off the bathroom floor, and when he put one on it covered him like an evening gown.

They were a hardy, sporting family whose quail and venison graced the dinner table and whose basement had been strung with bulbs of elk sausage. Hemingway had been a guest at the cabin, as they called the five-bedroom fortress, and the thirty-aught-six he had shipped to Roland in gratitude hung over the mantel. A wooden plaque identified its provenance: Papa.

And they were, it turned out, supremely Christian. Theirs was an unfamiliar practice to Albert, his own exposure having run to the darker end of the spectrum, and he dismissed their rosy outlook as unserious, a child's version of the faith, and their admiration for John's accomplishments, their genuine wonder not just at the amplitude but at the timbre of his *instrument*, as the Breckenridges referred to it, was an extension of that unserious worldview in which things were good or bad, beautiful or ugly, and complaisance masked an unchecked and vicious insistence on the rightness of their attitudes.

He and Sydney had spent three nights there before returning to San Francisco where Albert had client meetings. Mornings on the hunt; afternoons engaged in outdoor sportsmanship; and every night after dinner, Bron's mother had insisted on a song. John, Albert noticed, displayed none of the formality or reticence with his in-laws that defined communication with his own parents, and he would rise with a broad grin and walk to the hearth of the fireplace as though it had been constructed for the express purpose of his performance. Such was parenthood; you instilled the ideals that caused them to reject you. So be it.

The last night Albert glimpsed the true source of his son's pride, however. Instead of watching his son sing, Albert watched his daughter-in-law listen. She was enraptured, red-cheeked, face upturned to John as he lilted through a lied, her fingers clasped in her lap as though attempting to form a cage over the orgasm no doubt building in her wet little snatch. So that's it, Albert thought, and he reclined in the enormous leather chair and folded his hands over his belly, satisfied at his discovery, a tidy explanation of his son's good humor, his voice just another trick for getting laid. Of course the ruddy-faced Breckenridges couldn't see the truth, living as they did in the benevolent glow of their happy Jesus and his tum-tumming Negro band. Just remember it's the same Christ who smiles down on my son's bare ass while he pounds away at your little girl, Albert thought.

That day in Florida, it had fallen to Albert to phone Roland and Gerta Breckenridge. In the even, gray-flannel tones he'd have used with a client, he explained to the silent line that the little boy had fallen into the swimming pool that afternoon, efforts had been made to revive him, but he had been pronounced dead at the hospital. Roland had asked to speak to his daughter but Albert had said she'd been sedated and wasn't able to come to the phone. Roland asked to speak with John. Albert called his son over. John took the phone and walked with it through the nearest open door, which happened to lead to the bathroom. He'd yanked the cord in behind him and closed the door. Caldwell did not hear the light switch. His son remained in the bathroom for half an hour, and when he emerged said only that the Breckenridges would arrive the next day.

Together the two families flew with their terrible cargo to New York. They buried the boy. Roland and Gerta took their daughter back to California. She returned to New York only to appear at the divorce proceedings.

Sydney was dead within a year, like something from Shakespeare, killed by grief. Her heart broke: an arrhythmia. A failed surgery and she was gone. Gone before that, though.

And in the end, an unnatural state of existence, an inversion of the order of all things, the earth in orbit around the moon, rivers flying into the sky, hoary old Albert Caldwell living on, Sydney and the little boy cold in their graves.

For all their days together, Sydney had been his shepherd, unflappable, coaxing out conversation with her good humor, but after the boy's death, even she had been silenced. Tracy and Fil had retreated to what comforts they could find in their own families, John to his catastrophe. Albert's dinners with Sydney were concertos of silverware on porcelain, resonant mastication. He had already formulated the idea that the boy's death was his fault, but it was Sydney's silence that convinced him he was right.

Sydney's airless place was not unlike Bronwyn's, the stones packed tight around her chest. The frantic gasping for shallow breaths. The wild, hair-tearing agony of white pain that, like a nuclear flash, blotted out everything else with its light. Albert wondered what it was about these women that their collapse had to be complete, a total shattering of their psyches?

He would have done well to level the question at himself. What did he think he was doing, implanting his own ineffable sorrows in surrogates so that he might, via the twisted logic of the serial repressive, for once in his life experience his own feelings? Yes, he knew the language for it. Tracy and Fil had hurled it at him often enough, fresh from treatments he'd paid for, his attempt to soothe their spirits the only way he knew how: with money. Yes, that was love, a far better form than he'd been dealt, a demonstrable, calculable, tangible form of love that they so happily consumed, only to turn around and spew bile on him for loving them so callously, so incorrectly. You love us like you love a whore, Fil said to him at dinner one night not long after she and Tracy had graduated college.

You don't love a whore, Albert responded between bites of game hen.

What did I expect? Fil said. It's a trap. Everything is a trap with you.

If you don't want the money, don't take it, he said. You're an adult now. You can choose.

And if I choose not to? Fil said. What will you have on me then?

Then I'll have done my job.

Your job as a parent was not limited to paying whatever bills I incurred for the first eighteen years of my life. Can you even comprehend that?

Well, more than eighteen, wouldn't you agree? You'll see, Albert said, still scooping food into his mouth.

I'll see what? How easy it is to buy off my own kids?

Albert put down his fork, folded his napkin, and left the table, and later he'd hand-delivered the rent check for Fil's apartment in the West Village.

Daddy, she said, this is the whole problem.

I don't see a problem, he said.

She'd taken the check.

John would never take anything from him. Went to college on scholarship, Juilliard the same. Worked to pay rent. Insisted on his independence even though he lived only three blocks away. Albert had found out after the boy died—John as unwilling to take his money then as ever—that he and Bronwyn had been accepting money from *her* parents all along. Well, let him come begging now that the river's gone dry, Albert thought.

It was an accident, my father said to Albert. Your presence at the scene of an accident doesn't qualify you for the torments of hell. Is this Dickens? A plot you cooked up when you realized you were going to lose your mind, just to keep things interesting? It's absurd.

Albert absorbed my father's words with a placid, almost bored expression on his face. You're afraid, Albert said.

There's certainly something for me to be afraid of, isn't there? my father said. You kill yourself and I go to jail?

Oh, let's be men about this. You know I won't allow that. You're afraid, Albert said, because it would require you to modify your ethical model. I'm proposing a return to the old, vengeful gods. A life for a life.

Albert stole a glance at the clock, then resituated himself in his chair. You're afraid that if you go along with me, you will have to hold yourself to the same standard. Isn't that it? You have a pragmatic reason to fear my plans. These phobias of yours, your fear of the world itself, they all come from whatever unspeakable act you committed. What was it, I wonder? What could have been so terrible that you have sacrificed your sanity to make amends? We're actually in agreement here—you might not know it, but we are. You believe in a life for a life, too. But you haven't been able to kill yourself, not quite. Why is that, Erwin?

Because I'm a coward, my father said.

Yes, you are, Albert said. Don't you worry about the legalities. I guarantee that you will be amply protected.

I'm sure, my father said.

Before my father left that night, Albert told him a final story: A dirt baseball diamond in Central Park, 1956. John's team in the field, John playing second base, his jersey tucked into his dungarees like all the other boys, smacking his glove like all the other boys. Albert in the passel of parents behind the low fence along third, having walked up from his office on this blazing July day to watch his son, and John a little jumpier for it, but a little lighter on his feet, too, yelling No-Hittah, No-Hittah to the pitcher in the jacked-up voice that possessed them all when their fathers showed. John kept checking, and there he was, in a wool suit, a crisp white shirt and tie despite the crushing heat, his black shoes and hat, there among the other fathers in their shirtsleeves, shirts with their names sewn on the chest, which John, at ten, could decipher, as he could decipher a hat embroidered with a company name above the bill, or wearing the top two buttons of one's shirt open so that the curly hair formed a rude, isolinear wedge, all signals of a lack of fatherly fitness to John, of the working-class slob who sweated for his dough.

Two strikes and a ball into the count, the batter, rattled by the runt second baseman who wouldn't shut the hell up, let fly with a wild swing that bestowed all his animus unto the ball, a line drive that, miraculously, shot like a bullet directly at the loudmouth on second. John almost got his glove on it but his bony thigh took the blow, and the ball dribbled off toward first, where the hitter stood triumphantly with one foot on the bag, his round little fists on his waist.

John was writhing in the dirt. He looked once, twice toward his father, the other fathers turning to each other to make way for the one among them who would step up to the fence, awaiting the signal from the coach, a CUNY kid working at the Y for the summer, to summon him over. The coach crouched down by John and put a hand on him. He looked in the direction of the parents, his mouth open as he scanned the faces, the coach who really just wanted to get on with the game, kids these days go down like goddamn scarecrows, until Albert, despite his best efforts, with a wince of concern exposed himself as the father. Don't be shy, one father said. Man's down, go ahead, another one said. When Albert didn't budge, the others urged him on, gently at first. Once they realized that his unwavering gaze was not stoicism but dissent, they looked to each other. Getta load of this piece of work. Albert saw his son's tear-streaked face, and knew his son could see his face, and he waited for the boy to pick himself up, dust himself off, raise a hand to signal that he was fine. And that's what John did. He shook off his coach's helping hand, got up, limped around in a little circle to try to flush out the throbbing pain, wiped the snot off his nose, smacked the glove with his fist. His chest hitched once as he settled into position, and he held up his glove to the pitcher, who winged the ball to him. John caught it, flipped it back. Attaboy, one of the fathers said.

To occupy his hands, Albert removed his glasses and polished the lenses in slow circles. He was utterly defenseless when his love for the boy rushed forward at him, and he'd erected a high wall to protect John from his ruinous affections. He felt nothing but disdain for the men around him, who were muttering to each other, obviously about him. He hated the wisdom of crowds, the mob mentality, and he believed there was a striking power bestowed upon an individual who could turn against the crowd. Albert intended for his son to see it in practice so that he would better understand the reasoning behind a rebellion of one. To put it in elementary terms his son would understand, he later asked the boy, Do you want to be a milkman or Andrew Carnegie?

No one coddled their kids in those days. No one raised his son to be a musician. You wanted a physician, a statesman. But somehow he'd miscalculated. He'd taught the boy to cut against the grain, to think for himself. John had never come to him for advice because he'd taught him never to ask anyone for advice. Chose his own college, chose his own major, decided to sing, marry the girl, get a divorce—all of it without his father's counsel. News delivered after the fact, all. Once in twenty years did he come to Albert with a question, a real question riddled with confusion and uncertainty and need, real need, for the question was a dreadful one, the answer equally dreadful. Where to bury the child?

In my plot, Albert said.

23.

So my father had heard it all from Albert, but that night at Roosevelt Hospital, he didn't stop John from telling him again. As much as he didn't want to hear it, he couldn't help himself. He needed to hear where the son's and the father's stories diverged.

Before you ask, he'd been christened, John said. Odd, my father thought. Not a question that would have occurred to him. Why would he call John to account over the boy's everlasting soul? He felt outsmarted by the assumption, as though he'd misunderstood some essential part of his own character that was obvious to everyone else. Sorry? he said.

He'd been christened, John said. In Santa Rosa.

I think Albert might have mentioned, my father said, though Albert had not.

I didn't care. Wasn't my idea but I wasn't opposed to it, either. Now it seems like the only good thing I ever did for him. You know what we were doing when he died?

No, my father said without a moment's pause, having made the decision to lie his way through the entire conversation.

Having an argument.

You and your wife? my father said. Divergence one.

Me and my father. He was arguing with all of us. But mainly with me. Money. Always fucking money and why won't I take their money *for my son*, and he's getting nowhere with me so he turns to Bron, who wasn't brought up like this, you know, with all the yelling and threats, and she's near tears as it is, he's got my wife in tears right there in front of the whole family, people she's only known for a few years, people who are practically strangers, and right there in front of my sisters and their husbands and the kids, she hardly knows where she stands with anyone, and the son of a bitch takes the fight to her. To her! Enough, I said, you know? That was it. That was plenty.

And Tracy's married to this guy, hell of a nice guy, a real house of a guy. Played D-one football. She could not have found a better man, really, a prince.

This is Tad? my father said, lest he play too dumb.

Yes, that's right, John said. Tad. Really generous guy, big lovable bear of a guy, and he can't stand how my father's treating Bron. He's been on the couch with this look on his face—let me tell you, this look said it all. Here's a man who can do serious physical damage, a person *his* size. A real Southern gentleman, too, so there's that overzealous thing about taking care of women, but it's nothing compared to his respect for his elders, so he's in a spot with my father. Even though you can tell he wants to tear his head off, gentleman Tad holds his ground.

It's funny. Turns out I'd seen him play on TV once. Has that ever happened to you—you meet someone and then much later you cast your mind back and realize that this was someone you had actually seen on TV, or in a play, or whatever? It was the '63 Gator Bowl. And here's one of the stars of the game, sitting on the couch—it's embarrassing, to be honest, to have him witness our wreck of a family. I'm pretty damn sure his family doesn't operate that way. Which is why he's where he is today, and why his brother is where he is—brother's a congressman from Durham, got elected at something like twenty-eight—and why we're all where we are. But finally Tad's had enough. He gets up really slowly and he walks in the direction of the sliding door, probably thinking he'd like to run through it and never look back, and he's holding this sweaty glass of iced tea that looks like a test tube in his hand he's so huge, and there's something about it that's profanely uncomfortable, like it pains him to have to hold this stupid glass and act like a civilized human being in the midst of this insanity. So he sets it down on a coaster and he walks on over to the glass door.

He stands there for a second before he decides to go outside. Completely reasonable reaction. Like I said, he's a real gentleman. He believes in an ordered universe. If he has a fault, that's it, his belief in the system. He's never in his life raised his voice to an elder. Even if my father was wailing away on Trace, Tad would stand aside and swallow it. That's why Southerners are so goddamn passive-aggressive, you know. They have to stand there and swallow it because of the social order, the fucking system. It's bigger than all of them put together. And the system says fathers over daughters and old over young and white over Black, and god almighty over everyone. So for Tad to walk across the room is a display of almost heroic proportions. He's registered his disapproval of his own father-in-law. You see? And for him to actually leave the room, to walk out of the house entirely—you have no idea unless you've met this guy. He's broken with the system. He's taken the only yardstick he has for measuring his self-worth and he's snapped it over his knee. Snapped it just like that, the sense of duty to his family and elders, generations of tradition.

And does my father even notice? Of course not. Doesn't even notice because he's very calmly and logically working on Bron, dissecting her, working his appeal to her as a mother. You know him. You know that when Counselor Caldwell shows up there're going to be bloody chunks on the floor by the time he's done. He's going to get his way, hell or high water, he's going to put the screws to you and by god you'll submit or die. He's appealing to her childhood, her idyllic childhood in Santa Rosa—well, he doesn't know about how idyllic it *wasn't*. It never is, is it? Not with that much good cheer slathered all over everything. Her parents—her entire family—smell like candy apples. Complete con job.

My father listened to John's address thinking that it was a deflection, too polished, a speech worked over in the dark reflection of tragedy. Blame must lie somewhere. Perhaps the son has every right to indict the father. After all, that's the covenant of parenthood, isn't it?

So it was Tad who got to him first, John said. He walked out the sliding door, and like the gentleman he is, closes it behind him. Then he jumped in the pool. I saw him jump. We didn't know what the hell was going on. He'd finally cracked up, you know? Captain America lost his marbles, and it was our family that did it.

I think Trace laughed. She was right to laugh. It was funny. She's thinking he'd done it for comic relief. And she and I walked over to the glass to see what he was going to do next, but he didn't come up. And when he did, he comes out of the water with my son in his arms.

He brings half the pool with him. Like someone dropped a car in. He lays him down on the concrete and he starts to work on him. That's the other part—Tad drove an ambulance for a couple of summers, so he knows what he's doing.

You know, funny thing about Tad, John said. The next morning we're all sitting in the living room and Tad looks at Beatrice—this is my other sister's daughter, Fil's daughter, she's all of eight at the time, she's in complete shock, she's just old enough to understand what's happened—and Tad looks at her and reaches out and takes her hand, and he says, Bea, it's not your fault.

Tad thought he'd done some emotional calculus there that would help Bea out. He was thinking, Bea was the last person who was out by the pool with the boy, and even though that was an hour before, since she'd been out there with him, somehow she would think it was her responsibility, that her child's mind might believe it was her fault for not watching over him. No one had asked her to babysit him. No one would have given her that responsibility. And if you could have seen her face—it obviously had never crossed her mind. She'd never thought for a second it was her fault. No one had. And now, oh boy, that kid's face. Now it *was* her fault. She knows. She's sharp as a razor. So all of a sudden now she's bawling her eyes out, she's wailing and screaming, and Tad's looking around like he doesn't get it—and it's genuine. He really doesn't get it. It's not in him, that sadistic streak. That's my father's stock-in-trade, but it's inconceivable to Tad. He was only trying to help. He's sitting there, he'd been scouring his memory, trying to put together a timeline to explain how it happened, and he keeps getting hung up on one thing, that John and Bea had been splashing around on the pool steps together. And he thinks, Dear Lord, what if this kid thinks it's her fault? One of those things that hits you like a bolt from the blue and leaps out of your mouth, because what if that poor kid thinks it's her fault and she's sitting there silent as a mouse, keeping it to herself, and it's eating her up inside—he's got to let her know pronto that's crazy thinking, there's no way it's her fault, no one would ever think it was her fault.

But, my father said, the truth is, Tad did think it was her fault.

John nodded grimly. And now *she* thinks it's her fault. Beyond a shadow of a doubt. It's been five years, and you look at her now and it's all you see. It's in her forever, and nothing's going to convince her otherwise. She'll never eat cake or ride a horse or make out with a boy without that guilt sitting on her shoulder. She'll for sure never go to sleep without thinking about how it's her fault. Because that's how it works, right? A kid can't make an independent judgment about something that devastating, not the way an adult can. Not even a kid as smart as Bea. Kids are absolutists. With kids it's all or nothing.

Not just kids, my father thought.

The off-duty cop had sauntered over and was leaning against a concrete pillar. You looking for an elderly male? he said.

Albert Caldwell? John said.

The cop had at his disposal a vast arsenal of expressions to convey exhaustion, from existential malaise right up to full physical collapse, and he invoked two distinct efforts then, first a burping sigh, followed by a pinching of eyelids with the thumb and forefinger of his right hand, before saying, I can't confirm. Elderly man, Caucasian.

Yeah, John said.

The cop had a thick brush of a mustache and wild eyebrows, furrows of black hair across the backs of his hands, a shadow of growth along his jawline. He wasn't near retirement, but he'd been on the beat for a while. The gun and the nightstick weren't the sources of his authority.

So maybe this is your guy, the cop said. Vehicular theft. Took off in a cab. His. He lifted his chin in the direction of a sleeping hack melted across an orange plastic chair.

I don't think so, John said. Appreciate the help, but wrong elderly

Caucasian. My father couldn't drive fifteen feet in weather like this without putting the thing onto its roof.

The cop showed signs of life, the briefest inflection of a smile. Definitely the right guy, he said.

What? John said.

He took out a section of retaining wall as he was exiting the property, the cop said, smile widening.

Oh, for fuck's sake, John said.

The cop was chuckling.

Jesus fucking Christ, John said, setting off more life signs in old whiskers.

You're the son? the cop said.

Yeah. So where have they got him?

The cop, now fully awakened from his long winter's slumber, said, Got him? They don't got him anywhere. Stickshift McGraw there made a clean getaway!

He burst into laughter.

But someone's gone after him, or what? John said.

He stole a cab in a blizzard. Where's he gonna go? All the way down to the corner?

He's just out there, then? Out in all that? He's not a well man!

Really? Took out of here like he'd made a full recovery. What's he got?

John looked at my father and said, Everything. Everything that could possibly be wrong with him, is. But I don't even know what they brought him in for because Ratched over there won't tell me shit.

Whatever it is, the cop said, didn't dent the old fighting spirit, did it? He was laughing hard, hat in one hand, dabbing at his eyes with the knuckles of the other. Sweet mother Mary, he said when he regained his composure. So he's a real wildcat, is he? My pop's the same. Can't take your eye off him for a second or he's *pffft*, out the door, out the window, down the fire escape, whatever.

He could be halfway to Ohio by now, John said.

Nah, the cop said. Trust me. He's not going anywhere. GW's closed,

Triborough's closed, and you can't even get north of 90th Street, anyway. The plows are all downtown. He made it three whole blocks, I promise. Go out and look for him. The only reason *that* guy's not looking for him—he nodded toward the hack—is because he knows exactly the same thing I'm telling you. Tomorrow morning, his cab's going to be right around the corner with the keys in the ignition, just waiting for him to dig it out.

So you think my father's out there wandering around in a blizzard? John said.

You sit tight. He'll aim for home. They always do.

You don't know my father, John said.

All right, the cop said with a shrug, whatever you say. Gentlemen, have a good night, he said, and drifted back to his original post by reception.

My mother knew how to deal with him, up to a point, John said to my father.

She ever have to post bail?

Who does this sort of thing? This isn't a mental condition—this is a circus act. It's a circus act he's been training his whole life to spring on us.

He's not in his right mind, my father said.

As ever, John said. Why not just ask for a ride? Why not pay the nice man sitting in the front to drive you to your destination?

Because he's not in his right mind, my father said. If you don't mind my saying, whether or not he's the same man at the core, the fact is, he's not thinking straight. He's not operating rationally.

You seem to have a problem accepting the fact that I've known my father a little longer than you have, John said. He's a bully. He's a bag of TNT. Scares the shit out of people just for fun. You're sitting there in the den watching TV and the next thing you know, he's screaming about Pigmeat Markham and how the country's going to hell in a handbasket. I'll tell you what it was. He was out for vengeance. My whole life he's been out to avenge some wrong perpetrated on him by god knows who, and he's going to teach everyone a lesson along the way, just for good measure. But then Mom dies and he falls to pieces. Like we're supposed to take care of him now? And the sobbing about how everything's his fault? What am I supposed to do there? Tell him it's going to be okay? It's not his fault? Because it is his fault! So if you want to tell me he's got a mental condition that's altering his behavior, I'm not buying. My question is: Where do I go for my vengeance? Where do I get my pound of flesh?

John had turned to face the window near my father, standing at a measured distance so that he could see the double exposure of the lobby projected onto the snowfall, the fluorescent tubing stitched in bright dashes across the surface, his own ghosted face hovering in the foreground. He was muttering to himself, and after a while said, What are we supposed to do now? Wander around out there until we freeze to death? He'd like that. That would please him no end.

Either we go to the Twentieth Precinct, my father said, and wait for someone to bring him in, or we go home and wait.

John looked in my father's direction, intending to respond, but his eye caught something in the distance over his shoulder. My father swiveled his head to see, and John made a sucking sound. Don't! Eyes this way. This way, John hissed.

My father complied by staring again at the coffee machine, his posture comically erect, straining to hear something that might give him a clue what was going on. The intercom chattered over the crackly strains of something classical. On the far side of the expanse, the elevators chimed and the doors clunked open, closed. Slowly, with the deliberate nonchalance specific to a person attempting to draw as little attention as possible to himself and in the process making a real show of his acting chops, my father turned his head in the direction of the elevators.

No, John said. Be still.

John slowly sat down next to him and leaned back until his spine touched the glass.

Are you hiding? my father whispered.

Yes, John said.

It almost worked, but John's pipe, that elegant sine wave between his teeth, gave him away. Having exited the elevator, a cold pack lashed to his forehead by an Ace bandage, and having crossed the lobby toward the coffee machine, the counterman from the Cosmic's poor banged-up brain flashed a sign of recognition, and he opened his eyes wide, wider, and the mouth beneath his eyes shaped a word unvocalized but that my father, having by then no doubt about the source of the threat, unmistakably heard in the echo chamber of his own head: Motherfucker.

24.

Before evacuating to Grand Central for their suburbia-bound trains early that afternoon, Tracy and Fil had caught the IRT uptown to look in on their priest of complaint, dear old Dad, who, mounted upon his throne in the oak-paneled study, received them with the air of stoned inattention a prince might reserve for dignitaries of negligible rank who come grubbing down the embassy receiving line. They'd cleared space to sit among the piles of newsprint and journals on the sofas and taken the pneumatic descent into the ancient cushions, which reeked of cigar smoke. The four-hundred-day clock's pendulum spun and unspun on the mantel. Dust upon dust. The girl was not allowed to clean in here, and he had gotten rid of her anyway, though Tracy and Fil did not yet know it.

That morning he'd given his routines unusual attention. He'd shaved slowly, taking pleasure in the clean lines the razor scored into the cream. His mind had been clear, and he thought for a while on the purity that attended the lifelong practice of a skill, a simple act beatified by decades of repetition. He thought on the perfect unity of windshield wiper blades, the ticking of the rubber as it met the base of the glass. He considered the possibility that men who had lawns to mow might be the luckiest men in the world. They could tame chaos and impose unity in a matter of an hour. Window cleaners, whipping their squeegees in reaping arcs. What a job. To act and see the result right there in front of you. He supposed he'd missed out on the pure good of so much manual labor. The closest he'd come had been in his attention to a properly aligned collar, a properly knotted tie, and what were those things if not the labors of other men that he affixed to his body? All he'd had was the insignificant acreage of his face, which was no longer his but his father's.

The same routines but a newfound sense of significance. He moved intentionally that morning, attuned to the angle of the light, as if a film had been stripped from his eyes while he slept. Nothing rote about today, no. Feels like a court day, closing arguments, every nerve focused on the moment when you'll rise to deliver the oratory. The dread, the fear—it was a panther you were stalking; you allowed it to stalk you, too, you lured it closer, listening for the crackle of a leaf, the tensing of muscle before the death leap, and you kept vigilant, knife out. Routine was your camouflage.

A morning different in other ways. Erica had not cleaned the apartment. One day of the week she was off in the morning, but she straightened up first. No, not today.

And then Saltwater had not come, unusual after so long. It was Monday, yes. But he shouldn't have expected Saltwater, no. The week before, he had failed the test and the avalanche that would end him had slipped loose and begun to build speed.

When Erica moved in, Tracy and Fil's children, in the city for a Sunday afternoon visit with Grumps, had conducted a thorough sweep of her chest of drawers, closet, bed, bedside table, medicine cabinet, and turned up nothing that indicated secret habits or perversions, after which Beatrice, age thirteen, had declared her to be a banality in a world of bores. Bea's own nanny had kept a stubby bottle of olive oil and dog-eared copies of *The Sensuous Man* and *The Sensuous Woman* in her bedside table. Upon examination, both books had turned out to be disappointingly even-toned—educational, even—devoid of throbbing members or diamond-hard nipples. The olive oil, it turned out, was for her elbows and knees. Bores, all. The grandchildren hadn't bothered to go back to Erica's room again.

So it was that the day of the blizzard, wondering where Erica was, and unable to get a straight answer out of her father, Tracy intended to conduct a sweep of her own, though she'd only made it as far as the kitchen. She'd gone back and indicated to Fil that something was up. Fil rose, followed her—Albert tracking her with his eyes but still talking—into the kitchen.

Where are you going? he shouted after they'd left the room. I should address myself to the paintings now?

In the kitchen there were dirty dishes everywhere and bags of trash on the floor. See? Tracy said.

Don't look so happy about it, Fil said.

I'm not happy about anything, Tracy said, though she was weirdly pleased that the evidence was for once so obvious, when everything else with their father was a labyrinth.

Hm, Fil said, crossing back through the dining room, foyer, through the French doors, to her father's desk, where she began rifling through his mail.

Daddy, she said, where's Erica?

Excuse me, Filomena?

Tracy this time: Daddy, where is Erica?

Who in hell is Erica?

The girl who lives here, Daddy. The one who helps you. Long black hair, about yea high?

What are you talking about? How should I know where she is? Albert said, threading his fingers together beneath his chin.

You would be the only one who knows, Daddy.

Of whom are you speaking?

No, Daddy, Tracy said. Not this game.

Albert had to think for a minute. I don't see anyone else here, do you? Ergo, whoever you're looking for is not here, he said.

Daddy, what happened in the kitchen? Fil said.

How should I know? Albert said. The girl handles that.

So, again, Daddy, Fil said. Where's Erica?

I suppose she's no longer in my employ, Albert said.

Is that so? Fil said. According to?

According to her employer, that's who! Albert boomed. According to? According to whom do you think?

Take it down a peg, Daddy. You fired her? Tracy said.

She's not here, is she?

So you don't know what happened to her? Tracy said. Or are you pretending not to know?

Who's the caretaker in this scenario? Albert said. Now I'm supposed to keep track of some fifteen-year-old? You're asking me to speculate on her motivations? How would I know what the hell she was thinking? She made clear that she no longer enjoyed the terms of her employment and I suggested that she exercise her right to leave. She packed up her things and went. She relieved herself of the position. I'm sure she got a better offer.

Daddy, first of all, she's twenty-five, and she would have called me if she had found something else. What did you do to her?

I did nothing.

Bullshit, Fil said. What did you say to her?

What could I have possibly said to her? Albert said. She never listened to me for a second! She was like a cow. A fat, stupid cow with big black eyes, standing in a field chewing cud.

Fil couldn't entirely disagree. There *had* been something harmless in Erica's eyes, to be sure, the cultivated emptiness some girls exchanged for entrance into the world of men, and compared to Bea, who was a decade younger but nursing an adult-sized ulcer, Erica looked positively childish. Her clothes strained at the seams. When she sat, the placket of her shirt gaped between the buttons like little mouths. Her softness was that of a child bulking for puberty, her breasts folds of flesh atop her chest, her chin low, cherubic. She had a pug nose and lips that lacked the thin, adult severity of Bea's. Most of the time it wasn't a cow to which Albert compared her. He thought she looked more like a cartoon of a person than a person, a point she wouldn't have disagreed with. In fact, Erica would have laughed about it. She felt she had yet to take her permanent form. Her body was seeking itself in the birthright passed down from her mother and grandmother, the former a bowling pin, the latter a bag of leaves. No need to worry, you, she told herself. Not yet. In the meantime you do what you can. In a few years the clay would set, but for now she was between states, unsettled, intrigued by her own potential.

It was also true that she was not a superb listener. She was a monologuist, a skill she'd honed while caring for her mute, bedridden grandmother, and her primary subject was the neighborhood outside the Apelles' gates. To Albert's annoyance, she delivered her speeches in the tone of a tourist who, having returned from an expensive trip that had gone wrong in every conceivable way—boat sunk, hotel burned, passport and money stolen—insisted that the experience had been enlightening, even terrific in a way, a real learning experience. He hated her relentless optimism, the flood of naïve revelations about the kindness of the bums on Broadway and the shocking yet wondrous dangers of Riverside Park, the fascinating conversations she overheard when the old Jewish men settled in at the Cosmic's counter for their morning coffee. Oh, what a world, what a world. Albert wasn't shy about telling her to shut up, but given his facility with insult, he was surprisingly polite about it. Perhaps even Albert was softened by her wide-eyed delivery.

Erica? he'd shout. Please?

I know, I know, she'd say. This old mouth!

Like a wet leaf stuck to his shoe. She had gone everywhere with him: to the Cosmic in the morning for his coffee and bagel (she sat separately with her orange juice, scrambled eggs, rye toast), for walks in Riverside Park, to the doctor, to the dentist, to the Y for his twice-weekly swims. She tapped on the door when he spent too long in the head. She was gone for only a few hours on Monday mornings, and when she left, she alerted the doorman, who was under strict orders from Tracy and Fil never to allow their father out of the building alone. He'd had no choice, then, but to get rid of her.

I'm calling her, Fil said, phone in hand.

Please do, Albert said. I have nothing to hide.

Before Erica moved in, Albert spent most of his afternoons in the study, radio tuned to classical WQXR, a box of Cohibas at his elbow, his mind slathered with lust. Christ, it was all he could do not to think of women. Surely this was a side effect of going senile, water pulling back at low tide to expose the dark rippled mud just beyond the pristine beach. He would never have believed that after so many years there'd remain such a stockpile of filth within him, and he resented not having done a better job of depleting it. The midnight erections were not unpleasurable. But his powerlessness during those empty afternoons, voids flooded by an endless procession of rooms, beds, creaking slats, the recurring image of a stateroom on an Atlantic passage, three portholes in the bedroom alone, which hadn't been his (all he'd had to his name then was a shaving kit and a pinstripe suit), and the woman, who had at first been unfathomably old to him, a novelty, a married mother of four, white fissures in the flesh of her belly, and a lush, joyous way of pounding at him with her hips that transmuted the thudding noise from the ship's engine room, ever-present in his own sardine tin of a cabin, so that for years it was impossible not to think of her when he saw a painting of a ship or caught sight of the docks from a cab on the West Side Highway, impossible not to think of pistons, oil, steam. He'd been on his way to England, 1931. There were others. A field in rain, a park at night, the streaking sun on a brilliant white wall, clouds against the blue through a farmhouse window. Another open window, Yorkville, the breeze blowing in—and how there'd been a fan in the room in Italy, it dried the slickness between them and he'd yanked out the cord, yanked the wire right out of the plug, and they'd sweated through to the mattress, the taste of the sweat in her armpits, the rivulets coursing from beneath her breasts, and the moans, the concentrated effort, all his energies focused on the perfect delicate movement, and afterward the sound of the flies knocking stupidly against the ceiling, none of it was lost to him, it all came back in the sagging stillness of the afternoon. Merry revels for an old man in his waning years? Not for Albert, for whom it was all distraction, grease on the lens when he was trying to train his eye on his punishment.

There was an element of mockery to it that enraged him—mockery of his intellectual weakness, his moral decrepitude. He couldn't keep track of what day of the week it was, yet here was the girl he met in Berlin after the war, the light blue veins at the back of her knee, her leg draped so nonchalantly over his shoulder? That was thirty years ago. What was a body worth in those days? They would do it for a tin of beans, and what good was that? Slavery. A depraved, mechanical transaction that conjoined him to a catastrophe of a civilization, the utter debasement that had befallen the German people. A ragged, misbegotten country, deserving of all the malice the world had to throw at it. To fuck one of its daughters was to descend into a rotten, connubial malaise. How could there be such a thing as pleasure in a place like that? The girl had been lifeless as a rag doll, a receptacle to fill with the appropriate part of his own anatomy.

Sadistisch, sadistisch, she'd said. The infantry destroys. It's those who come after, bearing accordion folders and documents, the shaved, pressed, and dressed, who conquer. Berlin, was it? Or Nuremberg? Why was he revisiting these things? What sadist was behind all this? Oh for god's sake, don't pretend it's a punishment. What difference did it make who he thought about—he was nothing but an animal prowling old hunting grounds. No harm in it. They were pictures, not people. And then one day, in the doorway: Erica, as soft around the edges as a blurry photo, yet real, flesh and blood, a beating heart and a compassionate soul. God, how embarrassing, looking at her was like being caught peeping through a hole in the changing room wall, yet he kept catching himself doing just that. A little burst of shock and he'd turn his head, imagining himself to be disgusted. If nothing else, he had his iron will. Once that was gone, he was finished. He'd restrained his hands if not his eyes, and kept his comments to himself, and after she'd been with him a few weeks, the afternoon waters calmed. Sometimes he allowed her to sit in the room with him and read. She absorbed his loneliness, shuffling quietly through her copy of the *Post*, occasionally murmuring in dismay at a bus plunger or a smash-and-grab with casualties, and she made him feel that there was some life yet in the world. All those afternoons before her, his mind had gone to what was available in the archives, but now those memories had been sent back on their wheeled carts. He'd almost become fond of her.

More than fond. I know that he dreamt of being summoned to her room, where she would pull away the sheet and slide down the pillows, her parted fingers reaching for him in supplication, speechlessly beseeching as only someone unhitched from shame could, her body a pool of water for his thirst, her breasts, her belly, the dark saddle between her pliéd legs a feast, her thighs as thick as tree trunks, and she would be murmuring his name, begging for him.

The other memory, the one he meant to tend so carefully, was untethered and would arrive on its own schedule, flagellate him, evaporate, then reconstitute, a time-lapse shot of a cloud on an endless loop. The blue sky, the pool, the body. It came and went like the weather, and because when the memory was gone it left no trace, every time it reappeared it was a fresh pot of scalding water. This was the horror that he did not want to outlive.

When was it that he began to regard his inner life as nothing more than a slightly mysterious facet of his physical being? Love was an ache in the center of his mass. Lust, a hard-on. Sadness was a dragging, salty ache at the back of the throat, an emptiness like hunger. When emotions acted in a disorderly fashion, he put them in a headlock and choked them until they submitted to his will. He shoved them into the sunlight when he felt blue, whipped them when his courage failed, strangled his unmentionable desires, and applied exacting reason in those rare instances when he couldn't force the stubborn beast to correct its course. When confronted with an undeniable truth about himself, a jag in his otherwise linear existence, he reflected the inquisitorial beam back onto his family, his colleagues, whoever happened to be available to lash to the pyre and torch in sacrifice to the gods of self-ignorance. Feelings! Gibberish language, a translation of a translation of a translation, distractions no sane person needed to spend more than the bare minimum of time wrestling into submission. Feelings were a tactic women invoked when they didn't get what they wanted.

So inexperienced in matters of his own heart, he'd barely managed to develop a rudimentary language for the sorrow that came after the boy's death, but then when Sydney died he had to create yet another lexicon of grief, and that was beyond even the great mind of Albert Caldwell.

Someone was slamming cabinet doors in the kitchen. Albert listened, looked around, and waited for his brain to make sense of it. Fil was at his desk, one hand full of unopened mail, the other flipping through the checkbook ledger—platter-sized, three checks per page, green pleather with an embossed gold border.

She'd gotten through to Erica on the phone, but the girl would say nothing more than she no longer needed the work, about as naturally as a hostage reading off a cue card.

Stop bothering my things, Filomena, Albert said. Come back over here.

Daddy, last time. What did you do to Erica?

Albert leveled his eyes on her. I don't remember.

I'll get to the bottom of it, she said. Honestly, Daddy. Look, I've told you not to worry about writing checks.

What are you talking about? Albert said.

Daddy, I pay all the bills. Erica leaves them here for me. She held up the rubber-banded stack of envelopes.

Of course you do. What are telling me not to write checks for? I know full well you've robbed me of every adult responsibility.

Just stop writing checks. I'm leaving you a note here that says, No Checks, okay? And where in the world are you getting these numbers? Two forty-nine to D'Agostino's?

Delivery charge, he shot back.

Daddy, Erica shops with you. You two go to the store on Tuesday and Friday.

I'm fully aware of that, he said. He looked around for Tracy, hoping for confirmation that her sister was behaving unreasonably, but apparently Tracy was the one banging around in the kitchen.

Fil carried over the ledger and laid it in his lap.

What, Filomena, what? he said. I thought I wasn't to write any more checks. Get this off me.

Daddy, look here. If you want to get away with it, you'll need to stop documenting your crimes so carefully. These receipts. This one, and this one. You're too meticulous for your own good.

There it was, handwriting that exactly matched his own. A jolt, as if he'd touched a live wire. He flipped through the stubs.

Fil went back to the desk, opening and shutting drawers until she found what she was after. Good god, Daddy. Here, look. One drawer was packed solid with signed, uncashed checks. You really went on a tear this week, didn't you? Fil said.

Not so long ago he was still trying to mail them, but recently he'd taken to stashing them all over the desk, a disheartening adjustment, Fil realized, because it meant that the task of writing the check, addressing the envelope, sealing it, locating a stamp, and posting the letter had become too much for him.

She dropped the stack of checks onto the ledger in his lap. Albert glanced down at them, casually, as though assessing a bowl of peanuts put out by a bartender. Fil waited. He picked them up. There were about thirty, all bearing his signature. He hummed to himself as he went through them.

Even confronted with written proof, he could not bring himself to believe that it was *his* memory that had failed to retain the image of his pen scraping across the check's pale green surface. Surely it hadn't been he who had written all these. No, quite impossible. There'd be an imagistic flicker, a tickle somewhere in his brain. Surely it wasn't he who'd written the checks. It had been someone else.

This is outrageous, he said. It's the girl. She's been forging my signature.

Daddy, said Fil, her fingertip tapping at the ink, you wrote these checks. It's your handwriting. It doesn't matter that you've forgotten. Just acknowledge that you did it.

I'm not a child, Filomena.

Who said you were a child?

You're treating me like a naughty boy.

No one's treating you like a naughty boy. You're just making mistakes, do you get that? You're making mistakes and that's fine, but would you just admit it?

I'll do no such thing. This is a kangaroo court! Let's drag the girl before judge and jury and we'll see what she has to say for herself.

It was then that Albert's eye fell on a check he'd written for $10,000, made out to Erica Spindrake, a check she'd refused to take even though she'd agreed, in principle, to allow him to buy her out. He'd discovered during one of her monologues that her father had taken ill and for that very reason she was working as Albert's caretaker instead of attending classes at CUNY, and he offered on the spot to rectify the situation in exchange for her prompt resignation. He did not know what to make of the check now in his hand, but he could imagine, and when Fil turned away he hastily stuffed it down the side of his seat cushion.

Fil was threatening to take the ledgers with her if he couldn't stop himself from writing checks. Well, he said, if he wasn't even aware of the existence of the impostor who was writing the checks, presumably while he was asleep, then how the hell was he supposed to stop it?

Albert couldn't have recalled that this had first happened over a year earlier, or that this scene played out every week or so since, Tracy and her wet black eyes watching from her seat across the room. To Albert it was a fresh inquisition every time, and to Fil, ever more depressing. Her frustration had given way long ago to sorrow. She played frustration now, a dutiful daughter creating reality for her father. It was all a stage show and they were a ragged troupe hashing out the same old lines, entering and exiting, a spiritless production of a dusty old American tragedy. Yet Fil dreaded the day she'd search the desk and find empty drawers, a cheerful old man smiling wanly at her from across the room.

What Albert also failed to recall was that Erica, nowhere close to the dim bulb everyone took her for, had the previous Friday walked with him to the Chemical branch on 82nd Street and stood by as he'd withdrawn $10,000 in cash. She had packed and left that afternoon, only too happy to turn half of it over to her father (her whole take, for all the elder Spindrake knew), whose illness's primary symptom was a tendency to place bets on perennial losers at Aqueduct. With the other half wrapped in butcher paper and stashed in the back of her closet, she began plotting her own escape.

We're getting someone new, Daddy, Tracy said. I'm phoning an agency as soon as this storm's blown through. We're going to get someone who can put up with you. Understand?

Fine, fine.

As girls they had stood on tiptoe, one on either side of him, and he'd bent down for their kisses. Now Tracy knelt at his left, Fil at his right, and they crossed their arms over his chest and pressed their lips to his cheeks.

My girls, he said, folding his hands over their forearms.

As they rose, Albert did an unexpected thing. He caught them both by the wrists and looked into their faces, his great mottled head swiveling back and forth, and then he pulled them both down and embraced them.

They thought at first he was hallucinating, and they weren't all wrong. He'd heard a sound, something from far away, and he was holding them close the way he'd have held them as children, to keep them quiet, to silence the room, so he could identify the source. But he couldn't put his finger on it. He thumped them on their backs and released them.

If the trains are running, we'll be back tomorrow, Daddy, Fil said. Otherwise, we'll see you the day after.

Not if you're lucky, he said, his standard sign-off, plunging his girls into an ice bath before sending them out into the cruel world.

Bye, Daddy, Tracy said, kissing his cheek one more time for good measure. The floorboards in the hallway creaked as they made their way out, and the heavy maple door swept closed with a hermetic swoosh, the locks ticked, silence descended.

In the hall outside, Tracy said, I'm telling Manny not to let him out even if the building is on fire.

Hope you have some cash, Fil said.

One of us should stay with him tonight.

Are you nuts? Fil said.

Probably.

Because if you stay, you're going to be presenting arguments to hiz-zoner in there until three in the morning. And then you'll get to sit through the rebuttal, which should take you right through to breakfast.

Sounds like a good time to me, Tracy said.

You know he won't set foot outside the building unless one of us tells him *not* to, not in weather like this.

I know, Tracy said. I know. What are we going to do about Erica?

What's there to do? She's done. Finis, Fil said.

How many times are we going to have to go through this?

Once. We're getting him a muscle-head. A big dumb idiot. A big dumb idiot who doesn't speak English.

Tracy nodded.

One of these days he's just going to disappear, you know. He'll turn into a nice old man who can't remember his own name and he'll do exactly what we tell him to.

I know.

And we can empty his accounts and retire to Bermuda, just as we've always planned, Fil said, grasping Tracy's arm. We'll finally have those matching minks and—and—and we'll never think of home and we'll drink martinis all day and laugh and laugh!

We'll seduce the pool boys!

Oh yes, yes. One each.

Two each. And when we're done with them, *pffft*, Tracy said, drawing a finger across her throat.

And we'll flee to Monaco!

Poor Daddy, Tracy said. Murderesses for daughters.

You can't say we don't come by it honestly, Fil said.

Jesus Christ, Tracy said.

Alone in the oak-paneled den, among the piles of *Barron's* and the *Journal*, the weekend's cigar stubs leaning like drunk, fat little men against the ashtray's marble walls, Albert reached for the Bakelite radio on his reading table, and his fingers tapped against the grille but he did not turn it on. His daughters' presence was still draining from the room. People left no truly meaningful remnants; a person was either there or she wasn't, and a photograph or old dresses or drawers full of her stockings and sweaters were only artifacts, triggers for memories, and memories were morbid things, confirmations of loss. He had nothing left but absence. So it was just as well that he go.

Once he became accustomed to the room's silence, it was as if they'd never been there at all. Outside, the usual symphony of horns and sirens. The roar and scrape of the plow trucks.

Through the French doors he saw the baby grand in the corner of the living room, and from there his eyes drifted back to the sofa across from him, the rumpled basins left by his daughters' behinds. The Oriental rug, turned up at the corner, and on the coffee table, his own empty scotch glass. A water mark. He supposed the girl would put some mayonnaise on it, but as he filled his lungs with air to bellow her name, he wondered why it mattered.

All the same, he called after her, repeatedly, in a harsh, barking voice. She didn't answer.

Oh. Yes. The girl is gone.

He went to the sideboard, poured a scotch right up to the rim of the glass, and sat back down. He sat in his chair for another hour, the leather creaking when he shifted his weight, fingering the rivets at the end of each arm, not exactly thinking but allowing thoughts to skip across the surface of consciousness. The girls; vague screwball theories about commodity prices; images from a trip to Ireland he took with Sydney in 1966. His son, who never visited. He winced when he thought about his grandson, and he invited the memory to submerge him. All along, his mind was rummaging around for the plan.

How did it start, again?

Another hour passed. He nodded off, snapped awake, repeated the cycle. More snow slipped by the window. Intonations drifted from the heating grates. The pipes knocked in the wall. Night soil sliding down to the sewer. What causes the vibration of pipes filled with human waste? Something to do with vacuums, air pressure, he couldn't exactly be sure, but now he had an image, all the waste behind all the walls of his apartment, the dark mass in transit, surrounding him, a prison of excrement. When he'd arrived a scholarship boy at Tolver in 1918, he'd never used an indoor toilet. In those days, one became a man at thirteen. Today one could make a good living playing sports or popular music, one could dress in a T-shirt and tennis shoes, eat at 21 wearing blue jeans. Money had superseded the refinements of the upper class. Did this mean anything to him? No, only an observation. In this era a man's chief aim was to remain a child.

He sneered and exhaled through his teeth. Wasting time. He hated wasting time. Where was the girl? He consulted the small notebook he kept in his pocket. It was Monday. Was it Monday? Yes. His scotch glass was empty. He got up and refilled it.

The girl is gone.

He'd dismissed her, had he? Things would be different for her afterward. His daughters might file suit, but what could they take from her, sheltered as she was by poverty? Would she miss him? Unlikely that she'd ever visit his final resting place, or glance mournfully out at the river. If he failed to complete his task, he'd be institutionalized. He'd never see her again, either way.

The girl is gone. Good. So you've taken care of that.

He was trying to puzzle out what hospital to call when Erica appeared, an apparition floating down the hall like a whisper, turning the corner into his study with an imperceptible sigh. Efficient as ever, she moved to clean up the decimated *Times* scattered on the floor beside his chair.

I'm still reading that, he snapped.

She backed away.

You didn't use a coaster, she said.

It's my goddamn table. Put some mayonnaise on it.

Did you have a nice visit?

Yes, he said quickly before scrambling to recall who had visited.

Well, that's good. Did Fil make you something to eat?

He looked around, in part to gather more information so that he might answer, in part because he meant to show her that he couldn't see anything she couldn't, and that the question was stupid.

Doesn't appear so, does it? I need you to go out and get me something to eat, Albert said.

Albert, she said.

I'm hungry for sesame noodles.

You haven't eaten anything? It's late.

Is it? he said, though he was already looking at the clock. I was waiting for you, he said.

She laughed. Waiting for me to get your dinner, you mean. Albert, the snow. There's a blizzard. Nothing's open, not even Golden Palace.

You've confirmed this?

Albert, nothing's open.

You've confirmed it? he said.

Their secret: Albert survived on General Tso's chicken and cold sesame noodles. Four, sometimes five nights a week, she called in the order. Albert refused to let her tip more than fifty cents, but if the weather was bad, she added a quarter of her own.

I'm sure they're open. But they won't deliver. Not tonight, he said.

You're just making things up now. Stop it.

Prove me wrong, he said.

Fine. Let's call and see if anyone picks up.

I don't want to call them! Albert was gripping the armrests like a man undergoing a particularly hairy dental procedure.

Fine, Albert. Do you want to look at the photo album? Erica said.

Now? Albert said.

One last time before you go, she said.

Fine, fine, Albert said. What had she meant by that? he wondered. Did she know what he meant to do?

Erica perched on the arm of his leather chair while he turned the cardboard pages, tapping his finger here and here, breezily reeling off locations and dates. His identifications were inventions, words spoken with an authority intended to convince himself that he could go on. He recognized only himself and Sydney. Even their children, though they were obviously the children, were unfamiliar to him, and he said, Here are the children, and from a background or a dirt road or a farmhouse in the photo he would construct a location in terms vague enough to sound correct. If there were mountains, he called them the

Adirondacks; if he saw a boat or a fishing rod, the Finger Lakes; if a beach, Florida.

He'd gone on as long as he could, covering the lapses, but it was exhausting, an exercise as painful as push-ups on broken arms, and he began to lose heart. Confronted with a photo of his grandchildren, he'd say, Now, there's a fine boy. He reminds me of my schoolmate Irving Teller. Died in the war, Irving . . . And who could say otherwise? He knew Erica didn't care, and as with most deceptions, the bulk of his efforts went into convincing himself of the lie, though after a while it hardly worked on him, either.

His mind: a slow sinking, an insignificant tear in the hull that takes on only a gallon or two a day, but eventually the gunwales are even with the surface of the water, and eventually the boat disappears, descending through the depths, leaving Albert to scissor his legs and carve the water with his emaciated arms. He'll go down soon enough, he knows it. He's finished, he welcomes death.

Erica! Albert yelled. Where had she gone? He yelled again. This went on for a while until he looked at the clock, and suddenly she reappeared, leaning against the doorframe, arms crossed.

What's my dog's name? she said.

What dog? Albert said.

My dog. The only dog I ever had.

You've never mentioned it.

Only every day. What's his name?

Don't play this game with me. I'm starving.

What's his name, Albert?

I don't care what your dead dog's name is, Albert yelled. Go get me something to eat.

Erica nodded. Good, that's right, he's dead. What was his name?

Albert gripped his chair. You're taunting me. You're always asking meaningless questions. These doors you insist on making me unlock just to get a drink of water or a morsel of food—if my daughters knew the tortures you put me through, they'd have your hide. I refuse to comply. I refuse.

You don't complain to them, though, do you?

My conversations with my family are none of your business.

Albert, you know it's good for you. It's good for your mind. It keeps you sharp.

I'm a dead man. Who cares how sharp I am?

I do, and the sharper the better.

I'm pleased to be able to do you a service, then. Pleased.

Don't be such a little old lady, Albert. What was my dog's name?

Sparky.

That's right. Sparky.

Don't threaten me with Sparky.

No one's threatening you, Albert.

I was skinning rabbits when I was six. I could field-dress a deer when I was eight. My father had to hold me up to reach the hams. Don't threaten me with stories about your little dead dog.

Erica moved closer to his chair. Mind your manners, Albert.

He waved the back of his hand at her. I need to eat, he said. I need you to go get Chinese.

Erica put her hands on the arms of his chair and leaned in until her face was so close to his that her eyes became blurs. Their noses touched.

How much have you had tonight?

You think I can remember? he whispered. He felt her breath on his lips.

You want me to leave.

Yes, he said.

I've already left, Albert. Do you understand?

I understand.

I left so that you can do what you need to do.

I understand, he whispered.

I hope you'll have more courage when it comes to the rest of it.

I will.

This is what people do for people they love, she said.

I know, he said.

You've made a plan? You know what you're going to do?

Yes, he said.

You know what to do, Erica said. Her eyes were closed.

I do, Albert said. He had closed his eyes but opened them now. He gently pushed Erica back by the shoulders, only enough to be able to see her face clearly.

Didn't I already send you away? he said. Didn't I remove you from danger? You'd have tried to stop me, he said. I got rid of you for your own good.

I know what you're going to do.

You do? he said. Did she? he thought. Don't tell, he said.

Albert, you shouldn't go tonight. If you fall on a patch of ice you could break your leg. You could get lost. You could freeze to death. How are you going to find your way?

I'll find my way.

Go tomorrow.

No. You're trying to trick me. It must be tonight.

He turned his face away from hers, but she was so close, her body over his, that struggling was pointless. Her legs were astride his, her feet pinning his on either side. The silver cross around her neck tapped against the underside of his chin. Her hair poured over his face.

Tomorrow I'll have lost my nerve, he said. I feel it draining from me already.

He felt the wet of her lips against the dry granite of his own.

You've thought this through? she said.

Yes.

Hardheaded old man, she said. She pulled back.

What's my dog's name? she said.

Sparky.

You know how you're going to do it?

I know. It's clear in my mind. Go, he said.

And she went, like a vapor, back to the ether world she'd come from.

It was time. The rug beneath his feet was rotting flesh, the walls the sides of a dank tomb. Go.

Choices: Would he experience numbness, palpitations, shortness of breath, coldness in the extremities, burning of the bowels, blurring of vision, failure of vision, agita, tremors, organ malfunction?

He would call Roosevelt. He located the phone book and painstakingly worked his way through it. Every time his eye attached itself to a new name, he plunged into a dark well. What was he doing, again? He climbed back out and resumed the search. Finally, he arrived at the number. He dialed. He hung up quickly. Work out a dialogue first. Anything worth doing is worth doing properly. Prepare and strategize. He pulled out the Parker from his breast pocket and a legal pad from the side table.

Help me, I'm in agony, he wrote.

I'm experiencing shortness of breath. There is some numbness in my limbs.

He looked at what he'd written. He read it aloud, and struck out the last sentence.

I can't feel my hands! he wrote.

He ran through the dialogue a few times, found his address on the *Journal*'s delivery label, jotted it down, practiced the dialogue once more.

That sound again, barely audible, from far away. He recognized it this time. He knew exactly what it was. The river.

25.

My photographs of Vik are medleys of smudge and blur, thumbs effecting solar eclipse, plan views of shoelaces. When I managed to align focus and f-stop, I was a mug-shot artist. Videos, same: catalogues of a wide range of ground cover species, off-camera directions that always end with, Okay, ready? and as the frame swings up to capture the subject . . . blackout—or worse, when I captured him standing uneasily at the edge of a swimming pool, stage-mothering him to Do something, do something! Move around or, like, dance!, and he would, saggy trunks dripping all over the place, tentatively bouncing on one leg then the other as if testing their structural integrity, his mouth a rictus of mortal embarrassment.

Vik was director of our tripod-assisted sex tapes, all of them either metronomed by low-light warnings (though the audio has been, in years since, an effective enough lubricant if mixed with vodka; melancholy, sure, but what's the brain doing during masturbation, anyway, but pining after an absent set of hands, mouth, body, way of life?) or, when well lit, comedies starring a Parkinsonian ghost writhing abstractly about our mattress, disgorging here and there a foot or arm before redevouring the escapee; sexy snapshots, likewise, were lightning flashes of bleached landscape and shadow, a cloud of saltpeter storming on our affections, carving into the foreground horrors of cleft and gap.

It was if we'd undergone a training program for photographers of industrial flange and pipe-fitting catalogues, steeped in an objectivist

Jack Livings

approach that treated every bolt, bushing, and return bend equally, everything shot under the same flat illumination, a triumph of truth over perspective.

A person viewing our collected works could be forgiven for thinking it was all an intentional, if not quite realized, project, some hyper-ironic thrift shop approach to the saccharine naïveté of the knock-kneed, blepharoplastied Japanese hipster. But nope. Just bad composition and shyness, a headshot collection for the jacket flap of an anti-anagraphist manifesto.

Look at me. What a drag, a sullen mug mouthing the words at the back of a group sing-along. Stiff as a board at the Pantheon, exhibiting lifelessness on the Spanish Steps, idling uncomfortably in a gondola, tonguing a plasticine gelato. Wait, there's more! Here Comrade Hazel refuses to strike pose at Bolshoi! классический! Look there, poor madam impersonates a wilting rhododendron in the Yumthang Valley. Vik: There he stands, hands in pockets, shallow smile, a wax figurine, a chroma-key shot, an action figure propped against a rock.

If not for his friends, I would have no proof that he ever smiled. Their donations came in manila envelopes, email attachments, on CDs with accompanying thumbnails helpfully preprinted on glossy photo stock. Most are from the days before we were together, when our pasts ran parallel, back when my history didn't require a revision quite so desperately as it does now. Eventually our timelines merge and in some of those photos we stand together looking not entirely bloodless. Enough of them, at least, to assure me that we lived not quite so statutory a life as our portraits of each other suggest.

I'd sent the blanket request in advance of the funeral, and his friends, being competent and thoughtful types, top-notch custodians of their pasts, had responded with an archive, every shot suitable for framing, the deluge a long-overdue spring clean. I suppose his friends welcomed the invitation to initiate an act of catharsis. Dear man had been in hiding for fifteen years, what could they do? What could I do? Keep on stroking the organ responsible for pain, whichever one that is. The brain? The heart? An electric finger on the dorsal posterior insula, prodding mercilessly until it was a swollen, pulsing mass of signals, throwing off cyclones of barbed wire and hailstones?

The Pavlovian compact by which all Americans live, the promise that anguish is eventually terminated by an endorphin release, took a rain check on this one. Someone forgot to pay the electric on the effervescent promise that as long as I *worked through my pain* it would all *pay off in the end*, because anything that pays off is *worth it*, worth it because we are *made stronger by our suffering*.

Fifteen years they couldn't find Vik. He was everywhere and nowhere, scattered across Lower Manhattan in an untidy Bayesian distribution, no easier to locate for the blanketing effect of his disintegration, but eventually he emerged, and I have placed that artifact, the first and only, once a shard of bone, now a white powder reconstituted by a Fisher Scientific Sonic Dismembrator, treated to Bode Technology patented DNA-extraction procedures, the full arsenal of forensic science available to the New York City medical examiner's office, in an oak coffin, and I performed the ritual of mourning and remembrance. Correction: I put seventy-five percent of his remains, by weight, into the coffin. The other twenty-five percent I placed on my tongue.

Sure, he was a little late to the party, but we all remembered the steps, we being the widows, by then having put parts of thirty-six of Vik's colleagues in the ground. Vik had been elusive, that old fox, doping around in the shadows while I stood on the dance floor swaying to the dirge. Fifteen years.

In 2001, I had offered up personal item reference samples and bio samples, per instructions from the Office of the Chief Medical Examiner. I'd expected his blood relatives' spiral lattices to do the heavy lifting, but I obliged with the trinity of hairbrush, comb, razor, and a river card: the panties I wore Monday, the day before he was killed, and the spermatic deposits thereupon. Later, I discovered a fork in the dishwasher. I delivered it to OCME. A few weeks later I found hairs in the bed, bagged and delivered those. In December, a fingernail clipping revealed itself from within the padded confines of a ball of dust behind the toilet. I bagged it. I gave away every tangible piece of Vik I could find.

I was told that he, like his colleagues, was pulverized, reduced infinitesimally, reduced to dust. A finely sifted flour. Particulate matter.

A single particle. A speck floating among motes. He was made so small that photons in a sunbeam struck him like waves breaking over the bow of a ship. He was inhaled, expelled in a mass of phlegm, transported by Kleenex to waste bin, to garbage truck, entombed in a landfill to await the next millennium's archaeologists. Arguably, he still existed in some microscopic sense. What constituted *him*? Two molecules retaining their bond? A single molecule once associated with his cellular structure? And after his dust degraded and he was split into the component atomic elements, where was he then? When did he cease to be?

Elusive Vik. At first I forced myself to believe these things, to believe that he'd vanished into the mound of rubble, been pestled by the concrete slabs and plummeting I-beams. I forced myself to believe he'd been incinerated, his carbonized particles elevated in the pillar of black smoke, absorbed into the mesosphere. In the absence of a body, paperwork became his corpse. I had the DX certificate, official pronouncement of death by judicial decree. But what I wanted—what we all wanted—was the DM, the physical remains certificate. Eventually all the other girls got theirs. Goddamnit, Vik, where was mine?

Were they my friends, the other widows? If we'd been friendly before, cocktail party cohorts, left-hand partners at dinners requiring the presence of a full contingent, the smiling soft-serve ice cream our husbands brought around to please potential investors, now we were comrades, veterans of a flash battle that had wiped out half our battalion.

For everyone else, for the DMs, the problem wasn't that their husbands had vanished, but that they kept coming back. There was a white tent on 30th Street overlooking the East River, a high-quality aluminum frame shrink-wrapped in slick polyester. The remains were stored there until the memorial park was finished and they were relocated to subterranean shelf space beneath the plaza's selfie zone. Officers of the state tested and retested the remains, turning an infinite row of prayer wheels while chanting the mantras of forensic tech. When the universe granted a hit, they'd call. They'd call every time until you couldn't handle any more and signed the form begging them to stop.

I never saw the blue glow of the caller ID: OCME MTTN. But they kept pushing the prayer wheels, retesting, retesting—thousands of unidentified tissue remains, thousands of bone fragments. And there were millions more out there in the world, too small to detect. I kept up with the literature. I knew the technology was advancing toward infinite sensitivity. It was only a matter of time before they'd point a spectrometer wand at the sky and transmit me the coordinates of Vik's atomic remnants. There he is, hovering over Germany today, tomorrow Sweden, drifting Arcticward, catching a lift on the polar jet, circumnavigating the world's crown. There he is, parting the seas from atop a plankton's rostrum. Look there, in yonder deer gut, amongst the honeycomb of the reticulum. In a volcano, in a carburetor, under my fingernail. Everywhere, nowhere.

Unless you asked, they didn't tell you where they were finding all the new pieces. You had to go to the white tent and they'd point to a map. Your husband was here: The pit. Fresh Kills. A rooftop. Sewer. A shard here, a sliver there.

But after so long and no call, I'd formed some theories, some unsound ideas, by the time he came home. Ideas like: not dead, just gone.

On the occasion of the initial identification he returned with a herald. An officer of the NYPD, fidelis ad mortem, was in the lobby asking to see me. I told Peter, the doorman, to send him up and Peter, stooped Peter who could barely climb off his stool, escorted the officer himself. I didn't trust it, he said to me. A cop? You? No, I didn't trust it one bit.

Even so many years later, standard operating procedure still applied in the case of this particular mass-fatality incident. Upon identification of human remains, OCME issued the coveted DM certificate and notified NYPD, which was then compelled to notify me in person. So, there he was, an old hand from the Twentieth Precinct, wedding ring, removed his hat and secured the threshold, framed in full 3D by the jambs, which gave way to his elbows as he awaited my invitation, Peter doing his best impersonation of an octopus behind him. Come on in, I said. We sat, I displayed my government-issued identification, he said, no, not necessary while scanning it nonetheless, he on the couch, me on the ottoman—weird, right, my apartment, but with bad news/good news in the pipe we'd assumed stage positions intended, though unintentionally, to communicate to our audience, dear old Peter, that order and authority were in balance, all was right in the world, chaos held at bay for just a moment more. The officer did then address our rheumatic chaperone, whose pose of angular discomfort, one gnarled hand on the jamb of the French doors open to the living room, his body all juts and doglegs inside the uniform that fit him like a set of drapes, indicated that he was suffering a hell of spasmodic agony, to suggest that we could be left alone, and I, concurring, said something along the lines of, Thank you, Peter, as though I were dame of the manor in a perfect little Fieldian table setting of a screenplay. He took his leave hitchingly, and the cop, whose name, no kidding, was Postman, Officer Postman, a low-grade amusement on par with the doctor named Nurse or the funeral director named Lively, just a little distraction from the news at hand, of course, forgive me, because I was listening with one ear, as they say, comparing his dialogue to the teleprompter scrolling in my head, checking for deviation from the déjà vu, and my concerns shifted quite naturally to allowing him to complete his assignment with minimum delay, which, by the way, flying colors, old boy, direct, calm, and collected, no euphemisms, just the facts, ma'am, presented from his breast pocket, right, the precinct's card, the left being somewhat obscured by a terrace of gold bars atop the badge, the black-banded badge, certainly not in honor of Vik but some lawman recently departed, and I would of course, if asked, assign him high marks on professionalism, and though I wanted to ask if he'd been to the apartments of Cynthia and (the former) Evan Mask or Megan and (the former) Terrance Plenge, both located within the boundaries of the Twentieth Precinct, I restrained myself from undertaking that foray into the social macabre (if I cared enough one way or another I could just ask Cynthia or Megan if Postman had been their guy lo those many years ago, and had they, too, noticed the third finger, right hand, shortened by a single segment north of the knuckle, shop class/band saw, or perp/knife, or possibly something that had happened in the lengthy interregnum, goddamnit, Vik), and I showed him out, transferred the card from my right to my left hand so that I might present him with a firm handshake, with thanks, upon his exit, restraining myself from doing anything so bald as *ushering him out* or *hurrying him on his way*, because, after all, he's only doing his job, good news/bad news, pretty hairy stuff, plunging into these estrogen-soaked apartments where virtually anything could happen, these women, even all these years later they're grieving, you know, they're not moving on, they're not in their right minds, got to keep your wits about you, man, anything could happen, anything, shoot, stab, grope, smack the messenger, you've gotta stay on your toes with those gals, better send in old Postman, he knows his way around an NOK.

Yes. This is why we're here. They've found Vik. The snowdrift of photos on the bed. His shirts piled on the floor. And oh dear, yes, I have excavated from the back garden of my mind, grown over with weeds, that most unsound idea, nestled among the glimmers of hope, as they say, doses of magical thinking, the pathetic possibility that Vik had, on that day of all days, emerged from the subway and because of the remarkable and well-documented atmospheric clarity had been drawn toward the splendor of the Jersey City skyline, and in an entirely uncharacteristic display of nonchalance toward our financial well-being, instead of turning left into the North Tower, strolled right on down Vesey, all the way over to the river, where he'd boarded a ferry, aflame with the same poetic inspiration that had consumed him the night of the blizzard, and upon disembarking on the other side and seeing over his shoulder the dark poppy bloom, and having been spared the executioner's blade, had decided to keep going west, ever west, traversing the continent, boarding a ship at San Francisco bound for Guangzhou, from there walking westward across the provinces, up into the mountains, passing through Burma, over India, Pakistan, into Iran, and that until the moment Officer Postman arrived he'd been walking, while I'd been mentally tracking him, advancing his pixel a micrometer a day, ever traveling, ever safe.

Or, or, bear with me, or that he'd been mugged in a dark corner of a subway station on that terrible morning, received a blow to the head that erased his memory, and caught up in the chaotic aftermath of the attack had been deposited in a hospital where, unable to identify himself, he was eventually discharged to the care of the state, and after a brief stay at Bellevue allowed to reintegrate into society because despite his identity problem he retained his working knowledge of finance, and within a few years had established himself at some off-the-grid firm, probably in Boston because who would stay in New York after *that*, perhaps awaking in the middle of the night with ghostly images of my face floating on the backs of his eyelids.

Or—or! Or perhaps he'd simply been one of the survivors, one who got out just in time and seized his chance to start anew, and was living now in Phoenix, running a smoothie shop, feeding his neighbors' cats when they went out of town, contemplating, wondering, missing me but convinced it was all for the best. I would have preferred it. I would have preferred anything to this. Well, that little tin box had been excavated from the garden and its contents deemed inadmissible. News flash, Hazel: your husband is dead.

Part IV

26.

In my bag were five reel tapes, recordings of Turk's father's voice, made in 1961 by a doctoral student doing a rotation at Pickering. His daily rounds there were considerably more agreeable than the hand-to-hand combat he'd endured the previous year at Bellevue, though lacking the smorgasbord of schizoid antisocial behaviors available at the public institution, and he'd invented a side project to keep himself engaged between circle group meetings.

Curious, he'd thought, the narrative leaps made by schizophrenics. A schizophrenic, recollecting his day's activities for an interested party, would deliver a standard top-down tour of a Dadaist countryside, a game of narrative pachinko that offered the interlocutor gems like, Sally cow tank drank so much gasoline through her ball, and The empty crows and so many furrows in the doorways, the only safe place to land, the frying pan. Given enough time and coffee, any moderately inquisitive English major could parse meaning—indeed, a multiplicity of meanings—from a section of schizophrenese, but what happened in those gaps, those spaces between phrases where the speaker abandoned sensical connection, disappeared into the mist, and emerged again on the other side only to utter a completely unrelated word or phrase? What dark magic occurred in the silence? What meaning existed there, and how schizophrenic did the listener have to be to understand the leap?

So that he might have accurate transcripts, the doctoral student had been recording his patient interviews, thinking he might be able to get some grant money next cycle to have them transcribed. Which is to say, he didn't have much to show for his research beyond the stacks of tape boxes on his desk, when in wheeled Dr. Lazlo Brunn, the mad babbler.

At Pickering, not a revolving-door operation but a well-funded private institution that tended its flower beds and kept its kitchen floors clean, an intake was an all-hands affair by virtue of its rarity. That first week, Lazlo Brunn talked nonstop, and since no one quite knew what to do with him, the student figured he'd make some tape just in case it turned out the patient's diagnosis fell within the scope of his research. He wheeled his aluminum cart into Brunn's room, introduced himself, got some gibberish in response, asked in turn if he could record their conversation—more gibberish but no physical signs of disagreement— and proceeded with his first question: How do you feel today, Doctor Brunn? The patient took one hour and four minutes to deliver his logatomic response, and he was still talking when the tape ran out.

The student was named Asher Schiff, the same Schiff who would later treat my father, and I'd come into possession of the tapes when I'd made a research mission up to the Bronx to see him, hoping he could tell me something about my own state of mind in those days immediately after the Vornados' party.

The morning after the party, when I had emerged from my bedroom and asked who the man who'd been thrown over the balcony was, Schiff had been my father's first phone call, and he'd trudged through the snow to our apartment that same day. As I understood it, we'd talked for a long time, and then I'd been to see him in his office several times after, but I had no recollection of his face, much less our conversations.

He apologized for not being able to speak extemporaneously on the subject of our sessions, but he couldn't remember anything specific himself, and we descended into his basement, where he dug around in some old steel file cabinets until he found his notes, which weren't much help, either.

According to this, he said, we met five times. Twice I came to you, and the other three, your parents brought you to my office. I never wrote much down, for legal reasons—standard practice, not because of the details of your case. So there's not much here, I'm sorry to say. I see that I referred you to Sandy Stern. Did you see her for long?

I told him I had, about five years.

She's who you should be talking to, he said, but she passed away some years back.

Yes, I said.

You already knew that, he said, and smiled. Suddenly I remembered his smile—crooked, rumpled, compassionate, the smile of an inveterate listener. Do you want to talk about anything now? he said.

Oh no, I said. I've done plenty of that, thank you.

I had only a vague idea of what I was looking for. Some clue that he'd seen Albert Caldwell peering out from within me, I suppose. Some written proof that I'd spoken like a guilt-ridden old lawyer.

So, I said. We're like a couple of old war buddies who can't remember the war.

He gave me that smile again, and a shrug that either meant, Oh ho, I remember the war all too well and I'm not opening that can of worms, or else it meant, simply, I'm sorry. Either way, there was no more conversation about that night in 1978. So we talked about other things. He was a lovely man. He asked about my father. When I told him I still lived at the Apelles he asked if I happened to know anyone in the Brunn family. Sure, I said. Follow me, he said. Up we went to his office on the second floor, a room with books for walls, towers of ancient journals and papers begetting yet more papers, two desks obscured by a long, long career's worth of psychological detritus—the Egyptian reproductions, the old chess pieces, a graveyard of laptops, flowerpots where he'd cultivated twigs and dust. One smiling shelf was dentured with slender reel tape boxes, and he picked through them until he'd found the ones he was after.

You get old, you try to disburse, he said. The family might want these.

I thanked him for his time and took them home.

It took me a while to get around to the tapes. They slipped my mind, to be honest. I was a little preoccupied putting my house in order.

I'd finally managed to dispatch the hundreds of photos of Vik into manila folders. His shirts had gone to the mission on 82nd Street, the same place Turk had taken her parents' clothing. His coats, his shoes, all gone. I expected a sudden weightlessness, some bliss-of-purgation kind of uplift, a setting off on the open sea type of feeling. There was new space in the closet. Lightness in the drawers, extra shelves in the medicine cabinet. I felt the same.

It was as much out of a desire to avoid that sameness as any feeling of obligation to Turk that I went rummaging in my parents' basement storage, abstractly looking for their old reel-to-reel without any real concern over whether I'd find it or not. Maybe I'd listen to the tapes, maybe I wouldn't. Why did I bother? Why didn't I just take the tapes to Turk? When I think about how close I came to missing my salvation, how many ways I tried not to discover it, I'm only more convinced of the truth of what I found.

I camped out on the storage room's concrete floor for a few hours paging through old photo albums and pulling open the cloverleafed tops of unlabeled boxes. Even after I excavated the tape deck from a mountain of twine-bound *National Geographic*s and hauled it back up to the apartment, it sat on the floor in all its dusty glory for a couple of weeks before I carried it into the dining room and set it up on the table. I had to buy an adapter for my headphones, which put me back another week. But finally, finally, one night, somewhere in the concavity between 2:00 and 4:00 a.m., I spooled up the tapes and pressed play. I wouldn't say I was floored by what I heard in the five minutes I listened that first night, but it was obvious that Lazlo Brunn was not babbling incoherently—not at all. His noise had form and rhythm, to be sure.

A few days later I downloaded some software to digitize the tapes, thinking it would be easier for Turk to listen that way, if she wanted to listen at all. In a marathon session, two bottles of wine, an entire roast chicken from Fairway, I transferred all five tapes.

The software's enhancement suite was comprehensive, offering pitch, tone, and speed adjustment, layering, reversing, noise reduction. Pretty basic, I suppose, to any twelve-year-old with a laptop, but it wasn't until I, analogue-brained, remembered Gene Hackman in *The*

Conversation, twisting knobs so powerful that they could make the truth rise up from the magnetic surface of his tapes like ghosts from the grave, that I thought to use the software to manipulate the sound.

Why did I do it? Wine and sorrow. And boredom and idle curiosity. I certainly didn't expect to unearth ancient bones. Or did I? It's hard not to think I was somehow drawn to investigate the tapes, given what happened next, but let's be honest. I wasn't sleeping and you have to kill the time somehow.

First I tried giving the playback loop a little drag, slowing it until Lazlo's yammering was baritone yowling, then whale song. Then some more, until the sound fell away completely, the waveforms flattened, and his vocables lay down unmarked in the sonic boneyard.

I pushed the sliders in the other direction. I doubled the playback speed and got a Chipmunks Christmas album. Quadrupled it and got Twiddlebugs on helium. Quadrupled again. Mechanical chirps. At thirty-two times the recorded speed I sat back and let it play out, almost inaudibly high, sonic detritus emitted by the earth's crust, magnets serenading each other, the hour-long audio reduced now to about two minutes. And it was there, in the electrostatic ether, through the whistling cracks, that a voice spoke out.

Are, it said. I was quite sure my mind had fabricated it, that my sadness had finally metastasized inside my frontal cortex, but then came another word: *You.* Another ten seconds passed. *Speaking.* Another ten. *To.* And finally, *Me.* The recording ended.

What kind of whackadoo sci-fi bullshit is this? you might ask. Because I sure did. I slammed shut my laptop and went directly to bed. I was drunk, of course—that was it. Drunk, yearning for a voice from the beyond. I passed out and slept deeply, dreamlessly, and the next morning I had almost convinced myself that I'd heard nothing more than an echo off the inside of my own skull, a question I would have done well to ask myself. Who was I speaking to? No one. It was after dark when I approached the recording again. I put on my headphones and clicked play. The tangle of sound began. It was incomprehensible. How pleased I was not to hear a thing. What a relief, I was thinking, basking in the knowledge that I had fabricated the whole episode, when he spoke. I felt a shock strike the back of my neck, as real as if someone had slapped me open-handed. What kind of madness?

That night, sitting at the table in my socks and cotton shorts, slurping on an over-milked lukewarm coffee, how could I have comprehended what he'd done? My ears had not yet been opened. I could hear but I was not listening. I was a novitiate to Lazlo's order. It took a couple of months. I did everything I could think of to the tapes. I scrambled and descrambled them. I re-recorded his five-word question, sliced and diced it, ran it backward, forward, sped it up and slowed it down. I stretched, deconstructed, rebuilt, and inverted the sounds, all the while hoping that I could create another phrase, something that would prove I had made his words out of nothing more than coincidence and selective hearing. I recorded my own voice, trying to mimic the trick. I couldn't make it work. I deleted the software, packed up the deck and tapes, and stuffed them in the closet.

I took it all back out. I bought a new reel-to-reel deck, one that was capable of controlled high-speed playback, hoping to discover that all I'd heard was a fluke of the software. But the words were right there on the tape. Finally I had to accept the most likely possibility—the one that didn't point to coincidence and luck but to a carefully constructed truth: Lazlo Brunn had slipped outside a human perception of time. Not so complicated in the end, not so crazy, and completely within the bounds of modern scientific and neurological understanding of the brain. Researchers have known for decades that the smaller an animal, the more refined its perception of time. To a frog, the child's grasping hand moves in slow motion. To a flea, a minute is an endless expanse. To a microbe, a day is a lifetime, but one filled with endless variation and experience, a life no less astonishing in its scope than any human life. I'm not suggesting Brunn invented an anti-gravity machine or made himself invisible. I'm merely suggesting that he lived on, physically un-changed, silent as a mouse, occupying his room at Pickering until the day he died in 1982.

But within his normal human life span, he'd made himself immea-surably large, a perceptual giant, so that to him, the white-frocked orderlies would appear and disappear like lightning flashes. To him, there'd be a shimmer in the doorway; it would spit out a heartbeat's worth of incomprehensible blather, and vanish. Lazlo had shifted to geologic time. He'd become a glacier creeping across a landmass. For him, a day was the beat of a hummingbird's wing. A week was the length of a breath, and felt like pressure in the ears, relieved with a yawn. His own body must have been a thing of wonder, a blazing electrical arc that sparked from bed to wheelchair to bed and back without a thought. Did he even register the trays of food put before him? Wheelchair tours of the grounds?

Surely not. He did it all with an attendant at his side, his body nothing more than a carriage for his brain. The domestic rituals by which we mark the passage of our days became averages for him, a slur arcing across a line clogged with sixteenth notes. If he spent eight hours a night in bed, that added up to a respectable, and noticeable, fifty-six hours a week. But disconnected, each instance of sleep like a blink of the eye, did it all add up to a deep slumber? Or had he, unable to detect his body's daily motions, separated from the need for sleep entirely? Is it possible that by the end of his first week at Pickering he'd stepped out beyond the end of his own life and was living in a future after he'd died?

He would have spent a hundred hours a week in front of the white wall in his room. He would have seen the wall. He might have registered the sunlight racing across the plaster, the expansion and contraction due to humidity and temperature, the wall pulsing like a vein, the birth and growth of cracks that crept and spread, the subtle shift of color as the paint leached pigment. His body sat there for years, the wall all the while throbbing with life. Where was he?

In that first week, he still would have been evolving, thus capable of recognizing Schiff's presence, however brief. Lazlo's question, *Are you speaking to me?* took the duration of the first tape to complete. Each of the four remaining tapes was an hour and four minutes long, identical to the first. I ran them all through the same process, and did I get secret messages from the beyond? Messages to Turk, to his sons? Confirmation of his scientific breakthrough? Did he quote Goethe, the fly's thousand dead eyes? Smart's "Jubilate Agno"?

Blame Schiff for adhering to clinical procedure, leading off with the same question every day: How are you feeling today, Dr. Brunn? One tape a day for five days. Same question, same answer.

I called Dr. Schiff and asked if there were more tapes. I asked him if he had any recollection of the interviews, or any notes.

I could hear him smile and shrug through the phone.

The young Schiff didn't work weekends, and when he returned to Pickering the Monday following Lazlo's committal, the patient had gone mute. He never spoke again. I suspect Lazlo had entered a new phase of communication, an adaptation that took advantage of the disparity between his perceptual advance and his physical equipment. His further communications may yet be awaiting discovery, hovering somewhere out there in the future, encoded in the molten core of our planet, awaiting rebirth in a leaf. By that second Monday morning, could he even tell Schiff was there?

Are you speaking to me?

My beneficent madre-in-waiting, architect of the Gedanken, spending her peaceable retirement in repose, puffing on an assortment of electronic one-hitters and watching the Criterion Collection from bed. If not for the bathrobe, a garnet terry-cloth number that had become her day-lounge uniform, you'd have thought Turk a starlet in nova.

Darling, she said when she opened the door.

Hi, I said. I was aware that I might have looked—what, predisposed? Intent, in any case, a seeker arrived from a great distance, having traveled across the wastes, through wind and weather, beset by bandits, transformed by my journey into the foreigner now beseeching her from the doorstep, and it made me self-conscious, so I affected an attitude of perfect me-ness: casual, blithe, amicable.

Good god, what's wrong? she said, and pulled me inside. What happened, dear? Is your father all right?

Oh yes, I said. I assume he is.

Something downstairs? she said. Downstairs being her name for the business, because we had to call it, well, something.

No, no, everything's fine.

Is it?

Turk, I said, when your father was getting on, near the end, did he talk to you about his work?

Oh, here and there.

Anything about the device he was working on?

I see. I've been down this road, Turk said. And no, not that I recall. I tried to piece it together, you know, but only after he'd gone up to Pickering, after the tape decks were stolen—that put a real scare into me.

He never said anything to you about what they were supposed to do?

No, Turk said.

I have something for you, I said.

Oh? How exciting, Turk said sotto voce, folding her hands together as if she were a little old lady and not the immortal being that had created my world, as if she didn't already know exactly what I had for her.

I reached into my bag and handed the slim boxes, white with foxing, to Turk.

These are recordings of your father, I said. From Pickering.

Artifacts from the deep? Turk asked. You went to the institute to get them?

Asher Schiff, I said.

Really? she said. Isn't that something. How did you track him down?

It wasn't hard, I said. He used to treat my father.

So he did. I'd forgotten that. He's in good health, is he?

Seemed so, I said.

He was good with Father, Turk said. He was always helpful when I'd go up to visit. It's funny—years later I started to see him around, at Zabar's, out on Broadway. Finally I stopped him one day and reintroduced myself. This was ten years after we'd last spoken, and he remembered my father as if it had only been the day before. Turns out his office was just around the corner. I suspect we had some of the same clients. I saw him out once with his family. You fear for a psychologist's family a little bit, don't you?

Mhmm, I said.

You didn't go to him looking for these? she said, holding up the boxes.

No, I said. Just doing some personal excavation.

Did he tell you where the treasure's buried?

Not much help there.

Sometimes the wrong answer's more useful than the right one, Turk says.

Maybe.

So what's your plan?

What do you mean?

Sweetheart. You've been rattling around like a ghost since the funeral, doing god knows what. You're not sleeping, are you?

I shrugged.

All this detective work, Turk said. What exactly are you looking for? Something that can't be explained. What did you go up there to see Schiff for? Something about your father?

No, I said.

What, then?

Something about my past. The usual.

And you wound up with my past instead. What a shame.

Past, present, and future, I thought. I could have told her what I'd found on the tapes, but I didn't. I didn't trust her. Good Turk, who'd been like a mother to me. I could have asked her the central question that had been eating away at me like an acid since I'd found her father's question on the tapes, but she was right: I was trying to prove an unprovable. All the research, digging through my past, my father's past, Albert's past, all of it was a search for clues that might tell me what Turk, if I could trust her, could have told me in a single word, yes or no. The question: Wasn't everything that had happened to me since that night in 1978 a complication?

I knew, though, that if the answer was yes, Turk wouldn't tell me. If she'd created the complication and had adhered to its rules for this long, surely she wouldn't break them simply because I asked. Equally possible: She'd been part of it for so long that she would no longer recognize that she was part of it. This had been her life, too, this elaborate fabrication.

Does it sound far-fetched? Is it really any more absurd than what my father did, creating an analogue version of Hazel Saltwater, one that turned me into the unrecognizable, the impostor, the photocopy?

You need a little R and R, Turk said. Why don't we watch a movie?

I'm okay, I said. I'm going up to see Dad.

Thank god, Turk said.

Mm? I said.

That's the right thing to do. All this business—you've been barking up the wrong tree, dear. Go see your father if you want to know about the past.

27.

In Cornwall there is snow on the ground. My father's house, perched on a hill overlooking the Hudson, battered by the weather, appears to have recoiled slightly from the water, turned its face away from the source of all its trouble. Built as a small hotel during the spa boom in the late nineteenth century, it is solid, and it stays warm inside. From my father's discursions on timber joists and horsehair plaster, I gather that the ancient asbestos insulation is holding up fine. He moved into the old ruin when Vik and I got married, having sold us the apartment at the Apelles for a dollar.

Why did I expect to find the house empty? He is home, alive and well, for once not reading a book but watching, of all things, ski jumping.

He turns slowly to look at me, as though I've caught him in a state of meditation. His eyes long ago faded to a milky blue, the green and brown radials of his irises submerged in Caribbean waters. Struggle though it is through those presbyopic lenses, he still consumes books at a frightening pace. He doesn't write anymore, and in most respects he has mellowed, but when he is reading, he budges for neither love nor money. Won't answer the phone or the door, and on those occasions when I haven't been able to reach him for days on end, I've raced up the Palisades Parkway fearing the worst, let myself in expecting to find him facedown on the hall rug, only to find him absorbed in, say, some nine-hundred-page treatise on the formation of the Teutonic character, looking at me, as he is now, as if I'd roused him from an epic sleepwalk. Hello, dear heart, he'll say to the crazed woman standing in his living room. I understand how recollection is a riptide that can carry you far from shore, yet it does nothing to console me when he, accompanied by only his faulty cardiovascular system, decides to take a temporal vacation, close as he is to crossing that final threshold.

He holds out his hand to me.

He offers me some tea in the spare mug he has at hand not because he's prescient but because he always has a spare mug, just in case. I settle into the sofa, which is generously piled with quilts, as naps are an essential part of his day. He rocks gently in his leather armchair. With the mug of tea warming my hands, mint steaming up, sock feet tucked in lumps beneath my thighs, I feel as though I've been packed in cotton batting, and it's harder to feel as though I'm a fading image, someone about to crop myself out of the photograph.

If this visit is part of the complication, if it is a detail courtesy of Turk's grand plan for me, it is a generous gift.

My father points at the TV and says, I've never paid much attention to this sport. What an oversight! Once, not long after I moved up here, Charles Quail was going to take me to see some jumping up around Amenia, but when we got there, the ramp had turned to slush. I remember the structure had a certain utilitarian elegance—you can imagine, like the underside of a long pier—but nothing to recommend that it was capable of facilitating anything so sublime as this, he said, waving at the TV. Charles would go on endlessly about the sport, you know, with great passion, but to be confronted by that brown, dripping, wooden thing about as elegant as a shipwreck . . . We ate at a Wendy's and drove home. If only I could have seen them flying, I would have been a lifelong fan. How right he was. If anything, he undersold the whole enterprise. Imagine! All these years I could have been an enthusiast, if not for one too-warm day in February.

It suits you, I say.

Yes, speaks to my boundless appetite for danger, doesn't it?

Through the window I see a raven land in the field to the side of the house, stately, its feathers iridescent across the shoulders. In better weather they were always battling with the gulls, executing twisting dives to escape the larger birds. If a single raven was under pursuit, others would show up to harry the gulls. They're smart, ravens, but something about their intelligence, devoid of compassion, makes me dislike them. They are neither brave nor curious, merely efficient hunters equipped with bodies large enough to allow them to fend for themselves. The gulls attacked only because the ravens raided their nests. William Push had been a fan, and had lobbied to have the building named not the Apelles but the Raven.

Push was the guiding spirit behind the Apelles, and the reason I have come to visit my father. When the Apelles opened in 1915, Push intended it to be the most technologically advanced building in the city. He was an automat mogul, an engineer of renown, and his considerable wealth bought him a position as consultant to Black and Simms, the architects of record, who assigned him the responsibility of designing the pneumatic tube, waste disposal, ventilation, heating, and dumbwaiter systems, all of which, as he would eventually prove, enabled a resident to close the door of his apartment behind him and abandon the world to its self-destructive urges. Push died in 1938, having spent the last nine years of his life sequestered in his apartment. Why he did so can be chalked up to that distinctly human tendency to define oneself by the depth and breadth of one's discontent.

He considered the human organism to be inefficient and alarmingly fragile. According to his personal taxonomy of the world's beings, wild animals were far more advanced than *Homo sapiens*. Take, for example, the lion, which operated at maximum efficiency, lying at rest unless seized by a biological imperative. A lion, Push argued, had no desire to be anything other than what it was. If an un-lionlike thought ever put into the harbor of a lion's brain, it would be raided, burned, and sunk on the spot. If, by a perversion of nature, there should ever be a lion given to lolling about in the dirt thinking up poems, it would be quickly set upon by marauding elephants, tusked and trampled and left to dissolve into the savanna floor. Lions never looked at birds and wished for wings. They couldn't have spent years musing on the beauty of a tree if they wanted to. They were pure, the elegant result of evolution's dispassionate murder of any trait that didn't increase the lion's ability to hunt and reproduce. Likewise the raven, whose very image spoke to Push of ecological efficiency.

The note card my father had written on that night in 1978 when Turk's Christmas tree had blocked his way had itself been designed by Push. His pneumatic tube system once carried hundreds of them an hour all over the Apelles, and the job of sorting the cylinders fell to young women who worked twelve-hour shifts in a basement room. The job was notorious for inducing nervous diseases, in no small part because of the elevated swivel chairs designed by Push according to his interpretation of ergonomics, which dictated that the female's delicate anatomy required a wicker seat and a low wooden backrest that, in practice, crushed the kidneys and liver, threw the sacrum into disorder, and bit into the lower spine. No matter how the workers complained, he insisted they use the chairs, even though no sorter lasted more than a month, most leaving the building's employ for less physically debilitating occupations in sweatshops. As a consequence, few of the girls became competent in the job, and with forty containers a minute sluicing through the tubes at times of peak activity, messages rarely reached their intended recipients on the first try. For Push, these setbacks only confirmed his assessment of *Homo sapiens* as infuriating creatures whose utility had been weakened by centuries of miscegenation, inbreeding, and the insistence on caring for and even cultivating the weak and sick.

Over the decades, use of the pneumatic tubes dwindled, and by the time I was a girl, the system had been shut down. Hence the cards in the elevator lobbies.

Is it any surprise that Push's design included a set of tubes that allowed him to divert any branch of the system to a delivery bay in his apartment? When I was a girl I could tell something was weird about the empty room in our apartment, something beyond its antiseptic air of disuse. My parents could feel it, our housekeeper could feel it. They knew well enough to leave it alone. My father parked a few boxes of books in there, but otherwise it remained unused for decades. When Vik and I moved in, we avoided it.

As it turns out, it was waiting patiently for me, the one room in the apartment with no ghosts from my childhood, and no memory of Vik. A few months ago, when I decided to abandon the bedroom and move the bed to the empty room, the electrician, punching neat little squares on either side of the headboard for wall lamps, found Push's matrix of secret tubes. He said there was no way to run wire without ripping out the entire wall first. In every direction, his test taps struck metal. I told him I'd go with floor lamps, and I had a drywaller tear out the plaster, all of it. There, packed as tightly as cigarettes from one side of the room to the other, were vacuum tubes, and affixed to each were gauges, inlets and outlets, a series of interconnected flat handles that, like organ stops, opened and closed the valves that made possible Push's voyeurism.

In the Apelles, there are many ways to listen. The heating vents, the doormen who are only too happy for you to stop by for some gossip, old-fashioned hallway loitering, the pneumatic tubes. By manipulating the handles, I can pick up transmissions from all over the building. Most of the inlet slots in the apartments have been covered over, but even through plaster and paint they provide a little sonic connection. At night I open all the valves and let the building sing me to sleep.

What do people talk about? The contours of their day, how much they hate people who they wish liked them more. Money, their bowels. Eavesdropping is spiritual pornography, a novelty that ceased to interest me much after I realized that the source of my excitement was not the content of the conversations I overheard, but the power to overhear them. I prefer the insect hum of all the voices at once, the droning proof of life. A building full of people, a living entity.

I can only assume that William Push spent his last years, his decade of sequestration, sitting at the controls there, pulling levers, monitoring the gauges, sorting through his neighbors' pneumatic notes, playing the valves with the virtuosity of Rachmaninoff, teasing music from the building's residents, plucking each one like a guitar string, sounding discord on the ninth floor, generating joy on the third. He must have come to believe he was the composer of their desires, that their every feeling was an expression of *his* grand structure, his direction giving form to the unspoken, the unfelt, the unimaginable. Without him at the helm, the building's fragile organic systems would rot. Thus the trouble with endless observation—we come to mistake interpretation for creation. Even our own behaviors, so quaintly called choices, are nothing more than observation and reaction followed at light speed by a transformative brain trick that bends temporal perception: voilà, free will.

Old men are strange creatures. My father is ninety-three years old. When I begin to question him about his past, he answers readily, without suspicion. It is a little shocking how willingly he offers up his most heavily guarded secret, the locus of his shame, after a lifetime of keeping it locked away so deeply within himself. Perhaps, as a person ages, he cares less and less what others think of him. Only monsters are predisposed with their legacies, anyway. He never even asks why I want to know.

All the same, it doesn't arrive on a silver platter. He has to tunnel his way to the story at his core when I ask, with no preamble, whether he ever made his confession to Albert Caldwell, as part of their pact. In the book, I say, you just leave it hanging. You never say.

Oh, I couldn't have told him about Poland even if I'd wanted to, he said, much less write about it. In those days, it was all still classified. Make no mistake, I was far from ready to tell anyone—I didn't need any motivation to keep it to myself.

What about now? I say.

Oh, all activities have been declassified. I suppose I could tell anyone I wanted.

Have you ever?

No, he says. After a moment he says, Ah, I see.

He waves the remote at the TV until it mutes, and he tips his head back and breathes at the ceiling for a while. He is moving into a dream state; when we're talking, it's not unusual for him to sit there for minutes on end, examining the beams above his head, massaging the arm of his chair. We'll sit with the house creaking around us until he finds his way. And so I wait.

Finally he begins. After the war, he says, I went back to Princeton. This was the fall of '46. The dorm at night was like an asylum. Boys weeping in the showers, screaming in their sleep. Christopher Stanwyck stabbed his roommate with a fountain pen in the middle of the night, raving about the Japs. None of us were in our right minds that first year back, but we adjusted. Most of us did. The astonishing power of focus and intellectual engagement. And the elastic nature of youth. We'd argue about Sartre and Popper in the eating clubs with real vehemence—there'd be fistfights! Brawling over philosophy, can you imagine? But you have to understand, arguing about *No Exit* with boys who'd been POWs, boys who'd seen firsthand the worst impulses of humanity become manifest—they understood that these works were necessary to the survival of the species.

You didn't bring your own experiences into the discussion, that was poor form. But what happened was always there behind the curtain, whispering at us. Maybe it was a form of therapy, all the *not* talking about what we'd seen. And then there were those who hadn't come back, of course. Conspicuously absent at the beginning of the semester. You'd ask after someone's old roommate and he'd tell you. Okay, sorry to hear that. What branch, what theater? What a shame.

We were pretty well practiced in burying our memories of the dead.

On my freshman hall there had been twenty-four boys. In September 1946, eight of us were back at school. Numbers don't mean much, that's always the trouble with body counts. The empathetic drive does not engage with a number. Stories are the antidote. Everyone must have his story told.

I wrote letters to my mother for an hour every morning. There was a little oak-paneled common room, and in the winter, the caretaker, an old man named Pharaoh, lit the fire at five, so I'd be in there in my robe and slippers at six, scribbling away in a mohair club chair at the hearth. Supposedly I'd muscled all my problems into a cage while I was locked up at Casa Del Rey. But those letters. Mother kept them. You can see them if you'd like. You'd have thought I was at sleepaway camp.

I'd write things like, I didn't go out Saturday night because there were reports that the James Gang was going to hold up the Dinky! Jokey foolishness. I told her I avoided public places because the Junior Birdmen had warned against enemy activity. I thought that if I pretended to be a child I could shield her from what I'd become. I was really only deceiving myself, of course, believing that there could be anything childlike left in me. A new letter every day. I was a murderer in a clown suit.

So she sent Ben to check up on me. Of course, who was checking on Ben? He was only a few months out of the Navy himself and had his own terrors to contend with. Those poor boys on their floating bull's-eyes. At sea, everything signifies death—you're surrounded by it, the gray, depthless water that's ready to swallow you up, and the monotony is a form of death, too, weeks of routine as you steam across oceans, weeks of flat horizon, and then the enemy appears and it's as though the fabric of the world is ripped open right before your eyes. It must be almost impossible to believe. You must think at first that the enemy is an apparition. And the battles, like two prizefighters squared off toe to toe and slugging away until one goes down in a cloud of blood. My god, the fires, all the munitions aboard erupting like volcanoes. I've heard stories, though never from Ben. Never one word. He was at Midway, so he saw plenty, but he never said a thing about it. My own sea travels, thank god, were considerably less dramatic. A week to Liverpool, a week back.

Never uttered a word about what he'd seen. Of course, neither did I. He'd wait all day for me to get out of class, and we'd go directly to a bar and drink ourselves blind, stagger back to the dorm, and in the morning I'd get up and go to class. I suppose he slept most of the day or wandered around campus. No idea what we talked about. The first round of Nuremberg verdicts had come down, and we must have talked about that, about *those* numbers, which no one had believed during the war, even though Rabbi Wise and the Jewish press had been putting them out since '42 or '43. We must have talked about that. But I can't remember.

What I can remember is Ben's face at nineteen or twenty, clear as day—an odd thing. Marvelous black hair that he swept back like a singer, and no matter who was talking, his eyebrow was always cocked. A skeptic from the day he was born. Do you remember him? You were so little when he died. But of course you've seen pictures. Women loved him. Even when we were kids it was obvious that girls wanted to be around him. Right from the beginning, he had a natural ease, something that drew people in. Just the opposite of me. I do remember his face so well. I was in a fog for years after I got back but his face was always clear. I never would have said it, but I loved him. We were thick as thieves but it never crossed our minds to say that we loved each other. You understand how it was? You loved your mother or your girl.

And then Ben went back home. I believe he worked at a warehouse until he started school himself. We wrote sporadically. Once we'd left home we never lived in the same city again, you know. We visited at first, but in retrospect it's clear I made decisions that kept us apart. At the time—for decades, in fact—I blamed the demands of work and I blamed geography and I blamed timing. It's rarely the case that anything stands between you and family but that you choose it. When I finally admitted this to myself, I could have made an effort, but even then I thought, The ruts in the road have frozen hard, there's no changing now. God, the stories I told myself. The very mechanism which makes us unique as a species is the very thing that makes us impenetrable to ourselves. The ability to weave a story from only a few threads of detail, to make those connections, to invent actions that have not yet occurred—it can be a great hindrance to discovering truth, can't it?

I could only imagine painful outcomes were I to broach the subject with Ben—his eyebrow cocked, mocking. So many times I imagined the futile arguments about my good intentions, his dismissive responses, my own anger swelling, and it was as though I had lived it. What was I angry about? He'd done nothing to me. He'd said nothing. But I was angry that he'd not been a better inquisitor. I'd needed to tell him I was falling apart but I couldn't muster the strength to do it on my own, so I blamed him for being the gentle, unassuming fellow that he was. And I imagined giving him hell for it. Imagine an argument a thousand times and it rivals reality. Write it down and it *becomes* reality.

This is how we gained dominion over the animals, you know. Our ability to predict future behaviors based on our experience of the past. Our ability to make up fictions. We do live in the past and future simultaneously, don't we?

What am I talking about? Good grief, how do you put up with me? I'm sorry. But the context is essential. It is essential that you understand.

I agree, I say.

You're my child but you were never a child. I'm sorry for that. I'm beyond believing anything I could say would help you. That ship sailed a long time ago. But I'll tell you what you want to know.

I needed to unburden myself, my father says, but I couldn't tell Ben because I couldn't live with the shame of it, and something told me he'd suffered far worse than I had. What did I have to complain about? I had my life! I had my arms and legs! I didn't want to sound like some sort of coward. I certainly couldn't tell my mother or father. Never. But if we'd stayed close, Ben and I, I would have *had* to tell him. You see how these decisions are made? These deep, unspoken fears that govern our lives? Of course I'd have told him if I'd been near him, so in order to make that impossible, I engineered a life far from him.

And let me tell you something. To hell with prison. To hell with classified activities. That wasn't what stopped me from telling him. It was shame that stopped me.

What is it you would have told him, Dad?

Yes, yes. Even now I'm avoiding the subject, is that it? Fine, then. Fine.

My father looked again to the ceiling and said, You know that in '42 Donovan recruited me out of school because I spoke good Polish and had been to the country a few times when I was a boy—a professor in the Department of Slavic Studies put him on to me. He took four of us. Mazur, Wojcik, Bissel, and me, because we spoke the language and knew the country. I believe Wojcik had only been in the U.S. for a couple of years. Family had fled Poland for political reasons. So, it was because of your grandmother's bloodline that I was scooped up by OSS.

I was twenty years old. Certainly twenty was a different proposition at that time. But at twenty, regardless, experience plays no role in your decisions. If you were someone like me, what you called experience was

Hardy, Yeats, Graves, Edward Thomas. Hemingway, of course. But you didn't understand what they were trying to tell you. You're excited by the idea of dying on the field, dying for a cause. I believed their experience to be mine. So it wasn't my uniform I wore, but theirs.

I was based in Washington for a year, assigned to a branch that worked closely with British intelligence. Highly decentralized command structure. I don't think I saluted more than a handful of times. It was a real circus, that place. Donovan was a ball of charisma, and whenever he met a new man he became instantly smitten with the possibilities—this man would be the one to win the war. Then you left the room and he forgot all about you. Within reason, an intelligent person could do what he wanted at OSS. Do you know what I worked on?

You helped write manuals.

That's right. I was recruited for my Polish, but once I got there I sought out the writers, and they needed someone with a pulse to type up the Morale Operations manual, so I got myself taken off radio intercept work and put into the typing brigade.

After the Morale Ops manual was finished, they put the squad to work adapting a British field manual. This was the fall of '43. The British manuals were field-tested. They were clear, devoid of the usual military mumbo-jumbo, and they followed a distinct, very English line of reasoning. The language and structure of the manual itself taught you to think in the particular logical fashion they intended to teach you. Quite something.

Do you know what simple sabotage is? my father says.

No.

We had a two-pronged approach to sabotage, he says. Jordan in *For Whom the Bell Tolls* blowing up the bridge is sabotage work, full stop. You parachute into France, connect with the Maquis, spend a few weeks plotting in a hayloft, and then on the new moon you infiltrate a power plant, lay charges, cut the fuses, blow the turbines, and escape back to the safe house. Extraordinarily dangerous work.

The second type, simple sabotage, was a practical philosophy that was to be laid out in field manual number three, the one we were working on that fall. The goal was to turn average citizens into saboteurs without putting them at risk. The idea was that if properly motivated, anyone could do it. Factory workers, file clerks, plumbers. Anyone could fight the German war machine. And if everyone in the country is fighting the Germans, well.

My father tips his chin back and speaks again into the space above his head: *His arsenal is the kitchen shelf, the trash pile, his own usual kit of tools and supplies.*

That's ours, he says. We used it as a little code around the office, a little joke in the mess as we were filling our coffee cups. His arsenal is the kitchen shelf. It's more than sufficient, isn't it? Very catchy. Nice rhythm, wouldn't you say?

He is smiling crookedly at me, eyebrows arched, a look I know well. Professorial, my paternal interlocutor. I am supposed to puzzle out the line.

Ah? he says and dips his chin so that those misty blue eyes peer over the tops of his black frames.

His arsenal is the kitchen shelf, I say.

He whispers it back to me slowly, his hand pressing the rhythm into the skin of my forearm. His ARE senal IS the KIT chen SHELF.

Iambs, I say.

Good, he says, squeezing. The meter?

I repeat it in my head. Tetrameter.

Now, isn't that nice? he says. And the alliteration—do you hear the snake and the silence? *S, s, tch, sh.* Subversive, dangerous silence. You understand the attention lavished on every letter? All this care for a manual, a tool for outlining principles and objectives, a military booklet. Then "the trash pile." Bacchius, a trisyllable. Drops like a brick through the skylight. The trash pile, rank and smelly. Not "refuse heap." Too soft. Hard *t.* Hard *p.* It's jammed in there like a wrong note. And then back to iambs at the end. Great thought went into every line. I spent the better part of six months watching them work, and they worked urgently, these men and women. Before the war they'd been screenwriters, poets, journalists—published writers. They'd argue over a paragraph break for half a day, resolve the issue, then pick it up again the next morning because one of them was foolish enough to say, "Confirming the break in section B of paragraph two, page fifteen." Back at each other's throats. We worked until midnight and they went home to their screenplays and their stalled novels. They drank so much they had gills. By the winter of '44 you couldn't find whiskey anywhere, so they were on terrible stuff, bathtub hooch. Mornings were unpleasant. Those who drank at night were hungover, and those who drank in the daylight hadn't gotten warmed up yet. The couriers knew better than to knock before lunch.

I suppose I contributed in small ways. My job was to take notes, mark changes on the working document, and at night to type up fresh pages for the morning. I followed every peregrination, every line change, every rearrangement of the steps a field agent was to take in disseminating the sabotage message. It became a part of my existence—it's not unusual for the apprentice to know the form of the work better than the master, who has to create the form and is therefore occupied with all sorts of thorny questions of philosophy and craft. He's in argument with the medium most of the time. But I was free to absorb the manual's deeper questions and internalize its precepts.

A state of mind should be encouraged that anything can be sabotaged. That's from the introduction, and I took it to heart. It was an ideology and I was an idealist.

When it was finished, they ran a thousand copies and off it went to the field agents . . . the field agents—we tended to go a little slack-jawed when the field agents came through. They were mysterious, sublimely aloof creatures. The administrative officers were always at their wits' ends over the agents' behavior. They'd go tearing off through the French countryside, drop out of communication for weeks, sometimes months, with no regard for their orders, and back in D.C., command would be irate—smashing furniture, threatening to shut down entire operations—until lo and behold one day in waltzes the field man for debriefing and here's the admin officer, the CEO of Ohio Steel out in the real world, suddenly quiet as a mouse, fetching coffee for this twenty-year-old in full beard who hadn't even bothered to salute. We'd hear reports from China or Afghanistan about field officers marrying multiple women or running liquor, spending money like water, but did anyone raise a finger? Necessary evils of deep cover. An unholy mess, the whole thing. Donovan kept it all together by the force of his personality. He was very close to Roosevelt.

OSS did have a reputation—one we cultivated, I suppose—of being a New Haven social club where waiters in bow ties and waistcoats served sidecars on silver platters. But our agents' survival odds were abysmal. And if they did survive a mission, they were redeployed quickly, usually into a more dangerous scenario than the last. It was almost as if command was simply trying to see what it would take to kill you. So it took the edge off to pretend that we were a poetry discussion group, I suppose. A number of the field officers were foreign-born—liberated prisoners of Gestapo prisons, Spanish Republicans who'd landed in French refugee camps, what have you. The recruiting pitch was, We'll get you out of this dungeon, but you have to go back in for us, deal? Those boys and girls, let me tell you. They'd kill you as soon as look at you. They'd been to the white-hot center of hell and escaped Satan himself.

I didn't meet many field agents during my time at headquarters. That came later. Just fleeting glimpses of them in Washington. They were ghosts. They trained in Canada or on the Chesapeake, and then sailed to England for deployment. Most were captured by the Nazis, who classified them as terrorists, which according to the laws of war allowed them to carry out on-the-spot executions, but in most cases it was torture and interrogation first, then execution. We were aware of this, of course. No one who went over actually expected to return.

That was a grisly business, field operations. When OSS officers did the killing, they killed intimately, in darkness. You were trained to creep through the brush, clinging to the shadows, emerge behind a sentry, embrace him, slit his throat. You felt the struggle of the life draining out of the man when you killed that way, pulling him back into your body, your hand over his mouth, his blood pouring out over your arms. You felt the heat of it. And you knew that at any moment you could suffer the same fate. You could be killed going in, killed coming out. Your drop plane could fly into the side of a mountain. You could parachute into the sea. You could complete your mission, reach the extraction site, lift off, break through the clouds, and be safely on your

Jack Livings

way to England, and somewhere over the Channel have your plane cut in half by ME-109s. Any number of ways to die. The instructors trained you to deal with your fear by cultivating an uncompromising belief in your own immortality, which isn't all so difficult when you're twenty, is it? But all the same.

And of course I was jealous of them, those dashing young spies, and that helped me take the work seriously. I absorbed the lessons of that manual. Anything—anything—could be an instrument of sabotage, and anything could be sabotaged. Doing your typing job poorly was a form of simple sabotage. Being stupid—we intended to teach people to be stupid, to behave like idiots, as a form of subversion. A difficult proposition during wartime, when a factory worker whose deepest sense of pride—the only pride he has left now that the Nazis have plundered everything else he had—is invested in the quality of his product. A bolt or a tank tread or whatever it might be. Consider who one of these potential civilian saboteurs was. He was too old to fight in his country's army, or he was a cripple. For whatever reason, he's unable to go to the front with his neighbors and defend his homeland. He's left back home with the women and children. And his wages had been cut and cut, everything had been rationed, the food on his table was made of sawdust, his cigarettes tasted like kerosene, his alcohol was long gone. What little manhood he had at the beginning of the war had shriveled. German soldiers groped his wife and daughters. Was he angry? You bet. Was he angry enough to sacrifice the last of his pride, though?

That's the question the operative had to pose. The worker is in conflict with himself, and must be convinced to work slower, to make mistakes, to use his tools incorrectly, to dull their edges, to break them, to waste oil, to forget procedure, and to pretend to be confused and weak. He must be made willing to sacrifice his intellect and spirit for the cause. And what a cause! A cause which ends not with an explosion and a curtain of flame, but a secret, impotent, dim fizzle. It's quite a hurdle to clear. Yesterday, this factory worker was the best at his job—or at least competent. But now he must will himself to become even worse than the most contemptibly stupid son of a bitch in the entire factory. Other workers will all say, What the hell happened to old Tomasz, he used to be so efficient, and look at him now. And what can old Tomasz say? If he's committed to his role in fighting Hitler, he can only shrug the idiot's shrug. Unless, that is, he can convert his friends. And then you have something like the beginning of a revolution. That was the idea, at least.

Minuscule acts of subversion. Harass and demoralize. Millions of people, each one slashing a single Nazi tire. Delivering Nazi mail to the wrong address. An entire country slowly tipping over, felled by a plague of incompetence.

The manual went to press in January '44. I moved back to the Polish section to work on propaganda but I wasn't there long, maybe two weeks, before the field section started calling people in for interviews. I was called in first by the head of Morale Operations. I walked in and he said, Take a seat, Saltwater. Manual three, page fifteen, subheading E.

He had this way of speaking that made you feel the words were emanating from his chest, as though he wasn't even moving his mouth. I was afraid that if I answered incorrectly, I wouldn't be allowed to work on the next manual, so I closed my eyes and concentrated. Of course, I have no idea what's on that page he's asking about. I know the manual by heart, but I don't have a photographic memory, so I think, Well, that's somewhere in the Specific Suggestions section, and I worked it out from there, following the logic of the manual. Tools, lubrication, cooling systems, gas and oil, electric motors. A, B, C, D, E. So there I had it. Electric motors, I said.

I saw from his face I'd gotten it right and I felt a thrill, like a schoolboy who'd pleased his teacher. He wasn't quizzing me to evaluate my fitness for more editorial work, of course. They were up against the wall. I have wondered: If I'd gotten the answer wrong, what might he have done? Probably would have sent me anyway. They'd lost so many field agents in Poland, they were really scraping the bottom of the barrel by the time they got to me. I wasn't even an officer, but they hopped me right up to second lieutenant.

So I was off to Prince William Forest for A-4, Special Operations basic, without any clue why I was being put into an operational division. I knew there'd been losses—we all did—and I knew that my language expertise qualified me for a certain type of work, but I was no spy. They told me nothing. Go to SO, they said, then Fort Benning for jump school, then report back to D.C.

So that's what I did. I'm taught to conduct myself with stealth and lethality, how to fight in close quarters, how to infiltrate and extricate, lay charges. In order to graduate basic I had to sneak into a hydro-electric plant in Maryland, make my way to the turbines, and leave a calling card inside a fuse box just outside the control room. No one at the plant was warned. If I'd been caught, I could have been shot by the guards. But I completed the mission, and then it was off to Fort Benning. Training there was quick. Doesn't take long to learn how to fall out of an airplane. You know what they say? It's the landing that kills you. And once I was back in D.C., they sent me to an intensive Polish course, three weeks, eight hours a day. Slang, cultural touch points. Every night after dinner we watched two movies, Waszyński mostly, we studied for another two hours, and we went to sleep listening to recordings of shows from Radio Warsaw. The language instruction—that was Turk Brunn's father's outfit, you know. Small world.

My father takes his hand from my arm, where it has been transmitting a kind of gentle Morse pressure all along, and raises both his hands to his face to rub his eyes, those tired eyes, sliding his forefingers up his nose, beneath the frames of his glasses, gently working the inner canthus with the tips of his fingers, moving them out along the closed lid, massaging the cornea beneath. He resettles his glasses and drops his hand back onto my arm.

About a year earlier, he says, the Royal Air Force had flattened Essen's armament factories. They all but wiped out Krupp. Farben, Daimler-Benz, too. The Nazis had to relocate them to somewhere outside Allied bombing range, and whatever machinery hadn't been destroyed was disassembled, loaded on trains, and shipped to Western Poland, to Silesia and Sudetenland.

There was a camp in Silesia, a granite quarry, called Gross-Rosen. The Nazis set up the factories in towns nearby, and by early '44, they'd built about a hundred other sub-camps, all to supply slave labor to these factories. Gross-Rosen was a death camp—when you were sent there, you knew your end was the crematorium. In the sub-camps, maybe you had a better chance, because they needed live bodies in the factories. In the sub-camps there were Jews, but also Russian POWs, Ukrainians. French. Poles. Enemies of the Nazi Party.

The one I'm most familiar with was called Fünfteichen. It was three miles from the Krupp factory, and the Jews who worked there were marched back and forth twice daily. In weather like this—my father gestured at the snowscape outside the window—they wore pajamas. They wore pajamas year-round. They had these wooden clogs, but the mud sucked them off their feet, and when you're marching, you don't stop to pick up your shoes or you're shot, so most were barefoot. I don't have to tell you what it was like there. The daily meal was warm water in a bowl. A rotten radish was a godsend. This is all well documented. In the morning they'd march to the factory, having spent the entire night unloading trains, or standing at attention outside their barracks as punishment for an escape attempt. Beatings were a matter of course. They'd march to the factory through whatever weather, wearing their pajamas, barefoot, and once they were inside, if they survived the march, then the suffering really began.

We had reports from inside the factory, through the Polish resistance, about all this—the Jews were being starved to death, worked to death, beaten to death by the kapos and the SS. And every week there were industrial accidents, electrocutions and the like. Limbs severed, workers burned alive. But it was most common that they—they were slaves, so I should call them slaves—the slaves died by being beaten to death on the factory floor.

In late '43, Polish resistance intercepted a letter from Alfried Krupp, the chair of the company, to the Gestapo. If you can believe it, he was complaining about the conditions and the treatment of the workers. Ever mindful of his bottom line. "We've invested money and time in training these prisoners for our factories and your SS troops are killing them all! How are we supposed to make our quotas?" Krupp was crafty—he placed blame on the local administrators for mismanaging the factories, which gave the brass in Berlin a scapegoat. And sure enough, in early 1944, the old factory administration is kicked out, put on a train back to Essen, and the SS guards are reassigned. The execs at OSS thought it was our chance to inject simple sabotage into the bloodstream. Just so you understand: This was not an attempt to save the Jews, but to do further damage to the German armaments industry. As far as the War Department was concerned, the Holocaust was incidental.

So in February '44, they sent me to London. My instructors were British army and my classmates were all Poles who'd been conscripted by the Nazis but had managed to surrender to the Allied forces. These boys had extraordinary knowledge about the inner workings of the German military, from strategic arrangements right down to what kind of toilet paper the troops carried. Who better to turn into spies? We trained as two-man teams. A radio man and a field officer. My radio man was Tadeuz Zachurski. By then I knew exactly where I was going, of course.

At the end of February, Tad and I parachuted into Poland. We connected with the partisans who would transport us to Markstädt, the town near Gross-Rosen, where our mission was to collect intelligence and spread the gospel of simple sabotage.

My father, religious in his avoidance of elevators, a man who couldn't bring himself to ride a Ferris wheel with his own daughter, who once sat down in the middle of the sidewalk rather than cross the Brooklyn Bridge because he couldn't stop replaying the image of the span buckling, cables snapping, the whole thing collapsing into the river, a man so wedded to his fears that he could not leave the apartment without his lucky hex nut in his pocket. A man whose editors, as he got on in years, took the elevators down from their offices on thirty-three to meet with him in the conference room of the law firm occupying the second floor of their midtown building because, without question, my father would have taken the stairs all the way up, and they didn't want to be responsible for his cardiac arrest. Even at the Apelles, where he'd reached a perfunctory truce with the elevator at the end of our hall, he might yet detect a disharmony in the metallic scrape and jangle of the pulleys and say, Meet you down there. A resigned, guilty shrug of the shoulders as my mother and I stood in the hallway waiting for the doors to open: it was a force over which he had no control. One might be inclined to wonder why, if he was concerned about the mechanical integrity of the elevator, he would allow his wife and child to take it. Because he knew there was no real danger, no more so than actuarial tables allowed for, at least—it was just that he was nuts. That's how he put it himself. I'm nuts, sorry. Lips drawn tight, he'd disappear into the stairwell.

He'd pulled the same thing on flights for London, Bonn, a puddle jumper to Cape Cod. Sorry, he'd say, and he'd step neatly out of the boarding line and head back to the ticket desk to see what the rest of the week's schedule looked like. Can't go today. Just can't. He'd refused taxis, subways, trains, ferries, trams, funiculars.

Entire buildings failed to transmit the correct vibrations. It's the maintenance crews, he'd say. Look at their uniforms, he'd say, gesturing at some admittedly sartorially challenged guys champing on cigars in a loading bay. You think those guys sweat the details? Think they're sticking to the checklist?

And now I remember something. He once told me that most of what is considered evil in this world is nothing more than willful apathy. We had been walking on Riverside when he'd said that, and dusk had turned the buildings across the river into silhouettes, the sky shades of violet, and the air was still but crisp, everything around us obtrusively pensive. Even the traffic had seemed to hum in harmony. I was in college. He'd been explaining simple sabotage to me, the philosophy of ignorance, both blissful and malignant.

He'd been explaining it to me all along.

We were wearing mufti, he says. Every stich of it Polish cloth. I'd had a tooth pulled and replaced with a cyanide tooth.

What? I say.

He opened his mouth and inserted a finger. You know, a hollow molar, here, this one, he says. You remember, you old southpaw?

I nod, thinking, Yes, I do. Of course I do. How strange that you'd return to the night of the party, the night I sent your tooth down the heating vent.

We rendezvoused with the partisans, he says, who took us to a farmhouse about fifty miles from Markstädt. The idea was that we'd travel during the day in a horse cart loaded with sausage. Traveling at night was too suspicious. The partisans drilled us on every aspect of making krupniok before they'd let us set foot outside that farmhouse. Standard protocol because the Nazis were by then well attuned to the rhythms of a cover story. The day I'd arrived in London I'd been given a rusty knurled pipe and told to work it every night before bed so that I'd develop calluses. Can't claim to be a peasant with ivory palms. The Germans took note of these things. Neither Tad nor I had bathed in weeks. Our toenails were the appropriate shade of green. Our teeth were mossy.

Even on the open road, nothing but farmland for miles around us, Tad and I spoke Polish. We discussed nothing but the sausage and the details of our cover story. To be anything less than one hundred percent Polish was to ensure exposure and execution. The Germans at the checkpoints were only too happy to liberate us of some of our cargo. This was by design, smart thinking on the part of our minders, and we'd been given explicit instructions to complain, but not too much—just the right amount of hopeless griping. We had letters from our cousins, we had our papers, everything was in order. They waved us through. Off to see our family in Markstädt, heil Hitler.

We arrived and made contact with the partisans there, our cousins who'd sent word that there's work for us in town. We spent a couple of weeks selling sausage in the town market, letting everyone get a good look at us. Our cousins introduced us around. I got on as an apprentice to a master electrician who was part of the resistance.

I carried out my mission according to my training. Identify the disaffected, the bellyachers, and cultivate their sense of discomfiture. The Polish tradesmen were my primary marks. There was a pub where we all went for beer on Saturdays. Of course there were Germans there, too. We Poles played skat and drank and slowly, bit by bit, I formed bonds. A word here or there. It wasn't uncommon to commiserate about the rotten szkopy sitting five feet away, just over at the bar, and after a while I could capitalize on that. The trick was to find the Pole whose hatred of the Germans was at a low boil, a pot that required only a touch more heat to froth over. He might, in passing, tell you what kept him up at night, staring into the dark. A couple of weeks later, he'd mention it again. Then you find out the Nazis had shot his brother or sent his father to a work camp. Everyone had been affected, but a family tragedy at the hands of the Waffen SS, for instance—well, there you had your opening. You'd think the anger that came from having the Nazis squatting over your country, showering you with excrement day and night, would be enough. But there had to be something more. Because you could endure the rest. If the scalpel cuts slowly enough, you might not even feel the extraction of your most dearly held beliefs. Abnormality repeated becomes the norm. But the single traumatizing event, that's what breaks us, isn't it? You know this.

My father looks at me with terrible sympathy. His face. My father's kind face.

It's only a trauma if you can't process it, I say.

Like a computer? my father says.

I have this on good authority, I say. The best shrinks on the island have delivered their opinions. If you can't stop reliving it, it's trauma. I don't relive it. I just miss Vik.

Of course, he says. Different for me, you see. My father taps his head. Bad input. Faulty wiring.

So, I played the dutiful apprentice, he says, all the while gathering intelligence and identifying my marks. Within a couple of months I had contacts in seven factories at Gross-Rosen. I adhered to my training, cultivated relationships, and hoped I could lead a few of them to some minor acts of sabotage. You touch a spark to kindling, and if conditions are right, the fire spreads.

But I had no way of knowing if my efforts were doing any good. It wasn't like a bombing raid, with quantifiable successes defined by installations neutralized stroke body count. At best, I got something anecdotal from my marks, probably just bragging. I decided I needed to get inside a factory myself to assess the situation. This was a stupid idea, and my compatriots told me as much, but I persisted.

At the Berthawerke, the Krupp factory that made howitzers, there was a Pole, originally from Lodz, who had an administrative job. A bookkeeper. He was sympathetic to the cause—he'd been the one who'd passed along the letter that had landed me in Poland in the first place. He'd told us that after the administrative purge a new SS unit had been brought in, more SS guards who'd worked for Krupp in Essen, and their Polish was bad, which I knew would give me extra cover. The foremen on the factory floor were German, so the same held for them. They only spoke basic Polish.

The bookkeeper was staunchly against my plan. It was ludicrous and he told me so. The first thing he explained to me was that the factory's production hadn't improved an iota since the new administration's takeover. In fact, escape attempts were up, and the Russian POWs were running their own sabotage schemes. So what's there for you to see? he wants to know. Whatever you need to know, he says, I'll tell you! The Berthawerke was a crap factory, the German staff continually on report for loafing. The foremen purposely trained their underlings poorly, did whatever they could to make sure that materials and tools were mishandled. You see, if a worker showed some talent for a job, he might have become foreman himself—not a Jew, of course, but there were German prisoners, Eastern workers, the Russians. Self-preservation dictated that the foremen keep production low.

This is a fool's errand, this bookkeeper tells me. If anything, you'll be a danger to the prisoners. You'll ruin whatever plans they've already laid.

Obviously he didn't think much of me, and for good reason. I was only a kid, after all, and had done nothing to earn his respect. Simply setting foot on the floor, he tells me, you put the entire resistance in danger. He would yell at me: You're a child! You have no idea what goes on in a place like this!

He could not have been more right.

About half of the German foremen also served on B-Trupps, the roving guard squads who were called on to enforce the efficiency protocols—the same efficiency protocols they didn't want their workers to maintain. They carried truncheons, metal pipes sheathed in rubber, and they'd mercilessly beat anyone the SS told them required discipline. And among these German foremen, the bookkeeper told me, the most brutal, the most bloodthirsty, were the same ones slipping the prisoners extra rations, cigarettes. Who would call this arrangement anything but madness? What option did anyone have, with the crematoriums blazing, but to live from second to second, to play the cards you're dealt in that very moment? And what would happen to me in such a place, if I was found out, which I assuredly would be?

I didn't hear anything he was telling me. I was undeterred. The more the bookkeeper argued against it, the more insistent I became. The whole reason I was in Poland went back to the intercepted letter from Alfried Krupp—why wouldn't I take the initiative and try to gather information from inside the very same factory? I insisted, out of a sense of defiance that I believed to be valorous but that was nothing more than a boy's anger at being treated like a boy. Eventually I told the bookkeeper that I'd find a way into the factory with or without him, and he relented. It's a miracle he didn't have someone in the resistance kill me then. I was lucky that, in the midst of all that chaos, he'd held on to a shred of his humanity.

He said he'd get me in for the express purpose of reconnaissance. I was not to try to recruit anyone, I was not to breathe a subversive word to a soul. I agreed. They had their own prisoner-electricians at the factory, but as it happened, by and by there was some high-voltage work to be done on a milling machine and it had to be done correctly, so the master electrician from town was summoned, and as his apprentice, I went along to assist. The factory administration told us that under no circumstances were we to speak to the prisoners except to conscript them if we needed labor for the repairs.

The factory was cavernous. Furious noise and acrid air. Gray concrete and screaming machines carving steel. The first thing I saw when we walked in was a beating, a boy, a teenager, who'd fallen asleep at an inopportune moment and had been spotted by an SS guard. His legs were covered in open wounds, bruises. His feet were mangled.

Twenty-five on the backside with the truncheon. I couldn't believe that his heart didn't stop, but he appeared to be alive when they dragged him off. If he'd been killed, they would have rolled him against the wall until the end of the shift and then the others would carry the corpse back to camp. Then tossed in a truck and carted to the ovens at Gross-Rosen.

The master electrician leaned over and whispered to me, What's wrong? You look like you've never seen a slaughterhouse before. He hated me for bringing him to that place, for putting him in such close proximity to the horrors there, for risking his life. In fact, he never spoke to me again after that day in the Berthawerke.

It was a big job. The inside of the machine had been carbonized from a fire caused by a short, and we had to replace every inch of wire, from the heavy-gauge copper cabling down to the little switch wires for the on/off lights. Everything that wasn't steel had melted. Of course, it had been sabotaged at the behest of our bookkeeper from Lodz. Now, this machine was German. It had been brought in from Essen, and there were a number of recessed panels within the machine, and etched into the inside of each door was a schematic with detailed instructions in German. Neither the electrician nor I could read them, so we requested a translator, and a Polish Jew was assigned the task, a man named Stern—Janusz Stern. He was old enough to be my father, a ring of gray hair and steel-rimmed glasses, a gentle man. Patient. He'd been a teacher in Poznań.

He and I spent a considerable amount of time inside the machine together, in a space about the size of a phone booth, Janusz translating the panels aloud by flashlight, me with a pad and pencil taking transcription as he read, sketching up the schematics. He was all business. There was an SS guard standing just outside the hatch, and once we had a panel translated, Stern would crawl back out and wait by the guard. The master electrician would climb in to lay up the wiring. There were fifteen or twenty of these panels, each bank of instructions very detailed, and by the end of the day Stern and I had spent many hours together. To that point, as I say, he was all business, except for apologizing from time to time for his smell—it was wintertime, and he smelled no worse than I or anyone else, but it was his way of politely suggesting that he was something more than the prisoner crouching next to me. His hands shook from cold the entire time but there was nothing I could do for him, even though I had a nice warm coat and a hat. The guard might pop his head in at any time, and even if I'd only lent him the hat, that would be the end of Janusz. He didn't complain once, and went about the work pleasantly. He seemed to know intuitively when to pause to allow me to catch up, when to carry on, and his translations were very precise. He never had to rephrase anything. He must have been a superb teacher.

So we worked this way for the better part of the day, and as we finished up the final panel, he turned his face to me and looked into my eyes. He was between me and the hatch—there was no space for me to back into. I couldn't even lean away from him, it was so tight. I said nothing, but I tensed, ready for close-quarters hand-to-hand if he gave the slightest intention that he meant to do me harm. His face came closer and closer, moving so slowly that I could hear him blinking. Closer and closer, as though he was moving in to kiss me. Then his lips were grazing my ear. He grabbed my hand, the way you'd take a child's hand to cross the street. And in an almost imperceptible voice he whispered, *Szybko, szybko, powiedz mi żart. Quickly, quickly, tell me a joke.*

I didn't understand. Was it some sort of code? I shook my head. He said again, *Quickly, a short joke.*

A joke? Was this a trap? I had to decide on the spot. I say, loud enough for the guard to hear, Can you look at this section again? Is it correct? And he says, Yes, let me have a look, give me the pad.

I turn my head so that now my lips are against his ear. A joke, I say. He's as still as stone. I whisper: Field Marshal Keitel returns home from another long day at high command. He takes off his boots and coat, hangs up his hat, and calls out, Liebschen, I'm home! There's no response, so he goes up the stairs to his bedroom. He opens the door, only to find his wife in bed with Field Marshal Goering. Keitel lets out a heartbroken moan, unholsters his sidearm, and puts it to his own temple. His wife starts laughing and says, You idiot! And Keitel screams, Don't laugh, you're next!

This camp where the Jews were imprisoned—Fünfteichen. This was a place of absolute suffering. There were no Dantesque levels of punishment or Miltonian realms of existential pain. There was white, blinding horror, nothing more. There was no separation from god because the existence of the camp itself was confirmation that there was no such thing as god. In a place like that, each person was his own hell.

Yet I was told they prayed even as the guards beat the life out of them. Their lips moved. Because what else can a person do? Hitler hated Jews because he believed they were responsible for creating the individual. Did you know that? He blamed them for introducing philosophies that distracted human beings from constant race war, which he believed to be the natural order. In Hitler's philosophy, such as it was, the natural state was the state of the animal kingdom. The strong and fast devouring the weak and slow. The strong reproducing. Repeat. Hitler blamed Jewish philosophers for the invention of humanism. Self-knowledge was a Jewish disease. Hitler made them responsible for empathy and the principles that suggest all races might live together in peace. In Hitler's new era, there was no concept of empathy. There were no nations, either, only races fighting for dominance.

And what weaponry did I have to counteract Hitler's insane machine? I had tactics for some sort of theory war, a war fought while sitting at a table. Clogging pipes and dulling files? His arsenal is the kitchen shelf?

Of course, Hitler had already won. Within the walls of a concentration camp, everyone was an animal. He forced the Jews into a philosophy of immediacy, where an hour was a lifetime, where there was no thought, no contemplation, where there was only action, and every action had but a single goal: to live long enough to take one more breath.

So you see? With the camps, Hitler succeeded in returning the world to its primitive state.

And what had Janusz Stern asked me for? An inconceivable deviation from the unremitting beat of that Teutonic drum. A useless luxury, a joke. A profound subversion. And I gave it to him because it was nothing to me. Do you know what he did?

No, I say to my father.

He laughed, my father says. A whisper at first, a sort of wheezing, getting the bellows warmed up, and then his throat engaged, like a cough, and his body began to shudder—the sound was amplified in that enclosed space, but let me tell you, before I had time to cover his mouth, he was roaring, howling. There were tears streaming down his cheeks, he was gasping for air. To this day, I've never seen a person so consumed with mirth. He was writhing around, spasming. The guard was banging on the side of the machine, What's going on in there? Everyone out! Now! Raus jetzt! Raus jetzt! He reached in, one big German paw, and grabbed me by my coat, yanked me out onto the floor. Janusz was thrashing around, the sound pouring full-bore out of the hatch, as if the machine itself was howling. But not for long. The guard dove in, dragged Janusz out, screaming, Raus jetzt, over and over, his eyes popping out of his head, but Janusz couldn't stop. He couldn't even stand. He was possessed, flopping around in paroxysms on the floor. Another guard came running, and then one of the B-Truppers, and they're all screaming.

He couldn't stop. And that was the end of him. Just like that.

Afterward, they sent for another Polish Jew who spoke German. Through this man they asked me what I said to the dead Jew that was so funny. I told him a joke, I said. What joke? they said. And I tell them the joke, only I tell it the way the Nazi propaganda machine wrote it. A Polack comes home from work one day and hangs up his coat. He calls out to his wife but she doesn't answer. He goes up the stairs to their bedroom, where she's in bed with his best friend. From his chest of drawers he pulls out a pistol and points it at his head. You idiot! his wife says, laughing. Don't laugh, he says. You're next!

The Germans knew this joke well, and it was even more hilarious coming from the lips of the Jew interpreter. Of course, Janusz Stern had known the Nazi version, too. By some miracle, the Germans were satisfied by my explanation. They assumed he had gone insane. The guard tapped my forehead with the barrel of his rifle and said, No more jokes, Polack, or you're next. And they all had a good laugh.

Tad and I were called home not long afterward. Our greatest accomplishment had been eluding the Gestapo. Was the intelligence we gathered worth anything? Who knows? Probably not. Was the work I'd done to disseminate simple sabotage equal to the life of Janusz Stern? Well. We were instructed to make our way to Russia for extraction. When we left town, we passed by hundreds of Jews in the fields, digging pipelines for new factories.

At Kraków we sold the horse and cart and bought train tickets. We were accompanied by a man from the underground on the train to Lwów, where we were handed off to a new man, and within a week we were on a plane out of Russia. London, debrief, from there I sailed back to Washington. The very definition of a smooth extraction.

So I return to the Polish desk at headquarters. Nothing's changed. I'd been gone only a few months, but it felt like years. I moved back into my room on Twenty-Fifth Street Northwest, same bed, same sheets. The other two rooms upstairs were occupied by new tenants, young officers, attachés, but otherwise the house was the same. The towels in the bathroom smelled the same. They had a stiff way of hanging off the racks. On Saturdays our landlady, her name was Sadie Mott, took out the wash, did everything by hand in a big tub on the back porch. She used Ivory flakes. The rasping sound of the washboard. She hung the sheets on the lines in the backyard. The sheets were white with flowers. Yellow petals, brown florets. Sunflowers, I suppose. I could hear them fluttering on the line, exactly as they had before I'd left. I'd lie in my bed on Saturdays and listen. The bathroom smelled like Old Spice and Brylcreem. Memories reconfirmed. *Life* magazine on the side table in the living room. Casseroles, stews, the thin white curtains billowing while we ate. It was summer and everything was wide open. Dinner was at seven thirty on the weekends, late in those days, on account of the heat. I started to fall apart.

I didn't sleep well, which wasn't unusual, no one slept well, but no one complained. Everyone had troubling thoughts, nightmares, what have you.

I'd been thoroughly debriefed in Washington, too, of course. I confirmed the intelligence Tad had radioed in, and I told them what I could about the Berthawerke, about the conditions there, but, again, the War Department—you have to understand that winning the war was all that mattered. The war effort was about defeating the Axis, not about rescuing prisoners. It wasn't that they didn't have information from inside concentration camps, written accounts of mass executions, bodies dumped in mass graves. British intelligence knew from early on. They had been intercepting diplomatic mail for years. There were stories coming out of the Polish Embassy, for instance, about the ghettos. The U.S. government knew. But it wasn't until after the war, at Nuremberg, that a complete account of what had been happening at the camps became public. Who knew what, and when did they know it—this is all of tremendous importance, but in 1944 the government wasn't looking for new reasons to win the war. Do you know how many civilians died during the invasion of Normandy? Thirty thousand. Thirty thousand French civilians, all killed by American bombers. Two hundred thousand Allied troops dead. The context in which the camps existed at that time—to the left, millions of troops dead, to the right, millions of civilians. Mr. Roosevelt, the Germans are rounding up Jews and gassing them! And Roosevelt says, Defeat the Nazis. If you want to make it stop, beat the goddamned Nazis. Let's make a date to discuss the morality of our decisions after we've forestalled our own annihilation!

Did I mention that my debriefing was thorough? What did I see. What did I hear. When did this happen, when did that. When did shipments arrive. What did I know about the production rate on such and so week. How many successful sabotage attempts, and in what factories, and carried out by whom?

At no time did I bring up Janusz Stern. I had no doubt that Tad would give an account of the man's death in his debriefing, and the story would have made its way to OSS through the Polish underground, anyway, so if I deserved retribution, it would find me. But it never came—from an official standpoint, Janusz Stern was only one more body on a pile so high it was blotting out the sun. My involvement was incidental. There would be no consequences for admitting my role in his death, yet I had decided I would never speak a word of it to anyone. I'd decided this before he'd breathed his last breath, while he was lying there on the concrete floor of that factory, the kapo standing above him, his truncheon slick with blood. That man wasn't Janusz Stern's murderer. I was.

I was a coward who'd killed him with carelessness, and bravado, and a thousand childish decisions I'd made going back to the day I agreed to join OSS, an outfit I joined because it made me feel that I'd been chosen, that I was special—from that very first day I was a murderer. And even before then, I'd been sharpening my bayonet.

My debrief was one hundred and twenty-two typed pages. The name Janusz Stern appeared nowhere. I was told, as we all were, that everything I'd done, everything I'd seen, was secret. You were expected to take that information to your grave. No one spoke about the missions until they were declassified.

Forty, fifty, sixty years we kept our mouths shut, and where do you put that, where do you store those memories of what you've seen and done? Well, you're trained to keep secrets, and that's what you do. But let me tell you, it causes a fundamental rift within a person who is motivated to seek truth, of course, to lie by omission for that long.

Water will find its level.

At first, I couldn't sleep. I don't mean this colloquially—I wasn't *having trouble* sleeping. I stopped sleeping completely. By the middle of the second week back in D.C. I'd come undone. It was obvious to everyone at command that I wasn't fit for duty. I was a babbling mess. Hallucinating. At night I sweated through the sheets, flopping around like a fish, staring at the dark. In the morning, drag myself in to work, sit down, nod off at the desk, bolt awake. Over and over, all day long. I took medicine. I drank. Nothing worked. I was seeing eyes in the shrubbery. I was being followed by the Gestapo. My food was being poisoned. The girl behind the reception desk was a double agent. This was shameful to the whole outfit, you understand. Field officers were supposed to be hard as nails. They were selected for their mental stability. That was a fundamental requirement. I was a complete failure on all fronts—not only was I falling apart, I was dragging down morale in the office. So they got me out of there posthaste, packaged me off to Fairfax for evaluation. The doctors didn't even let me go back to D.C. for a change of clothes. Diagnosed with operational fatigue and sent directly to Santa Cruz with an escort.

At least I finally got to sleep. They shot me full of barbiturates and put me in a private room at the Casa Del Rey, which had been converted into a naval hospital. A deep, empty sleep without dreams. I woke up and I felt like myself again. I talked to psychologists, but of course we couldn't get at the problem. They'd give you a shot of sodium amytal in those days to dredge up the root of the neurotic behavior. Or the psychologist would hypnotize you and take you back to the battlefield. But they couldn't use those methods with me. My work was classified. So the shrinks did their best and I did my best with the little charade. After about two weeks, they declared me well enough for some day passes. I'd made a friend by then, a sailor from Idaho who'd lined us up a couple of dates, nurses, and we went out for an afternoon on the boardwalk. It was the Fourth of July.

My father reaches into his pocket and pulls out the hex nut he's carried with him for as long as I've been alive. Do you know where I got this? he says.

You said it was part of a roller coaster.

That's right, he says, and smiles. The roller coaster was in Santa Cruz.

It was not a good date, he says. The nurse I was paired with was named Marcy. Marcy Plotkin from Clearwater, Florida. Her friend was light-hearted, you might say, but Marcy had a kind of haughty distraction about her, something I suspect she'd developed long before she joined the Nurse Corps. I had no idea how to talk to her. No doubt I was quoting Shelley, trying to work her into an elegiac froth, but this Marcy Plotkin couldn't be bothered to humor me. She tended to convalescing sailors and soldiers all day and night. The things she must have seen in that hospital. What'd she want with poetry? It's a funny thing, because *she* of all people would have been pretty well suited to listen to me talk about what was really on my mind, but of course that wasn't possible. What a date.

We all rode the roller coaster, the Giant Dipper. It was a creaky, rattling wooden contraption. Surely it's collapsed by now. Mind you, it was about as frightening as a pet bunny, but as soon as we went clicking up the first little incline, I was in a panic. I felt death all around me, as palpable as the sweat on my skin. It was everywhere, pressing in on me. I was too terrified to even scream. Thank god I didn't or old Marcy might have thrown me overboard.

A roller coaster! A ride for kids. But for precisely the reason that it was designed to be harmless, I seized on the idea that the probability of a malfunction was astronomical. See, during the war, maintenance would have been done by some old codger who could barely get up on the catwalks every morning. Probably half blind. Every bolt and screw would be loose, the boards soaked in salt air, axles inadequately lubricated—the possibility of something going wrong felt absolutely guaranteed. I'd never considered such things before Poland, before I'd worked on the manual.

If you'd asked, I would have said that I trusted that the mechanical world held together because otherwise capitalism would fall apart. You can't make any money selling shoddy machinery, so you design a better piston than the next guy, manufacture it to a higher tolerance than the next guy, you test it thoroughly and refine it so that, left untouched, it would operate correctly for decades. And every company operated this way, a perfectly synchronized aperture of industry, opening and closing with exacting precision. I would have said there was some elegance to it. Maybe I would have said that our machines were gleaming proof of the quality of our national character. It's American, by god, best in the world. I believed in the constructed world, in the intelligence behind our superior designs. I believed that every cog was machined to mesh perfectly with every other cog. I believed in efficient systems.

This was my brother's influence, you know, my beliefs. He thought like a scientist from the time he could talk. Do you know how many patents Ben had filed by the time he retired?

No, I say.

Thirty-one. Dow owns them, almost all of them polymer structures, but they're his work. Well, no longer did I believe in the divine nature of calculus. The scales had fallen from my eyes. It was suddenly obvious to me that simple sabotage was *simple* because the manufactured world already strove toward entropy. We can't conquer natural laws, I realized. It's a gargantuan feat to build a city, it takes hundreds of years, infinite quantities of human thought and labor, and it can all be leveled in a flash. We are, on our best day, only a hair ahead of chaos. The natural order is rubble. Left alone, everything finds its way to ruin.

Was it Janusz Stern who'd made me think this way? Certainly. Certainly it was. Through his death I had become aware of the carelessness behind the decision to induct me into OSS. The carelessness that had put me in a position to make such a foolish mistake. The total lack of thought that had gone into my insertion into Poland. I was just another body thrown at the Nazi machine in hopes that I'd clog the gears before being mashed to a pulp—this was how the world operated. As a child, I trusted that my world was the result of thoughtful planning, but in Poland I understood unequivocally that as a race we are in a constant state of panic and last-ditch efforts, everything a stopgap measure, everything an act of faith.

Well, I started jawing away about all this right there on the roller coaster, but guess what, Marcy's not interested in hearing about entropy and rubble, and as soon as we set foot back on the boardwalk, she and the other nurse took off. My buddy from Idaho took off after them, and I stood there, sweat pouring down my shirt like I was standing on the surface of the sun, and I'm shivering, my teeth rattling around in my mouth. I looked around and the only safe place I saw was the beach. What was sand, after all, but pulverized civilizations, vegetable and meat and mortar all reduced together on their journey back to nothingness? The next stop after you're a grain of sand? Atoms. Subatomic particles. Then you were done. You were returned to origin, broken and scattered. That was our natural state, not this random propagation of flesh and bone. Silence and nothingness was the pinnacle of existence, not animation, not thinking, not creating.

There was a big band in a shell up on the boardwalk playing patriotic standards. The gulls were crying and the sea was breaking on the beach with these little plashes. Sun was shining. The sand was hot, there was a breeze. It all helped. Eventually I began to calm down. And then I started thinking about the Japanese saboteurs lying just off the coast in their little subs.

Thank god I took a pill and fell asleep on the sand before I worked myself into another state. When I woke up, the band was playing "Song of the

Volga Boatmen." I was between a couple of umbrellas. There were girls under them, or families, people, in any case, I suppose, and puffs of their conversations came to me when the wind shifted. It was getting toward evening. I could feel a little breeze on the wet cloth between my shoulders.

I looked out at the sea, out where the submarine nets were. Up and down the coast there were gun batteries and watch posts. Full-time coastal defense. If I'd been a sub commander, I would have parked beyond the nets and after dark put an insertion team in an inflatable. They could have landed right there, right where I was sitting. Piece of cake in blackout conditions. From there, easy to get to the rides on the boardwalk. The hospital was across the street, but in an operation like that, you'd be more interested in the high-visibility objective, the one with psychological impact. Blowing up hospitals is pretty despicable work, even for saboteurs. If it had been me, the roller coaster would have been the first thing I'd hit. Guaranteed success: loosen a few nuts, pry-bar the joints, pull some nails, take a hacksaw to a couple of joists. It wouldn't take much to kill an entire Cub Scout troop or some Rotarians and their wives. You sabotage a few other rides, just to eradicate any possibility that it was a freak accident or a maintenance oversight, and suddenly up and down the West Coast there's full-scale panic.

So that night I went back. Everything had been locked up tight, and I scaled the fence and wriggled into the area there beneath the tracks. There was a spot inside all the crosshatching, like a nest. It was dark as pitch but I could feel that the concrete was covered with nuts and bolts. I was revolted, as though I'd been feeling around under the fridge for a quarter I'd dropped and discovered a blanket of dead roaches. The flags were popping in the wind. I heard the waves. And voices, very faint at first, hushed, and the shushing sound of something being dragged over sand.

My father presses the hex nut into my palm.

The voices got closer and I began to sweat. The same cold, shivering sweat as earlier. The dragging sound of the raft was distinct—there was no question in my mind that I was hearing canvas on sand. I didn't know what to do, so I did nothing. I cowered there inside the roller coaster, in the dark, praying that I wouldn't be killed, but knowing that as soon as they swept their red filters across my face I'd be shot. They came closer, and I heard shushing, one voice shushing another, and the hissing of the canvas, more whispering. And then giggling. I lifted my head and made out figures moving against the moonlit water, only about twenty feet away. They tumbled down onto the thing they'd been dragging, which I could see then was a big, flat raft, and I realized what I'd heard was nothing more than a soldier and his date looking for a place to bed down.

Look at this Finn, my father says to the television. He's like a UFO. Do you think the skis are designed primarily as airfoils or as vehicles for achieving maximum speed on the ramp?

I don't know, Dad.

And is there an ideal speed at which to launch, or is it simply, Go faster, fly farther?

I really don't know, Daddy. Probably works according to a logarithmic scale. Weight times speed divided by height times speed.

Probably so, he says. I'm sure they have the drag coefficients worked out to the thousandth decimal point.

He shakes his head at the pointlessness of such precision.

Sleet ticks at the window base. The raven is standing in the middle of the blank field, as still as a painting. Suddenly it extends its wings to shiver off the precipitation, then goes back to standing sentry.

I believe that, like Lazlo Brunn, I need to shift my perception of time, to arrest my perception so that a glacier's progression toward the sea emits a grinding screech that sets my heart racing; so that the moon is a blur zipping around a wildly oscillating earth, so that an oak grows and dies in the span of a breath. Stellar time, rock time, radioactive half-life time. I need to stride over generations, two hundred, three hundred at a time. This isn't grief but a new way to survive.

Explain, I say. Are you part of it, Daddy?

Part of what? he says.

The complication, I say. This *thing* that's between me and my real life.

My father stares at me, as I expected he would, admittedly the correct response to what would sound like insanity to him if he is, in fact, part of the complication. In that case, he would be no more conscious of it than a character in a book is conscious of the book.

Your life doesn't feel real to you? he says after a long pause, channeling old Dr. Schiff.

Plenty real, but I have my suspicions, I say. Around the edges it can seem a little hypothetical.

What is a father's response to the knowledge that his only child has lost her marbles? For mine, it is to rise, slowly, glacially, in fact, and shuffle over to the sofa. He sits down next to me and pulls me close to his bony flannel frame, and he grows to twice, three times his size, enveloping me in peace, and I cannot but help thinking that I am doing nothing more than transferring my tragedy to him, this lovely old neurotic catastrophe who failed at every turn to protect me from the onslaught of the world because he could not even protect himself. Charged by bulls, he threw books; beset by floodwaters, he built levees of paper. He told a joke that killed a man. He gave a test that turned out to be a suicide note. He was too distracted to save his own daughter from destruction. The catalogue of his failures is a heavy tome.

Neither you, he says, nor I, nor Vik, nor anyone, is a thought experiment.

Prove it, I say into his arm.

Impossible, he says, And that's the staunchest proof I know. Proof by contradiction. I cannot simultaneously exist and not exist, ergo . . . How can I posit the possibility of my existence if I do not exist? Therefore, I exist because I don't *not* exist. Except, of course, when I go to the post office. Twenty years and I'm still invisible to that woman behind the counter.

I have to go, Daddy. It's sleeting.

Just stay here tonight.

Have to go, Daddy, I say.

Do you believe me when I tell you what happened in Poland was real? he asks.

Of course I believe you, I say.

You've read that story before, so you might be inclined not to believe it, he says. But it's true.

I've read a version of it. In *Slingshot.*

The version you read was fiction. Now you know the truth. Do you believe me?

I believe you, I say.

And this business about a hypothetical life? he says.

I'm working on it. I'm righting the ship.

How's that?

I'm rewriting *The Blizzard Party*, I say.

Are you? he says and sits up, his face bright.

I'm all but finished, I say.

Well, this is news, he says. This is wonderful news. When can I read it? Do I get to see it before you're done?

You'll see it soon, I say.

I hope so. What an undertaking. Correcting the sins of the father and all that?

A corrective, yes. I never did understand why you thought fiction was the way to tell the truth about what happened. Maybe I understand a little better now.

Are you sticking to the facts? he says.

I've tried to.

You've taken no liberties?

Maybe one or two.

And have you found that they grow? They're like seeds, aren't they? Before you know it, you've got a forest.

That might be true, I say.

We like to believe we can control the story, he says, or for that matter how we live, not that there's really any difference. But we don't. The truth comes when it's ready. It hides when it's not. Don't confuse fact with truth. That book—it's always needed you to make it right. You've always been the thing that's missing.

The raven pumps into the spitting sky when I start my car. There's a little choo-choo-train puff of smoke from my father's chimney, the forest behind the house a gingerbread fantasyland of evergreens dripping with icing.

Back to the city, praising Audi all-wheel drive the whole way, the silver four-ring logo staring at me from the steering wheel, cousin to Krupp's triclopean hoops, brother to the Olympic loops, chains all, methods of restraint—but these are only idle observations, distractions to occupy my mind as I slice southward toward the city, as I slide into the tollbooth lane, greened for EZ passage, as I barrel down the West Side Highway, hugging the river, past my favorite sloop, *Ishtar*, my signal to exit, weirdly having reappeared at its mooring in the dead of winter, and east to the Apelles. The city is producing some slushy precipitate mess, nothing worthy of being called snow, but portentous.

28.

Albert Caldwell was thirty-nine when Japan bombed Pearl Harbor, too long in the tooth, and too well connected, anyway, for the infantry, thus inducted as an officer in 1942 and assigned to the Judge Advocate General's Corps. Discharged 1945, he was called back in 1947 to work on the "subsequent proceedings" against Alfried Krupp at Nuremberg. The primary proceedings had failed to win a conviction against Gustav, the family patriarch and head of the firm, whom the court had deemed mentally unfit, and the U.S. was bringing a new case, one in which his son, Alfried, was charged with four counts: crimes against peace, crimes against humanity, use of slave labor, and conspiracy. Albert worked on the team prosecuting Krupp for using slave labor in its factories both within and outside Germany.

Albert's discovery notes for Cecelia Goetz, the counsel in charge, were accurate, carefully executed, and surprisingly absent the condescending tone that crept into the notes of many of Goetz's subordinates (men, all). Albert respected Goetz deeply, though his motivations were hardly noble. He'd never worked for a woman before, and never again would. He knew as well as anyone that back home no private firm would hire a woman, thus he wasn't competing with her for an office in New York. This knowledge afforded him the ability to work calmly, with no concern for his own future. It was the only time in his life he felt comfortable conversing with another lawyer about questions to which he had no answers. He and Goetz endlessly discussed the intractable problem before the prosecution: What punishment could possibly equal the crimes Krupp had committed? Albert was adamant that a death sentence was far from adequate. What was a hanging? A quick jolt and then darkness. A firing squad? A painless moment of shock. A quick death was no punishment at all. Death should be a reward dangled at the end of a stick until the convicted begged night and day for it. But how to push a convicted Nazi to that point? Flaying? Boiling? Catherine wheel? They were hardly even beginnings.

That each of the perpetrators could die only once was, for Albert, a powerful argument against a natural state of justice. How many times would each member of the executive board of the corporation need to die to make up for the suffering and deaths of tens of thousands of people? How weak the mechanism for exacting revenge we have been granted, and how unimaginative our solutions, he'd said to Cecelia, who took a more measured approach: Punishment was imperfect because it required concessions to the humanity of the punishers. Of course there was no natural state of justice—justice was a human creation, and relied entirely on human behavior to define its parameters and enforce its boundaries. To think otherwise was naïve. Were it in her power to dole out torture, to do so would erase her own humanity, turn her into a monstrosity, and pervert the very rights she'd sworn to protect.

Albert interviewed a number of witnesses, including Jewish survivors of camps at Fünfteichen and Markstädt, which had supplied the bulk of the labor to the armament factories in Poland. Among the stories he recorded: a Polish Jew, Janusz Stern, assigned to work at a Krupp factory and beaten to death on the factory floor for laughing at a joke. Albert crisscrossed southeastern Poland searching for an electrician's apprentice, the lone surviving non-German eyewitness, but in the end could only determine that he'd disappeared near the Russian front.

Albert worked two years on the case. Krupp's sentence: twelve years and forfeiture of property. Not even three years later, General John McCloy ordered that Krupp was to be freed from Landsberg, his property restored. The only thing worse than a Nazi was a communist, and Stalin's shadow was creeping across the continent. The U.S. needed a strong, industrialized Germany between the Reds and the free people of Western Europe. Cecelia Goetz was right. Justice is a concession to the humanity of the punishers. If we were made to atone for the sins of our fathers, there'd be no one left.

I understand now that my father was trying to atone. He might not have burned and broken his body, but his illogical fears, the terrors that controlled his movements through the world, were punishments, daily reminders of his sin. His books were shrines to the death of Janusz Stern. Every crooked word he wrote was an act of remembrance. Every malformed character, every faulty structure, every looping metafictional roller coaster. For decades he failed to write a single word of truth, and that was his lasting memorial to what he'd witnessed in that Krupp factory. The book he hated most, the one he always said was the biggest lie of all, the one that made him famous, made him wealthy, and forced him to create yet another version of himself in order to deal with the praise, *Slingshot*, was the story of a Jewish teacher who escaped the Nazis, set in Poland in 1944. All those years he was writing negatives, reverse images. The more he lied, the more books he sold. A person could be forgiven for thinking that the whole world is inside out.

29.

The air had frozen and cracked open so that it could spontaneously generate snow without need of the clunky cloud-based apparatus, a spectacular advance in meteorological destruction, a full-bore whitewash, wall-to-wall cotton sludge, a ubiquitous visual plane that induced in my father an acute claustrophobia because he couldn't—yes, it was true—see his hand in front of his face. Whiteout conditions! he thought (he couldn't help himself from naming everything, however banal; he was sure that even as he drew his final breath he would be cataloguing the room, Table, Chair, Wife, Window, and his dying words would be something profound like Ceiling Fan) and went on to consider that on the ice caps this was how explorers died, lashed together by a length of rope, sausage links snaking blindly around in wobbly parabolas, spirograph patterns, tangled knots that enfolded the fools in their open-air tomb, though it *was* easier to recover the corpses when the thaw arrived several months later . . .

He wasn't going to die. He knew that. Didn't he? The streets at that moment safer than they'd been in years, and he was never more than thirty feet from the door of a building, though the physical insistence of the storm was extraordinary, fire-hose-level insistent. Since his last step he'd been suffocated, encased in Styrofoam, buried alive, disinterred, drawn and quartered, plunged whole into an icy lake, battered by shovels, whipped and spun and trampled and given a righteous slap on the ass to get the lungs fired up again, and when he ventured forth another tenuous step into the void, perhaps following John in a northernward direction, perhaps charting his own new trail west to the Hudson, matters of velocity and heading having been delegated to the murky realm of telepathy and Tarot, cardinal points having become remnants of a lost age, he had the sense that he very well could be stepping off a cliff. On the upside, he was pretty sure that the mental patient chasing them wouldn't be faring any better.

Well, he was mostly right about that. The counterman from the Cosmic, who, with all the precision of an inadequately tranquilized rhino, had come weaving across the hospital lobby at John, plowing into chairs, flattening a revolving wire stand of reproductive health brochures, his bruised brain a tangle of sparking wires that resolved into carbonized, half-formed curses, many of which, if salvaged, might have proved innovative, even poetic, packed as his quiver was with a broad spectrum of linguistic twists and cultural biases, and had, bummer for him, caught the attentions of the off-duty cop, Mr. Mustache, Officer Kissler when on the beat, not just another stick of lobby furniture to be trashed by our mercury-tongued counterman as he prepared to sing his polyphonic aria of profanities, which had begun with the aforementioned silently intoned *Motherfucker* but that, afterburners alight, would soon enough soar to the perilous heights from which the terminator becomes a haw closing over the land and sea, exposing in the wake of the shadow's blade all the voices of all the peoples, amplified by the shimmering black glass of the sky, an anthem of curses and blasphemies rising from the surface, funneled through the raw red throat of this prophet, humble diner employee, head wound victim, who had only just formed the word *Horse* in his cottony mouth when Officer K. stuck out one Bates steel-toe three-quarter patrol boot and brought him down hard. A knee in his spine, left arm in wrench-lock hold, the counterman wriggled and tried to throw the bastard off, but the officer gave a little tug and his shoulder socket became a fiery ring and he cut that shit out but fast.

John and my father, having fled before the takedown, had plunged into the storm like a couple of foxes diving for lemmings and didn't know they'd been saved, so their antagonist existed at that moment in the pseudo-quantum state of lying in forced prone restraint position on the filthy linoleum back at Roosevelt while simultaneously pursuing the two of them in the snow, if only in their imaginations—though their shared belief that at any moment a pair of iron hands would pincer their shoulders and they'd be in short order eating their own teeth must count as a shade of reality in which the counterman's existence was as real as the genuine article's. My father would have something to say about the third and fourth state of the counterman's existence, the one here, in these pages, and the one there, in his pages, but if you really want to play around in the garden of meta, try *The Horseshoe Crab* or his first one, *El El Narrows*. (It's 1968, Mexico, and el-el protagonist tarta-mudo, Duo—the el el additionally a play on the ⌐L of Longshore Laredo, the U.S. company pouring funds into the Dirty War—hamstrung by his tripping tongue, has ceased talking and is instead writing a bil-dungsroman, protagonist of which is a character named Duo. Halfway through *El El Narrows* [coincidentally, also the title of Duo's novel], writer Duo is shot by a soldier on a dark street, in a neighborhood col-loquially known as Los Estrechos, the Narrows. In the closing pages, which come quite early, we learn that it was Duo's own brother, Salmar, who pulled the trigger. Duo's novel is left unfinished, another unfertil-ized egg destined for the frying pan. I digress, but you get a sense of what I'm dealing with.)

My father had lost sight of the younger, swifter companion as soon as they'd hit the open air, and he'd trudged dutifully down the hospital's arcing driveway and into the street, where it seemed possible that the snow might be shallower. He'd turned right, to what he felt assured was the north, and had been staggering blindly, with every step ex-pecting said cliff, when a dark form appeared at his elbow. In his fright, he pitched face-first into the snow, his shoes carving channels, and he flopped around in the powder, his sweater failing to forestall the ava-lanche up his torso while his pants committed the same act of betrayal on his nethers.

Oh mother of Christ, he shouted around a mouthful of snow, and rolled onto his back, where at least he might be able to fend off the attack with some sort of pawing/kicking action, and it was from that position that he made out a familiar beard, a hat, and an extended glove, which grabbed his hand and hoisted him up. It was John, of course, who'd been right there all along.

You're going the wrong way, John yelled through his scarf.

Yes! my father shouted back. Am I?

John possessed a couple of preternatural physical talents, one of which was an instinctual connection to the earth's magnetic fields, which granted him an ability to navigate perfectly under any circumstances (the other was hawk-like eyesight; on a planar stretch of Nevada highway, he could read a billboard at two and a half miles), and his gut told him thataway to the Apelles. I wonder now if John, like a chess piece, was capable only of certain proscribed movements that night; if perhaps his directional gift was nothing more than an expiration date. Looking into the past, aren't we all chess pieces? Why shouldn't the same hold true when we look into the future?

Together they trudged northward, and after a couple of blocks unmolested by the counterman, they assumed he had surrendered to the blizzard. My father arrived back at the Apelles around 2:00 a.m. John, who made a detour, arrived around 3:00 a.m.

The timeline is what allows me to see clearly through the aged panes of wobbled glass, straight through to that night. Sure, temporal triangulation is an analgesic, a distraction from this ragged sack of retrospection I'm dragging along the concrete behind me. But the precise timing, everyone's movements that night executed as if according to an exquisite plan—we were even then a complication, each one of us a gear locked in rotation with all the rest, marching forward in conjunction, pausing, marching forward, pausing, none of us any more or less culpable than any other. Just a grand machine executing a design.

30.

o you remember Marcel Duchamp's *Nude Descending a Staircase*, 1913, caused a real ruckus at the Armory Show? It was one of my mother's favorites. It is one of my favorites because of Duchamp's precise expression of superposition, of the possibility of multiple physical states occupying the same position at the same time—the nude not at the top and bottom of the staircase simultaneously but *possibly* in either place, or somewhere in between—it fills me with hope. The nude is both everywhere and nowhere. I've come to understand that if my perception could be altered, I might be able to see exactly where she is, which is to say: everywhere. Perhaps then I might be able to see where I am. A fundamental truth of my life, probably obvious to you by now, is that I have never been able to determine my own position.

I have, however, finally discovered a solution to that fundamental problem, and to Albert's fundamental problem, and to the fundamental problem at the root of humanity's grossest failings, which is that we exist only *now*, in this very moment, and while we are capable of remembering the past, we cannot physically *be* in the past because we cannot be in more than one place at a time, or time at one place.

My solution is hardly an innovation. Back in the '60s and '70s, the lab at Camp Hero was conducting experiments to combat the same tragic problem. Turns out that the conspiracy theorists had the right idea, but the wrong mechanism. Military researchers weren't strapping crusty old Montauk lobstermen into rocket planes and launching them into wormholes. All they were doing was selling them weed with extra ingredients. What could be more natural, and what better cover for a perception-altering experiment? After you toked up and the military-grade sedatives kicked in, agents would enter your residence, strap you and your buddies to gurneys, transport you to the base, and the lab coats would run their tests. After a long, weird night you'd be deposited in a thicket out at Culloden Point, where you'd awaken in the dawn light and shrug it off as the perfectly normal conclusion to a Tuesday night at Doug's house.

Long-term effects became apparent years later. Test subjects saw all manner of spooks, specters, blurry ghosts zipping around at the periphery, and some began trading stories about abductions, wild visions of leather straps and filmstrips run at high speed. Sal Fumoso, proprietor of Cinema West and a son of Montauk, claimed to have been one of the abductees.

Lazlo Brunn's desk at the Apelles had faced east; when he ran his tape deck experiments, I have no doubt that his inner eye projected beyond the river, past Brookhaven National Laboratory, all the way out to the dark fingertip of Montauk. His binaural research was done under contract to the lab at Camp Hero. Maybe Krupp money was deep behind the Army's research. Surely, given the decades that had passed since Lazlo and Magda's escape to the United States, word would have gotten back to his relatives. Maybe it did and maybe they didn't care. Bygones. Maybe Krupp had nothing to do with the robbery of his decks and tapes. War at the heart of it all, though. Destruction, domination, pulverization.

31.

Ghosts? Blips on the scope, a weak glow as the green wiper swished by trailing its veil of excited electrons? Symbols, the imaginings of a long-dead futurist, a dream they were sharing, an acid trip? Were they even out there or was it just a superior hallucination courtesy of the ministry of snow and ice? There was nothing to see, everything to see, it was prisoner's cinema, frothing forms that coalesced and evaporated, and my father was awaiting the famed Third Man, who would any second appear to guide them home through the knee-deep soufflé when he walked right into the back of John (fuck, the hell, ow!), who'd stopped dead in his tracks because while my father's mental radiator popped its cap back there at the hospital, John's motor had a copious snort of sweet green ethylene glycol pulsing through its hoses, maintaining chambré, and despite the gravity of dread, his dead son hair shirt, and despite the hairline fracture in his third metacarpal due to his spill at the Cosmic (cutely: scrapper's fracture, well-known to ER docs working third-shift Saturdays), which manifested a dull, full-paw throb punctuated with exciting, unpredictable doses of electrocution-level zaps that ran clear to his collarbone and, despite the knowledge that his father was out here, somewhere, possibly entombed in a mound he'd already tromped over, despite those distractions—wait, no, it was *because* of them, in fact—his young brain had been purring along like a dream, operating at max efficiency, and he had had a moment of insight, a flash, an eclipse, a black pupil in a fiery iris, a sense of absolute clarity at the edge of the snowy hyperspace tunnel hurtling past him, and he'd run smack into his own bloody realization (oof, hey!) that he should turn around and go back to the hospital.

He had to pull away his scarf and put his lips very close to my father's ear to communicate his intention, the snow adhering to a hardline horizontalist platform, pegging each word like a dart and whisking it southward, and by the time he'd finished explaining, his declarations had carried deep into the theater district; a few unlucky syllables caught by downdrafts were dashed against the drifts and lost forever, but some were cross-winded to the river, snagged on looping updrafts and corkscrewed into the convulsive digestive tract hovering over the city, pummeled and twisted through the inner workings of the cumulonimbus before being funneled into the inverted colon of frigid air rising toward the nailhead moon like a fistful of confetti, and ejected into the constellate sky to wander the aether for eternity, dodging cherubim and decommissioned telsats.

Thus, he repeated himself until my father got the gist and had to decide, then, whether to follow hoary Ahab or to carry on in a homebound direction. Didn't take a heartbeat. He patted John on the shoulder, wished him godspeed, and pushed on home. Always a moment of terrible import in the historical record, two intrepid explorers agreeing to divide, exercising free will, the wages of such shortsightedness their inevitable demise. But wait. A juke, sidestep: not everyone's demise, only Albert Caldwell's, John's, and mine.

Vik had by this time already led Albert back to the Apelles. The elder Caldwell had abandoned the stolen taxi in Riverside Park after punching a hole in an unseen iron fence on Riverside Drive and smashing through a bench before shushing downhill toward the water. He might have slid all the way into the Hudson if he hadn't run into a gargantuan drift that ate the car and forced him to exit via the window. He'd gone the rest of the way on foot, and had been working south along the railing at the river's edge, stopping to peer down at the Hudson every few feet, seeking a spot where he might throw himself in, because the river wore a skirt of ice thirty feet wide, and Albert, not thinking clearly, barely thinking at all, in fact, operating in a hallucinatory state brought on by exhaustion, alcohol, and incipient hypothermia, had decided he might as well jump down onto the ice, a twenty-foot drop, and from there proceed to the water's edge, when he came into Vik's sight line.

Vik didn't leap into action immediately, fearing at first that he'd been backtracked by the poet-terror from Cinema West, but after a moment observing the man, he decided that this was another classification of nut entirely, one who intended to commit an act of self-harm, as Albert was by then attempting to straddle the railing, with minimal success. Vik was only about twenty feet away, a distance that somehow made him responsible for Albert's well-being, and he called out to the potential fence-hopper: Excuse me!

Albert: Who's there?

Vik: Over here! Do you need help?

Albert squinted into the storm. It seemed to him that the trees themselves were speaking. He drew back his leg from the railing and replied in code. He said: There are a lot of people who don't know how to read a newspaper!

Vik moved closer, toward unknown dangers, driven by an empathetic impulse, a genetic flaw that drove Bonny to drink over his son's chances for survival in the wolvish arena of, well, everything: school, import/export, love. Wrong paternal instinct, Bonny. You should have deprogrammed his unyielding punctuality. Vik said: Sorry?

Albert, now apprehending the non-tree before him: I say, a lot of people who don't even know how to read a newspaper!

Vik, desperately trying to understand: Illiterates?

Albert: No idea that it's all fibs. They get so exercised.

Vik, clueing in: Oh yes, I understand.

Albert: Other than newspapers, however, where would one get one's information?

Vik: The television?

Albert: Fool! The television hasn't even been invented!

Vik: Sir, do you need a cop? (And none of that New York smart-ass on the *sir*, either.)

Albert: Certainly not. They are the last to know. If they knew anything about how to do their jobs, they'd arrive before the crime, wouldn't they?

Vik: Do you live nearby, sir?

Albert: Why would I go home?

Vik: Because it's cold out here.

Albert: Why would I go home?

Vik: To see your family.

Albert: At the Apelles?

Vik: The big place on 78th?

Albert: The Apelles, yes.

Vik: That's where you live?

Albert: I suppose so. I suppose I should go home? Is that it?

Vik: I think so?

See? Easy, simple, nothing sinister in their exchange, just a decent kid helping a senile old man on the worst night of the year. Their little story might have rounded out a blizzard box deep inside the *Times*, nestled in there among the rowdy Queens runts chucking snowballs at the police cruisers (say hey, whaddya want, city kids, amirite?) and Stella Kilgore age ninety-seven's first-person account of the great blow job of 1888 (ma'am, you have to stop saying that, no, what, never mind, go ahead, I'll just put down . . .), a bridge club from Hartford on their way to Key West for a tournament, stuck at JFK for the night but guess what they did? Played bridge! Enterprising bartender invents the Manhattan Whiteout to delight of trapped guests at the Plaza! Etc.

Nothing pulls the city together like a natural disaster. Metro section, B5:

Apology Accepted: Blizzard Thaws Hearts

By A. L. KNAPP

John Caldwell, 31, involved in an altercation at the Cosmic Diner on the Upper West Side Monday afternoon, later sought out his adversary at Roosevelt Hospital to apologize. Caldwell attributed his decision to a change of heart, and made a peace offering of a cup of coffee.

"I thought it was decent of him," said the employee of the Cosmic, who asked that his name be withheld, having been released after treatment for a mild concussion. "I don't know I would have done the same thing."

When asked why he and the Cosmic employee had tangled, Caldwell had no comment. One witness to the reconciliation noted that it was "a sort of good will to man kind of night."

"Drugs," said a nurse who spoke anonymously, as she was not authorized to speak to the press. "They're all on drugs."

32.

We reach the hot, molten center of my discord. Vik, age thirteen, had deposited Albert Caldwell, age seventy-four, a man on a mission of self-erasure, alone in a bedroom with me, age six. It was the innocent mistake of a boy to whom an old man was an authority, trustworthy by virtue of age alone. He said later he thought my presence in the room might have been a solace to Albert.

The revel was thumping away just outside the door. I was facedown, the razor-sharp creases of my uniform skirt's box pleats bowed suggestively open or snapped suggestively shut, my shirt untucked, a sliver of glowing skin exposed at my waistband, the line of skin at the bottom of my leggings, the buttons of my elbows, the radii of my wrists as delicate as tulip stems, every inch of it an enticement. The dried blood on my scalp some sort of symbol. Albert, whose eyes no longer functioned as traps for light, didn't see me, but he sensed me. He removed his clothing.

Albert was practiced in the art of occupation. He was receptive to the thoughts and feelings of the child in the room with him, postmaster to my mental correspondence. Chief among these communications was my dream, the dream of Slade, again pawing along the high beam in the barn. Already Albert had entered the dream, a silent observer, and I was aware of him but there was no cause for alarm, no more than I'd express over the sudden appearance of a tree or an old cow. He stood behind me on the dusty floor of the barn, in the hazy gray light, and while

I watched Slade, he watched me. There was no water in my dream, which is perhaps what had attracted him most, some need to equalize by his presence the absence of that essential element, to soak the brittle straw and corn husk, to give weight to the dust, to tamp down the atmosphere's lightness. He was sodden, his cell walls shredding as water broke through mesothelium to drown his organs, swell his muscle fibers to exploding, insinuate his bones, turning them to mealy pulp, filling his fingers, his palms, his arms, a spring cracking the stone within him and flooding his every thought, straining away color and texture, rendering him featureless, smooth as an eyeball.

I was dry, dry, dry, and he was overwhelmed by my scent. I was earth and altitude, the smell of cold astringency and absence, of life itself, unstained. His urge to fill the dryness with himself was overwhelming, an army marshaled to slaughter reasoned thought; compared to this, the urge to procreate was a pebble in his shoe. I was drawing him like a source of gravity, capillary action absorbing him into the dream, and the barn filled with water, I filled with water . . .

And I was kicking to the surface, which was thick with a skin of dust and straw. I punctured it, reached for the beam, and Slade was there, his tail twitching, the water still rising, and what did Slade do? He flew. I held tight to his small soft body and we soared through the loft doors, above the water, and as we escaped the roaring ocean consuming the topography below, dialing up the sides of houses and sinking the peaks of roofs, swallowing trees, telephone poles, flattening and darkening the world, I turned my head to the side and I saw a lone jag of rock jutting out of the dark sea. We flew closer and I saw that atop the angle of stone there was a birdbath, and sparrows were perched there, dipping their small bodies and flipping diamonds of water off their wings, oblivious to the flood.

Slade and I zoomed away from the water but not in fear, for we could fly forever, we could live in the sky, but it was troubling me, the water's gelid menace. It was alive. It could send up a silvery palm and slap us out of the sky, and I urged Slade higher, until we were so high

I was sure we were unreachable, as high as the tallest buildings I knew of, the World Trade towers. Good Slade!

I knew that Albert, like a dog that had treed a raccoon, snarling jaws white with foam, would starve, freeze, burn, waste away waiting for me to descend. I knew it was him, the old man who lived downstairs, trying to tempt me down, cooing liquid sibilance, Devonian soundings that rose and fell like wind, mere Hertzian insinuations because, after all, he was already in my head. That is to say, even in the dream, I knew that he already inhabited me, and the clear eyes I once used to view the world clouded and I was awash in metaphor. Yes, I understood the water was not water but Albert, and also that his voice was not a voice but a song in my memory, that I was dreaming, that nothing in the world was only itself, but a twin, that everything, even my own self, had divided into the real and the imagined, and that the two were interchangeable and that it was impossible to tell which was which.

33.

Real or imagined: I was the only credible witness to the murder of John Caldwell. Yes, John, who had turned back to the hospital to make peace with the counterman, driven by a strange attraction to difficulty, or by a sense of guilt, or a need to be forgiven, or by that flaw universal among those who are drawn to the stage: a desperate desire to be loved by strangers. And then propelled again to his father's building by the same impulse. John, whose impeccable and atrocious timing, whose every second at the hospital making amends to the counterman from the Cosmic, whose every snowbound step over to West End and then north to pick up his dining table from the package room at the Apelles, or to check to see if his father had returned, or some other mix of bad fate and benevolence (conjecture, as he's unavailable for interview, long gone), whose every hitch, every lurch, every scarf adjustment, whose every pause to clear his nostrils became, on the timeline of his existence, overweighted with import as he approached the Apelles, accreting dread suspense, as his path drew him ever closer to the spot in the snow where his father, traveling at a high rate of speed on the x-axis, would intersect finally with his own plot on the y-axis, an empty set fixed at an exact point on the night's grid.

When John reached the Apelles, he saw the Vornados' terrace-tossed furniture sticking out of the snow. He stopped to pull a teak chair out of a drift. He found the little French café table. Another chair. His apartment had only a fire escape landing, certainly no outdoor space for patio furniture. For whatever reason, he was arranging the chairs in a row when his father came down out of the sky and crushed him.

Egon Larder and his wife, Saska, acquaintances of Bo's, had just skied up, and were only about twenty feet away. Under his parka Egon was dressed in a suit and tie, and had skied down from 89th wearing a plastic Tricky Dick mask, its protuberances hyperbolized with snow, the eyeholes and tic-tac slot breathing hole having suffered from accretion and clogging issues, and at the moment of impact he was conducting a vigorous boring-out of same with his gloved fingers. Saska (thrown together Dolly Parton/Elly May Clampett) was yanking on her left binding, drunkenly fumbling with the hinky clasp that never seemed to open except when she was downhilling, and then, usually, catastrophically. They had come from another party just up the block. Even over the wind, the sound of Albert hitting John made an audible thud, like a dictionary closing. A mattress, Egon thought. Neither of them having witnessed the actual event, they moved in for closer inspection and at that point discerned that the object in question was a body. They counted the legs and arms—two bodies. This all came out later—their inability to state unequivocally that they'd seen Albert fall from the top of the building was the heart and soul of Sid Feeney's defense.

The prosecutor—tall, thin, dangerous-looking Adam's apple—had a witness list as long as his chimpanzee-proportioned arm. One by one, party guests ascended the stand, recounted to their best recollection the events of that evening, climaxing at Sid Feeney's ejection of Albert Caldwell, and one by one, they were dismantled on cross by Feeney's lawyer, who reminded them of their oath before asking them if they'd ingested any foreign substances on the night of the party. One by one, they descended from the stand with their eyewitness accounts broken in two. And, if it please the court, if not one soul who claimed to have seen the alleged murder was a reliable witness, then how could anyone say with assurance how the two bodies had materialized there in the snow, dead as doornails? Perhaps the crowd on the terrace had experienced a collective hallucination that coincided with the suicide of a senile old man who unfortunately—terrible tragedy—ended the life of his own son in the process. Perhaps, for all a reasonable person could deduce from the evidence, they had been arranged there just so by a sidewalk-level assassin who meant to thwart an investigation. Perhaps it had been a suicide pact, a deal sealed in blood between a father and son who, let's face it, had all the reason in the world to share a bleak state of mind. Perhaps— Give it a rest, counselor. We get the picture.

A bunch of rich, amoral assholes saw a guy get thrown off a balcony and they kept right on partying? The papers went bananas. "BLIZZARD PARTY BUGOUT!" "SNOWBLIND MURDER!" "SKI NO EVIL, HEAR NO EVIL!" (the last accompanying a photo of Monteller Lavange, louche inheritor of a minor fortune, who'd skied over to the party and famously tried to plead the Fifth from the witness box).

It was all going Feeney's way until the prosecutor put me on the stand and I told the court what I'd seen, and when Sid Feeney's lawyer ambled over, introduced himself, and gently asked me if I'd had anything to drink or if I'd taken any drugs that night—did I know what drugs were? Yes, they're pills, I said—and I responded that I had, indeed, had a drink and some drugs, his dim old eyes relit and he pressed on for details, so I told him orange juice and two Children's Tylenol for the cut on my head. There was some laughter, and the judge gaveled, and the lawyer thanked me and went back to his table. On close, he argued that Feeney had meant to be my savior, that he'd acted valiantly in my interests, and that his own molestation as a child predisposed him to overreact in stressful situations, but no one on the jury thought any of it made it okay that he'd thrown Albert Caldwell off the roof of a building and killed John Caldwell in the process.

A noteworthy detail, the reason Feeney wasn't my savior: Albert was dead before he went over the edge. You'd be forgiven for thinking that, from a legal standpoint, this might work in Feeney's favor because, after all, you can't kill a dead man. Albert wasn't naked for the reason Feeney suspected, not at all. The chief medical examiner for the city of New York, whose office I would years later have occasion to visit no fewer than fifteen times, testified that his forensic work showed the elder Caldwell to have expired not from the shock of impact but from hypothermia. His limbs showed evidence of discoloration and his lungs the presence of pulmonary edema. He was naked because of a late-stage symptom called paradoxical undressing, not because he had sexual designs on me. Well known among alpinists, paradoxical undressing is the last stop before death, though it is sometimes accompanied by a symptom known as terminal burrowing, wherein a person will attempt to squeeze into a very small area—an opening in a tree trunk or a rock face, for instance—just as an animal finds a tight spot for hibernation. The chief medical examiner testified that Albert was dead before he reached that stage. But had anyone asked, I could have told them that Albert did, in fact, find an impossibly small space to squeeze himself into, and that he lives there to this day.

Albert's reasons for being out in the blizzard that night barely even came up in court, and my father, who never even showed up at the Vornados' place, never had to divulge his role in Albert's suicide plans. As far as anyone knew, his motivations for walking to the hospital with John were entirely altruistic, and his book did nothing to disabuse anyone of that notion.

By the time Albert went over the parapet, my father had already settled into his chair, cleared his desk, dropped his novel about the Buddha's life, seven years of work, into a drawer from which it would never emerge, and started typing what would become *The Blizzard Party*. Thus, he was no use as a witness.

My mother and the Jahanbanis, who were among the few people at the party capable of stating with any authority that they were not blasted on pills, had retreated to Bo's office to talk art. So when it came to telling the cops what they knew about the incident in question, they could only frown and shake their heads. All the same, the court didn't take kindly to the idea that I'd been left to fend for myself, and when I finished my testimony, the judge ordered my mother and father to stand up so that he could take a look at the loving parents who'd abandoned their daughter in the court of Caligula.

And Vik? Vik had met Bo, who was rummaging in the kitchen pantry for a package of Nilla Wafers, while searching for the elusive someone—anyone—who could give him a straight answer about where Mr. Caldwell lived. Bo, stoned but far from mentally incapacitated, inquired as to how this Indian kid, still wearing his overcoat, pockets bulging, came to be the minder of the old crank, and Vik, being Vik, explained what he'd been doing out in the snow, where he'd come across Mr. Caldwell, and why he'd felt motivated to help: Because it seemed like the right thing to do. Vik actually said that. It seemed like the right thing to do.

Okay, Bo said. We'll take him downstairs together. But first I want to know is, is that a gun sticking out of your pocket?

Oh no! Vik said, shocked at the suggestion.

Later, when a guest drifted into the kitchen and casually mentioned to Bo that people were tossing his patio furniture onto West End, Bo indicated only that they were to stay the hell away from his Finnish smoker.

He and Vik were busy scooping snow off the windowsill and ferrying it to the refrigerator, which they'd disemboweled, racks and all, in the name of science, and where Vik had arranged the Tami and the black velvet on the vegetable crisper. And that's where *they* were, peering at snowflakes, when Albert went over the railing.

34.

One last stroll through the apartment, the sharp cedar/pine of floor polish, the aura of wool in the living room, of heating oil by the vents, mildew on the kitchen sponge, the curry and cumin in the cabinet, the vegetal aroma beneath the sink, ozone and tea in my father's old office, the rank humanity of the laundry bag, the scent of impending snow in the bedroom I shared with Vik.

A place you spend your whole life becomes a memory vault, its walls hung with images encased in ice. At the front door I loop a finger around a coat hook and give it a tug. It's seated as firmly as ever, as indestructible as the Apelles itself, for it *is* the Apelles itself, just as the faucets and floorboards are, each fixture as eternal as stone, each one laden with the past, and I feel as though I'm pulling them all along behind me, every last scrap of wallpaper, every sink and window. I wonder, as I have so many times, if Lazlo Brunn, time traveler in the great beyond, has ever spent one of his thousand-year seconds here, brushing his fingers over the coat hooks, passing through the door of his old apartment to sit with Turk, however briefly, a life being such a brief thing, quicker than a thought to the old doctor. Or would he have been wiser than that, too aware of the dangers of a place so freighted with the past, the near impossibility of escape?

The familiar heft of the front door, the solid whoosh-click of oak and steel, the sonic death of the carpeted hall to the elevator, the cool, almost imperceptible resistance of the call button. The elevator arrives empty and I press ⓛ, and for old times' sake I release a bloody scream into my balled-up cardigan from around 12 to 2. In the lobby I nod to Peter and divert past the brassy grid of the mailboxes to the service elevator, press, board, and down I go. Past the storage cages, into the boiler room, unlock steel door, close and lock steel door, down the stairs, ever downward, more steel opening, slamming shut behind me. No one waxes poetic about a basement. Beyond the cellar door lies the realm of rot and fear. If you're lucky, the domicile of your enemies. A pit, home to mold and decay, host to sewer, worm, and root.

Another short flight of stairs, another steel door, the handle cold, two locks and a keypad. It opens directly into my office. No diploma on the wall, but two of my mother's canvases keep watch over each other from opposite sides of the room. There's nothing here you wouldn't expect to find on the C-suite wing at any moderately sized producer of exportable plastic componentry. No windows, of course, but tuned lighting does a passable imitation of Central Park on a clear fall day.

The *Nutcracker* soldier I lifted from the Vornados' house all those years ago occupies a position of honor on my desk, a four-drawer fiddleback number that belonged to Turk. Beneath the paintings, which are unobtrusive color studies, interesting but not distracting, there are marble-top work surfaces. A pair of sofas face each other in the middle of the room, White House style, for client meetings. When I bought out Turk and became the sole proprietor, I only made one upgrade: the floor. I had the oak planks ripped up and the concrete jackhammered, which dropped the surface six inches. One industrial iron step, diamond plate, brings you down from the main office.

In 2001, there were two earthquakes in Manhattan, one in January, one in October, and though initially I assigned them no meaning, over the years I began to think of them as bookends to that day in September, a pair of memorial shrugs of the mantel, neither of which moved the needles at the Columbia Earth Institute more than the towers' collapse, as though out of respect, and I confess that by the time I took over from Turk I felt a strange affection for the bedrock beneath our streets, and wanted to be as close to the schist as possible.

Thus my office floor is the roof of the Hartland Formation, its gray burr ground smooth and buffed to a dull sheen. Most people wouldn't notice a floor, and if they do I assume they see concrete. I've been generous with the rugs, low-pile, natural hues, and you would really have to be on your geologic game to recognize that you're standing on Cambrian schist, an ancient layer in the St. Nicholas thrust zone, just west of Cameron's Line. When you stand in my office, you stand on the earth's crust. It's a beautiful volcanic rock studded with garnet and flecks of quartz that wink in the light. Copious deposits of magnetite.

Tanawat's office is on the other side of the lobby, the decor decidedly unchanged since Turk brought him on as chief of operations back in the '90s, Tanawat being an archconservative when it comes to the preservation of his own personal history. He maintains, for instance, a full arsenal of functioning bongs dating back to his years at Columbia. He also has a shelf heaving with family photo albums. It is because of him that I have no concern about the company's ability to provide our clients the same level of service as ever, whether I'm here or not. By all rights, the company should be his, anyway. He's the one who manages relationships with the vendors, keeps abreast of the latest trends in tech and fantasy, and ensures that the clients get exactly what they need, even if that's not what they want. He tends to spend as much of the winter as possible on the West Coast, so I haven't seen much of him lately, but he'll know what to do.

I feel as if a hundred pilgrims who had set off decades ago, each from a different corner of the globe, are approaching their final destination. There is a cohesive presence, a warmth in the air. Surely I was part of the blueprint from the start, a structural element drawn in by William Push, a truss at the apex of a larger idea. My preparation long predates my knowledge of it, that's for sure. What more could I have asked for: A father who taught me to mistrust probabilities in favor of coincidences. A mother skilled in the interpretation of signs and symbols. From Vik I learned the secrets of dispersion. From Turk, an understanding of the methods of complication. From Lazlo I received the mechanism for transformation.

And from Albert, who rather than surrender his guilt transformed me into his surrogate, Albert, who devised a mysticism all his own, who, like Lazlo, managed to outsmart mortality itself, the master complication, who escaped by engineering his own expulsion, shedding his own skin and putting on mine, I received the final dose of knowledge. Sometimes a suicide is not meant to be an end to suffering but its extension. And while I do not intend to suffer any longer, I do intend to extend myself infinitely.

I had lost myself in my father's and Albert's and Vik's murky recollections, but now I am found. And though I understand that my life has already been written, all of it preordained, I confess to some trepidation about what lies ahead. It has become difficult to keep myself separate from the world. I've got real issues with the observable universe right now due to this marriage of the minds, and I suspect this would be only the beginning, like the striated mixing of paint, eddies of Albert swirling into eddies of my father, Vik bleeding into Hazel, blending at the edges, distinction vanishing. Maybe my father was protecting me from this very thing with his fictional version of Hazel. Maybe I've done this to myself. It doesn't matter now. I know what's coming if I stick around. I know it like I know foot is foot and hand is hand. Soon enough, foot will be paper clip and hand will be soup and I'll be lost to myself. Before that happens, I must evacuate this body. This is ancient business, it's witches and cauldrons on the heath. I finally have my chance to invite the seraphim of amnesia to settle on the crown of my skull, to chant, Forget, Forget, Forget, do its egg scramble number down in the brainpan, the old Moniz mash, the leucotome twist, one-two, look, I'm a roux.

I have rewritten myself and now I must focus on the solid forms before me, on the proper preparation of the tools that will aid me on my passage, the consecrated elements.

Headphones, quartz, copper, and electricity. The quarter-inch tapes are spooled, Urdu on the right, German on the left. I have cross-wired the dual decks exactly as Lazlo wired his, not out of sentimentality but because I wouldn't dare try to outsmart this mystical communion I am undertaking. I'm not so arrogant as to think that there could be a better way to do this, some modern, digital substitute. There is only one way to be sure it works, and that is the old way. I have procured a pair of

Koss SP/3s, the same headphones Lazlo used, because where understanding ends, myth begins. How else do we recognize the horizon line of the sacred if not by our inability to comprehend? A lifetime of devotion to auditory hermeneutics would not begin to demystify the inner workings of the spiritual-mechanical elision I'm about to undertake.

To Lazlo's machine I have added a conduit, one that will transport me into the Apelles herself, and from there I will make my way into the magnetite beneath my feet, into geologic time, into the world of the subatomic. I stand at the edge of a cliff, a diver peering down at the flashing water so far below. I have constructed a sturdy platform, but the execution of the dive is up to me.

A bomb vest is but a means to achieve divine elevation. The same for the knife drawn across the neck of the sacrificial lamb. The rocks hurled at the martyr. Tools. I have been wondering if the men who killed my husband were properly prepared. An airplane's aluminum fuselage is no more divine than a horse cart unless the pilot has prepared himself for the metamorphosis. Did they transform?

I will seek out the remnants of Mohamed Atta. I will seek out the remnants of my husband. For I have prepared properly. Of that much I'm sure. I have been preparing for so long! What is a complication but a preparation for its end? Once I am free, I will create infinite complications within my complication. Surely I am already free. Surely I will never be free. I am everywhere and nowhere. Permutations upon permutations for three hundred sixty generations. Blood and bone, iron and steel, disease and cure, atoms enjoined and split asunder.

I am ready.

Soon I will exist outside the boundaries of what my father wrote, outside of Albert, Vik, this building, my life.

I will follow the path of Lazlo Brunn. I will don the headphones and press the keys. I will listen, and once I have slowed myself sufficiently, I will close my mouth around the strand of heavy-gauge copper wire, thick as a thumb, that is poised on the wooden stand like a cobra before me, and I will inject myself into the Apelles via the heavy current converter I have affixed to her electrical conduits, having secured the connection with the hex nut my father gifted me, and my being will be transformed into a flowing stream, all sense and sensibility erased, all memories flayed to shreds, cohesion rent asunder, and I'll pass into her foundation, and from there into the Hartland schist.

Yes, my body will smolder and die, but don't mistake this for suicide. It's simple sabotage, a pinprick to the foot of an elephant. A pinprick, but I am one of many. I will exist, reconstituted on the same plane as Vik, reduced, reformed, a free radical passing through stone and air, burrowing in, reconstituting in a leaf, superheated at the core of the earth, a part of everything living, dead, fired like a shot out of the sliver of existence we call humanity into the wilderness of natural time. I don't know why I didn't think of this sooner. But, of course, I didn't have to think of anything.

ACKNOWLEDGMENTS

For the gifts of time and space to work, and for bringing me into contact with extraordinary artists and scholars, thank you to the American Academy in Rome, and to the American Academy of Arts and Letters for awarding me the John Guare Writer's Fund Rome Prize for Literature. My deepest thanks also to PEN America and the family of Robert Bingham for the PEN/Robert W. Bingham Prize and for the financial support attached to the prize.

My thanks to Lee and Cynthia Vance, and to Carol Paik and Daniel Slifkin, who have over the years repeatedly lent Jennie and me quiet places to write. And my love and thanks to Larry and Mary Yabroff, whose dining room table is its own writer's retreat.

Thank you, Jason Siebenmorgen and Christoph Meinrenken, for friendship and generosity beyond compare.

Dr. Ukichiro Nakaya's snow crystal classification system was a constant companion as I wrote, as was the snowflake photography of Wilson Bentley. The work of Dr. Charles Merguerian, Professor Emeritus of Geology at Hofstra University, on subterranean Manhattan was invaluable in creating the world under Hazel's feet.

Of the many helpful documents and books I consulted, several proved to be indispensable: the National Oceanic and Atmospheric Administration's *National Disaster Survey Report 78-1*, which was key in building the novel's chronology and was a fascinating account of the meteorological science behind the storm itself; the *SOE Secret Operations*

Acknowledgments

Manual; the Field Manuals of the Office of Strategic Services, especially No. 3, which describes the methods of simple sabotage; *The Abandonment of the Jews: America and the Holocaust, 1941–1945*, by David S. Wyman; and *Herr Krupp's Berthawerk*, by Theodore H. Lehman, essential for its descriptions of imprisonment at Fünfteichen and of labor at the munitions foundry.

I am grateful to the supporters and staff of the USC Shoah Foundation's Visual History Archive Online and to the British Library Sound Archive's National Life Stories / Living Memory of the Jewish Community project, both of which provide free online access to their many interviews with Holocaust survivors.

For your intelligence and infinite patience, thank you to everyone at Farrar, Straus and Giroux with a hand in the publication of this book, especially Gretchen Achilles, Rodrigo Corral, Hannah Goodwin, Olivia Kan-Sperling, Alexis Nowicki, and Stephen Weil.

Thank you to Sean McDonald for wading through multiple drafts and thousands of pages, and for fielding endless questions with grace and generosity. Thank you to Antoine Wilson, whose friendship and enthusiasm have forestalled countless crises of the spirit. And thank you to Anna Stein for always answering, always humoring, always looking forward.

To my children, who are, in ways mysterious and undeniable, at the center of everything I write, and to Jennie, who is in every sentence, every word, my love.

A NOTE ABOUT THE AUTHOR

Jack Livings is the author of the short story collection *The Dog*, which was awarded the 2015 PEN/Robert W. Bingham Prize and the Rome Prize for Literature. He lives in New York City with his family.